AUTHOR

CLEARY, J

CLASS 12 DEC 1997

AF

TITLE

Dragons at the party

DRAGONS AT THE PARTY

It is Bicentenary year and Australia is having the party of a lifetime. Detective Inspector Scobie Malone, hero of three other Cleary books, would far rather be out on Sydney Harbour with his family, watching the fun. Instead he is on duty, investigating the murder of an aide to President Timori, who is in exile in Australia with his glamorous wife Delvina following a coup on the Spice Island of Palucca. Clearly the bullet was meant for the President, and Malone has the task of tracking down the hit-man before he takes a second shot.

Malone identifies the would-be assassin as international terrorist Miguel Seville. He also suspects that Seville is in contact with a young Aboriginal rights activist. But who is paying Seville, and why? Prime Minister Phil Norval turns out to be an old flame of Delvina's from the days when she was a dancer and he was a TV star, and businessman Russell Hickbed seems to have his own reasons for wanting President Timori protected.

In this gripping new novel Jon Cleary has set an ominous cat-and-mouse game in a sophisticated city intent on celebrating. But carried on the wind at the edge of the city, fire is scorching the bush and destroying people's homes. And somewhere between the opulence of Sydney's Point Piper and the slums of the impoverished Aborigines, a gunman is preparing to kill.

JON CLEARY

DRAGONS AT THE PARTY

COLLINS
8 Grafton Street, London W1
1987

William Collins Sons & Co. Ltd
London · Glasgow · Sydney · Auckland
Toronto · Johannesburg

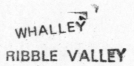
BRITISH LIBRARY CATALOGUING IN PUBLICATION DATA

Cleary, Jon
Dragons at the party.
I. Title
823[F]   PR9619.3.C54

ISBN 0-00-223246-4

First published 1987
© Sundowner Productions Pty Ltd 1987

Photoset in Linotron Times Roman by
Rowland Phototypesetting Ltd
Bury St Edmunds, Suffolk
Made and printed in Great Britain by
William Collins Sons & Co. Ltd, Glasgow

For Jane
(1949–86)

ONE

1

When they took the bag of emeralds from the pocket of the murdered man, the President sighed loudly and the First Lady, who had been taking French lessons with her sights on asylum on the Riviera, said, '*Merde!*'

All this Malone learned within five minutes of arriving at Kirribilli House. Sergeant Kenthurst, the leader of the detail of Federal Police who were guarding President and Madame Timori, might know next to nothing about homicide but, coming from Canberra, had a sharp ear for detail and expletives.

'It struck me as a bit off-colour,' he said.

'It would have been a bit more off-colour,' said Russ Clements, who had taken high school French, 'if she'd said it in Aussie.'

'Righto, Russ, spread yourself around, see what you can pick up.' Malone and Clements had started together as police cadets and Malone sometimes wondered if Clements, with his basic approach to everything, didn't have the right attitude. There had been a time long ago when his own approach had been irreverent and somehow police work had been, or had seemed to be, more fun. 'Are those protestors still outside?'

'They've been moved further back up the street. I'll see what I can get out of them. It may have been one of them who did it.' But Clements sounded doubtful. Demonstrators didn't bring guns to their outings. You didn't volunteer to be manhandled by the pigs with a weapon in your pocket.

As the big untidy Homicide detective lumbered away, nodding to two junior officers to go with him, Kenthurst said, 'Is he a good man?'

Malone sighed inwardly: *here we go again.* He was a patient-looking man, always seemingly composed. He was tall, six feet

7

one (he was of an age that still continued to think in the old measures), big in the shoulders and still slim at the waist; he had that air of repose that some tall men have, as if their height accents their stillness. He was good-looking without being handsome, though the bones in his face hinted that he might be thought handsome in his old age, if he reached it. He had dark-blue eyes that were good-tempered more often than otherwise and he had a reputation amongst junior officers for being sympathetic. He suffered fools, because there were so many of them, but not gladly.

'Don't they teach you fellers down in Canberra to be diplomatic?'

The Federal Police Force, headquartered in the Australian Capital Territory, was a comparatively recent invention. Being so new, it had had no time to become corrupt; based in Canberra, it had also been infected by the virus of natural superiority which, along with hay fever and blowflies, was endemic to the national capital. The police forces of the six States and the Northern Territory, older, wiser and more shop-soiled in the more sordid crimes, looked on the Federals in much the same way as State politicians looked on their Federal counterparts, smart arses who didn't know what went on in the gutters of the nation. The cops of Neapolis, bargaining with the pimps of Pompeii, had felt the same way about Rome and the Praetorian Guard.

Kenthurst blinked and his wide thin mouth tightened in his long-jawed face. He never liked these assignments here in New South Wales: the locals were too touchy. 'Sorry, Inspector. I didn't mean to criticize –'

'Sergeant, if we're going to get on together, let's forget any rivalry. I'm not trying to muscle in on your territory – looking after a couple like the Timoris would be the last thing I'd ask for. You called in the local boys from North Sydney and they called us in from Homicide. I don't want to take your President away from you. This is the biggest weekend of the year, maybe in Australia's history, and I was looking forward to spending it with my wife and kids. So let's co-operate, okay?'

Kenthurst nodded and looked around to see if anyone had overheard the exchange. But Malone did not tick a man off in

8

front of his own men. He had his own diplomacy, of a sort.

Malone looked down at the sheet-covered body. The police photographer had taken his shots and the body was ready for disposal; Malone could hear the siren of the approaching ambulance. 'Masutir – what was his first name?'

'Mohammed. He was a Muslim, same as the President. He was a kind of second secretary, a pretty innocuous sort of guy as far as I can tell.'

'Poor bugger.' Malone looked around the grounds of the old house. All the lights were on, but there were big patches of black shadow under the trees. The grounds sloped down steeply to the waterfront and just below them a ferry, lights ablaze, drifted in towards the Kirribilli wharf. Once upon a time, before he and Lisa had started their family, they had lived just up the ridge from this house and he had caught that ferry to work. 'Looks like the shot could have come from that block of flats.'

Kenthurst looked towards the block of flats just showing above the trees on the street side of the house. 'It would have to've been from the top floor. I think the local boys are over there now.'

'What was Timori doing out here?'

'I gather he always liked to go for a walk after dinner – he wanted to go up the street, round the block, but we put the kybosh on that. He was famous for it back home in Palucca. No matter where he was, he always went for a walk after dinner. Just like President Truman used to, only *he* used to go for his walk before breakfast. Timori is a great admirer of Harry Truman, though I don't know Truman would have liked that.'

It was Malone's turn to blink, but he made no comment. Kenthurst might turn out to be a mine of inconsequential information; but Malone knew from experience how sometimes a nugget could be found amongst all the fools' gold. 'What happened when this feller went down? Did anyone hear the shot?'

'No. Those galahs outside were chanting their usual stuff. *Go home, Timori,* all that crap.'

'How has Timori been taking the demos?'

'He just smiles – I guess he's used to it. I gather the Paluccans were a bloody sight more vocal and violent than our galahs.

9

He'd given up taking his walks the last couple of months in Bunda.'

'What about Madame Timori – did she scream or faint or anything?'

'Nothing. She just got angry, started swearing – she knows a lot of words besides *merde*. She's a real tough cookie.'

Kenthurst was about the same age as Malone, forty-two, but Malone guessed they looked at different television programmes. Kenthurst, a smart dresser, looked as if he might be a fan of *Miami Vice*, where all the girls were tough cookies. But he had said 'galahs', so he wasn't entirely Americanized. Malone was glad of that. He himself wasn't anti-American, but he had grown tired of the standards for his own work being set by *Hill Street Blues* and *Miami Vice*. Police work, 99 per cent of the time, was plod, plod, plod and the music was slower than an undertaker's jingle. The New South Wales Police Force had its critics, but it wasn't the worst police force in the world, far from it.

'Why are the Timoris here at Kirribilli House?'

'It's only temporary. The PM wanted them taken to Canberra, kept on the RAAF base there or even at Duntroon, so we could keep tight security on them. Madame Timori wouldn't have a bar of that. Sydney or nothing, she told them. So they shoved them in here till they find a place for them. It's been a bloody headache.' He gestured at the sheet-covered corpse. 'Maybe they'll be glad to move now.'

'Let's go in and talk to them.'

They walked up the gravelled path to the steeply-gabled stone house. It had been built just over a hundred years ago by a rich merchant with the commercial-sounding name of Feez and in time it had been acquired by the Federal Government as a residence for visiting VIPs. Then a certain Prime Minister, chafing that such a charming house in such a beautiful situation right on Sydney Harbour should be wasted on visitors, some of them unwelcome, had commandeered it as his official Sydney residence. The present Prime Minister, who hated The Lodge, the main official residence in Canberra, spent as much time here as he could, being a Sydney man. Malone wondered how Phil Norval, the PM, felt about these unwelcome guests.

10

The Timoris were in the drawing-room. They were a handsome couple in the way that the ultra-rich often are; money had bought the extras to the looks they had been born with. Only when one looked closer did one see that Abdul Timori's looks had begun to crumble; his bloodshot eyes looked half-asleep in the dark hammocks beneath them and his jowls had loosened. Delvina Timori, however, looked better than when Malone had last seen her close-up, ten or twelve years ago; she had never been strictly beautiful, but she had a dancer's arrogance and grace and there was a sexuality to her that fogged-up most men's view of her. Only their womenfolk looked at her cold-eyed.

'Scobie Malone, isn't it?' she said in the husky voice that sounded phoney to women and like a siren's song to their tone-deaf escorts. 'I remember you! Darling, this is Mr Malone. He used to be in the Vice Squad when I was with the dance company. He thought all we dancers were part-time whores.' She gave Malone a bright smile that said, *You never proved it.* 'I hope you've changed your mind about dancers, Mr Malone. Especially since Australia is now so *cultured.*'

Outside, on the other side of the harbour, the fireworks had begun. The sky was an explosion of illumination. The city turned red, white and blue, the colours of the British, the founding fathers; someone had forgotten to light the green and gold rockets and local patriotism, as so often, remained in the dark. The citizens were still getting used to the idea that their nation was two hundred years old this week, not sure whether it was a good or a bad thing.

The ambulance had just come in the gates and in a moment or two Mohammed Masutir, the dead man, would be lifted into it and carted away to the morgue; but as far as Malone could see, Madame Timori had already forgotten him, had put his murder out of her mind.

'I'd like to ask some questions, Mr President.'

'The President is too upset at the moment to answer questions,' said the President's wife and, belatedly, made her own effort to look upset. She dabbed at her eyes with a handkerchief; Malone noticed it came away unmarked by any of the thick mascara she wore. 'Poor Mr Masutir.'

11

'Yes.' Malone noticed that she, notorious for her jewels, wore none tonight. She was crying poor mouth, silently. But there were the emeralds that had been taken from Masutir's pocket. He said bluntly, 'The bullet was meant for the President – we can be pretty sure of that. Do you know of any organized opposition group here in Australia that would be likely to try and kill you, sir?'

'Start asking that trash in the street outside –'

Timori raised a tired hand, silencing his wife. He took a sip of Scotch from the glass in his other hand; he was one of those Muslims, Malone guessed, who bent his religion to his own tastes. Malone, a Catholic, knew the feeling.

'Mr Malone, I have enemies everywhere. Tell me a ruler who does not. The President of the United States, your Prime Minister –'

'I don't think Philip Norval thinks of himself as a ruler, darling,' said Madame Timori. 'Does he rule you, Mr Malone?'

Malone gave her a smile and looked at Kenthurst. 'Sergeant Kenthurst could answer that better than I can. He's from Canberra, where everyone rules. Yes, Sergeant?'

Clements had knocked on the door and put his tousled head into the room. 'Can I see you a moment, Inspector?'

Malone went out into the hall. With the edge of his eye and mind he was aware of the furnishings of the house; it was the sort of place he wished he could afford for Lisa and the kids. Then he consoled himself: the voters could kick you out of here quicker than any foreclosing bank. 'What is it, Russ?'

'None of those out in the street know anything – I'm inclined to believe them. We've been into those flats opposite – some of the owners are away for the weekend. Those that are home said they heard nothing because of the noise of the clowns up the street.'

'What about the top-floor flats? That'd be the best bet where the shot came from.'

'The whole of the top floor is owned by an old lady, a –' Clements looked at his notebook '– a Miss Kiddle. The bloke below her thought she should be home, but we can't raise her.'

Malone looked at the burly, greying sergeant in uniform behind Clements. 'What do you reckon, Fred?'

12

Thumper Murphy was a senior sergeant in the local North Sydney division. He had played rugby for the State and for Australia; his approach to football opponents and law-breakers was the same: straight through them. He was the last of a dying breed and Malone sometimes wondered if the Force could stand their loss. 'We could bash the front door down. I've got a sledge-hammer in me car.'

'I thought sledge-hammers had gone out of fashion.'

'Not on my turf,' said Thumper with a broken-toothed grin.

'Righto, get in any way you can. But don't scare hell out of the old lady.'

Thumper Murphy, accompanied by Clements, went away to get his sledge-hammer and Malone went back into the drawing-room. The President had lapsed back into the bleary-eyed look he had had when Malone had first walked into the room; the whisky glass in his hand was now empty. Madame Timori took the glass from him, slapped his wrist lightly as if he were a naughty child, and glanced at Malone.

'I've suggested to Sergeant Kenthurst that the President be allowed to go to bed. He's worn out.'

Malone looked at Kenthurst, who somehow managed to shrug with his eyebrows, *What could I say?* 'All right, Madame Timori. But I'd like to see the President again in the morning. By then I hope we'll know where we're going.'

Timori was helped to his feet by his wife; he suddenly looked ten years older, sick and tired. 'You don't know where you're going, Inspector? Neither do we. Good night.'

He brushed off his wife's helping hand and walked, a little unsteadily, out of the room. Madame Timori looked at the two policemen. 'We've been through a lot this past week, as you've probably read.'

And it hasn't put a hair of your head out of place, Malone thought. Surviving a two-day siege of their palace, then a successful, though not bloody, coup, seemed hardly to have fazed her at all. Exile, however, might do that.

'You may have to go through a lot more, Madame. This may not be the last attempt on the President's life. Or on yours,' he added and waited for the effect of the remark.

She did not flinch. 'I've had three attempts on my life in the

13

past three years. One gets used to it.' It was bravado, but Malone had to admire it. 'I suppose we were careless this evening. One just doesn't expect assassination attempts in Australia. Except character assassination,' she added with a smile that would have cut a thousand throats. 'Now, is there anyone else you'd like to question?'

She had taken charge of the investigation. Malone grinned inwardly: Lisa would enjoy the police gossip in bed tonight. If he got to bed . . . 'Anyone you'd care to suggest?'

Madame Timori gave him a look that would have demoted him right back to cadet if she'd had the authority. 'The household staff?'

'I think we can leave them till last. I'd like to talk to the staff you brought with you from Palucca. They'd know more about your enemies.' He was treading on dangerous ground. He was aware of the warning waves coming out of Kenthurst, the Canberra man. *You're dealing with a Federal Government guest, a personal friend of the Prime Minister.* 'That is, if you don't mind, Madame?'

'You mean am I going to claim diplomatic immunity for them?'

'I don't think they'd want that. Not if they want to know who is trying to kill their President.' *Even if he's only an ex-President now.*

'You sound so efficient, Inspector. So unlike our own police back home. I suppose, then, you should start with Sun Lee.'

Sun Lee was the President's private secretary, a Chinese in his mid-forties with a skin as smooth as jade and eyes like black marbles. He was just as cold as both those stones. 'I have nothing to tell you, Inspector.'

Malone looked at Madame Timori, who gave him a smug smile. Then he looked back at the Chinese. 'Maybe you could show me Mr Masutir's room?'

Sun frowned, a thin crack in the jade. 'He shared a room with me – the accommodation here is limited –' He spoke with all the expansive snobbery of a man accustomed to a palace. 'There is nothing in Mr Masutir's room but his personal belongings.'

'Those are what I want to see.'

14

Sun glanced at Madame Timori, but she said nothing. Then he turned abruptly and led Malone out of the room and upstairs. The house, for an official residence, *was* small. Australia did not believe in any grandeur for those it voted into office; that was reserved for those forced upon it, the Queen's Governors and Governor-General. There was a substantial mansion right next door to Kirribilli House, but that was the Sydney residence of the Governor-General and no place for a deposed President. The Queen, through her representative, only entertained exiled monarchs. A certain protocol had to be observed, even in disgrace.

The room was comfortably and attractively furnished, but Sun obviously thought it was a converted closet stocked from a discount house. 'There is no room to move . . . Mr Masutir's things are still in his suitcase. We were only allowed to bring one suitcase each.'

'I read in the papers that the RAAF plane that brought you was loaded with baggage.'

'The newspapers, as always, got it wrong. We brought packing cases, but they are full of official papers – records, files, that sort of thing. President Timori wanted to leave nothing for the vandals who have taken over the palace.'

'What about Madame Timori? Did she bring only one suitcase?'

'Madame Timori has a position to uphold.'

'I thought she might have. The papers said she brought twelve cases and four trunks. But women never travel lightly, do they? So they tell me.'

Masutir's suitcase, a genuine Vuitton or a good Hong Kong fake, Malone wasn't sure which, was not locked. Malone flipped back the lid, was surprised at how neatly everything was packed; had Masutir been packed for weeks, waiting for the inevitable? Most of the contents told Malone nothing except that Masutir had always bought quality: the shirts, the socks, the pyjamas were all silk. In a pocket in the lid were Masutir's passport and a black leather-bound notebook.

Malone flipped through the passport. 'Mr Masutir had been to Australia before?'

'I understand he had been here before.'

15

'Six times in the past –' Malone looked at the earliest date stamp '– eight months. Did you know about those visits, Mr Sun?'

If Sun had known about the visits he didn't show it now. 'No. Mr Masutir was more Madame Timori's secretary than my assistant. Back home in Palucca she was a very busy woman, as you may know.'

'Are you a Paluccan, Mr Sun?'

'Fourth generation. My family came to Bunda from Hong Kong after the Opium War.'

'Which side were they on?' Sun looked blank and Malone added, 'The war?'

Sun still looked blank, made no answer. So much for being a smart arse, thought Malone; but the quietly arrogant Chinese was beginning to get under his skin. Malone flipped through the black notebook, saw a list of Sydney addresses and phone numbers. He decided against asking Sun about them.

'I'll take this. I'll give you a receipt for it.'

'Can you do that?'

'Do you want me to find out who murdered Mr Masutir?'

The tiny frown was there again, but just for a moment. 'Of course. But how will his address book help you?'

'We have to start somewhere, Mr Sun. Every murderer has a name. Our murderer's may be in this.' He held up the notebook, then slipped it into his pocket. 'I think that'll be all, Mr Sun.'

Sun looked surprised, and Malone was surprised to see him capable of such an expression. 'You don't want to question me?'

'I'll be back to do that, Mr Sun. In the meantime you prepare your answers.'

He went ahead of the Chinese down the stairs, not bothering to look back at him or say anything further. He sensed there might be something in Masutir's notebook which might worry Sun Lee. A night to think about it might put another crack in the jade face.

When Malone reached the front hallway Clements was waiting there for him. He read the bad news on the big man's face

16

before Clements said it. 'We bashed the door down and found the old lady. She'd been strangled.'

'Any sign of the killer?'

Clements shook his head. 'He'd left his gun, though. A Springfield .30, with a telescopic sight. He was a pro, I'd say. I've rung Fingerprints, they're on their way.'

'What about the old lady? Had he knocked her around?'

'No. It was a neat job, with a piece of rope. He'd come prepared. Like I say, he was a real pro.'

'Righto, I'll be over there in a while. In the meantime, give this to Andy Graham, tell him I want every one of those Sydney addresses and phone numbers tracked down. Tell him to tell them to stand by when he finds out who they are. I'll want to interview them.' He handed the notebook to Clements, aware of Sun standing behind him and hearing every word. 'Something doesn't add up here. Maybe they meant to kill Masutir, after all. You think so, Mr Sun?'

The mask was flawless this time. 'It would be presumptuous of me even to guess, Inspector. I am not a detective.'

Clements watched the small exchange, but his own wide open face was now expressionless. 'I'll wait for you over the road, Inspector.'

Malone went back into the drawing-room, said directly to Madame Timori, 'There's been another murder. An old lady over in the flats opposite.'

She just nodded. She did not appear disturbed; the handkerchief was not even produced this time. She stood up, giving herself regal airs if not a regal air, which is different; she was the most common of commoners but she had always had aspirations. She had always wanted to dance the royal roles when she had been with the dance company; nobody would ever have believed her as Cinderella. 'I'm retiring for the night.'

I'd like to retire, too, thought Malone; or anyway, go to bed. 'I'll be back tomorrow morning, Madame. I hope the President will be well enough to answer some questions.'

'What sort of questions have you in mind? I'm sure I could answer them all.' She paused, as if she might sit down again.

'You must be tired,' said Malone, not offering her any

17

further opportunity to take over the investigation. 'Good night, Madame. I'll see you in the morning.'

He went out into the warm night air. There he exchanged information with the two other Homicide men who had come with him and Clements. One of them was Andy Graham, a young overweight detective constable who had just transferred from the uniformed division. He was all enthusiasm and ideas, most of which were as blunt as Thumper Murphy's sledge-hammer.

'I've got the notebook, Inspector.' He brandished it like a small black flag. 'I'll have 'em all waiting for you first thing tomorrow morning.'

'Not all at once, Andy. Use your judgement, get the big ones first.'

'Right, Inspector, right.'

'Take Kerry here with you. Divide up the addresses and numbers between you. Be polite.'

'Right.'

As he and Clements crossed the road towards the block of flats, Malone said, 'How come you never say *right* to everything I say?'

'Do you want me to?'

'No.'

'Right.'

The old lady had been taken away in the same ambulance that had taken the dead Masutir; the holiday weekend casualties were starting early and these two not for the usual reason, road accidents. Up towards the corner of the street a large crowd had now congregated behind the barricades that had been thrown up. The protestors had stopped demonstrating, jarred into silence by the sight of the two bodies being pushed into the ambulance, and the crowd was now just a large restless wash of curiosity. Double murders just didn't happen in Kirri-billi: the local estate agents would have to work hard next week to continue promoting it as a 'desirable area'.

The fireworks were still scribbling on the black sky, but the crowd seemed to have turned its back on them. A band was playing in the open court at the northern end of the Opera House and the music drifted across the water, banged out at intervals by the explosions of the fireworks. The waters of the harbour were ablaze with drifting lights: ferries, yachts, rowboats, the reflected catherine wheels, shooting stars and lurid waterfalls of the fireworks. Malone wondered if the local Aborigines here on the Kirribilli shore had waved any firesticks in celebration on the night of that day in January 1788 when Captain Arthur Phillip had raised the British flag and laid the seed, perhaps unwittingly, for a new nation. As he walked across the road Malone looked for an Aborigine or two amongst the demonstrators, with or without firesticks to light their way, but there was none.

The Fingerprints men were just finishing as Malone entered the top-floor flat past Thumper's handiwork, the splintered front door. 'Can't find a print, Inspector. We've dusted everything, but he either wiped everything clean or wore gloves. He must have been a cold-blooded bastard.'

'Have you tried the bathroom?'

'There's two of them. Nothing there.'

'Try the handle or the button of the cistern. I don't care how cold-blooded he was, he'd have gone in there for a nervous pee some time.' The senior Fingerprints man looked unimpressed and Malone went on, 'It's the simple, habitual things that let people down, even the most careful ones. I'll give you a hundred to one that a man doesn't take a leak with a glove on.'

'I couldn't find mine if I had a glove on,' said Clements with a grin.

The Fingerprints men looked peeved that a Homicide man, even if he was an inspector, should tell them their job. They went away into the bathrooms and two minutes later the senior man came back to say there was a distinct print on the cistern button in the second bathroom. He looked even more peeved that Malone had been right.

'The second bathroom looks as if it's rarely used, maybe just for visitors. The print's a new one.'

'Righto, check your records,' said Malone. 'I'll want a report on it first thing in the morning. Sergeant Clements will call you.'

Malone was left alone with Clements, Thumper Murphy and the sergeant in charge of the North Sydney detectives, a slim handsome man named Stacton. 'Okay, so what have we got?'

Clements pointed to the dismantled rifle which lay on the table in the dining-room in which they stood. 'He must have brought it in dismantled and put it together once he was in the flat – it's a special job. Then after he'd fired the shot, he dismantled it again and put it in a kit-bag, the sort squash players carry. Nobody would've noticed him if he'd come in here behind those demonstrators.'

'Where'd you find the bag and the gun?'

'Under the stairs, down on the ground floor. Someone must've come in as he was going out and he had to hide.'

Malone looked at Stacton. 'Would it have been one of your uniformed men?'

'I doubt it, Inspector, but I'll check. They were busy holding back the demo. And I gather there was a hell of a lot of noise – no one heard the shot.'

'There's no security door down at the front?'

'None. People ask for trouble these days.'

'How did he get into the flat? I noticed there's a grille security door on the front door.'

'I dunno. There's no sign of forced entry. The old lady must have let him in.'

'A stranger?' Malone looked around him. The furniture was antique and expensive; it had possibly taken a lifetime to accumulate. It was the sort of furniture that Lisa would love to surround herself with; he found himself admiring it. The paintings on the walls were expensive, too: nothing modern and disturbing, but reassuring landscapes by Streeton and Roberts. Miss Kiddle had surrounded herself with her treasures, but they hadn't protected her. 'This is a pretty big flat for one old woman.'

'She has a married nephew who owns a property outside Orange. I've rung Orange and asked someone out to tell him. It's gunna bugger up his celebrations.'

'It's buggered up mine,' said Malone and looked out the window at another burst of fireworks. The past was going up in a storm of smoke and powder, you could smell it through the open windows. The kids would love it, though the grown-ups might wonder at the significance. It took Australians some time to be worked up about national occasions, unless they were sporting ones. The Italians and the Greeks, who could get worked up about anything, would enjoy the fireworks the most.

'Well, I guess we'd better make a start with our guesses. Any suggestions?'

Clements chewed his lip, a habit he had had as long as Malone had known him. 'Scobie, I dunno whether this is worth mentioning. I was going through some stuff that came in from Interpol. You heard of that bloke Seville, Miguel Seville the terrorist? Well, Interpol said he'd been sighted in Singapore last week. He got out before they could latch on to him. He'd picked up a flight out of Dubai. They managed to check on all the flights going back to Europe after he'd been spotted. He wasn't on any of them, not unless he'd got off somewhere along the way. Bombay, Abu Dhabi, somewhere like that.'

'He might have gone to Sri Lanka,' said Stacton. 'He's always around where there's trouble.'

When Malone had first started on the force no one had been interested in crims, terrorists then being unknown, outside the State, even outside one's own turf. Now the field was international, the world was the one big turf.

'The betting's just as good that he came this way,' said Clements.

Malone said, 'Who'd hire him? The generals who've taken over in Palucca have no connection with any of the terrorist mobs, at least not on the record.'

'Seville is different. That's according to the Italians, who've had the most trouble with him. He's not interested in ideology any more. He's just a bloody mercenary, a capitalist like the rest of us.'

'Speak for yourself. We're not all big-time punters like you.'

Clements grinned; his luck with the horses was notorious, even embarrassing. 'You pay Seville, he'll organize trouble for you. A bomb raid at an airport, a machine-gun massacre, an assassination, anything. Someone could have hired him to do this job.'

'Righto, get Fingerprints to photo-fax that print through to

21

Interpol, see if it matches anything they might have on Seville. Have we called in Special Branch yet?'

'They arrived just as I was putting me sledge-hammer away,' said Thumper Murphy.

'A pity,' said Malone and everyone grinned. 'Well, it looks as if we're all going to be one big happy family. The Feds, the Specials, you fellers and us.'

'I always liked you, Scobie,' said Thumper Murphy. 'They could have sent us one of them other bastards you have in Homicide.'

It sounds just like Palucca must have sounded, Malone thought. Each faction wanting all the others out of the way. He sighed, just as Kenthurst had said the President had sighed when the emeralds had been taken from Masutir's pocket. Only then did he remember he hadn't asked anyone about the emeralds.

'Where are the emeralds?'

'Kenthurst said he gave 'em back to Madame Timori,' said Clements. 'She asked for them.'

'She would.' He wondered how many tears had been shed for the Mother of the Poor, as she had called herself, when she had left Palucca.

2

Palucca was the largest of the old Spice Islands. Columbus was heading there when he accidentally ran into America; he had coined the phrase, 'Isn't it a small world?' and thought he had proved it when he finished up some 11,000 miles short of his intended destination. The Spice Islands survived his non-arrival, but European civilized types, led by Ferdinand Magellan, arrived in 1511 and from then on the aroma of the Spices began to change. Nothing has ever been improved by the advent of outsiders, nothing, that is, but the lot of the invaders.

The Portuguese were succeeded by the Spanish, the Dutch and the British; the Islanders just shrugged, learned a few words of the newest language and dreamed of the old days when they were barbaric and happy. Their paradise had been

spoiled by the Europeans who, seeking profits, had come looking for the spices that would, in addition to the sweet taste of
profits, make their putrid and indigestible food edible. The
pepper, nutmegs, cloves, mace, ginger and cinnamon, added
to what the Europeans ate back in what they thought of as
civilization, saved the appetites and often the lives of the
civilized millions. Spices were also used by physicians to treat
diseases of the blood, the stomach, head and chest; sometimes
a cookery recipe was mistaken for a medical prescription, but
it made no difference anyway. The patient usually died and the
family got the bill, the physician's bill being larger than the
grocer's.

The Dutch stayed longest and eventually the Spice Islands
were absorbed into what became known as the Dutch East
Indies. The Japanese came in 1942, were welcomed but soon
wore out their welcome and were gone in 1945. The Dutch
came back; but they, too, were unwelcome. In 1949 the Indies
obtained their independence and became Indonesia. The Paluccans, however, declared their own independence and the rest
of Indonesia, tired of fighting the Dutch and just wanting to
get on with the post-war peace that the rest of the world was
enjoying, let them go.

The Timori family, which had been the leading family in
Palucca for centuries, were pains in the neck anyway. They were
conspirators, connivers, meddlers, and corrupt: ideal rulers to
deal with the Europeans, Americans, Chinese and Russians
who would soon be coming to court them.

Mohammed Timori, Abdul's father, had himself elected
President for life, a title he chose in preference to Sultan, to
which he was entitled by inheritance; he was prepared to make
a bow towards democracy, though it hurt every joint in his
body. He moved back into Timoro Palace, the family home
that had been commandeered by the Dutch a hundred years
before. He said public prayers of praise to Allah, but privately
he told Allah He had better come good with some United
Nations aid or Palucca would be in the hands of the Chinese
money-lenders before the next crop of nutmegs.

Allah came good with better than United Nations hand-outs:
oil was found on the north coast of the big island. It did not

23

make Palucca a rich country, because the oil reserves were judged to be only moderate; nonetheless, Palucca was suddenly more than just a source of ginger and nutmegs and the oil companies of the West came bearing their own aromatic spices, bribes with which to start Swiss bank accounts. The Timori family were suddenly rich, even if their country wasn't. They shared their wealth like true democrats, 10 per cent to the voters and 90 per cent to the Timoris, and thought of themselves as benevolent, honest and born to rule. They were no different from all the Europeans who had preceded them in Palucca.

Mohammed Timori died in 1953 on the same day as Josef Stalin, which meant he got no space at all in Western newspapers. The Americans, prompted by John Foster Dulles, decided to compensate for that lack of regard; they established a naval base and named it in his honour. Abdul Timori, who was then twenty-five, was called home from Europe to succeed his father. His election as President for life was no more than a formality, like high tea, monogamy and other European importations, and was looked upon as just as much a giggle.

Abdul Timori had been labelled by the Fleet Street tabloids as the Playboy of the Western World, though Synge would have disowned him. His mistresses were laid endlessly across Europe and America; love-making was his only successful sport. He owned a string of racehorses that invariably finished without a place; bookmakers quoted them at prices that embarrassed both the horses and the jockeys who rode them. He took up motor-racing and drove in the Mille Miglia, the Targa Florio and the Le Mans 24-hour event; he finished in none of them, managing, miraculously, to emerge unscathed from crashes that earned him the nickname Abdul the Wrecker. His father, however, had insisted on his death-bed that Abdul should succeed him, and the ruling party, its faction leaders all afraid of each other, had agreed. They had assumed that Abdul would be no more than a playboy President and they, splitting the spoils between them like true democrats, could run the country as they wished.

They were mistaken. Abdul turned out to be a better politician than any of them; and a despot to boot, a boot he used to great effect. The two jails of Bunda, the national capital,

were soon full of party men who thought they could be independent of him; common criminals were hanged, to make way in
the cells for the jailed politicians. The latter, however, did not
remain there long. Nothing changes the mind of a pragmatic
politician so quickly as his having to share a prison cell with his
rivals; it is more upsetting than sharing a voting booth with a
citizen voting against you. All at once they were born-again
Timori supporters, shouting hallelujahs, or the Muslim equivalent, to the skies. The army generals, already wooed by Abdul
with promises of long courses in Britain and the United States,
smiled cynically at the venality of politicians and swore to
Abdul that he had nothing to fear from them.

Abdul, in turn, was wooed by the Americans. Recognizing
that anyone who raised the anti-communist banner was going
to be saluted by Washington, he invited the Americans, for a
consideration, to enlarge their naval base. For the next thirty-
four years Palucca enjoyed a stable existence, a state of affairs
accepted by all but those who believed in freedom of expression,
honest government and democracy. Since Abdul Timori believed in none of those aberrations and the Americans forgot
to remind him of them, nothing, it seemed, was going to disturb
the Timori delusion of his own grandeur.

He married the daughter of another old family, but it was a
marriage of inconvenience: he found she got in the way of his
mistresses. He divorced her by clapping his hands and telling
her she wasn't wanted; a procedure that several foreign ambassadors, whose wives were a hindrance, marvelled at and
envied. Timori married again, this time one of his mistresses,
but she at once turned into a wife and after a year he got rid
of her, too. Finally, ten years ago, he had married Delvina
O'Reilly, who had come to Bunda as a speciality dancer, a Mata
Hari whose intelligence work was only in her own interests. Her
mother had been a Malay, her father an RAAF sergeant-pilot;
she had been educated in a convent but had never learned to
be a good Catholic or even a good girl. At dancing school it
was said that the only time her legs were together was during
the execution of an *entrechat*; one smitten choreographer tried
to write a ballet for a horizontal ballerina. When she married
Abdul Timori, in a wedding extravaganza that *Paris-Match* ran

25

over five pages, she let him know it was for good: for her good if not his. Abdul, to everyone's surprise, not least his own, accepted her dictum.

Then the plug fell out of the oil market and Palucca's economy slid downhill on the slick. The Americans were suddenly more interested in Central America than in South-east Asia; Washington also, at long last, began to have pangs about the corruption in the Timori regime. Abdul and Delvina Timori began to assume the image of a major embarrassment. The Americans, belatedly, looked around for an acceptable alternative, meanwhile pressing Timori to resign on the grounds of ill-health. Madame Timori, who was in the best of health, even if her husband wasn't, told the Americans to get lost, a frequent location for them in foreign policy. The British, the French, the Dutch and all the lesser ex-colonial powers sat back and smiled smugly. As a mandarin in Whitehall remarked, nothing succeeds in making one feel good so much as seeing someone else fail.

Then the Paluccan generals, all too old now for courses at Sandhurst and West Point, tired of army manœuvres in which never a shot was fired, decided it was time they earned the medals with which they had decorated themselves. They staged a coup, asked the Americans to fly the Timoris out of Bunda and promised a brand new future for Palucca and the Paluccans.

That was when the trouble started *outside* Palucca.

3

'Nobody wants them,' said Russ Clements. 'The Americans wouldn't fly them out and they leaned on Canberra.'

'Kenthurst was telling me last night,' said Malone, 'that everyone down in Canberra wishes they'd move on. Including Phil Norval.'

'Canberra is going to be even more shitty when we tell 'em what came in from Interpol this morning.'

When Malone had arrived at Homicide this morning Clements had been waiting for him with a phone message from Fingerprints. The print on the cistern button in the Kiddle flat had been positively identified: it belonged to Miguel Seville.

'Are there any mug shots of Seville?' Malone asked.

'Just the one.'

Clements took a 5 x 4 photo out of the murder box, an old shoe carton that over the years had, successively, held all the bits and pieces of the cases he had worked on. It was falling apart, only held together by a patchwork skin of Scotch tape, but he held on to it as if it were some treasure chest in which lay the solution to all murders.

'It was taken about twelve years ago, when the Argentinian cops picked him up. That was before he became a mercenary, when he was with that Tupperware crowd. Tupperware?'

'Tupamaros.'

Clements grinned. 'I was close.'

'I know a Tupperware lady who wouldn't thank you for it.'

Malone looked at the photo of the curly-haired handsome young man. He would have been in his late twenties or early thirties when the photo was taken, but already the future was etched in his face: a defiance of all authority, a contempt for all political and social morality. Malone wondered if he had ever had any genuine belief in the Tupamaros' fight against the Argentinian junta and its repressive rule.

'He's taken the place of that Venezuelan guy,' said Clements. 'That Carlos. Whatever happened to him?'

'Special Branch said the rumour is that the Libyans got rid of him. Maybe we should ring up Gaddafi and ask him to get rid of this bloke, too.'

'You reckon he'll try another shot at Timori?'

'Depends how much he's been paid. And who's paying him.'

Malone looked out the window, over Hyde Park and down to the northern end where Macquarie Street ran into it. That street was where the State politicians conducted their small wars; but there was no terrorism. There might be vitriolic and vulgar abuse that made other parliaments look like church meetings, but there were no assassin's bullets. Now Timori, the unwanted guest, had, even if involuntarily, brought that danger to Sydney.

'Did The Dutchman have anything to say this morning?' So far Malone hadn't looked at this morning's newspapers. He

27

was not a radio listener and he usually got home too late to look at the evening TV news. When he got the news it was usually cold and in print, but he had found that the world still didn't get too far ahead of him. There was something comforting in being a little way behind it, as if the news had somehow been softened by the time it got to him.

'His usual garble. I dunno whether he's for or against Timori.'

'If Phil Norval's for him, The Dutchman will be against him.'

The Dutchman was Hans Vanderberg, the State Premier, an immigrant who had come to Australia right after World War Two, had become a trade union official, joined the Labour Party, got on well with the Irish Catholics who ran it, taken on some of their characteristics and ten years ago had become Leader of the Party and Premier. He was famous for his garbled speeches and his double-Dutch (or was it Irish?) logic; but he was the best politician in the country and he and everyone else knew it. He was also a magnificent hater and he hated no one more than Prime Minister Philip Norval.

Malone looked at his watch. 'We'd better get over to Kirribilli. What time do Presidents have breakfast?'

'I know what time I had mine. Six o'bloody clock.'

Malone grinned; he always liked working with Russ Clements. 'You'd better get used to it, sport. This looks like it's going to be a round-the-clock job.'

'How does Lisa feel about you working on the holiday weekend?'

'She wouldn't speak to me this morning. Neither would the kids. I'd promised to bring them all in to The Rocks to see the celebrations.'

'I was going to the races. I've got two hot tips for today.'

'Put them on SP. Where do you get your tips?'

'From a coupla SP bookies I used to raid when I was on the Gambling Squad.'

'How much are you ahead this year so far?'

'A thousand bucks and it's only January twenty-third. They'll be holding a Royal Commission into me if it keeps up.'

'What do you do with all your dough?' Clements always looked as if he didn't have his bus fare.

'Some day I'm gunna have an apartment in that block down

28

at the Quay, right there above the ferries. People will point the finger at me and say I made it outa graft, but I won't give a stuff. I'll pee on 'em from a great height and if some of it lands on some crims I've known, so much the better.'

Malone grinned, wished him well, stood up and led the way out of Homicide. The division was located on the sixth floor of a commercial building that the police department shared with other government departments, most of them minor. Security in this commercial building, because of the shared space with other departments going about their mundane business, was minimal. Malone sometimes wondered what would happen if some madman, bent on homicide towards Homicide, got loose in the building.

They drove through the bedecked streets of the city. The citizens held high hopes for the coming year; it was no use living in the past, even though they were celebrating it. They had just come through the worst recession in years; they had been told to tighten their belts, torture for the beer-bellied males of the population, but for this week they were letting out the notches. There is nothing like a carnival for helping one forget one's debts: banks are always closed on Carnival Day.

They drove over the Bridge, above the harbour already suffering a traffic-jam of yachts and cruisers and wind-surfers, and turned off into the tree-lined streets of Kirribilli. This small enclave on the north shore of the harbour, directly opposite the Opera House and the downtown skyscrapers, had had a chequered history. In the nineteenth century it had been the home of the wool merchants. In the 1920s middle-class apartments had been built on the waterfront. After World War Two it had gone downhill till in the late sixties it had become a nest for hippies and junkies. Then real estate agents, those latterday pioneers, had rediscovered it. Now it provided *pieds-à-terre* for retired millionaires, luxury apartments for some prominent businessmen, small town houses for young executives and their families and, almost as a gesture of social conscience, two or three rooming houses for those who couldn't afford the prices of the other accommodation. Kirribilli, an Aboriginal word meaning 'a good place to fish', also provided Sydney havens for the Governor-General, the Prime Minister and ASIO, the national intelligence organization. It was natural that the local elements, including those in the rooming houses, thought of themselves as exclusive.

The dead end street leading to Kirribilli House was blocked off by police barriers. The television and radio trucks and cars were parked on the footpaths of the narrow street. The anti-Timori demonstrators were jammed solid against the barriers; there was a sprinkling of Asians amongst them, but the majority were the regulars that Malone recognized from other demonstrations; in the past twenty years protest had become a participation sport. Standing behind the demonstrators, as if separated by some invisible social barrier, was a curious crowd of locals, some of them looking disturbed, as if already worrying about falling real estate barriers. Murder and political demos did nothing for the exclusivity of an area.

Standing just inside the gates of Kirribilli House was a group of thirty or forty Paluccans, men, women and children. They were all well dressed, some in Western clothes, others in Eastern; they looked nothing like the photos Malone had seen of those other refugees of recent years, the Vietnamese boat people. Yet for all their air of affluence they looked frightened and lost.

'They're probably the lot who came in with the Timoris on the RAAF planes,' Clements said. 'They've had them out at one of the migrant hostels.'

'Better question them, find out if any of them were missing last night. Get Andy Graham and Joe Raudonikis to talk to them.' Then Malone noticed the three Commonwealth cars parked in the driveway. 'Someone's here from Canberra.'

Someone was: the Prime Minister himself. As Malone and Clements walked towards the house, Philip Norval, backed by half a dozen staff and security men, came out of the front door with Police Commissioner John Leeds.

The Commissioner, as usual, was impeccably dressed; he was the neatest man Malone had ever met. He was not in uniform, probably as a concession to the holiday weekend, but was in a beautifully cut blazer, slacks, white shirt and police tie. Why do I always feel like a slob when I meet him? Malone thought.

30

Then he looked out of the corner of his eye at Clements, a real slob, and felt better.

'Ah, Inspector Malone.' Leeds stopped with a friendly half-smile. He nodded at Clements, but he was not a man to go right down the ranks with his greetings. He turned to the Prime Minister. 'Inspector Malone is in charge of the investigation, sir.'

Philip Norval put out his hand, the famous TV smile flashing on like an arc-lamp. He gave his greetings to everyone, even those who didn't vote for him. '*Scobie* Malone? I thought you'd be out at the Test.'

'Maybe Monday, sir. If . . .' Malone gestured towards the house. He had once played cricket for New South Wales as a fast bowler and might eventually have played for Australia; but he had enjoyed his cricket too much to be dedicated and ambitious and, though he never regretted it, had never gone on to realize his potential. In today's sports world of ambition, motivational psychologists, slave-master coaches and business managers, he knew he would have been looked upon as a bludger, the equivalent of someone playing on welfare.

Norval said, 'I'm going out there later.'

He would be, thought Malone. Though he had never shown any talent in any sport, Philip Norval never missed an opportunity to be seen at a major sporting event, preferably photographed with the winners. There had been one dreadful day at a croquet championship when, not understanding the game or the tally count, he had allowed himself to be photographed with the losers; in the end it hadn't mattered since they had all turned out to be conservative voters. He occasionally was photographed at an art show or at the opera, but his political advisers always told him there were no votes in those camera opportunities.

He was fifty but looked a youthful forty. Blond and handsome in the bland way that the electronic image had made international, he had been the country's highest paid television and radio star for a decade, the blow-dried and pancaked tin god host of chat shows and talk-back sessions, with a mellifluous voice and no enemies but the more acidic and envious TV critics who, if they were lucky, earned one-fiftieth of what he

31

was paid. A kitchen cabinet of rich industrialists and bankers, looking around for a PM they could manipulate into the correct right-wing attitudes, had taken him in hand and within six years put him in The Lodge, the Prime Minister's residence in Canberra. He had been there five years now, was in his second term and, though known as the Golden Puppet, so far looked safe from any real opposition.

'We have a problem here, Inspector.' He was famous for his fatuities: it came of too many years of playing to the lowest common denominator.

'Yes, sir.' Malone looked at Leeds, his boss, who was entitled to know first. 'We have a lead. We think the killer could be Miguel Seville.'

'Seville?' said Norval. 'Who's he? Some guy from Palucca?'

'He's an international terrorist, an Argentinian.' Leeds was perturbed, looked searchingly at Malone. 'You sure?'

'It's a guess, sir, but an educated one.'

Norval looked at one of his aides for his own education: it was tough enough trying to keep up with the voters' names, let alone those of terrorists. The aide nodded and Norval himself then nodded. 'Oh sure, I've read about him. But how did he get into the act?'

'I don't know, sir,' said Malone. 'I'm just going in now to put some more questions to President Timori.'

'Take it easy, Inspector,' said Norval. 'You'd better explain what we've decided, Commissioner. Keep in touch.'

He shook hands with Leeds, Malone and even Clements, looked around to make sure he hadn't missed an outstretched paw, then went up the driveway to the waiting cars. Just inside the gates he stopped and raised his arms in greeting to the crowd at the barriers. The demonstrators booed and jeered and suggested several unattractive destinations. He just gave them the famous smile, aware of the newsreel cameras advancing on him, then got into the lead car and the convoy moved off. The Golden Puppet might be manipulated in significant matters, but no one knew better than he how to juggle the superficial.

'What's been decided, sir?' said Malone.

'Would you leave us alone for five minutes, Sergeant?' Leeds

32

waited till Clements had moved away, then said, 'The PM would like us to have hands-off as much as possible.'

'What the hell does that mean?'

'Don't get testy with me, Inspector –'

'Sorry, sir. But why?'

'Politics. You and I have run up against them before. I understand the dead man, Masutir, had a bag of emeralds in his pocket, a pretty rich packet.'

'I wouldn't even guess – none of us knows anything about gems. I could ask Madame Timori. Sergeant Kenthurst, from the Federals, said she grabbed them as soon as she saw them.'

'She's not going to tell us anything about them. That's part of our problem – they've landed out here with what seems like half the Paluccan Treasury. The RAAF who brought them out of Bunda also brought six packing cases. Customs went up to Richmond last night, to the RAAF base, and went through the cases.'

'I thought the Timoris would have claimed diplomatic immunity.'

'They would have, if they'd known what was happening. It wasn't a ministerial order. Some smart aleck in Customs, one of the left-wingers, overstepped the mark. The cases were opened and the contents down on paper before the Minister got wind of it. You know what happens when something goes down on paper in a government department. It becomes indelible and then multiplies.'

Malone grinned. 'I thought that's what happens at Headquarters?'

'Do you want to finish up as the constable in charge of a one-man station in the bush?' But Leeds allowed himself a smile; then he sobered again: 'The Timoris brought out an estimated twenty-two million dollars' worth of gold, gems and US currency.'

Malone whistled silently and Leeds nodded. Though there was a considerable difference in rank, there was an empathy between the two men. Twice before they had been caught up in politics, with Malone as the ball-carrier and the Commissioner, in the end, having to call the play. Malone began to wonder how far he would be allowed to carry the ball in this game. Perhaps he should send for Thumper Murphy and his sledge-hammer.

'There's a rumour they have a couple of billion salted away in Switzerland. It's no wonder the Americans didn't want them.'

'How did we get landed with them?' Malone said.

'I thought you knew. Madame Timori was an old girl-friend of the PM's.'

Malone could feel the ball getting heavier. He looked over Leeds' shoulder and saw that Madame Timori, in white slacks and a yellow silk shirt, had come out on to the veranda of the house and was gazing steadily at him and the Commissioner.

'Well, I'd better get it over with. Just routine questions?'

'Unless you put your foot in it again, like you used to.' Leeds buttoned up his blazer. The morning was already hot, the temperature already in the eighties, but he looked as if he might be in his air-conditioned office. 'Your tie's loose.'

'Yes, sir.' Malone tightened his tie. 'I'm afraid Madame Timori may want to hang me with it.'

'Don't look for me to cut you down. Good luck.'

He went out of the gates and Malone was left feeling alone and exposed. Twenty-two years ago, in his first representative game for the State, he had gone in as the last-wicket batsman to face two of the quickest bowlers in the country. One of them had hit him under the heart with his first ball and he had gone down like a pole-axed steer. He had somehow recovered and seen out the rest of the over and on the last ball, foolishly, had scored a run to bring him to the other end. There he had been hit twice in the ribs by the second bowler and he had found himself wondering why he had taken up such a dangerous sport as cricket. The bruises had taken two weeks to fade.

He walked towards Madame Timori wondering how long the bruises she would give him would take to fade.

34

TWO

1

Miguel Seville hated Australia and Australians. Not on political or ideological grounds; it was difficult to take seriously the parish pump policies of this backwater. No, he hated the country, or anyway Sydney, because it was so brash, materialistic and uncultured compared to his own Buenos Aires; he hated the people for the same grating faults. He had been here once before at the secret invitation of an Aboriginal radical group; he had found the blacks as objectionable as the whites. Loud, brash, with opinions on everything: nobody wanted to learn, especially from a foreigner, even an invited one. With the disappearance of Carlos, he had become the top man in his trade; but the Aboriginal radicals had wanted to argue every point with him. In the end he had walked out on them and gone back to Damascus.

That was where he had been two weeks ago when the phone call had come from Beirut. He had gone down to that ruined city and in an apartment in the Muslim quarter met the man who had phoned him.

'You will be paid one million American dollars.'

Seville tried to show no surprise; but it was difficult. His price was high, but it had never been as high as this. All at once the recent dreaming might come true: he could retire, go back to Argentina and be amongst his own again.

'Less my ten per cent.' Rah Zaid was a thin, thin-faced, thin-eyed man who always, no matter what the weather or the time of year, wore a neatly-pressed black silk suit and an Arab head-dress. He had a husky voice that suggested over-exposure to desert sandstorms; the truth, less romantic, was overexposure to American cigarettes. He was smoking now, almost shutting his eyes against the smoke. The air in the apartment

35

was acrid, but that could be the after-effects of the Christian shell that this morning had wiped off the balcony beyond the living-room's french doors. 'As usual.'

'The client is also paying you commission, I suppose?' Seville didn't resent what Zaid made out of the contracts; he was the best contact man in the trade that employed them. Utterly amoral, he was nevertheless utterly to be trusted. If he were not, he would have been dead years ago. Seville could have been the one to kill him.

Zaid smiled thinly behind the cigarette smoke: everything about him seemed to be squeezed tight to make the least possible impression. 'We have an understanding.'

'Who is the client?' Seville knew better than to ask, but he always did.

Zaid shook his head. 'In this case you aren't to know. Even I don't know. You are to kill President Timori either in Bunda or, if he abdicates and leaves Palucca, you are to follow him and kill him at the first opportunity.'

'I thought only kings abdicated?'

'I gather he thinks of himself as one. If he does, they have no idea where he'll go. Nobody wants him, not even the Americans.'

Down in the street there was a burst of automatic gunfire, but neither man flinched or got up to investigate. Beirut now had different everyday sounds from those of other cities. A breeze blew in from the bay but there was no smell of salt air, just cordite.

'When do they want me to leave?'

'Immediately. Things will come to a head this week in Bunda.'

'How will the money be paid?'

'Half a million to your usual account. The rest on completion of the job.'

'Did you nominate the price or did they?'

Zaid gave another thin smile; Seville, who had been happy as a child, wondered if the Arab had ever laughed aloud. 'I had to do some bargaining, but that's what I enjoy.' Seville could imagine the bargaining: it was second nature to an Arab. 'These people, whoever they are, hardly quibbled – their go-between

36

came back to me within ten minutes. They must be desperate to be rid of him.'

'But if he abdicates, why kill him?'

Zaid shrugged, lit another cigarette. 'Perhaps it is the Americans. It would save them the embarrassment of having to give him political refuge.'

It was Seville's turn to smile. 'I don't think so. They would pay someone a million dollars to kill *me*.'

'The client doesn't know who you are. I was just asked to find an assassin.'

Seville got up and walked to the french doors. He walked with a slight roll, like a man who had spent a long time at sea; but he was no seaman, indeed he hated it. He had a knee-cap that had once been broken by the Argentinian secret police; it gave him little trouble now, but it had affected his walk. He was good-looking in an anonymous way; he grew on women slowly, which was the way he preferred; women, for more than just professional reasons, should always be approached cautiously. He was slim and of medium height and had a cool air to him that was often taken for quiet arrogance and rightly so. He had contempt for a good deal of the world and its citizens.

He looked out across the Bay of St George to the steeply rising mountains. This had once been the most beautiful city in the Levant, a mixture of influences laid like a diorama of history, from the Phoenicians to the French and now the Syrians, on the slopes between the mountains and the sea. Now it was a battlefield, a city of ruins that, if the present madness prevailed, might never be rebuilt.

'Once I thought of retiring here.' He had wanted to retire for at least a year; he had tired of the game. But there had not been enough money to retire on; there was no pension fund for freelance terrorists. Indeed, there had been very few commissions for him in the past year; the terrorist groups had started to employ expendable fanatics who cost nothing. He had been fast approaching the point where he would be in debt, an Argentinian national habit but one which he had never indulged. Of course there was the family money, but he would have to wait till his mother died before he could claim any of

37

that; and that would not be easy, because half a dozen police forces would do their best to follow the trail of money to him. It might be years before he could collect it.

Now this windfall was being laid in his lap and he could think seriously of retiring. 'But I'll be in my grave before Beirut is peaceful again. Don't you think so?'

'Yes,' said Zaid, who preferred not to talk of the grave. No commission ever came out of a cemetery.

'What happens if something goes wrong? Whom do I contact?'

'I promised them nothing would go wrong.'

Seville shook his head, smiled almost as thinly as Zaid. 'You know I try to be as near perfect as possible. But something can always go wrong, especially if the target doesn't co-operate. You may not know it, but there were six attempts to kill Queen Victoria, but something always went wrong.'

'Assassins have improved since then – the technology is better. You won't fail, Miguel. Just think of the million dollars.'

Seville drew an advance from Zaid, went to a local bank and bought $3,000 worth of traveller's cheques; he did not believe in over-loading himself with money. Police had a bad habit of confiscating money when they picked up a suspected terrorist. He did not sign the cheques, because he could never be certain what name he would be using when it came time to cash them. The bank knew better than to insist that he sign them; in Beirut money was always being withdrawn for reasons better left unqueried. As he came out of the bank a car bomb exploded at the far end of the street. He stood watching the black smoke vomit up in slow motion; then the terrified figures came running out of it. A man was jumping towards him on one leg, the stump of the other streaming blood behind him; suddenly he stopped, balanced like a dancer on the good leg, then fell over. There were screams and shouts and, as if it had been waiting just round the corner for the call, the wail of the siren of an approaching ambulance. He turned and walked away, wondering who the one-legged man had been and why, even as he walked away and the man was behind him, the image of him should be so clear in his mind. He could not remember taking any notice of the victims of his own bomb plantings. Was he to be haunted by memories in his retirement?

He had returned that night to Damascus, going up the Aley road and down through the Bekaa valley through the Syrian troops' roadblocks. He left Damascus the next day as Michele Rinelli, the sales manager of an Italian computer firm, and, going via Dubai, arrived sixteen hours later in Singapore. There he checked into the Raffles; he preferred the older style of hotel, they reminded him of the hotels in Buenos Aires. He wondered what the hotels were like in Bunda.

Then a contact in the Singapore police told him he had been sighted and a watch posted at Changi airport. He had moved out of the Raffles into a small hotel and lain low for a week; then the news had come through that the situation in Palucca had worsened and President Timori was expected to flee to Australia. Seville had shaved off his moustache, dyed his dark hair blond, donned steel-rimmed spectacles and got out the passport that fitted his new identity. He had waited till it was certain that Timori was headed for Australia. Then he had bought a business class ticket for Sydney, gone through passport control as Michel Gideon, a French-speaking Swiss business-man, and boarded the crowded Qantas jet. He had been aware of the two plainclothes officers standing in the background as he passed through passport control, but they had not stopped him. Eight hours later he had come undetected through Immi-gration in Sydney; visitors were flocking to the city for the bicentennial celebrations and six 747s had landed within a few minutes of each other. He had collected his two bags, one with the dismantled rifle hidden in a false bottom, and, having nothing to declare, had been waved through by the over-worked Customs men.

The Timoris and their entourage arrived twenty-four hours later. The local press, with a fine disregard for security, had already told Seville where they could be found; they were tired of stories about the bicentennial celebrations, this was an entirely new subject to Australians. The country for years had been a haven for refugees, but they had always been of the lower orders; no President had ever asked for asylum. So they welcomed the unwanted bastard with banner headlines.

Seville had scouted the surroundings of Kirribilli House and decided he needed the top floor of the block of flats across the street from it. He had checked the number of the top-floor flat, then checked the name against the number on the mail-boxes: Kiddle. On the afternoon of the Timoris' arrival he had stood amongst the already present crowd of demonstrators and watched the small convoy of Commonwealth cars, trailed by the newsreel vans and cars, come down the narrow street and swing in through the iron gates. Madame Timori, mistaking the demonstrators for glamour-loving fans, had waved and been roundly booed. The waving hand had stopped in mid-air, looked for a moment as if it might turn into a two-fingered salute, then dropped out of sight. The gates had closed behind the cars.

Seville went back to the suburban hotel where he was staying, looked up Kiddle in the phone book, then dialled the 922 number. 'Mrs Kiddle?' he said to the woman who answered.

'*Miss* Kiddle.' It was an old woman's voice, he judged. 'Yes?'

'This is Security at Kirribilli House. We are just checking that the demonstrators are not worrying you?'

'The demonstrators? Oh, is that what they are? No, no. They *are* noisy, but they're not worrying me. Has President What's-his-name arrived yet?'

'Yes, ma'am.' She sounded as if she wanted to give the President her regards. 'We'll be in touch, Miss Kiddle, if the demonstrators get too noisy.'

'Oh, don't worry. If I were younger, I'd join them. Tell President Timori to go home.'

Seville smiled and hung up. He could not imagine his mother, God damn her soul, saying that; she would be out there waving a flag for President Timori, for any President. He packed the Springfield in the squash kit-bag he had bought that morning, added the length of stout cord he always carried, put in his black kid gloves and zipped up the bag. He dressed in jeans and a navy-blue tennis blouson, put on dark glasses and went out to kill.

The day was hot and the crowd of demonstrators listless; the police watching them were equally listless. No one stopped Seville as he pushed through the crowd and walked along towards the block of flats. He went into the cool hallway of the old thick-walled building and climbed to the top floor. There was no lift and he wondered how Miss Kiddle, if she was old, managed this climb.

There was a security grille door guarding the front door of the top flat. It took him less than a minute to pick the lock; a man who carried a dismantled Springfield rifle carried other tools as well. Seville was a professional: he knew better than to gamble on doors being left unlocked.

Then he pressed the bell beside the door. There was no answer and for a moment he hoped that Miss Kiddle had gone out: he had an aversion to close-up killing, such as a strangling. Then a voice said, 'Who is it?'

'It's Security from Kirribilli House, Miss Kiddle. We called you an hour or so ago.'

'Oh yes – just a moment.'

There was the sound of two locks being snapped back, then the door was opened. Miss Kiddle stood there, white-haired and frail; somehow he had expected someone more robust. He smiled at her, then pushed against the door and stepped into the flat, kicking the door closed behind him. She didn't look frightened or startled by his abrupt entrance; she was smiling at him when he took the cord from his blouson pocket and wrapped it round her neck. She died without protest, but he stood behind her, his head turned away till she went limp.

He laid her out gently on the floor, pulled a shawl off a grand piano and covered her with it. He opened the front door, locked the security door, and closed the front door again, locking it. Then he looked around the room in which he stood.

It was a big room and it reminded him of his mother's house in Recoletta in Buenos Aires: the antique furniture, the grand piano with the shawl on it, the dark drapes aimed at keeping out the too-bright sun; Miss Kiddle, like his mother, had preferred to live in the past. He crossed to one of the windows and at once looked down on Kirribilli House. Trees obstructed part of the view, but he couldn't ask for a perfect situation: assassins, by the nature of their trade, rarely do have perfect situations.

He put the rifle together and sat down to wait till the opportunity presented itself to kill Timori. It might be a long wait, but sooner or later Timori would emerge from the house. Twice the phone rang, but he ignored it, though he sweated through the second ringing, which went on for almost two minutes. He felt in need of a leak after that and he got up and went into the bathroom off the main bedroom.

But the room was full of a woman's private things: he couldn't face them, suddenly felt an odd respect for Miss Kiddle who possibly had never had a man, other than a plumber, in this most private of rooms. He went out, found a second bathroom, relieved himself, pressed the cistern button and went back into the living-room. He had taken off his right glove to handle his penis and now he put it back on again as he settled back at his post.

It was almost dark when President and Madame Timori stepped out and began their after-dinner stroll. They stood for a moment looking down at the spectacle of the lighted boats on the harbour. Seville raised the rifle, found his target distinct against the cross-hatch of the 'scope. The Timoris were standing close together; there would be the opportunity for two shots in quick succession. He would present Madame Timori to the client as a bonus at no extra charge.

The demonstrators, evidently alerted that the Timoris had come out of the house and were in the grounds, were now shouting and chanting at the top of their voices. 'Death to Dictators!' was one chant, and Seville took it as encouragement. His finger eased gently on the trigger, then tightened. At that moment he saw the other figure come right into the centre of the 'scope, but it was too late to hold the shot.

When Seville realized he had shot the wrong man, panic, something he had never felt before, shot through him. His hand trembled; he looked at it with amazement, as if it didn't belong to him. By the time the shaking had stopped it was too late for another shot. He hastily dismantled the rifle, fumbling in his haste and cursing himself for his awkwardness. He stuffed it into the squash bag, took a quick look around to make sure he had left nothing behind, then headed for the front door. He let himself out of the apartment and ran down the stairs.

He had reached the bottom flight, was halfway down it, when

he saw the elderly couple outlined against the glass front doors. They were about to come into the building, but had turned back for a last look at the demonstrators.

Seville missed his step, almost plunged down the last few stairs. He swung round at the bottom and turned back behind the staircase. There was an alcove there, a storage place for buckets and brooms for the building's cleaner. Seville pressed himself into the small dark space, waited for the elderly couple to come in and go to their flat. He had recovered his composure; he was prepared to kill again if he had to. It would be another close-to death, perhaps two, but that could not be helped.

The front door was pushed open and the elderly couple came in. Seville could not see them, but he could hear their hesitant footsteps on the stairs above his head. And their remarks:

'I'd lock 'em all up,' said the elderly woman.

'Those fellows across the road?' said her husband. 'Norval and his gang? I've been saying that for years.'

'No, stupid. Those young people in that crowd. Making all that noise and what for? What did noise ever do for anyone except give headaches? Have you got the key?'

'No, you have it.'

'I gave it to you, stupid!'

'Keep your voice down. You're making a noise.'

They had stopped on the first-floor landing. Seville stepped out from the alcove, then froze. A uniformed policeman stood right outside the front doors, clearly seen through the glass. Seville hesitated, then he shoved the squash bag back into the alcove, dropping it into a bucket. His mind had worked swiftly. He did not want to be stopped and questioned as to what he was carrying in the bag. The noise from the demonstrators had suddenly stopped as they realized something had happened in the grounds of Kirribilli House. The police would be more alert now; even as Seville looked at him, the policeman suddenly moved off at the run as a whistle sounded. Seville stepped across the front lobby and out into the street.

The demonstrators were being herded back up the street. They were going quietly, some of them looking shocked; they had evidently been told of the shooting. Seville hurried to catch up with the stragglers. A policeman appeared out of nowhere

43

and grabbed Seville by the arm. His first reaction was to stop and struggle, but the policeman, a big burly man with cauliflower ears, was too quick for him.

'Don't try any rough stuff, son, or you'll finish up in the wagon!' He gave Seville a shove, then a boot up the behind. 'Git!'

'Don't argue with him,' a young girl warned Seville. 'That's the Thumper – he's a menace to democracy.'

'You're bloody right I am!' said Thumper. 'Now git before I put me boot up your bum, too!'

The girl jerked her fingers at the sergeant, but ran up the street, dragging Seville with her. A moment later he was lost in the crowd of demonstrators, losing the girl too.

Now, twelve hours later, he sat in this small bedroom in a pub in Rozelle, two or three miles from the heart of the city. He had found Sydney booked out for its 200th birthday party; it was an obliging taxi driver, after driving around for an hour, who had found this drinking hotel which, miraculously, had a room to rent. It was not an establishment that catered much, if at all, for accommodation; it made its money out of drinkers, not guests, and it entertained the drinkers with rock bands that had no talent but thunderous volume. The noise and the surroundings had done nothing to decrease Seville's dislike of Australia and Australians.

He was cursing the loss of the rifle; he still had the task of killing Timori but now he had no weapon. He had coolly walked through security screens before, in Rome, Milan, even Tel Aviv; but he had never done so carrying a weapon immediately after an assassination or massacre. This job had come too quickly, Timori's movements had been unpredictable and Seville had had no time for proper planning. He was a precise killer and this time he had been anything but that. He was not accustomed to failure and it hurt like a bullet wound.

He was forty years old and perhaps it was time to retire. But he could not go out on a botched job, with the target still alive and walking around. He needed another gun; but where did one buy a gun in Sydney on a holiday weekend? Guns were being fired all over the city, but they were firing blanks for celebration. Then he remembered the black militants he had met on his last visit to Sydney. The Aborigines, if they were like the Indians of Argentina, would be the last people taking a holiday to celebrate the rape of their country.

2

'This house is so *small*,' said Madame Timori, trying to look hemmed in and not succeeding. 'Our palace back home has eighty-eight rooms.'

'Perhaps Australians have a better sense of modesty than us.' President Timori, homeless, was doing his best to be polite. He was training for exile, just in case the worst proved permanent.

'I'm Australian,' said his wife. 'Or anyway half-Australian. Do you live in a modest house, Inspector?'

'It's no palace, Madame.' Malone thought of the three-bedroomed house in Randwick that would fit almost twice into this one.

'Do you have a swimming pool?'

'Yes, a small one.' That had been a gift for the children from Lisa's parents, a gesture that at first he had resented.

'This house doesn't. Can you imagine, a Prime Minister's house with no pool? An *Australian* Prime Minister's! I'll bet there's a barbecue somewhere, though.'

She's more than *half*-Australian, Malone thought. She's one of those expatriate Aussies who can't resist knocking their home country. He wondered if she ever mentioned Malaysia, her mother's country. He was not chock-a-block with patriotism himself, but a little of it didn't hurt, even a traitor.

'You can always go next door and bathe in the Governor's pool,' said the President.

'The Governor-General.' She had a passion for accuracy: she wouldn't have missed if she had been firing at her husband. 'But who'd want to? He hasn't sent one word since we arrived here. He's probably waiting on the Queen to tell him what to do. And you know what *she's* like, so damned stuffy about protocol.' Then the First Lady seemed to remember some protocol of her own. 'I hope you're not taking any of this down in your little book, Inspector.'

'No, Madame. Now may I ask the President some questions?'

They were sitting out on the terrace on the harbour side of the house. Out on the sun-chipped water the yachts were already gathered like bird-of-paradise gulls; once, Malone remembered, the sails had all been white but now a fleet looked like a fallen rainbow. A container ship, all blue and red and yellow, was heading downstream towards the Heads, its hooting siren demanding right-of-way from the yachts, which seemed to ignore it till the very last moment. On the far side of the water the expensive houses and apartment blocks of Darling Point and Point Piper, silvertail territory, sparkled like quartz cliffs in the morning sun. There was little breeze and the heat lay on the city like a dark-blue blanket. It was going to be a scorcher of a day.

'I don't see why it's necessary,' said Madame Timori, throwing cold water.

Malone ignored her. 'Mr President, we have a lead on the man who tried to shoot you. We think it is Miguel Seville. He's an Argentinian, one of the world's leading terrorists. Maybe *the* leading one.'

Sun Lee had come out of the house to stand in the background just behind Timori's chair. The rest of the Presidential entourage, the men, women and children who had spent last night in one of the immigrant hostels, had moved down from the front of the house and stood in a group in the shade of some trees, looking as if they wanted an audience of the President but were not game to ask. But Malone noticed that they were all suddenly still, as if they had heard what he had said, and behind Timori the private secretary seemed to stiffen.

Timori raised an eyebrow, but that was all. He was dressed in white slip-ons, white cotton slacks and a blue batik-patterned shirt: he could have taken his place on any of the cruising yachts out on the harbour or at any one of the barbecue picnics out in the suburbs. Except for his face: there was no holiday spirit there. He looked sick, older even than he had yesterday. Last night's bullet hadn't hit him, but he had read his name on it: it was unfortunate that poor Mohammed Masutir had had involuntary power of attorney.

'Why would they hire a foreigner to kill me?' He sounded

46

affronted as well as puzzled: for all his corruption he was a true nationalist.

'Perhaps it was the Americans,' said his wife. 'The CIA will hire anyone. Remember those Mafia they hired to try and kill Castro?'

'But they *were* Americans,' said Timori. 'No, it wouldn't be the CIA. President Fegan is my friend,' he told Malone.

'I'm sure he is, sir.' Malone did not voice his truthful opinion, that in top politics there were no friends, only expendable partners. He could not believe that Timori had read no history. 'Have you had any trouble from terrorists in Palucca?'

'None,' said Madame Timori. 'I told you there were to be no political questions!'

Pull your head in, Delvina. But Malone's voice was still mild: 'It wasn't meant to be political, Madame Timori. I'm just trying to build up a picture in my mind so that we can do something about catching this man Seville before he makes another attempt on the President's life.'

'You think he'll do that?' Timori had a soft silky voice; now it was just a whisper. 'What sort of protection can you give me?'

'I can give you none, sir. That's up to the Federal Police and our Special Branch.'

'What do *you* do, then?' Madame Timori's voice was neither silky nor a whisper. Over under the trees the group was leaning forward, ears strained.

'I'm afraid we're always called in too late to prevent anything. That's why we're called Homicide – after the crime that's been committed.'

'Homicide? I thought you fellers had finished here?'

Malone turned his head as the newcomer passed him, shook hands with Timori, then kissed Madame Timori on her up-turned cheek. He was a barrel of a man, a mixture of muscle and fat, dressed in blue slacks and shirt and a raw silk jacket. Amongst all the sartorial elegance on this terrace – even Sun Lee looked like an advertisement for one of Hong Kong's best tailors – Malone felt like someone who had just stepped out of a St Vincent de Paul store.

'I'm Russell Hickbed.' He was the sort of man who would

never wait for someone else to introduce him. His broad, blunt-featured face had no smile for Malone; the pale-blue eyes behind the horn-rimmed glasses held no hint of friendliness. 'You're –?'

'Inspector Malone.' Malone didn't stand up or offer his hand. He sensed at once that only by remaining seated was he going to keep control of this interview with Timori.

'Well, didn't you get the message, Inspector?'

Malone had never met Hickbed before but he had seen him on television, on *Four Corners, Sixty Minutes* and on the Carleton-Walsh show. Always laying down the law on the economic situation, on foreign policy, on equal rights: he was a nineteenth-century mind who shamelessly used a twentieth-century medium to preach his arch-conservative message. He had made his fortune in Western Australia in the construction business and the resources boom, then come East to take on the Establishments of Sydney and Melbourne and, according to his own estimate, beaten them to a pulp. Other Sandgropers, as Western Australians were called, had done the same, with varying degrees of success. The others still kept their bases in Perth, the Western capital, as if needing the moral, or immoral, support of their fellow millionaires; but Hickbed, folding his mansion tent on the Swan River, had settled in Sydney, buying an even bigger mansion on the shores of the harbour. Nobody knew how much he was worth, but if he lost a million or two on Monday he had usually recouped it by Tuesday. He had the rich man's magnetism for money.

'What message was that?' *He's expecting me to be a mug copper, so I'll be one.*

Hickbed looked at the Timoris. The President seemed uninterested; but the First Lady was tense and angry. 'The police here seem to be a law to themselves!'

Hickbed took off his glasses and wiped them; somehow his face looked blank and less aggressive without them. 'Is that so, Inspector?'

'Perhaps you should ask the Premier.' Malone knew that Hickbed and The Dutchman were enemies who would cross an ocean to avoid each other. 'The politicians make the laws in this State.'

48

'This has nothing to do with the Premier or New South Wales.'

'I'm afraid you don't know the law, Mr Hickbed. Homicide is a State offence, not a Federal one. I think it has something to do with States' rights.'

Hickbed recognized the barb. Before he had come out of the West he had been one of the nation's most vociferous advocates of States' rights. Then he had finally realized the real power would always remain in Canberra. That was when he had become leader of the kitchen cabinet that had taken charge of Phil Norval.

He put his glasses back on, looked threatening. 'You're making trouble for yourself, Inspector.'

Malone looked at him, then at Madame Timori, finally at the President. The latter might appear uninterested, but it struck Malone that he had missed nothing of the exchange between himself and Hickbed.

'They warned me of that the first day I put on a uniform. A policeman's lot . . .'

But Hickbed had never listened to Gilbert and Sullivan. 'You're a pretty uppity policeman, aren't you?'

Malone put away his notebook and stood up. 'It must be the surroundings. I was once in the Mayor's mansion in New York – I got a bit light-headed there, too. I must be more ambitious than I thought.'

'Oh, you're *that* Malone!' Hickbed looked at him with new interest, if no more respect. 'The one whose wife was kidnapped or something with the Mayor of New York?'

'With the Mayor's wife, actually.' Malone turned away from Hickbed; he also turned away from Madame Timori. 'I'm not giving up on the case, Mr President. I'd still like to nail this feller Seville before he tries to kill you again.'

Timori stood up, getting out of his chair with the stiff movements of an old man. But his eyes seemed to have come alive; he put out his hand to shake Malone's and his grip was firm. He smiled, a gold tooth that Malone hadn't seen before all at once suggesting the raffish look he once must have had. He's a bastard, Malone thought, corrupt as a rotten mango. But you might find yourself liking him.

49

'I'd be grateful if you can – nail? – him, Inspector. It was always my ambition to die in bed, preferably beneath a beautiful woman –' The gold tooth winked at the First Lady; she gave him an unladylike glare and Hickbed, unexpectedly, looked embarrassed. Malone just grinned. 'I don't want to die from an assassin's bullet. I hate surprises.'

'We'll do our best, sir. Well, I'd better go. Just one more question –' But he looked at Sun Lee, not at the other three who had been expecting the question. 'You've heard of Miguel Seville, haven't you, Mr Sun?'

Sun hadn't been expecting the question: he wasn't entirely ready with his answer. 'Me, Inspector? I – why should I have heard of him?'

'You must read the newspapers, Mr Sun, even in Bunda. Did you ever hear of him coming to Palucca? Private secretaries usually know all the gossip. At least they do in this country.'

'Mr Sun has no time for gossip,' said Madame Timori, who had once provided so much of it and still did.

Sun took his cue from her. He shook his head, gave Malone a cold stare: 'I know nothing about Mr Seville.'

Malone returned his stare, then nodded and turned his back on the Chinese. He said his goodbyes to the Timoris, ignoring Hickbed, and left the terrace, going round the corner of the house past the group still standing like an abandoned bus queue in the shade of the trees. In the front of the house, his jacket over his arm and his tie loosened, was Russ Clements, talking to Detective-Inspector Nagler of Special Branch.

'G'day, Scobie. You don't look happy.' Joe Nagler was a thin dark man with a sad face that belied his sense of humour. He was one of the few Jews in the force, but that didn't prompt him to waste any sympathy on the newer ethnics in the community. He divided the world into, as he called them, the goods and the bads and where you or your ancestors came from made no difference. 'Madame Timori been rubbing you up the wrong way?'

'You too?'

Nagler nodded, smiling sadly. 'Imagine her and Boadicea Thatcher running the world! Or one or two of the ethnic dames we have out here.'

50

'I didn't know you were a misogynist. Does your nice Jewish mother know?'

'She put me up to it. No Jewish mother wants her son loving another woman.' Nagler was happily married to a nice Catholic girl and had five children: the Pope, as he said, always got into bed with him and the missus. He changed the subject: 'So we're looking for this guy Seville?'

'You got any other bets?'

'He's good enough for me. This isn't a job I'd have picked as my favourite. Let's find him, wrap it up and go home.'

'And where do the Timoris go?'

'Who cares?'

Malone grinned. 'You fellers are special in Special Branch.'

'I thought of transferring once,' said Clements. 'They wouldn't have me.'

'You should have had a Jewish mother. She got me in. Well, I'm glad we're all working together.'

'What about the ASIO spooks?' said Malone. 'Anyone invited them in?'

ASIO, the Australian Security Intelligence Organization, had its Sydney headquarters half a block up the street in another converted waterfront mansion. The Federal Government looked after its representatives here in Kirribilli. Through the trees Malone could see the magnificent nineteenth-century pile that was Admiralty House, built by another of the colony's early merchants, a more successful one than Mr Feez of Kirribilli House. Yesterday the Governor-General had been in residence, but this morning Malone saw that the tall flagpole in the large gardens was bare. The G-G had folded his flag and fled, turning his back on his neighbours.

'Half the demonstrators outside are ASIO spooks, under-cover,' said Nagler, and Malone and Clements smiled agreement with him.

The talk was inconsequential, but they all knew they were sitting on a landmine of a type they had never met before.

'The trouble is,' said Nagler, 'there are certain people just across the water who'd love to see this whole thing blow up in Phil Norval's face.'

51

THREE

1

'Bugger 'em,' said The Dutchman. 'I run the police in this State, not Phil Norval.'

'I shouldn't let myself be quoted on that,' said John Leeds.

Hans Vanderberg grinned. It was a marvellous grin, a mixture of malevolence and friendliness, of cynicism and paternalism: each voter could take what he liked from it. He was a small man, with a foxy face and thick grey hair with a high quiff, a style that Leeds thought had gone out at least fifty years ago. It was Saturday, there were no official functions till this afternoon, so he was casually dressed: the brown slacks of one suit, the blue jacket of another and a shirt that suggested a drunken holiday on the Barrier Reef. He was a living denial of the latterday maxim that the voters voted for the electronic image; on a TV screen he looked like a technical fault. He was the very opposite of his arch-enemy the Prime Minister.

'You know what I mean, John. Phil Norval's up to something and he ain't gunna get away with it, my word he's not. We've got to grab the bull by the balls –'

'By the horns,' said Ladbroke, his political secretary, who was known to the Macquarie Street columnists as the Keeper of the Faux Pas.

'What's the difference? You ever had a bull by the horns in a china shop, John?'

'Offhand,' said Leeds, 'I can't remember it.'

'What's Phil Norval's connection with the Timoris? He's not doing this for them just because the Yanks asked him. Who's in charge of the case?'

'Inspector Malone.'

'Scobie Malone. I remember him. Get him to do some digging.'

52

'I'm sorry, Hans, you know I won't let any of my men get into political work.'

Vanderberg grinned again, but this time it was purely malevolent. He swung his chair round and looked out the window, but Leeds knew he wouldn't be looking at the view. They were in the Premier's office on the eighth floor of the State office block, with a magnificent view right down the harbour to the Heads. But they were too high up for The Dutchman: if he was out of shouting distance of the voters he was looking on a barren landscape.

'Just my luck to have an honest Commissioner. I oughta been Premier back in the old good days.'

'Good old days,' murmured Ladbroke, but only to himself.

'You know nothing about those days,' said Leeds. 'You're always saying history doesn't mean anything.'

'It's true. A voter, he goes into a voting booth, he doesn't remember the last election, he's voting on what his pocket tells him today. He don't want to know about yesterday, dead kings and prime ministers and Magna Carta, all that stuff. Neither do I.' He swung his chair back to face Leeds. He might not have a sense of history, which really is only for statesmen; he did, however, have a wonderful memory, which a successful politician needs more than an arm or a leg. 'Wasn't Madame Timori, whatever her name was before, Delvina Someone, Delvina O'Reilly, that's it – wasn't she a TV dancer before she got her name in the papers with that dance company?'

'I don't know,' said Leeds. 'Where did you learn that?'

'*TV Times.*' He might have, too, Leeds thought. He would read anything, even a bus ticket, if it contained information against an enemy. 'There's something going on there, I dunno what. Russell Hickbed's been to see 'em twice.'

'Was that in *TV Times*?' Leeds stood up. It was time to go, before he got into an argument with the Premier. They respected each other's ability, but they would never be friends. 'I'll keep Malone working on the case, then.'

'You want to get this feller Seville, don't you? Jesus Christ, he might try for me next! Phil Norval would pay him.' He grinned at the thought, relishing the sensation of his own death.

'I don't think the bullet's been made that could put a dent in you.'

Vanderberg grinned again: with pride this time. Somehow it looked uglier than his malevolence. 'Maybe I shoulda been a copper.'

Leeds managed a smile, said goodbye and left. He was going out to the Cricket Ground to watch the Test match for an hour or two and he hoped he wouldn't run into the Prime Minister again. He had had enough of politicians for the day.

When the door had closed Vanderberg looked at his political secretary. 'He's a good copper. It's a pity he's so honest. A little larceny never hurt anyone, right?'

'Right,' said Ladbroke, who had known all about larceny before he took this job; he had been a political columnist and had seen the State's best practitioners at work. He was a plump, anonymous-looking man in his late thirties who had no illusions left but didn't miss them. 'I've got Jack Phillips and Don Clary at work. If there's any dirt, they'll dig it up.'

'Oh, there'll be dirt, I'll bet your boots on it,' said Vanderberg, who never bet anything of his own. He stood up, looking pleased. 'It would make a great Australia Day if I could topple the Prime Minister, wouldn't it?'

'Great,' said Ladbroke, and the headlines broke in his head like a blinding light. He was a lapsed Catholic and for a moment he thought he'd had a vision.

'Do the press know about this bloke Seville?'

'Not as far as I know. The police want it kept quiet for the time being.'

Vanderberg thought for a moment. 'Well, we'll see. We might leak it, just to keep things on the boiling.'

'I'll prepare something, just in case.'

'I'm going home for a coupla hours.' The Dutchman lived in his electorate on the edge of the inner city. Glebe had once been a middle-class area, then for years it had been home for the working class and had become a Labour stronghold. Now the trendy academics from nearby Sydney University had moved in, bringing their racks of Chardonnay, their taste for foreign films and their narrow view of any world but their own. They voted Labour, but laughed at The Dutchman. But they knew and he knew that none of them would last two rounds with him in the political ring. 'We might have a good weekend.'

Avagoodweekend was a TV slogan for a brand of fly-spray. Ladbroke wondered if Phil Norval, the TV hero, knew he was about to be sprayed.

2

Malone was greeted at his front door by a four-year-old centurion in a plastic breastplate and wielding a plastic sword. 'Who goes there? Fred or foe?'

'Fred.'

'Fred who?'

'Fred the Fuzz.' He picked up Tom and kissed him. His own mother Brigid had probably kissed him as a very small child, but from Tom's age he could remember no kisses from the hard-working religious woman who loved him but was incapable of public sentiment. He sometimes wondered how often she had kissed his father and if she still did. Malone himself made a point of being affectionate towards his wife and children. 'Where's Mum?'

'Here.'

Lisa stood in the kitchen doorway silhouetted against the late sunlight coming through from the back of the house. She was in shorts and a halter-top and at thirty-seven she still had the figure she had had at twenty-seven. She swam every day, summer and winter, something he didn't do in the unheated pool, and she went to a gym class twice a week. She was more beautiful than he knew he deserved, but she was not vain about it nor was she fanatical about keeping fit. She had been born in Holland and she had the Dutch (well, *some* Dutch) habit of discipline. She and her parents were as unlike Hans Vanderberg as it was possible to be.

'A bad day?' She could recognize the signs.

He nodded. 'What did you do?'

'Mother and Dad took us all to Eliza's for lunch, then we came back here and swam all afternoon. They're out by the pool with Claire and Maureen. Your mother and father are here, too.'

Malone rolled his eyes in mock agony. 'Now I know how the Abos felt on that first Australia Day. Who's going to be the first to tell me what to do with Timori? Dad or your old man?'

'You're my old man,' said Tom. 'The kids at school call you that.'

'You've got a pretty bright lot at your kindy,' said Malone. 'They know an old man when they see one.'

He changed into his swim-trunks, went out to the back yard, kissed his daughters, said hello to his parents and his in-laws, swam half-a-dozen lengths of the thirty-five-foot pool, then climbed out, sat down and waited for the avalanche of opinion.

Con Malone pushed the first boulder. 'All right, what's he like? When they let crims like him into the country, it's time I went back to the Ould Country.' Con had been born in Australia, had never set foot outside it, but was always threatening to go back to Ireland. He was sixty-eight years old, every year stamped there in the square, creased face with its long upper lip; he was built like a tree-trunk (he had once been a timber worker) and he still couldn't say no to a fight, anyone, any time, anywhere. Only his age and the shame of younger opponents saved him from a licking. 'Him and Phil Norval are a good pair.'

'Oh, I don't think Norval's corrupt or a criminal. He's too stupid for that.' Jan Pretorius was a Liberal voter, that is to say a conservative one. When, some decades ago, the conservative party, looking for a new image, had usurped the name Liberal for itself, the ghost of Gladstone had climbed out of his grave in England but, with Australia already full of English ghosts, had been denied entry to protest his case. The name did not worry Jan Pretorious; he voted for the party's principles, which suited his own conservative outlook. He had a respect for politics and politicians that over-rode his contempt for some of the latter. He was still European, and not Australian, in that attitude. 'Someone is putting pressure on him to allow President Timori to stay here.'

'The bloody Yanks,' said Con Malone, who would blame the Americans for everything and anything.

'You think so?' Pretorious looked at his son-in-law. He was a distinguished-looking man, with silver-grey hair and a florid face that, despite his having been born in the tropics, had never become accustomed to the Australian sun.

'I think it might be closer to home,' said Malone.

'Who?' said Brigid Malone and Elisabeth Pretorious together. They had no interest in politics, but they had a *parfumier*'s nose for a whiff of gossip.

Malone smiled, dodging the question and gave his attention to his daughters who, wet and slippery, slid over him like young dolphins. He looked at Lisa, who had the centurion in her lap. 'I'm going to be working all weekend.'

'Awh-h-h-h Daddy!' his daughters chorused and Tom waved his sword threateningly.

'Why don't you apply for an administrative job, a nine-to-five one?' said Pretorious.

'Because he'd be unbearable to live with,' said Lisa.

'He oughta never been a copper in the first place,' said Con Malone, who had taken years to live with the shame of being a policeman's father. 'I done me best to talk him out of it.'

Malone, above the heads of his daughters, studied the two old men. They were the gold, if from opposite ends of the reef, that was the decency of this celebrating nation. Con Malone was the almost archetypal working man of the past: class conscious, prejudiced, scrupulously honest about his beliefs and passionately dedicated to mateship. He had recognized that the world at large had enemies: Hitler, Tojo and, later, Stalin. There was, however, only one real enemy in his eyes: the boss, any boss. Now that he was retired, living on his pension, he sometimes seemed at a loss without an enemy to hate. He and his son fought with words, but he would only raise his fist for Scobie, never against him. Malone loved him with a warmth that, like his mother, he would be too embarrassed to confess to the old man.

Jan Pretorious, too, was retired; but he had been a boss. He had been born in Sumatra of a Dutch family that had lived there for four generations making money out of rubber, tea and the natives. He and Lisa's mother had come to Australia after Indonesia had gained its independence; he had brought

57

little of the family fortune with him because by then there had been little of it left. At first they had not liked Australia and, when Elisabeth found herself pregnant, had gone home to Holland. A year there had convinced them they could never live in the northern climate and, with the baby Lisa, they had come back to Australia. He had gone to work in the rubber trade, at first working for Dunlop, then starting his own business making rubber heels. By the time Malone had married Lisa, half of Australia, including its police forces, were walking on Pretorious heels. Jan had once had all the arrogance of a colonial imperialist, but Australia had mellowed him; it had been that or get his face pushed in by the likes of Con Malone. He still occasionally dreamed of the old days, but he was dreaming as much of his adventurous youth in the Sumatran jungle as he was of a dead and gone imperialism. He and Con had one thing in common: they would like to turn the clock back, though it would not be the same clock. Scobie did not love him, but he felt an affection for him and a respect that was almost like love.

'I don't like the looks of that Madame Timori,' said Brigid Malone, who read only the *Women's Weekly* but never truly believed what it told her. 'She's all fashion-plate and nothing underneath it.'

'She's just a decoration for *him*,' said Elisabeth Pretorious.

Their husbands looked at them, wondering if and when they had been decorated.

How wrong you both are, thought Malone, looking at his mother and mother-in-law.

Brigid Malone and Elisabeth Pretorious had nothing in common except, perhaps, a distant beauty. They had once been pretty girls, but the years of hard work, two miscarriages, another child dying in infancy and her bitter disappointment at the way her trusted God had treated her had crumpled and smudged and almost obliterated, except to the sharpest eye, that Brigid Hourigan of long ago. She now spent her time visiting her grandchildren and once a week going with Con to the senior citizens' club in Erskineville, where they had lived for fifty years and where she and Con railed against the immigrant newcomers whom neither of them would ever call Australians.

President Timori could have been a Catholic saint but Brigid Malone would never have made him welcome, not in Australia.

Elisabeth Pretorious had kept some of her looks. Money and a less arduous life had enabled her to do that; also she had had fewer disappointments than Brigid. Her God had been a comfortable one who, through the sleek smug priest in the suburb where she lived, never asked too much of her. She was a Friend of the Art Gallery, a Friend of the Opera and she was forever mentioning her good friends the So-and-So's; but as far as Malone could tell she had no friends at all and he felt sorry for her. It struck him only then that she and his mother might have something else in common.

'Do we *have* to have them here?' she said.

Malone shrugged, let his daughters slide off his lap. They jumped back into the pool as if it were their natural habitat. 'What would you do? Would you let them stay?'

'No,' said his father-in-law.

'They claim they're political refugees.'

Pretorious gave him a sharp look: almost forty years ago he and Elisabeth had made the same claim for themselves. 'I think we have to draw the line somewhere. The man's a murderer. Or his army was.'

'It's his army that's kicked him out.'

'Are you on his side?' said Con Malone suspiciously.

'Christ, no!'

The centurion leaned across and whacked him on the knee with his sword. 'You told me not to say Christ. That's swearing.'

'Indeed it is,' said Brigid, smiling sweetly at her four-year-old saint.

Lisa had been sitting quietly and Malone knew she was studying him. Some husbands are unfortunate in the way their wives study them, but those wives are those who know they could have done better. Malone knew, however, that he was being studied in a different way: Lisa had come to know *him* better. He had very few secrets left that she did not know.

Later, after the Malones and the Pretoriouses had left, when the children were asleep and the old house was showing its age as the heat of the day creaked out of its timbers, she said, 'You wish you weren't on this case, don't you?'

59

'A holiday weekend – what do you think?'

'You know what I mean.'

They were in bed in the high-ceilinged main bedroom, a sheet covering only their lower halves. The house was not air-conditioned; they had an air-conditioner mounted on a trolley, but they rarely brought it into the bedroom. Malone, an old-fashioned man in many ways, had a theory that air-conditioning only brought on colds. He was also sensual enough to like a sweaty woman beside him in bed, a compliment that Lisa at certain times didn't always appreciate.

He said slowly, 'I think I could be getting into a real mess with this one. Nobody seems to care a damn about the poor bugger who was shot.'

'I met Delvina once.' He turned his head in surprise, looked at her profile against the moonlit window. They had not drawn the drapes, to allow some air into the room, and he knew they would be woken early by the morning light. 'I did a PR job for the dance company when she was with it. We didn't get on well – I featured another girl instead of her. I thought she was too obvious, didn't give the company the right image.'

'Where's the girl you featured, now?'

'Probably married, with three kids and living in the suburbs. Delvina was never going to finish up there, in the suburbs.'

'She may finish up with her head blown off.' He lifted the sheet and fanned himself with it. 'I've never worked on anything like this before. It's all strange territory.'

'Here be dragons.'

'Eh?'

'On ancient maps, when they came to the unknown parts they used to write, Beyond this place here be dragons. Australia would have been one of those places once.'

'Tell that to Phil Norval. He claims to've got rid of inflation and everything else. He can add dragons to the list.'

'Delvina has probably already told him. She used to sleep with him when he was still in TV. Mrs Norval would be able to tell you about that.'

'I can't back down now, Russ. I've got to walk tall in this.'

'For crissake, Phil, you're only five feet eight – forget about walking tall!'

Philip Norval and Russell Hickbed were in the Prime Minister's private residence, a property he had bought at the height of his TV fame and to which he retreated on the rare occasions when he wanted to escape the trappings of his office. It was a large mansion in grounds that held a hundred-foot swimming pool, an all-weather tennis court, a jacuzzi, a sauna and, as one TV rival remarked, everything but his own natural spa.

'We've got to get him back to Palucca,' said Hickbed. 'Christ knows what those bloody generals will do. They're already talking to Jakarta!'

'Is there much danger in that?' Foreign affairs were not Norval's strong suit; Jakarta had never figured in the ratings. 'I'd better talk to Neil Kissing about that.'

Kissing was the Foreign Minister and no friend of Hickbed. 'Leave him out of it. We don't want Cabinet interfering in this – you've got too many do-gooders in it.'

'Who?'

'Never mind who. Just let's keep this between you and me. We're the ones with something to lose, not the bloody government. Have you talked to Delvina?'

'Not alone – I haven't had a chance. Abdul doesn't seem to want to talk. Except about how the Americans let him down.'

'So they did. If they'd sent their Fleet in, a couple of thousand Marines, the generals would have stayed in their barracks and Abdul would still be in Timoro Palace sitting pretty.'

'Fegan would never have sent the Marines in. He told me last September in Washington that he wanted Abdul out of the way. He's an embarrassment, Russ –'

'Who – Fegan?'

'No, Abdul, damn it. He's so bloody corrupt –'

'Now don't *you* start being mealy-mouthed . . . Phil, corruption is a way of life up there. Everybody's underpaid, so you slip 'em a bit on the side to get things done.'

'How much did you slip Abdul? The *Herald* this morning said he's rumoured to have three billion – three *billion* –' Like all TV chat hosts, and politicians and priests, he had been taught to repeat points: one never knew if the audience was dozing. Though he had never known Russell Hickbed to be anything but wide awake. 'All that salted away in Switzerland or somewhere. That's quite a bit to have made on the side. More than you or I ever made.'

'Unless we get him back to Palucca we're going to make a bloody sight less. Or I am.'

'Just what have you got there in Palucca, Russ? You've never told me.'

'You don't need to know.'

'Meaning it's none of my business? I think it is, if you want me to shove my neck out on this. My popularity rating is dropping, Russ – it went down three points last week, just when it should be going up, with the Bicentennial going on. They don't think I can walk on water any more. If this Timori business goes on too long I could be up to my arse in water in a leaky rowboat. And I don't think you'd be rushing to bail me out.'

Hickbed took off his glasses and polished them. They were in the library, a big room stacked on three walls to the ceiling with books and video cassettes; on close inspection one saw that virtually all the books were to do with some sort of show business and the cassettes were of Norval's own TV shows. The few novels on the shelves were detective books and popular bestsellers. It was not a room where its owner got much mental exercise, but he had never sought it.

There was the crunching of gravel on the path outside as two of the security men went by. This was a safe area, but one never knew. This was the North Shore suburb of Killara; North Shore being a social state of mind more than a geographical location, since its boundaries began some five miles from the northern shores of the harbour. Kirribilli, for instance, right on the north shore, was not North Shore. Killara itself had once been considered the domain of judges and lawyers, a leafy outpost of the courts and chambers of Phillip Street, the city's legal centre. It was said that at Christmas the local council workers shouted, 'Let justice be done!' and the judges and barristers, mindful of their sins of the year, rushed out and thrust Christmas boxes on the jury of dustmen. Of later years advertising men, TV celebrities and even successful used-car salesmen had moved into the suburb: the tone may have been reduced but not the wealth or the status. It was still North Shore, safe and secure.

In the big living-room across the hall from the library one of the house's six television sets was turned on; four of Norval's staff were in there. Hickbed looked at the blank screens of the two sets in this room, then he looked back at the Prime Minister, the puppet who was now trying to jerk his own strings.

'If it hadn't been for me you'd still be in that awful bloody studio hosting your awful bloody TV show and going in five mornings a week to listen to dumb bloody housewives on talkback.'

'I was making a million bucks a year. It bought all this –' he gestured around him; he needed his possessions to identify himself '– and a lot else besides.'

'When you retired from all that, who would remember you? Yesterday's TV stars are like Olympic swimmers – nobody can remember them when they've dried off. You always wanted to be remembered, Phil – you love being loved by your public. You'll be remembered as the most popular PM ever. That is, unless you stuff up this Timori business.'

'You still haven't told me what you've got there in Palucca.' Norval looked genuinely stubborn and determined, something he had always had to pose at on camera.

Hickbed put his glasses back on: he was getting a new view of his puppet. He liked Norval as a man, as did everyone who met him: the TV star and the politician had always been more than just professionally popular. He had, however, never had any illusions about the PM's political intelligence and, indeed, held it in contempt. It struck him now that Norval might have learned a thing or two since he had been in office.

'I've got a twenty per cent interest in the oil leases off the north-east coast.'

'Who has the eighty per cent?'

'Who do you think? The company's registered in Panama, with stand-in names for me and the Timoris. I've talked to them about it and there's five per cent for you.'

Norval wanted to be honest, to be pure and uncorrupted; but he had been asking questions all his professional life. 'How much is that worth?'

'Several million a year, if we put the Timoris back in Bunda. Bugger-all right now, since the generals have confiscated everything. I've got nearly sixty million tied up there one way or another, the oil leases, construction, various other things. I'll be buggered if I'm going to lose all that without a fight.'

'How did you get in so deep?'

'Who do you think's been staking the Timoris since the Yank firms were warned to pull out by Washington? Delvina came to me – what could I say? You know what she's like.'

'Don't we all,' said a woman's voice.

Hickbed turned as Norval's wife came in the door. 'Hello, Anita. Just got in?'

'I've been visiting Jill and the grandchildren.'

There was no love lost, indeed none had ever been found, between Anita Norval and Russell Hickbed. When she had met Norval she had had her own radio programme on the ABC, the government-financed network, and when she had married him there were those on the ABC who thought she had married beneath her. She had truly loved him in those days, as had millions of other women; the other women might still be in love with him, she didn't know or care, but she knew the state of her own heart. There had been a time when she had thought she could rescue him from the trap of his own self-image; then Russell Hickbed had come along, taken the image and enlarged it till even she was trapped in it. She would never forgive Hickbed for making her the Prime Minister's wife.

'Nobody would ever take you for a grandmother. Neither of you.'

'Thanks,' said Norval drily.

He had stood up beside Anita; she knew they made a good-looking pair. He handsome and blond, she beautiful and dark, both of them slim, both of them expensively and elegantly dressed even on this warm holiday night: the image now, she

64

thought, had become a round-the-clock thing. They had a daughter who had married early and a son who worked in a merchant bank in London: both of them had escaped the image and refused to be any part of it.

'What's happening with the Timoris?' she said.

Norval chose a problem that had not yet been discussed this evening. 'We have to find them somewhere else to stay. We're supposed to move into Kirribilli House on Monday.'

'You should never have put them there in the first place.' She didn't want to crawl into a bed where Delvina Timori had slept; she had, unwittingly at the time, done that years ago.

'It was all that was available. Everything else is full – hotels, apartments, houses. They *would* land on us when Sydney's never been more chock-a-block.'

'Why can't we move them in here?' said Hickbed.

'No!' Anita almost shouted.

'I don't think that would be a good idea, Russ,' said Norval, not wanting another problem, closer to home.

Anita recovered, said sweetly, 'What about your place, Russell? You'd have room for them in that barn of yours.'

'A good idea!' Norval was almost too quick to support her.

Hickbed shook his head. 'What about security? It'd be too risky.'

'That could be fixed,' said Norval. 'I'll get the Federals to double their detail. It's the solution, Russ, I don't know why we didn't think of it before –'

'It's no solution. It'll just be a bloody great headache.'

Then Dave Lucas, one of the PM's political advisers, short and lugubrious-faced, a basset hound of a man, came to the door.

'There's just been a news-flash on TV. The Dutchman's put out an announcement that it was that guy Seville who tried to murder Timori.'

'Shit!' said Hickbed, who didn't speak French.

'Not on my carpet,' said Anita Norval and left the room, all at once glad that everything was going wrong.

65

It took Miguel Seville some time to reach Dallas Pinjarri. The Aborigine, it seemed, moved around as much as the Argentinian: militant radicals were the new nomads. But at last he had Pinjarri on the phone, though the latter sounded suspicious and unwelcoming. 'Who's this?'

Seville knew better than to identify himself: none knew better than he that yesterday's ally was often today's betrayer. 'A friend in Libya gave me your name.'

'What friend?'

Seville named a man in the Gaddafi camp, the contact who had sent him to Australia two years ago.

'You still haven't said who you are.'

'My name is Gideon, I'm from Switzerland.'

'Swiss? That's a new one. I always thought you jokers just went in for watches and cheese and fucking law and order.'

'Some of us have other ideas. Can we meet?'

There was silence at the other end of the line; Seville guessed a hand had been put over the mouthpiece. Then: 'Okay. You know the Entertainment Centre? No? Well, get a taxi, the driver will take you there. Eight o'clock. Wait in the lobby in front of Door Three. What do you look like?'

Seville described himself, having to close his eyes in the stuffy phone-box while he tried to remember his new looks. It was curious that he had never become accustomed to the sight of himself, when he looked in mirrors, in the various disguises he had to adopt.

'Okay, but you better be fair dinkum, mate. You're not fooling around with a tribe of fucking amateurs.'

Seville smiled to himself: Pinjarri hadn't changed. 'I'm sure I'm not.'

That evening Seville caught a taxi into the city, but, having looked up the Entertainment Centre in a directory he had bought, had the taxi drop him some distance from the Centre and walked the rest of the way. He took off his jacket and carried it over his arm: even the Swiss were known to relax occasionally.

He passed a gun shop on the way, but didn't pause. He had gone looking for such a store when the city had closed for Saturday afternoon; he had found two, including this one, but his practised eye had told him they were too well secured to be broken into. It was then that he had at last decided he had to risk contacting Pinjarri.

On the last part of his walk he was drawn towards the Entertainment Centre by the crowd heading there. He went down past Chinese restaurants and shops; a dragon with illuminated red eyes stared at him from a window and in the doorway beside it a Chinese girl smiled invitingly. Then the Centre loomed over him, an auditorium that looked like a dozen others he had seen in other parts of the world. An ideal place for a bomb scare, he remarked automatically. Just like all the others.

The crowd was pouring into the big building. All of them young, some of them bizarre in their dress; he stood out amongst them as if he were in fancy dress. Tonight was the first night of the Australian Pop Festival: the stars of the show were Dire Straits, direct from their American tour. Affronted nationalism hadn't kept the hordes away; they poured into the wide lobby as if the First Fleeters had come back to play the Top Ten of 1788. Seville took no notice of the irony: he was the true internationalist in the crowded lobby, the terrorist without patriotism.

He had been standing below the steps leading to Door 3 less than five minutes when he felt the tap on his elbow. 'Mr Gideon?'

The Aboriginal boy could not have been more than fifteen or sixteen; he was light-skinned and he reminded Seville of the Arab boys he had seen in the guerrilla training camps in the Bekaa valley in Lebanon. He looked just as serious and apprehensive as those boys.

'Yes, I'm Gideon. Am I supposed to follow you?' The boy looked surprised and Seville smiled. 'I've done this before. Many times.'

They pushed their way through the crowd, going against the stream. I may be in dire straits myself before the night is out, thought Seville wrily; but danger was an old ambience and he never felt uncomfortable in it. He followed the boy out into the busy street and they turned left. Five minutes' more walking brought them under what Seville took to be a traffic fly-over. There the boy, without a word, suddenly darted away.

Seville moved into the shadow of a pylon, stood waiting. He flexed the calf of his right leg, felt the knife in its sheath strapped there. If Dallas Pinjarri brought trouble, he would be ready for it.

Above his head he could hear the swish of tyres and the occasional rumble of a heavy truck. Through the pylons he could see the bright lights of the Darling Harbour complex, a new development since he had last been in Sydney. All cities, he decided, were beginning to look alike with their tourist projects; you travelled thousands of miles to look at buildings and display temples just like those you had left behind. In a thousand years, digging amongst the ruins, archaeologists would wonder in which country they were working.

Pinjarri appeared as silently and swiftly as the Aboriginal boy had disappeared: maybe it is an Aboriginal thing, Seville thought. He came through the bands of light and shadow; Seville thought he saw other shadows within the shadows, but he could not be sure. He waited, wondering if he would have to use the knife.

'Mr Gideon?'

'Hello, Dallas. Have you brought some friends with you, back there behind those pylons?'

Pinjarri peered at him in the shadows. 'I don't recognize –'

'I had another name when I was here two years ago.' He could not remember whether he had used his own name; his memory must be going. 'I also wasn't blond or Swiss –'

Pinjarri peered even closer. Then: 'Shit, is it really you? Miguel?'

'I might be,' said Seville, smiling. 'But call me Michel. I told you, I'm Swiss.'

'Sure, sure, whatever you say.' Pinjarri was a good-looking man in his late twenties with black curly hair and a complexion only slightly darker than an Arab's: a white man had stayed some time, maybe only for a night, in the family bed. He had a broken nose, a relic of a year as a professional boxer, and the sad dark eyes of a born loser. Yet he could still smile and it was a pleasant one. 'Sometimes I wish *I* could be something else. I'm a half-caste, half-educated, half fucking everything.'

Pinjarri hadn't been self-pitying when Seville had last been here; things must be going badly for the black militant movement. 'You wouldn't feel at home with the Swiss. No one ever does. Perhaps that's a better defence than an army.' Then he said, 'I need a gun.'

Pinjarri made a clucking noise. 'I always thought you'd have everything on hand. You said we were the fucking amateurs when you were here last time –' So he hadn't forgotten. 'You told us what a lot of shits we were –'

Seville was fluent in six languages and foul-mouthed in none of them; the obscenities grated on his ear. He was unconvinced that violent language achieved anything, except perhaps to help the speaker's own macho image. In the mouths of women it struck him as just ugly comedy. He was a prude in many ways, except in the matter of killing.

'I need a gun,' he repeated quietly. 'As soon as possible.'

Pinjarri stopped his abuse, looked at him curiously. 'You gunna kill someone? Or ain't I supposed to ask? Okay, forget I asked. What sorta gun? A Schmeisser, something like that? They're not easy to get –'

Seville doubted if Pinjarri had ever seen a Schmeisser: he was just airing his knowledge of the catalogues. 'I want a high-powered rifle, one with a telescopic sight. A Springfield or a Winchester or a Garand. What do your kangaroo-shooters use? I've seen them on television in those animal welfare propaganda films.' He could never understand why people should be so concerned with the slaughter of animals. 'I need something reliable and I need it at once.'

'I been 'roo-shooting meself. I used a Sako .270, it's a Finnish job –'

'I know it.'

'How soon do you want it?'

'Tomorrow at noon?'

'Shit, I dunno . . . It'll cost you.'

'How much?' He knew the price of a Sako: he had seen one

in the window of one of the gun shops he had inspected: $800.

Pinjarri hesitated, then said almost pugnaciously, 'Five thousand bucks.'

'That's a lot for a gun. I don't want to buy a battery of them.'

'Look, Mick, you know it ain't just for the gun. Our movement's in a fucking bad way – we need money any way we can make it . . .'

Seville smiled to himself. He thought of the money that was available to the PLO and the IRA. He had been in Beirut in 1982 when the Israelis had moved up into Lebanon; Rah Zaid, who knew of such things, had told him the PLO in four days had moved $400 million out of Lebanese banks into Switzerland. He felt tempted to bargain with Pinjarri, but the joke was too sour.

'Five thousand,' he agreed. 'But only if you deliver it by tomorrow noon and not a word to anyone whom it's intended for. Otherwise . . .'

'Otherwise what?' Pinjarri grinned. 'You wouldn't kill me, mate. I'm not worth anything.'

'So you wouldn't be missed.'

The grin faded. 'Okay, how will I get in touch with you?'

'I'll phone you at eleven. Dismantle the gun, bring it in some sort of bag. And a box of ammunition.'

'I'm not a fucking nong,' said Pinjarri, trying to sound like a professional. But what had he ever done? Seville asked himself the question and imagined Pinjarri asking it, too. A few demonstrations, the blowing up of a power-line pylon erected on an Aboriginal sacred site . . . It was difficult to be militant in a country that ignored you. 'You'll have it, no worries, mate.'

'I trust you, Dallas.' He had never trusted anyone, but it was always easy to say it.

'Sure, sure.' Then: 'You're not here to have a crack at Timori, are you? That wasn't you bumped off his sidekick last night, was it?'

Seville looked at him. 'You know better than to ask that.'

It was a threat more than a statement and Pinjarri recognized it. 'Sure, sure, forget it, forget I said it. But why didn't they ask us to do it, it's our territory? Okay, eleven o'clock tomorrow morning I'll hear from you. Hooroo.'

And he was gone: Seville wondered if *hooroo* was an Aboriginal farewell. Australians at times spoke a language all their own. Once more he longed to be back home, speaking Spanish, being *himself*. Whoever that had been: he had forgotten.

He went back to the hotel in Rozelle, pushed through the drinkers standing on the pavement outside, went up the back stairs on the storm of rock music being blasted out of the main bar. The building seemed to shake with it: the world was being white-anted by decibels. He closed and locked the door of his bedroom and the noise came up at him through the floor.

He turned on the small television set that the pub-owner, being obliging, had lent him and watched a movie about some Australian soldiers in the Boer War in South Africa. History was repeating itself there, except that blacks were being killed instead of whites, and he wondered why the movie's producers should have considered the subject worth while.

Then the movie was interrupted by a newsbreak: 'Premier Vanderberg has just announced that the prime suspect in the killing of President Timori's aide last night is Miguel Seville, international terrorist . . .'

He sat and stared at the small screen. The rock music came up through the floorboards and the tatty carpet like a rapid-fire barrage. He began to wonder how many people he would have to kill before the job was done and he could go home.

FOUR

1

The bicentennial celebrations were in full swing, building up to the climax of Australia Day only two days away. Flags flew everywhere; the city threatened to be airborne under the pull of fluttering bunting. Citizens walked around with bemused smiles, as if wondering how they had arrived at this anniversary: history is not comfortable if one has to wear it personally. The Lucky Country over the past year had begun to question its luck.

'Phil Norval must be questioning his luck,' said Malone. 'Being landed with Timori just as he's about to have his biggest shindig.'

'What about *our* luck?' said Kenthurst. 'We've got to move him out of here by tonight. The PM wants Kirribilli House back for the big day on Tuesday.'

'Where are you taking him?' said Joe Nagler.

'We haven't been told yet. We suggested we take him back up to Richmond, to the RAAF base – security would be much tighter there. But Madame vetoed that. I gather she wants to be somewhere around the harbour, so they can see all the celebrations.'

'What's she got to celebrate?'

'Twenty-two million bucks, for one thing,' said Malone. 'What are Customs doing about all that loot?'

'What can they do?' said Kenthurst. 'The Timoris didn't declare it, sure. But none of it's a prohibited import – they'll have to pay sales tax on the gold and gems, but the currency's okay. The rumour is that Customs want to grab the lot, but Canberra, or anyway Phil Norval, won't be too happy about that.'

'He should pick his friends more carefully,' said Malone.

He and Russ Clements had come across to Kirribilli again this morning and were going over the murdered Miss Kiddle's flat, hoping they might find something that had been missed on the night of the murder. The Forensic men had been here all day yesterday, searching every square foot of the building, and had come up with nothing. Malone, however, had decided to have a last look for himself. He and Clements had been in the flat only five minutes when they had been joined by Kenthurst and Nagler.

Russ Clements came through from the main bedroom. 'Nothing, Scobie. He was a real pro, except for that print on the dunny button.'

'And leaving his gun behind,' said Malone. 'That means if he wants another crack at our friends across the road he's got to get another gun.'

'I checked all the gun shops yesterday morning – I've got a list of everyone who bought a rifle or a hand-piece.' Clements might look like an amiable, slow-thinking slob, but he was usually one or two steps ahead of those who under-estimated him. Malone glanced at Kenthurst, but the latter's face showed no expression. 'His best bet would be to buy one from some crim. But how would he know any?'

'I don't think he'd try them,' said Malone. 'Terrorists like him don't have much time for the ordinary crim – every game has its snobs. No, I think he'd go looking for some mob of militants.'

When Lisa had been kidnapped in New York several years ago, Malone had had plenty of opportunity to study the terrorist mind. Since then he had kept up the study, certain that one day there would be terrorism in Australia just as there was in other countries. He knew that Joe Nagler agreed with him.

'We never had anything definite on him, but there was a rumour Seville was out here a couple of years ago.' Nagler looked diffident, an expression that didn't sit well on him; Special Branch were not supposed to deal in rumours. They might inspect them, but never spread them. 'That crowd who call themselves January Twenty-Six were supposed to have invited him. We talked to them, that guy Dallas Pinjarri and a couple of others, but we got nothing out of them. You know what a darky's like when he doesn't want to tell you anything.'

Nagler had his colour prejudice; Malone knew some whites who could be just as inscrutable as any darky. 'Is Pinjarri still in town? He comes and goes. The last time I heard of him he was up in the bush, Moree or somewhere, doing a bit of stirring.'

'I could find out –'

'No, leave it.' Malone didn't want Homicide pushed aside; this was still their case, two murder jobs. 'Russ, how'd you go on the hotel check?'

'A blank so far. I've had the boys go through the guest list of every hotel and motel in the city and up as far as Chatswood. The trouble is, I can't draw on the local stations. Every cop in Sydney seems to be on special duty for the bloody celebrations.' He had his own sense of priority, he would rather solve a murder than salute a flag. 'Every hotel and motel is full, been booked out for months. He'd have had trouble getting in anywhere.'

'Unless he's staying with some friends,' said Nagler. 'Pinjarri or someone like that.'

'Maybe,' said Malone. 'But we'll keep checking the pubs. Try the ones that still keep two or three rooms open – they've got to do that under the licensing laws.'

'I was hoping you wouldn't suggest that,' said Clements. 'That means every bloody pub within a radius of fifty miles.'

Malone looked at Nagler. 'Do you have trouble with the bludgers in Special Branch, sergeants who never want to work?'

'I'm a sergeant,' said Nagler. 'I bludge all the time.'

They all grinned, feeding on their sense of humour to keep them going. Malone led them down out of the building and across the road to Kirribilli House. The demonstrators were still behind the barriers further up the street, but they were quiet this morning; perhaps, thought Malone cynically, some of them had just come from church where they'd been praying for a better shot next time from the assassin. Police cars were parked on both sides of the street, but there were no Common-wealth cars. That meant Canberra had decided to take Sunday morning off, to leave the Timoris to their own devices. Of which, he thought, there would be many.

He stopped to be interviewed by two TV newsreel reporters and half a dozen radio and press reporters. He had nothing to report, he said, except that progress was being made.

'You've got a lead on the terrorist Seville?' said one of the TV reporters, a pretty girl who was dressed as if she had stopped by on her way to a barbecue or a yachting picnic. 'Are you hoping for an early arrest?'

'Oh, we're always hoping for an early arrest,' said Malone and grinned at one of the older press men standing in the background. That man knew the score and, an honest reporter, never expected too much of the police. 'We'll let you know when anything further turns up.'

'Are you getting any co-operation from the Timoris?' said the old reporter.

'Couldn't ask for more, Greg,' said Malone and knew the reporter didn't believe him. 'I'm going in now to talk to them. A charming couple.'

Madame Timori, with all the charm of a Paluccan cobra, attacked him at once. 'Back again, Inspector? We were told the case was to be closed. Poor Mr Masutir – he would have hated all this fuss over him.'

She wiped a dry eye with her handkerchief. She was imperial, or liked to think of herself as such; exile had gone to her head, which had been newly set and blow-dried. She was still not beautiful, her eyes were too small and cold, even on this hot morning, but there are some men who rarely look above a woman's shoulders. Malone was not one of them.

'How is the President this morning?'

'Still alive,' said Timori, coming into the drawing-room where they sat; or rather, where his wife sat and Malone stood. He was dressed all in white this morning and looked a little healthier, as if he might have slept well last night. 'Have they buried Mr Masutir yet?'

'I couldn't say, sir.' Burials were not his province. They obviously were not Timori's province, either, otherwise he would have known more about the disposal of his aide's remains. He had brought thirty or forty here with him to Sydney, so maybe one wouldn't be missed. It was hard to imagine that a man could be so callous, but then Malone had had no previous

75

experience of dictators. 'Mr President, we're still trying to find this man Seville. Do you think the generals back in Palucca would have employed him?'

'Why would they have done that? They have already got rid of me.'

'No, darling,' said Madame Timori. 'I think Inspector Malone has a point. There is more to this than a simple *coup d'état*.'

'I never thought *coups d'état* were simple,' said Malone, making a good imitation of her pronunciation; foreign phrases usually clung to his tongue.

'Neither they are,' said Timori, who seemed amused that his wife and Malone did not get on well together. 'I have more enemies than I thought, Inspector. Not all of them back in Palucca.'

Malone took a risk: 'What do you mean by that, sir?'

Timori smiled at him. 'You'd never be a diplomat, would you, Inspector?'

'I've been told that several times. But as far as I know, diplomacy never solved a murder case.'

There was a flash of anger in the dark eyes, but it was gone in a moment. It suddenly struck Malone that Timori was too defeated to worry about insolence, even if unintended, from some minor policeman. The man had been accustomed to power for so long that he was naked and afraid without it. Power corrupts . . . Malone had heard it somewhere (Hackton? Acton? Someone had said it once): but it also sustained. He had seen it amongst politicians and amongst criminals. Timori was both and now he had lost what had been his strength.

Then his other strength spoke up; she said, 'We can do without your insolence, Inspector. That will be all.'

Malone looked at her, then back at Timori. 'All I'm doing, Mr President, is trying to catch Seville before he makes another attempt on your life.'

'I think I have enough protection,' said Timori. 'Your Federal police, your Special Branch . . . Let Mr Masutir rest in peace.'

'Oh, I'll do that, sir. It's his murderer I'm after.'

He nodded to both of them, turned sharply and went out of the room and the house. As he came out the front door he almost bumped into Sun Lee.

'Mr Sun,' he said without any lead-up, 'who, back in Palucca, would profit by having the President killed?'

Sun gasped softly, as if the question had been a punch. 'I don't know, Inspector. Perhaps a hundred people – some might do it for –' he hesitated, as if to say the word was traitorous '– for revenge.'

'If they'd do it for revenge, why employ an international terrorist? There must be plenty of professional killers in Palucca.'

'Paluccans are gentle people, Inspector,' said Sun. 'Or how else would I, a Chinese, have survived amongst them? You don't know much about Asians, do you?'

Malone realized he had blundered: this was not a good morning. 'It could be someone who is not a Paluccan who hired Seville.'

There was just the faintest flicker of Sun's eyes. 'You mean a Chinese, perhaps?'

'Perhaps. Or Americans or Englishmen or Dutch or even Indonesians.'

'Or Australians?' said Sun, smiling. 'There were Australians in business in Palucca. Many of them.'

'Really?' Malone had thought there was only one. 'How's your memory? I'd like a list of them.'

'My memory is very bad, Inspector.'

'Give it a try, Mr Sun. Maybe another shot from Mr Seville will give it a jolt.'

Oh mate, you're really giving it to them this morning. In a bad mood at his own heavy manner, he jerked his head at Russ Clements, who stood in the shade of a tree over by the wall, his jacket off, a button on his shirt undone over his bulging stomach, his tie loosened.

'You look like a slob,' said Malone as he led the way towards the gates.

'This was supposed to be my day off,' said Clements, not yet attuned to Malone's mood. 'I was gunna spend it out at Bondi, floating around down at the southern end and admiring all the bare boobs. Instead . . .'

'Instead,' said Malone, 'we're going into Redfern.'

'Redfern? Oh Jesus. Why can't the Abos live beside the sea?'

'They used to, until fellers like you and all the bare-boobed sheilas came along and took it away from them.'

Clements looked at him. 'Sorry. I'd forgotten you used to be on their side.'

'I'm not on anyone's side,' said Malone wearily. Except perhaps that of law and order, but it would sound priggish to say it. He had the Australian fear of being explicit about the verities. One could be demonstrative about a sporting win, could shed tears at winning an Olympic gold medal but never about principles. You were certainly never expected to shed any tears over the Abos, not in the Police Department. Russ Clements was not a racist, just coloured in his views. 'Let's go and find Dallas Pinjarri.'

The demonstrators in the street let them through to their unmarked car. 'If I'd known that was a police car,' said one of the demonstrators, a girl dressed for the occasion: old clothes that wouldn't suffer when she was hauled along the ground to the paddy-wagon, 'I'd have let your tyres down.'

'Lie down and I'll run over you,' said Malone, forgetting about law and order.

They drove back over the Bridge and through the city to Redfern. It was an area on the edge of the uptown business section and had never been anything but working-class. It had always been rough and tough and it had succeeded in frightening off the gentrification that had overtaken other inner city areas. Malone had been born in nearby Erskineville, another tiny district that kept out the middle-class restorers and titivators with their Sydney 'iron lace' railings and their bright yellow doors. Malone was sure that his father Con, who lived behind a plain brown door and a plain wooden fence, had single-handedly kept the middle class out of Erskineville.

The advent of the Aborigines had been the final bar to any gentrification of Redfern. The radical chic would march in demonstrations for land rights and other compensations, but they preferred not to live amongst those they supported. Social conscience did not mean one had to have the right address; they had land rights of their own. The Aborigines had lived in Redfern for years; Malone could remember them as a kid, tolerated if not loved, a dark part of the community on which

78

no one ever wanted to shine a light. Then twenty years ago Redfern had become a magnet for Aborigines drifting into the city, driven there by intolerance in the country towns and the desire to share in the then boom being whipped up by the whites, the invaders of two hundred years ago. With this return to the original battleground came the radicals, belligerent, vocal and anything but chic.

Malone and Clements drove down a narrow street between terrace houses that looked as mean and suspicious as some of the people who stood lounging in the open front doors. This street was nowhere near as mean and desolate as some of the overseas slums Malone had seen on television: the South Bronx in New York, for instance. But the residents were just as suspicious of outsiders, especially cops.

Though he and Clements were in plainclothes and their car was an ordinary unmarked Holden, Malone knew they had already been identified as police. The local elements might have lost their bush skills and couldn't track a dingo in a sand-pit, but they could smell a copper at a hundred paces and probably round a corner.

'I'll stay in the car,' said Clements, 'just in case.'

Malone got out, feeling the heat hit him at once, crossed the pavement and knocked on the open door of one of the terrace houses. As he did so half a dozen Aborigines converged on the house, coming from several directions, unhurriedly but with purpose. They were all young men and all had the same sullen belligerence in their dark faces.

'You wanting someone, mister?'

'I'm looking for Jack Rimmer.'

'I'm here,' said a voice from the dim hallway of the house and then Rimmer stepped out on to the narrow strip of veranda that separated the house from the pavement. 'Oh, it's you, Inspector.'

'Can I have a word with you, Jack? Alone?'

Rimmer took his time looking at Malone. He was a full-blood, his face dark as an old saddle, the cheeks smooth on the bones but with deep lines running down from his nose to his mouth. He was in his fifties, but his almost black eyes looked centuries old; he had lived a dozen lives, none of them truly

79

happy. He was a government social worker and his work only increased his unhappiness with the world in which he had to live. Sometimes he dreamed of going back to the bush where he had been born, in the channel country of western Queensland, but he knew he would be lost there, too.

Then he nodded and glanced at the six young men on the pavement. 'It's all right, boys. Inspector Malone ain't the enemy.'

He led Malone into the narrow house. It smelled of bodies and cooked food; it was his private home but it was also a doss-house for Aboriginal kids arriving from the bush. He led the way through into the kitchen, waved Malone to a chair beside the table in the middle of the room and put a kettle on the gas stove. 'Tea or coffee?'

'Tea. Jack, I'm looking for Dallas Pinjarri.'

'He been up to something?' He had a soft, gravel-throated voice, as if someone had once tried to strangle him. Which, perhaps, they had.

'Not as far as I know. I just want some information from him.'

'You'll never get anything outa him. He's the tightest-mouthed bastard when it comes to talking to youse guys.'

'Not always,' Malone grinned. 'He once called me every name he could think of, in twenty-seven tribal dialects.'

Rimmer grinned, gap-toothed. 'That'd be him. He's an angry young bastard. He could make something of himself, but he's too busy being angry. Waddia you wanna know?'

'Jack, did the militants ever have anything to do with a terrorist named Miguel Seville?'

Rimmer had his back to Malone as he spooned tea into a broken-handled pot. 'That the guy mentioned in the papers this morning?'

Malone saw the Sunday papers lying on a battered couch against one wall, front pages up. Seville was more than mentioned: his name was a big headlined shout. 'That's the one. There's a rumour he was out here a couple of years ago.'

'He coulda been.' Rimmer turned round. 'If he was, they didn't bring him around here.'

'Jack, I'm not looking to hang anything on you. I don't care what happened a couple of years ago – if anything happened at all. I'm trying to prevent something happening today or tomorrow.'

'Like what?'

Malone hesitated. 'Can I trust you?'

'That's your risk, Scobie, not mine.' The kettle whistled and he turned his back again.

Malone stared at the thin bent back. He couldn't blame Rimmer for trying to protect his own. Very far back in the past they had all belonged to a tribe, several tribes: never a nation, but at least they had been owners of this land, of the bush that had become Redfern, become Sydney, become Australia. This weekend was an anniversary for them, but not a celebration. This week all the tribe had to be protected, even the rebels.

Malone said, 'We think Seville's going to have another crack at killing President Timori. We think he's looking for another gun and he's got to find someone who'll supply it.'

Rimmer poured the tea, brought two cups to the table and sat down opposite Malone. 'Milk? Sugar? Timori deserves to be bumped off. Best thing could happen.'

'Jack, I understand your sentiment. But passing judgement isn't my job.'

'Some of the kids outside would disagree with you.' But Rimmer smiled; then he sobered. 'Dallas never carries a gun, he's too smart for that.'

'He could get hold of one.' Malone stirred sugar into his black tea. 'Tell me where he is, Jack. I can keep him out of trouble if I can get to him in time. What's Dallas got to gain if Timori is killed? Palucca's not going to do anything about land rights for your mob. Tell me where I can find him.'

Rimmer stirred his tea, milk with no sugar, looking at it as if the leaves might flow to the surface and tell him the future before he had drained the cup. 'The stupid young buggers – they'll never succeed, trying it their way. There are millions of you, less than half a million of us . . .' He looked up, his eyes full of pain. 'If I put you on to him, will you promise you won't take him in?'

Malone again hesitated: policemen should never make promises. But he could not make Rimmer's position untenable: he did too much good work for that. 'I promise, Jack. All I want is to talk to him.'

Rimmer stood up. 'Stay here.'

Malone sat and waited, poured himself a second cup of tea. He wondered how Clements was doing out in the sweat-bath of the car, suffering the aggressive stares of the young Aborigines. He looked around the kitchen, saw the crude posters but didn't examine them. Some of them were violent in their demands, but he doubted that Jack Rimmer believed in them.

Rimmer was back in ten minutes with Dallas Pinjarri. The latter came into the kitchen, slumped down on a chair and shoved his legs out; the pose was so theatrically belligerent that Malone wanted to laugh. But he had experienced the same attitude from young white punks: rebels now got their image from TV just like politicians.

'I wouldn't of come if it hadn't been for Jack.'

'I'm grateful to him,' said Malone and nodded his thanks to Rimmer. 'Relax, Dallas, this isn't a bust. All I want is some information.'

Dallas Pinjarri came of a generation whose mothers had named their children, black and white, after American movie stars or American cities. At one time, Malone had remarked, the entire forward packs of Sydney rugby league teams seemed to be made up of Garys, Waynes and Carys; one had to dig to the bottom of a ruck to find a Fred or Clarrie. But the next generation would be worse: Malone shuddered at the ghastly thought of Jons, Jasons and Justins running on to a football field. Dallas had done his best to restore the balance by changing his name from Smith to Pinjarri.

'Have you had any contact with a man named Miguel Seville?'

Pinjarri's eyes flicked towards the newspapers on the couch, but his face remained set. 'The guy in this morning's papers? Why would I know anything about him?'

'We know he came out to see your crowd two years ago.' It never hurt to sound positive.

Pinjarri laughed, but Malone caught the uneasy note in it. 'What good would he do us? We wouldn't want him. Why d'you think he'd be contacting us now?'

'Possibly to buy a gun from you.'

Pinjarri straightened up, shook his head. 'That's it, you're trying to fucking bust me. I'm not selling no gun – I dunno this guy from Adam . . .'

'You could be in bigger trouble than just selling a gun, Dallas. You've read what this feller's up to –'

'You got no proof of that. It's just like you bastards, laying something on him before you got any proof – you dunno he's even in the country –'

'How do you know we don't?' Malone knew now that he had the Aborigine worried. 'An accessory before the fact of assassination – that wouldn't help the rest of your mob, would it?' He looked at Rimmer. 'Talk some sense into him, Jack.'

Rimmer, leaning against the kitchen sink, shrugged. 'I been trying to do that for months. He never listens to me, do you, Dallas? Wake up, son. You're gunna get your arse pushed in on this one if you play stupid.'

But Pinjarri was stubborn. 'I dunno the guy.'

Malone sat a moment staring at the young Aborigine. Then he sighed and stood up. 'Righto, Dallas. Just remember – when we do bust you for this, I tried to help you. Thanks, Jack. I think your job's harder than mine.'

'I wouldn't argue with that, Inspector. Only the pay's different.'

Malone grinned. 'I'm the right colour, Jack. Take care.'

He looked once more at Pinjarri, hoping for a last-minute change of heart; but there was none. The young Aborigine was staring out the kitchen window at the tiny yard: he saw nothing, Malone was sure of that. His stubbornness, his total distrust of the police jacketed him in an attitude that would eventually bring him to disaster. For a moment Malone felt sorry for him, but it lasted only a moment: pity, they had told him years ago, should never be part of a policeman's equipment. They had been wrong, of course, but he had learned to use it sparingly.

He went out into the street, climbed into the car and felt the sweat start on him immediately. 'Any trouble?'

Clements looked out at the dark young men lounging against the veranda railings of Rimmer's house. 'Why do we bother with 'em? Why don't we just round 'em all up and send 'em back to the bush. They'd be happier there.'

'Let's go, Russ.' He didn't want Clements' remarks overheard. The big man's heart probably wasn't racist, just his
tongue. It was the tongue, however, other people's tongues,
that caused half a policeman's problems. He'd lost count of the
number of murders that had begun with verbal abuse. 'Maybe
they don't like the bush any more than you do.'

Clements nodded, unconvinced. 'You get anything out of
Pinjarri?'

'Nothing. But I'll bet he's had contact with Seville. I want
him watched.'

He looked sideways at the big man and Clements raised his
thick eyebrows in shock. 'Who, me? In this heat? Ah Christ,
Scobie, let's call up some young joker –'

'You're it, Russ – you're younger than me. There's no time
to call in anyone else – I need a tail on him *now*. Pull up.'
Clements pulled the car into the kerb. 'Now's your chance to
prove you're a better black tracker than any of the blacks.'

'I can remember when you and I were mates, Inspector,' said
Clements, getting out of the car.

'It's the rank, Sergeant. It's always breaking up beautiful
friendships. Good luck, Russ. Ring me at the office in an hour.
I'll have some young fellers to relieve you by then.'

He watched Clements go back to the corner of the street,
stand there a moment, then disappear. He slid over into the
driver's seat and drove the car back into the city. He felt the
trail to Seville was warming up, though it would be Clements
who would be feeling the heat the most. He turned on the
air-conditioning and was surprised it was working. It was a good
omen.

2

'You've made it just that much tougher for us to catch this
man,' said Commissioner Leeds.

'Tough titty, John,' said the Premier. 'I had my reasons.'

I'm sure you did, thought Leeds. Politicians, particularly
ones like Hans Vanderberg, never did anything without a
reason. The voters might never understand the reasons, but

that did not matter. Though in this case the voters might understand: The Dutchman had never made any secret of his enmity for Phil Norval.

'This country's in a helluva state, John,' the Premier went on. 'The celebrations don't mean a thing. Anything that will get rid of that crowd in Canberra will be good for the country. I'm doing it for Australia,' he said and tried to look full of patriotism. But he was only a quarter-full of it and the emptiness showed.

Leeds tried not to throw up. 'It would be a feather in *our* cap, the State's, if we managed to catch Seville. The rest of the world has been chasing him for ten years.'

'That would be fine if you coppers were running for office. But you're not. I'm the one who's got an election this year. I got to get up to all the skulbuggery I can.' He looked at his political secretary and grinned evilly. 'But Roger here tells me I'm a dead certain to get back in.'

'Skulduggery, certainty,' Ladbroke whispered under his breath. He sometimes dreamed of going to Britain and working for a British Prime Minister: they always sounded so articulate and literate. But maybe they wouldn't appreciate his skills in skulduggery, or skulbuggery, whatever you called it; and he knew he would miss the opportunities to practise it. He loved the bear-pit of this State's politics. He said aloud, 'They're moving the Timoris out of Kirribilli House this afternoon.'

'That's news to me,' said Leeds.

'Where's he going?' said Vanderberg.

'He's moving over to Russell Hickbed's place at Point Piper. They've had trouble finding a place for him, nothing's on offer around the harbour.'

'Hickbed, eh?' The Dutchman spun his chair round and looked out the window. He could see Point Piper from here, a finger of silvertail residences poking out from the south shore of the harbour. He imagined he could see Hickbed's mansion, though he had only seen pictures of it; he had certainly never been invited to visit. It was within shooting distance, he would bring up the field guns tomorrow. 'I wonder how much of a hand he's got in the pie? I wouldn't trust him if I could throw him far.'

85

Ladbroke didn't attempt to translate that. 'We've got nothing definite, but he and Madame Timori are supposed to be business partners.'

'Are you going to pass on to us all the dirt you dig up?' said Leeds, and felt dirty asking such a thing.

The Premier swung his chair round to face Leeds. 'That'll depend, John. You don't want to get mixed up in anything political, do you? All you fellers have got to do is catch this Seville.'

'You've practically ruined our chances of that.'

'Then he may go home without taking another crack at Timori,' said Ladbroke, and Vanderberg nodded.

'If he does, then we may be stuck with the Timoris for ever. You won't like that, will you?'

'If I can bring down Phil Norval, the Timoris won't stay,' said The Dutchman. 'I'll see to that, my word I will.'

'There's one item Jack Phillips and Don Clary have dug up,' said Ladbroke and smiled as if he might next lick his lips: fat on gossip, he fed on it. 'There was a donation of fifty thousand dollars to Phil Norval's last campaign fund. The cheque came from a company called Da Gama Exploration. The principal shareholder is D.R. O'Reilly. Delvina Rose O'Reilly.'

The Dutchman clapped his hands: he looked like an ugly schoolboy who had at last seen the school well ablaze. 'Oh, I hope they don't kill Timori! Not till I can bury Phil Norval in the manure heap!'

3

Precisely at eleven o'clock Seville phoned Dallas Pinjarri. He was not being Swiss, but himself, the Argentinian. He had learned from experience that punctuality was essential in the trade of terrorism. The bomb that went off too early or too late never did anyone any good.

Pinjarri picked up the phone after it had rung only once; he must have been standing right by it. 'That you, Mick?'

Seville wished Australians were not so familiar, so matey, to borrow one of their own expressions. 'Did you get the package?'

'Sure, I got it here. But . . .'

'But what?'

'The pigs are on to you. I was quizzed by one of 'em this morning, about an hour ago, a guy named Inspector Malone. He asked me if I was gunna supply you with a gun.'

Seville pushed open the door of the public phone-box; he suddenly felt very warm. Or at least he was sweating, something unusual for him. 'Are they watching you?'

'I dunno. I can send someone out to look.'

'Do that. Stay by the phone. I'll call at eleven-twenty.'

He hung up and stepped out into the heat of the Rozelle street. A young girl brushed by him and went into the box; she dialled a number, then settled herself against the glass wall of the box for a chat. She lit up a cigarette and stared out through the glass at him as if challenging him to move on and leave her to her privacy.

Seville looked at his watch, then decided to go for a short walk; he did not want to remain in the one place long enough to be observed and perhaps later identified. He could feel uneasiness weakening him like a virus: too much was going wrong with this assignment. He was not himself; but it was not the Swiss disguise that had altered him. Perhaps he had been at the game too long, perhaps it was the environment; everyone blamed the environment these days for all their ills. He was lost in these drab, sunburned streets where everyone looked so casual and unafraid. He felt more at home in terror-stricken Beirut.

He stopped in at a newsagent's and bought a paper. The Timoris were still page one material, though they were not the lead story. He had no feelings about Timori, his corruption and his downfall. He was totally cynical about men in general; some were just worse than others. He was, however, intrigued by Madame Timori: one met so few successful evil women. He had watched her on television and she had sexually stimulated him. Love-making for him had always been a risk, a gamble with betrayal; he worked on the principle that there were two places where a man was always vulnerable to attack, in bed and in the bath. On top of Madame Timori was one of the most vulnerable places he could think of.

He walked back to the phone-box. The girl was still on the phone, one leg propped up against the wall opposite her, the box's air thick with cigarette smoke. He looked at his watch: 11.18. He waited a minute, then tapped on the door. The girl took no notice of him: he could hear her chatter: 'Nah, you know what he's like, at it all the time. I dunno where I'd be if I wasn't pinching Mum's pills . . .' He knocked again and she glared at him, poking out her tongue. It occurred to him only then that she could have been no more than fourteen or fifteen, a child.

He opened the door, smelled the smoke and the heat. 'May I use the phone, please?'

'Get stuffed,' she said.

He felt the knife-sheath rub against his calf. 'My mother's very ill. I'm trying to call the doctor –'

'Why didn't you say so? I gotta go, Shirl, see youse t'night.' She came out of the box. 'What's the time?'

'Eleven-twenty,' he said and stepped into the suffocating box, closing the door in her face. He dialled and Pinjarri answered on the first ring. 'Well?'

'There's a pig up at the end of the street and we think there is another down the other way. What do I do? I just as soon forget all about it, Mick.'

'You don't want the five thousand?' He stared through the glass at the young girl; she was listening to the conversation, waiting to hear if he'd got the doctor. He lowered his voice. 'Is the item dismantled and in a bag?'

'Yeah, nobody'd know what's in it unless I was picked up.' There was silence for a moment, then: 'Have you got the five grand on you?'

'No. Don't you trust me?'

'What if they pick you up after I've delivered the gun to you? What's in it for us then, eh?'

'I can give you a deposit of a thousand dollars in traveller's cheques, American dollars. The rest I'll see comes to you in a bank draft.' He would have to be careful with his money if this job dragged on. He had expected to be on his way back to Damascus by now. 'You need the money, Mr Pinjarri. You told me so. Trust me.'

There was hesitation, doubt, on the line: it was tangible, one could almost feel it. Then: 'Okay, a thousand dollars down. But I ain't coming out with the bag in daylight . . .'

'I wouldn't expect you to. Ten o'clock tonight –' He had already chosen the meeting place from the street directory, had been there and scouted it. He had just expected the meeting to take place at noon, instead of having another long wait ahead of him. Timori might die of old age before he got to him. 'Central Railway Station. Stand outside the cocktail lounge. If you can't lose the police, don't bother to turn up. Go home and I'll call you at eleven o'clock.'

He hung up and stepped out of the box, his nose dry from the smoke and his eyes smarting. The young girl, smoking another cigarette, snarled at him. 'You wasn't calling any fucking doctor.'

'No, my dear. You're going to learn that life is full of liars and cheats. Give my love to Shirl.' He sounded Australian in his own ears, but the girl, a true Aussie, just jerked her thumb at him and went back into the box.

Seville went back to the hotel, sat in his room and watched television, read and slept. He felt safer there; he was losing his confidence, he even felt unsafe in his disguise. When someone knocked on his door and said, 'Mr Gideon?' he jumped; but it was only the publican's wife asking if he was ill, would he like a cuppa coffee? He got up, opened the door and there she was with a tray.

'It's only instant, but it's better than nothing. I was in Switzerland a coupla years ago, me and my husband – we go away every so often. You Swiss make beautiful coffee, I used to drink it by the gallon. There's some iced vo-vo's, too – they're our national biscuit. You see? They've got our flag on them, for the Bicentennial. You're all right?'

'It's just the heat. I'm not used to it.'

'No, I guess you wouldn't be, coming from Switzerland.' She wanted to stay and talk, to find someone different from the pub's regular drinkers.

He put a hand to his head. 'I've got a headache. I think I'll drink the coffee and then lie down again. Thank you, you're very kind.'

She smiled, a plump woman with prematurely grey hair and a friendliness to her that was genuine, not the professional *bonhomie* of a publican's wife. She told him to take care and went back downstairs to tonight's rock band, which was just warming up. He drank the coffee, which made him grimace, ate the biscuits, chewing on the Australian flag, and switched on the television again for the seven o'clock news.

The celebrations were the main news, though the Timoris were the second item. Efforts were being made to find them a permanent haven: Holland, Switzerland and Singapore had said no. France, with Gallic bluntness, said it already had ex-President Duvalier and it was time someone else had a go. America was leading the effort to find them sanctuary, but offering none itself; sanctimony flowed out of Washington like the foetid air of two hundred years ago before the swamps of the Potomac were drained. Britain, a haven for everyone else, waited to be asked so that it, too, could say no; but Madame Timori, who had tried London once and found it frigid, climatically and socially, vetoed any suggestion about Britain. Australia, meanwhile, was stuck with them, though the ABC didn't say that.

A face Seville had seen once before on the news came up: Detective-Inspector Scobie Malone. 'Are you still looking for the terrorist Seville, Inspector?'

'Still looking,' said Malone.

'You're sure he's your man?'

'I'm never sure about any suspect. That's why he's only a suspect.'

'Have you any leads?'

Malone smiled: it seemed to Seville that he smiled directly at him, a challenge. 'We'll let you know.'

Seville watched the rest of the news, but took none of it in. He switched off the set, but Malone's face, that dry knowing smile, remained fixed in his mind's eye. Timori was still the target, but he knew now who the enemy was.

The rock music, like earth tremors high on the Richter scale of intensity, came up through the floor and drove him out of his room at eight o'clock. There was still light in the sky, but he was not afraid of being picked up; not yet, not till he had to approach Central Station in two hours' time. As he walked away from the hotel he did not see the police patrol car pull up and the two officers get out and go into the hotel.

In the bar the publican's wife, Mrs Brigham, shouted above the bombardment of the music, 'What? A foreigner?'

The two police officers, both young, jerked their heads and led her out into the private hallway. They showed her a copy of the photo of Miguel Seville; it had suffered in the reproduction and even his own mother might not have recognized him. If she had wanted to . . . 'Is he staying here? Or someone resembling him?'

'No, the only foreigner we have here is a Swiss gentleman. Mr Gideon. He's blond and wears glasses. Who's this bloke?'

One of the officers wrote down Gideon's name. 'A terrorist named Miguel Seville.'

'Oh, the one on the news?' She took out a pair of rimless glasses, peered again at the photo: she looked like a schoolmistress checking a pupil's drawing. Then she shook her head. 'Nothing like him.'

'Could we talk to him?'

'He's gone out, just a few minutes ago.'

'Can we have a look at his room?'

'You got a warrant?' She had once lost a good paying tenant, an SP bookie, by not asking the raiding police for a warrant.

'No.'

'Then no. Come back with a warrant, but I tell you now, you're wasting your time. You want a drink before you go?'

'We're on duty,' said the young policemen, but waited with their tongues hanging out while she brought them a middy of beer each, low alcohol, of course.

Seville wandered about the city for an hour and a half, stopping occasionally to watch the burst of fireworks over the harbour. He wondered what the fireworks bill would be for the celebrations; the country seemed to be going up in smoke. The city streets were thronged on this Sunday night; everyone seemed to be working up steam for the Big Day, the day after tomorrow. A crocodile of young people, half-drunk on equal parts of grog and nationalism, snaked its way down George Street, disrupting traffic. A Vietnamese boy stood at a kerb selling Australian flags, one of them wrapped round his head as a scarf. Two young men, everything tight about them, their clothes, their hair, their smiles, walked by hand in hand and were jeered at by two girls, who had everything loose, including one breast hanging out of a man's blue singlet. A fire engine came up the street, siren blaring, and everyone clapped and cheered, thinking it was part of the celebrations. Seville was outside it all, though he smiled at strangers who, infected with friendliness – 'We are all mates at a time like this,' Prime Minister Norval had told the nation at his last televised conference – smiled at him. But, with a few exceptions, most people in these crowds looked self-conscious about their gaiety. He remembered a Carnivale he had gone to in Rio de Janeiro, remembered the utter abandon. Suddenly he was homesick for South America again, even for a country that was not his own.

The party would come to a climax on Tuesday. He had to kill Timori before then; there would be too many police available after Tuesday. He didn't want to be caught in the cleaning-up, caught amidst the broken beer bottles, the husks of double-bungers, the condoms on the grass. He *had* to get the gun from Pinjarri tonight.

He went uptown, approached Central Station cautiously, coming up the sloping roadway from Central Square to the station itself with its tall clock tower. The tower, like so many of the city's landmarks, was flood-lit; the clock itself was a bright-faced full moon. It was 9.50, time for him to reconnoitre the station surrounds.

He saw no police cars; nor any unmarked cars in which men sat or by which they stood. If there were any police staking out the station, they were well hidden. He went into the big building, passing through the deserted outer area under the wide awnings and coming into the almost deserted main departure hall.

He stopped just inside the west entrance and surveyed the hall with its high vaulted ceiling. It looked as if it had been restored a year or two ago; late-Victorian stations usually didn't look as clean and attractive as this one. A few people sat on the big semi-circular brown and orange benches; it was difficult to tell whether they were travellers who had missed their trains

92

or homeless unfortunates waiting to bed down for the night. It seemed that all the trains had either left or arrived: there was no movement on the dark platforms beyond the glass entrance booths. There was also no sign of Dallas Pinjarri.

Seville went back and round outside the building. He was under the huge canopy that covered the wide roadway where passengers were set down or picked up. Two taxis pulled up and some people got out of them and went into the station. The taxis drew away, leaving the area deserted again. There were half a dozen cars parked on the far side of the roadway and there was another car parked on the footpath just along from the entrance to the main ticket hall. Seville had passed it when he had come round from the west entrance, but had taken little notice of it. Parking on footpaths seemed to be an Australian habit.

He went in through the ticket hall, came out into the main hall and looked along towards the cocktail lounge. He saw Dallas Pinjarri come out of the lounge carrying what looked to be another squash bag. He paused, looked around him, then set the bag down and leaned back against the wall behind him. At this distance Seville could not tell whether Pinjarri was ill at ease or not.

Seville scanned the big hall: there was no sign of any police. He was about to step out into the open, turning towards Pinjarri, when the voice behind him said, 'Sir?'

He turned, every muscle tightening. The young policeman, in shirt sleeves, cap pushed back on his sweating head, gun still in his holster on his hip, was smiling at him. 'Is that your car parked outside on the footpath?'

'No.'

'Are you sure, sir? I observed you coming away from it.'

Where had the young officer been? Seville hadn't seen him; perhaps there were more of them *observing* him. He had glanced into the car as he had passed it, to check there was no one hidden in it; but he could not remember stopping by it. The police, later, would learn that the car belonged to a drunken station employee who had been about to drive it into the main hall, smashing through the entrance doors; only another employee, slightly less drunk, had stopped him. They had been caught up in the city's party mood, had been drinking since last night and then this evening dimly remembered they were supposed to report for duty here at Central. The men were later reprimanded and docked a week's wages, but by then the damage was done.

'Would you mind stepping outside with me, sir?'

Seville hesitated, looking around for the squad of police to emerge. But none appeared, and abruptly he knew what he would have to do. 'All right, officer. It is mine. I'll move it.'

'If you wouldn't mind, sir.' The young officer was in a good mood: he would be knocking off soon, going to his own party.

'I'll need a hand to get it started. The battery's almost flat. If you wouldn't mind giving me a push?'

Seville's mind was accustomed to working fast; it had never worked faster than now. They went back through the ticket hall and out into the setting-down area. An empty taxi drove up, paused, then drove on. The area was deserted again. Seville knew he would have to work fast, have luck on his side.

Without looking directly at it, he was aware of the policeman's pistol in its holster on his hip. He walked towards the car, going in on the driver's side, between the car and the wall. He bent down and slipped the knife out of its sheath on his leg; he palmed it with the haft up his sleeve; he was thankful he was still wearing his jacket. He went to the back of the car and the young policeman followed him, coming round from the outer side.

'I don't think you're going to have room to turn her around, sir –'

Seville stabbed him in the heart, the knife going up under the ribs. It was another close-up killing; but Seville couldn't turn his face away this time. He stepped back as the policeman fell on to the boot of the car and slid down to the ground. Seville grabbed him and dragged him between the car and the wall as another taxi pulled up.

He crouched down over the body, heard the laughter and a shouted goodbye and the taxi was driven away. Between the car and the wall, as if through a narrow window, he saw a young man and a girl, arms round each other, go into the ticket hall. As they reached the door they paused and he stiffened, waiting for them to look at the car and then come towards it. But they just clung to each other, kissed and then, laughing again, went into the ticket hall.

He let out a quick sigh of relief. Then he flipped open the holster and took out the policeman's pistol. It was a short-barrel Smith and Wesson .38, good only at short range: no weapon at all for a long range assassination. But it *was* a weapon and he needed more protection than the knife could give him. He slipped the gun into his jacket pocket, took the extra six rounds of ammunition out of the pouch on the officer's belt, then stood up and looked out past the car.

No one had seen the killing. He moved out into the open and went back through the ticket hall. He pushed open the inner doors and stepped into the main hall and looked along towards the cocktail lounge. There was no sign of Pinjarri: he had disappeared.

Then Seville saw Inspector Malone and two other men in plainclothes come into the hall no more than thirty yards away.

4

The tail on Dallas Pinjarri had been lost. Clements, who had been relieved at noon and then came back on watch at eight o'clock, having spent the interim doing paper-work at Homicide, had seen the Aborigine come out of his house in Redfern at nine o'clock carrying a canvas bag. Pinjarri had walked up to Cleveland Street and then turned up towards the University. Clements had kept him in sight; at the same time he had kept in radio contact with the two junior men in the unmarked car that kept within range of him, but out of sight of Pinjarri, two hundred yards behind him.

Pinjarri had disappeared into the grounds of the University. The big campus was deserted; it was the middle of the Long Vacation and, due to the holiday celebrations, there were no summer classes. Clements had put on pace, cursing the warmth of the summer night, about which he could do nothing, and the fact that he was over-weight, about which he had been promising himself for months to do something. He went in through the unguarded gates, wondering where the security men were, and soon found himself in the shadows of the neo-Gothic buildings, the Victorian attempt to bring Oxbridge Down Under. He had never got even close to attending university; indeed, this was only the third time in his life he had ever been on this campus, the oldest of the city's three universities. A university might have graduates who went on to vice, fraud and homicide, his subjects, but those crimes rarely occurred on campus. He wondered why he had an inferiority complex each time he came up here.

There was no sign of Pinjarri: the black had melted into the black shadows of the big stone buildings as easily as he might have melted into the mulga scrub in a black Outback night. Clements flicked on his radio: 'I've lost him. I'm going right through the grounds to Parramatta Road. Meet me there, down past the Footbridge Theatre.'

'Right, Sarge.' That was Andy Graham.

Clements kept on through the dark, occasionally lit grounds; there were a few lights in some of the buildings, but not many. He went down past the sports ovals and along to the Parramatta Road gates. They were locked and too high for him to climb over. He cursed and was about to turn back when he saw Pinjarri on the far side of the wide main road. The Aborigine was hailing a taxi, which pulled in beside him with a sharp squeal of brakes. Clements strained his eyes, trying to read the company name on the side of the taxi; but it was too far away and there was too much passing traffic. The taxi pulled away into the traffic stream, heading north towards the city proper.

Clements cursed into his radio: he had lost contact with the follow-up car. Then it came on the air: 'Where are you, Sarge?'

'I'm locked in – the bloody gates are locked. Where are you?'

'Up by the theatre, where you told us. Are you on to Pinjarri?'

'He's just caught a cab, going north.'

There was silence for a moment: the young men in the car were working out where north was. 'Right, you mean back to the city?'

'Jesus wept!' Clements held on to his temper. 'Get Headquarters to call all the operations boards of the taxi companies.

See if any cab radioed in that it had picked up a passenger in Parramatta Road opposite the gates to University Oval. Find out where it took him.'

'What about you, Sarge?'

'I'll find my way out of here. Go back to the main gate – I'll meet you there.'

'Right.' Then a pause: 'We'll have to do a U-ie, Sarge.'

'Then do a bloody U-ie! When have you ever worried about the traffic laws? What do they teach you at the academy these days?'

He could imagine his comment going out on the open air, being picked up all over Sydney; he hoped the Commissioner wasn't listening in. Then he grinned at the thought of the police car trying to do a U-turn in the Sunday night traffic on Sydney's main western artery. He had to grin at something: there was precious little else to smile about. He could already hear what Scobie was going to say to him for losing Pinjarri.

But Malone had very little to say; he seemed to be remarkably philosophical. 'Never mind, we just have to hope Dallas is somewhere here inside the station. If he isn't, we can only guess Seville's already met up with him and Pinjarri has passed him a gun. That means Seville's got to come out into the open again if he wants another crack at Timori.'

'I just wish I hadn't lost Pinjarri.'

Legion Cabs had, in answer to the police enquiries, reported that one of their taxis had picked up a man in Parramatta Road and delivered him to Central. Yes, he had been an Aborigine and he had been carrying a bag of some sort. He had told the driver he was fed up with the city and was going back to the bush. Clements was waiting for Malone at Central when the latter arrived from his home, having been called just as he was about to fall into bed. In the circumstances Clements could only marvel at Malone's patience and he suddenly wondered if his chief cared whether Seville was picked up or not.

Clements had already asked for back-up, he told Malone when the latter stepped out of his own car in the setting-down area of the station. 'Six SWOS guys are also on their way.'

Andy Graham came out of the ticket hall. 'No sign of Pinjarri, Inspector.'

'Seville?' Malone had no real hope that they would recognize the terrorist.

'No, sir.'

The Special Weapons Operational Squad arrived in their wagon, pulling in behind Malone's car. The SWOS men tumbled out, a little too self-conscious in their eliteness; they barely looked at the men in plainclothes and the four uniformed men now converging on Malone. Their sergeant approached Malone and was briefed on where to post his men.

'Try and not frighten the natives, Sergeant.'

The sergeant gave Malone a look that said he and his men knew how to treat the natives; then he snapped an order and the men trotted away. Clements looked after them. 'They're all so bloody *keen*.'

'Righto, Rambo.' When Malone looked at Clements he always thought of himself as in peak condition; when he saw the SWOS squad he wondered if he should retire as an acknowledgement of his age and debilitation. 'Let's go inside. If you sight either Pinjarri or Seville, no gunfire unless they shoot first. I don't want half a dozen dead bystanders on my report sheet.'

He led Clements and Andy Graham in through to the main hall. A blond man in glasses passed them on his way out, but Malone stopped him. 'Excuse me, sir?'

Seville stopped. 'Were you speaking to me?'

'Yes, sir. We're police – we'd like everyone to remain in the station for a few minutes.'

Seville hesitated. He had seen the SWOS men in their flak jackets and with their rapid-fire weapons come trotting past him; he knew if he made a run for it now, they would blast him before he got out of the main hall. He decided to gamble: life had been a gamble for him ever since he had joined the Tupamaros all those years ago. He had headed straight for Malone.

'Certainly, officer.'

But then as he turned to go back into the hall he felt the weight of the dead policeman's gun in his jacket pocket. It was a lightweight linen jacket; the material did nothing to hide the bulge of the gun. He could feel it standing out on his hip like

98

a giant heavy tumor. It was too late, however, to turn and run.

It took Malone's men less than two minutes to round up all those who had been waiting in the hall, the cocktail lounge and the rest rooms. The SWOS men, meanwhile, had scoured the empty platforms and come back to take up their posts around the hall. Seville, standing in the middle of the group of civilians, felt that every gun in the hands of the SWOS men was aimed directly at him.

He was hemmed in by those around him; he was glad of their closeness. Two young detectives were trying to get the group to sort itself into a line, but several were rebelling at being marshalled like that: they had their rights, what was this all about? A young detective stood in front of Seville and said, 'May I have your name, sir?'

'Hey, what about me?' said the young woman next to Seville. She was heavily made-up, wore a cotton-knit shirt with no brassière so that her nipples showed through like press studs and she smelled of a heavy perfume that suggested it could be bought in family-size bottles. 'I gotta go – I'm late for a date –'

'Business, love?' said Andy Graham. He looked at Malone, who had just come up behind him. 'We need to keep the ladies, Inspector?'

'Do you know a man named Dallas Pinjarri, miss?'

'Who? Never heard of him. I was just passing through to go downstairs to catch the train to North Sydney –' Seville remembered her now. She had been standing beyond Pinjarri outside the cocktail lounge, waiting for any rough trade that might come by.

He was studying Inspector Malone. There was experience there in that bony face with the wide, good-humoured mouth; it showed in the dark-blue eyes and the patient way he looked at the cheap little whore. He was not treating her as a whore and the girl, unexpectedly, seemed to appreciate it. Seville guessed that Inspector Malone would be a very good man at gathering information from any source.

'You might have seen him here. A young Aborigine, light-skinned. He was carrying a bag of some sort.'

The girl frowned, brushed her long blonde hair away from her face. 'Yeah, come to think of it . . . He come outa the

99

lounge there. I looked at him, but –' She stopped: she wasn't prepared yet to admit she was on the game. 'Then he saw the young pig – sorry. The young cop – policeman –'

'Which young policeman was that?' said Malone.

Seville felt he was holding his head in place so that it would not swivel round to look out through the ticket hall to the area where the car was still parked. Where, since there had been no commotion, the young policeman's body was still wedged between the car and the wall.

'I dunno. I looked away and when I looked back, he'd just gone. He wasn't there.'

'Who? The officer or the young Aborigine?'

'Both of 'em, I guess.'

Seville's arm suddenly seemed to ache as he willed his hand not to stray towards his pocket and the gun.

'Find the officer,' Malone said over his shoulder to Russ Clements. He nodded to the girl, smiling at her. 'Righto, miss, thank you. Just give your name and address to Constable Graham. Come on, Russ, let's go round the traps.'

He glanced at Seville, looked along the straggly line and then walked away after Clements. Graham took down the girl's name and address, which she gave with some reluctance.

'Can I go now? I got this date –'

Seville put a hand on her arm, hoping he had guessed right: if he hadn't, he was done for. 'Wait for me – I shan't be long –'

'Who are you, sir?' said Graham. 'Do you know this young lady?'

'I came up here looking for her. I was told over at the hotel where I'm staying –' He tried to look knowing and at the same time embarrassed, a businessman looking for a cheap pick-up. Behind him an elderly woman clicked her tongue disapprovingly; he heard someone snigger. The girl just looked surprised that perhaps the night was going to turn out to be more profitable than she had expected. 'My name is Gideon, I'm a visitor –' He was giving away his identity, but it didn't matter; he had two other passports, two other choices of identity, to take him out of the country when the time came. 'I was just looking for some company. The celebrations, you know . . .'

Graham was writing in his notebook. 'What hotel, sir?'

'The one across the square.' He had seen it when he had walked up to the station. 'The Plaza something.'

'You don't know its name?' Graham raised an eyebrow.

'A taxi driver took me there. I had no booking, I was fortunate to get in.'

'Where have you come from?'

'Melbourne.' He hoped he wouldn't be asked any questions about Melbourne. He hadn't the faintest notion what that city was like, he only knew it was some thousand kilometres away to the south. He could feel himself beginning to panic, just as he had after he had realized he had not killed Timori.

'Have you any identification?'

Seville, steadying a hand that threatened to tremble, produced his passport. Graham took the particulars of it and handed it back. 'Okay, you two can go. Have a good night.'

The elderly woman clicked her tongue again, but Graham just grinned at her. 'It's the celebrations, mum, everyone wants to enjoy themselves. What were you doing here?'

The elderly woman swung her handbag and caught Graham on the side of the head. In the confusion and laughter that followed, Seville took the girl's arm and pulled her after him. The girl put her arm in his and followed him.

'My name's Dolores. Where we going? Your hotel?'

They went out through the ticket hall. A taxi drew up in front of them, deposited a soldier with a kit-bag, and Seville pushed the girl into the taxi and jumped in after her. 'Geez, you're eager!' she said.

'Pitt Street,' said Seville, grabbing at any destination.

'Which end?' said the taxi driver, a Tongan as lost in Sydney as his passenger.

'The bottom end.' Whichever that was.

The girl snuggled up to him, then instantly drew away. 'What's that? In your pocket.'

'Just protection. You don't need to worry.'

'Did you think I might have a pimp or something?' She was indignant that she couldn't be trusted.

By now the taxi was at the bottom of the ramp that led up to the station, halted at traffic lights. Seville took out his wallet and gave the girl twenty dollars. Then he passed five dollars to the driver. 'Take the young lady wherever she wants to go.'

'Five lousy fucking dollars!' said the young lady. 'How far d'you think that'll take me?'

'Out of my sight,' said Seville, opened the door and got out.

He walked quickly away. He had no idea where he was going, all he wanted was to be as far away from the police as possible. His panic had subsided; he was now angry and frustrated at how things had gone wrong. He was only thankful that Pinjarri had had the sense and intuition to be gone before the police could catch him. But now he had to be found again: he still had the rifle.

5

Russell Hickbed was separated from his wife. She was a down-to-earth country girl whom he had married when he had first started out in the construction business as a supplier of ready-mixed concrete; she had never become accustomed to their wealth and his greed for power. She had come to Sydney with him, but she had never been comfortable in the huge mansion at Point Piper or amongst the eastern suburbs Society, with a capital S, its semi-precious vowels and its opinion that anything two or three miles further west of its own domain was Ultima Thule or the Aboriginal equivalent. She had returned to Perth and a generous allowance and left her husband to his ambitions and his occasional mistresses.

Hickbed stood at the huge picture window in his immense living-room and looked down across his flood-lit gardens to the eighty-foot cruiser moored at his jetty and cried poor mouth: 'We're going to lose everything, Abdul, if we don't get you back to Bunda.'

'We have already lost everything,' said President Timori, to whom money was not *quite* everything. 'My reputation.'

'Abdul, for crissake, you never had a reputation, except a bad one.' Hickbed would bow the knee to no one, except perhaps the Queen; he hankered after a knighthood, but so far his friend the Prime Minister hadn't nominated him for one. Norval, the glad-hander, sometimes took egalitarianism too

102

far. 'Let's talk money,' he said and looked at Madame Timori, who was fluent in it. 'If we don't get you back to Bunda, you owe me quite a lot.'

'What's quite a lot?' Her tone was frigid, that of an Antarctic bank manager.

'Several million. That's not counting what I've got invested in Palucca.'

'We can't afford anything like that.' She had a reputation for extravagance, but not towards other people.

'Russell,' said Timori, who, having lost all his oil income, still had to pour oil on waters troubled by his wife, 'we are grateful for everything you have done for us. But it is too early to talk of repayment. Friends don't speak in those terms.'

Hickbed backed down. 'I didn't mean I wanted it *now*. But things aren't going well –'

'No. Someone is trying to kill me.'

'Yeah, there's that,' said Hickbed, who hadn't been thinking of that priority. 'I hope to Christ the security is tight enough here. But I mean otherwise. Money-wise. You heard the news tonight. The bloody generals are going to try and freeze your funds. The States, Switzerland, everybloodywhere.'

'Not Australia?' Madame Timori sounded apprehensive, a tone foreign to her.

'I dunno. I don't think Phil will allow it, but you never know. He has some mean-minded bastards in his Cabinet, real bloody Lefties.' There were no left-wing ministers in the Norval Cabinet, but Hickbed had his own standards. 'What are you going to do about your holdings in Switzerland and those other places?'

Timori looked at his wife. 'You're the treasurer, my dear. What have you done to protect our pension?'

'It will take months, even years, to trace it all.' Once she had had money to handle she had become magical at it: millions disappeared into thin air and foreign banks. She fondled the bag of emeralds as if they were loose worry-beads; she carried the bag with her since the unfortunate accident of their discovery in Mr Masutir's pocket. The bag looked like a pot-pourri sachet, so she had sprayed the emeralds with 'Joy' to further the illusion; it would have been sacrilege to have used a lesser perfume on such gems. 'We don't have to worry, not at the moment. It's the real estate that's conspicuous.'

'What about the stuff in the crates up at Richmond?' said Hickbed. 'That's beginning to smell.'

'Money never smells, Russell.' Neither did gold nor gems. She felt certain they would lose none of their possessions to the Australian Customs. She had forgotten that though the local natives were no strangers to corruption, it was not endemic amongst them as it was in Palucca. 'Philip will fix everything.'

'I wouldn't be too bloody sure about that. He's trying to sound independent. He's on the phone to Fegan twice a day.'

'That doesn't sound like independence.' Timori, an ex-President, no longer had any faith in Presidents still in power. He sighed, tired out already by exile. 'I'm going to bed.'

He kissed his wife, said good night to Hickbed and left the room. He was the quietest, most relaxed of the three of them; yet when he left the room it seemed disproportionately emptier. Besides being a president he had been a sultan, and sultans, like kings, occupy a larger-than-normal space. His wife, never a sultana, a title she found ridiculous though fruitful, had her own space but it still had to expand. She had been working on that when they had been deposed.

Hickbed went back to the window, looked out and saw the Federal police, two of them, down on the jetty. He knew there were six of them on duty at any one time and there were two New South Wales police cars parked out in the street, each with two men in them. If ten men couldn't protect Timori in this house, then Seville deserved to get his target. Then Hickbed became aware that, standing exposed in his own huge window against the lights behind him, he himself was a target.

He pressed a button and the white silk drapes slid across the window. The room, indeed the whole house, had been furnished by an interior decorator at great expense; nothing in it reflected Hickbed's personality. He was rough and ready; the house was smooth and slick. He only felt at home in it because it told him, in every gold-plated nook and cranny, that he could afford it.

He crossed the room, a small journey, and sat down next to

104

Delvina on a couch that would have held ten people. 'I'm not happy about you being here, love.'

She made a *moue* of surprise; she could occasionally appear girlish, but it was atavistic. 'I think the arrangement's ideal. I don't know why we didn't come here in the first place.'

'Del, how do you think I feel? You're in the same house with me, *my* house, and I can't get into bed with you.' He took her hand, the one not holding the bag of emeralds. 'I could screw the arse off you, just looking at you.'

'You're such a romantic lover, Russell. Who taught you? Your wife?'

She knew how to throw cold water. He dropped her hand, sat back. 'Don't mention her!'

'You mentioned my husband, if only by inference. I can't be unfaithful to him, not now. Not while someone's trying to kill him.'

'Who do you think it is?'

'Why the generals, of course. Who do you think it might be?'

'You.'

She hit him hard across the cheek; fortunately, with the hand free of the bag of emeralds. Then she said quietly but coldly, 'I could kill *you*. Make a remark like that in front of anyone and I shall kill you myself.'

He felt his cheek, then straightened his glasses, which had been knocked askew. 'Everyone's a suspect. Including me.'

'You're not married to Abdul. We're a pair, people always speak of us in the same breath. Like – like Tristan and Isolde.'

'Who are they – a couple of Paluccans?' He had never been burdened by culture; the only legend he was interested in was the one he was trying to build. He tried another tack, but only slightly to windward: 'If he is killed, we're buggered.'

'Not necessarily. One or two of the generals can be bought.'

'You've tried?' He was surprised, but he should not have been.

She nodded. 'They've said no, but that's only because they're not certain about the future. They'll listen if we go back again. One of them, General Paturi, is coming to talk to Philip about getting rid of us.'

'I didn't know that!'

'Neither does Philip.'

'How do you know, then?'

'I have my sources.'

He didn't doubt that. She had learned of the generals' plot two days before it had happened; she had telephoned Washington, Canberra, anyone who would listen. Everyone had listened; it wasn't that they disbelieved her, they just didn't want to help. She had her sources, but not to the hearts, or what passed for their hearts, of her political friends.

'Phil won't see him, not till after the celebrations are over. He's not going to let anyone spoil his Big Party. You and Abdul have already done enough. Maybe we can invite General Paturi up here?'

'Abdul would shoot him on the spot.'

'What with? Christ, he hasn't got a gun, has he?' He saw her sly smile and he shook his head; he was out of his depth with a woman like her. He was out of his depth with any woman, even his wife, but he would never admit it. 'I never know with you two . . .'

'No,' she said, 'the only gun you have to worry about is the one that man Seville has.'

'The police have that.'

'Do you really think he won't get another?' She stood up, kissed him on the lips; her kiss was cold, even though she slid her tongue into his mouth. He felt he had been kissed by a snake and shuddered; all at once he lost all desire for her. 'Good night, Russell. Don't worry. Everything will turn out all right.'

6

Six of the seven generals who had staged the coup in Palucca sat in the presidential reception room of Timoro Palace in Bunda, the nation's capital. It was a highly decorated room, a marble menagerie of elephants, tigers and monkeys that seemed to hold up its four walls. Abdul Timori's great-great-grandfather, who had built the palace, had been to Europe and been impressed by the use of marble in the palaces there; once all the marble statuary had been installed it had struck him as cold and dull and he accordingly had filled in the spaces between with gilt and gold-leaf. The effect was of elephants, tigers and monkeys ready to jump out of a rather dirty sunrise.

It had been another whim of Abdul the First's that the Equator should run right through the middle of the presidential reception room; he had liked to stand with his legs apart on the imaginary line and boast that his influence spread in both directions as far as the Poles. The Dutch, who had the real influence, had humoured him.

The generals now sat on either side of the line and General Kerang, the oldest of them but with no influence at all, sat astride the Equator. It was an accident of place and he was seemingly unaware of it.

'We have to turn over the palace to the people,' said General Guruh. His name meant *thunder,* but he was the mildest of all seven of them in temper, an idealist out of place in the junta.

'Not yet.' General Simupang was the ring-leader, though the others involved in the plot had not thought of him as such; he would only become that if the coup failed and they were all brought to trial. 'We can't rush things.'

'We have to give them democracy in small doses,' said General Mustopo from the southern hemisphere. He adjusted his chair, put a leg over the Equator. 'I think we should stay here in the palace till things settle down.'

They had occupied the palace as soon as the Timoris had departed. They had brought their families in with them and, with six wings to choose from, as if the architect of 150 years ago had anticipated them, had each taken a wing. It was another accident, or so it seemed, that it was General Kerang who had got the wing that had been the Timoris' personal accommodation. There he and his elderly wife slept in the empire-sized bed beneath the green silk sheets and under the canopy decorated with birds-of-paradise plumes, looking like two corn husks in a giant jewel-box. Madame Kerang was still amusing herself going through Madame Timori's many wardrobes, counting the seemingly countless dresses, coats and accessories therein. The wives of the other generals, deprived of that opportunity, sat in their wings and sulked and wondered why power, which had

107

never occupied their thoughts before, had to be shared in the name of something called democracy. They began to have a secret admiration for Delvina Timori, who knew a good thing when she grabbed it.

General Suwondo, in the northern hemisphere, watched a small green lizard circle his boot and then head south. He could smell the cloves outside in the gardens and, the financial mind of the junta, he began to wonder what money the harvests would bring this year. 'We're bankrupt, you know. I don't think we can start talking democracy till we have some money in the Treasury. That's what democracy's all about, money in the people's pockets. That's how they vote. I read that somewhere,' he added lamely as all but General Guruh looked at him accusingly.

'We've sent Paturi to Canberra for money,' said General Godigdo, who sat beside Suwondo. He had a talent for stating the obvious, no drawback in a general.

'What if he doesn't come back?' General Kerang had not fired a shot in anger since 1942 when, as a junior lieutenant, he had killed a Japanese soldier who had been trying to rape his wife. He had since risen through the ranks to be a wise general. He might know little or nothing about strategy and tactics, but he was an expert on the venality of his fellow officers.

'Oh, he'll come back. He's the most trustworthy of us all,' said Simupang, who was the least trustworthy.

Now that doubt had been raised, Mustopo said, 'Can we trust the Australians? They may be the ones who are trying to kill Abdul. They may kill Paturi. Or even us.'

Suwondo shivered; it was winter in his hemisphere. 'Are they so devious as to plan something like that? Inviting the Timoris and then Paturi to get rid of them?'

'They didn't invite either of them,' said Godigdo, stating the obvious again.

'The Australians aren't devious,' said Guruh. 'All the British deviousness they inherited has been bred out of them on their sports fields. In another generation or so it will be better, when the Italians and the Greeks and the Lebanese have bred it back into them.'

108

'Don't forget us Asians,' said Simupang proudly.

'They still have the Irish, too,' said Mustopo, who read the Australian papers, especially the *National Times*, the national muck-raker.

'We still have to raise money,' said Suwondo doggedly. 'Paturi has to get that twenty-two million back from the Australians. It's not much against the overall debt, but it'll pay the troops.' And themselves, the leaders of the troops.

They sat in silence contemplating the bankrupt country they had been foolish enough to take over. In the background, against the far walls of the huge hall, amongst the elephants and tigers and monkeys, the palace servants hovered like ghosts from the past; which they were. Outside, beyond the palace gates, the crowd clamoured for rice, democracy and a share in the national wealth, all in short supply at the moment.

'Do we send him on to New York and Zurich?'

'Garuda gave him an excursion round-the-world ticket.'

'Garuda don't go round the world.'

'Let's ring up Lee Quan Yew and see what Singapore Airlines can do for us. We all might get tickets. Just in case.'

'Lee's not taking any calls from us, not since we asked him if he'd take the Timoris.'

'The same with Suharto in Jakarta. He'll be furious with Garuda when he hears they gave Paturi a free ticket.'

They sat in silence again for a while, pondering their isolation. The clamour outside subsided and there came the faint tinkle of temple bells on the warm breeze that blew in the open windows. The servants came forward with tea and cakes and the generals' wives came in from their respective wings, floating in like large pigeons, six of them looking to see what the seventh was wearing. Madame Kerang, however, had not yet plundered Delvina Timori's wardrobes.

'Let's hope they kill the Timoris,' said General Kerang, astride the Equator. 'Both of them.'

'They?' said the wives. 'Who?'

'Anyone,' said the generals and looked at each other, wondering who was paying Seville, the foreigner, to kill their ex-friend.

FIVE

1

Malone came awake, his mind still soured by Sunday night's failure. He had felt certain they would nab Seville along with Pinjarri. He did not claim to be an expert on the terrorist mind; that was for the psychologists, virtually all of whom had never met a terrorist at large. But he did know the criminal mind, the thinking that ran counter to society's rules and morals, and he knew how desperate it could become when events turned against it. He had banked on Seville's coming out into the open to meet Pinjarri, but Pinjarri, the unwitting Judas goat, had disappeared before the prey had been sighted. Or had he been sighted and let go?

When Malone had come back to the group of civilians, after going round the traps with Clements and finding nothing, he had noticed that the group had diminished. 'Where are they?'

'I let 'em go, Inspector,' said a suddenly dismayed Andy Graham. 'They all looked in the clear. I couldn't hold 'em — there was one old duck who belted me, said she was gunna sue . . .'

'In future, Constable, ask me for instructions, okay?' But he knew he had been wrong in not giving instructions without being asked.

Then there was a shout from the far end of the waiting hall. The body of the young policeman had been found wedged between the abandoned car and the wall. When Malone and Clements reached the car and looked down at the blood-stained body, the pale-blue shirt a dark ruby from just below the breast-pocket down to his belt, Clements said, 'Pinjarri? He'd carry a shiv.'

'Maybe. But so might Seville. The wogs carry knives, too.' He was tired, fed up: all his latent prejudices, his father's, came

110

out of him. He would be ashamed of it later, but for now it was said. 'This is getting to be a massacre. Three murders.'

'Christ,' said Clements, and chewed his lip, 'there goes the holiday. We're gunna be working on this for weeks.' He, too, was tired: he was unaware of his insensitivity till Andy Graham, the enthusiast, looked at him. 'What's the matter with you?'

'Jesus, Sarge, the man's dead!'

'Don't I bloody know it! Christ Almighty!'

'Right,' said Graham, suddenly sensitive to Clements' tiredness.

'Calm down,' said Malone and led the two of them away from the body, leaving it to two of the dead man's uniformed mates. When they were some distance from the car he said, 'Seville was here, I'll bet on it. Did he get the gun from Pinjarri or not?'

'The dead guy's gun was gone,' said Clements.

Malone shook his head. 'Seville's not going to use a handpiece to kill Timori. I read that report on him from Interpol – Joe Nagler sent it across from Special Branch. Seville's not going to sacrifice himself by getting close to Timori – he's not that sort.'

'What sorta bastard is he?' Clements sounded bewildered as well as tired.

'I don't know. Cold-blooded, I guess is one description. But I suppose that applies to most terrorists, the ones who plant bombs in cars and blow up women and kids. Seville has done that, but for the past two years he seems to have become a solo hit-man. He just specializes in political killings. He wouldn't have anything to do with the Mafia or the Chinese triads, any of those mobs.'

'Maybe that's why he's lasted so long,' said Graham. 'Because he works solo.'

'He *works* solo – but not for himself. Someone pays him. Maybe we'd do better looking for whoever is paying him for this job.' He looked back towards where the dead policeman was being laid out on a stretcher someone had brought from the station's first aid room. Nobody had paid Seville to kill the young officer; that had been something Seville had paid for. Or would, Malone vowed. 'Do a report on that young feller,

111

Andy. Ask one of his mates to inform his next-of-kin, whoever it is.'

'Right,' said Graham and walked briskly away.

Malone winced and looked at Clements. 'Right?'

'No bloody fear,' said Clements. 'Nothing's right. Can we go home now?'

Now Malone had woken up beside his wife. He had lain staring at the ceiling for some minutes; when he turned his head he saw that she was awake and gazing at him. She said softly, 'Why don't you give up?'

'Give up?'

'Take a desk job. You take everything to heart so much.'

'I'm not taking this to heart. I don't care a damn about the Timoris.'

'You care about that old woman and that young constable last night.'

He said nothing for a moment, then he nodded. 'Why should those two die because of something that doesn't concern them in the least? What have Timori and his generals got to do with them? I wonder how the politicians are feeling now? Does Phil Norval still want us to have hands off?'

'That'll depend on what the papers say. He's very touchy about editorials.'

'They won't say much in this morning's editions. What happened last night would have been too late for any editorials. The *Sun* and the *Mirror* will have a go this afternoon.'

She put her arm under his head and drew him to her. 'It's only seven o'clock. Forget about the afternoon papers.'

He could feel the soft warmth and comfort of her. As always when he held her close to him like this, his crotch told him he was home. He rolled over, felt her and knew she was ready for him without any lead-up. He slid between her legs.

Then someone landed on his back, almost giving him a rupture. 'Who goes there? Fred or foe?'

With Tom still clinging to him, he rolled off Lisa while she burst into near-hysterical laughter. Then Claire and Maureen were bouncing on the foot of the bed and love, or any love-making, went limp beneath the sheets.

'We saw you on TV last night,' said Maureen, seven years

old and a TV addict. Though Lisa forced books on her, she never read a line; but she could reel off commercial jingles and the characters in soap operas as if facing an invisible prompter. She was blonde and bouncy and Malone could only hope that her abundant energy would eventually drag her away from her TV addiction, though he doubted very much if she would settle down to a book, good or bad. Lisa had tried switching off their set, but then Maureen had just gone in next door, where the neighbours' two kids were real TV junkies. 'You looked quite good. Miranda thinks you're better than Sonny Crockett.'

Miranda was the eight-year-old hophead next door. Malone looked at Lisa. 'Who's Sonny Crockett?'

'I think he's in *Miami Lice*.'

'*Vice!*' yelled Maureen. '*Miami Vice!*'

'What's Vice?' asked Tom, now sitting on his father's chest.

'It's all the bad things,' said Claire, the reader, the lover of books, 'drugs, rape, porno movies –'

'Righto,' said her father, 'get out to the kitchen and eat your cornflakes.' He thrashed a threatening hand and the children, squealing and laughing, tumbled off the bed and ran out of the room. He lay back beside Lisa. 'For God's sake – porno movies, rape . . . What sort of books do you let her read?'

'Mills and Boon.' Lisa got out of bed, slipped off her night-gown, stood nude. 'Relax.'

Malone looked at her, admiring her and, as ever, marvelling at his luck. 'How can I when you flaunt yourself like that?'

'I don't mean your crotch. I mean, relax about Claire and the others. They're all right. They're all pretty sensible – for a policeman's kids.'

'What d'you mean by that?'

But she just smiled and went into the bathroom. Women, he had learned, always liked the last word or gesture. Then Claire came to the bedroom door and threw the morning paper at him. He opened it and Madame Timori stared out at him. She had been photographed with a long-range lens entering the front door of Russell Hickbed's mansion. Someone must have called to her, for she had turned her head and was staring straight at the camera, her mouth open in what he knew would have been an angry and caustic last word.

He put the paper down and listened to the noise coming from the kitchen. The children were squabbling, but laughing at the same time: it was a sound he had come to love, but that he heard too seldom. In the bathroom Lisa was half-singing, half-humming under the shower. The number was 'Moon River': she could not have been more than a year older than Claire was now when she had first heard that. He listened to the small inconsequential sounds: they were like balm on the wounds he felt. He should take a desk job, give himself more time to listen to such music.

An hour later he was driving into town, through a morning that presaged another hot day. The *Herald* had told him there were bush-fires raging on the city's outskirts; the residents out there and the volunteer firefighters would not be celebrating anything. Tonight's fireworks might be a bitter joke.

He expected, he *hoped*, it would be a morning of paper-work and maybe some interviews in the office; he did not want to have to do any leg-work in the promised heat. He turned on the car radio, something he rarely did because he did not like being chattered at and preferred to drive in silence. Someone was chattering at him this morning, one of radio's sages:

'I'd like to ask how many innocent Australian citizens, ordinary people like you and me –' an ordinary citizen on two hundred thousand a year at least, Malone thought '– how many of them are going to be killed because foreign politics have been brought into this country? The police, I'm sure, are doing their best –'

Malone switched off the radio. There would be more of the same during the rest of the day; the newspaper editorialists and the columnists would be sounding the same message; they had run out of things to say about the Bicentennial. Phil Norval was now treading on dangerous political ground; pretty soon even his admirers would be asking questions. Who was more important, a foreign ex-President seeking asylum or ordinary Australian voters wanting no more than a safe ordinary life? Foreigners could kill each other, that was acceptable: Australians had always been tolerant in that direction. But it was a different matter when the bullets started to stray, or the rope and the knife claimed the lives of the natives.

114

Clements and Graham were waiting for him at his desk in Homicide. Clements still looked tired, but Graham might have just come back refreshed from a month's leave. 'We've come up with something, Inspector! I've been going through the computer lists of everyone we've checked in the hotels –'

Malone hung up his jacket, loosened his tie and sat down. 'What have you come up with?'

'A name – Gideon. Michel Gideon, a Swiss. He's on the hotel list, in a pub out at Rozelle, the –' he checked his notebook '– the Coach and Horses. I've also got his name here in my book – he was in that group at Central last night, but he told me he was staying at the Central Plaza!'

Malone wished his own excitement could match that of Graham; but all he felt was a sense that they were already too late. 'Who was he?'

'A blond guy in some sort of white jacket – he was standing next to that troll you questioned.'

Malone stood up, reached for his jacket. 'Righto, let's go out to Rozelle. You come with me, Russ. Get back-up, Andy, the same as last night.'

'SWOS men?'

'We'd better have them. Let's go out the back way. There's some reporters outside – let's see if we can do this without any publicity. At least till it's over.'

'I wouldn't count on it,' said Clements. 'Those bastards are like ferrets.'

Today was not a public holiday; but absenteeism was a form of patriotism. The crowds were already on their way into the city hoping for a preview of what they might miss tomorrow. Clements drove through the streets at a good pace and Malone, beside him, began to feel the excitement mounting in him. Maybe they would not be too late after all, maybe by tonight this whole mess would be over and done with, at least as far as he was concerned. There would still be the Timoris, but they were the politicians' problem.

They turned off a main road into a side street. 'Is this it?'

'The pub's down the far end,' said Clements. 'I raided it years ago when I was on the Gambling Squad. All the pubs around here ran SP.'

115

'Righto, pull up. We'll walk from here. I don't want to get too close before the back-up arrives.'

They got out of the car and walked down the street, past the narrow-fronted houses and the occasional cheaply-built block of flats. This was a working-class area, inhabited by the ordinary people who would resent intruders like the Timoris and Abdul's would-be assassin. Many of the locals had been foreign-born, but they had chosen this life here and they did not want it disturbed or, even worse, violated by the sort of violence that many of them had left behind them.

This was the sort of street where none of the houses had a garage. Cars lined the kerbs on both sides; men in singlets and thongs were tinkering with engines or washing the cars. Children were playing in the street and some women stood at a gate gossiping. As Malone and Clements passed them, the women abruptly shut up, turned their heads and looked after them.

'Police,' said one of the women in a foreign accent and the others all nodded and looked worried as well as curious.

Fifty yards short of the hotel Malone paused and looked back. 'Hold it!'

Four police cars had come in from the main road, followed by two SWOS wagons. Instantly, though no sirens were blowing, front doors opened and people came out to their gates. Then three TV vans and four radio cars, followed by three taxis, swung in from the main road. 'Bugger it!' said Malone and stepped out into the middle of the street.

All the vehicles pulled up, creating their own traffic jam. Pressmen jumped out of the taxis at the end of the jam and came running towards Malone; they were followed by the radio reporters and the TV cameramen, the latter with their cameras growing out of their shoulders like a second square head. Malone turned to Clements, who had come out into the middle of the street beside him.

'Get everybody back! Jesus, what a balls-up! Why didn't they come in with their bloody sirens blaring? Where's the SWOS sergeant?'

'Here, Inspector.' He was a different man from last night, a bony muscular man in his mid-thirties with close-cropped hair

116

and a thick black moustache. 'Do you want us to go in first?'

'Better not. We don't want to frighten the pants off the pub owner.'

'I'm afraid the element of surprise has gone. I'm sorry about that. We got no instructions on the terrain, no battle-plan.'

He's got to be ex-army, thought Malone, or I'm out of touch with the new approach. 'My fault. I shouldn't have called you in till I'd looked over the place. I was just afraid he'd do a bunk. If he hasn't already . . . Put your men in position to cover me. I'll go in and see the pub owner, see if Seville is still there.'

He waited while the SWOS sergeant deployed his men and the other police who had arrived. Clements had ushered all the spectators back into their houses, telling them to close their doors and stay away from the windows. 'You'll see it all on TV tonight. Do what you're told and stay away from the windows. There may be some shooting . . .'

If Seville is still in the hotel, Malone thought, he's got to have heard or seen what's going on out here. There was no uproar, but there had been the revving of engines as Andy Graham had cleared all the traffic away from the middle of the street. Two of the police cars had gone on down past the hotel to block off the other end of the street; two others had gone back to station themselves across the entrance from the main road. All the private cars were still parked along the kerbs on both sides and the TV, radio and SWOS vans had been backed further up the street. We should have sent him a telegram, Malone thought. Christ Almighty, wasn't *anything* going to go right on this case?

He walked down the street, on the footpath now and keeping close to the fences along the fronts of the houses. An old man, a twin of his own father Con, inquisitive and aggressive, stood at an open front door.

'What's going on, mate?'

'Better get back inside, dad.'

'Who you telling what to do?' He stood amongst his geraniums and zinnias on his front porch, king of his own castle.

You'll always find one of 'em, Malone thought, the man or woman who couldn't stand authority, especially from a copper.

117

'Get back inside,' he snapped, 'unless you want your bloody head blown off!'

He didn't pause, just kept walking, and was relieved when he heard the front door slam behind him. He came to the hotel on the corner. The door to the bar was open and the footpath outside it was glistening with water, steam rising from it in the heat; someone had hosed it down in the last ten minutes. There were no drinkers outside the pub and Malone hoped there would be none in the bar. He loosened the flap on his holster, looked over his shoulder to see that the back-up men were in position, then he took a deep breath and pushed open the door to the bar, swinging it wide, and stepped in.

There were already half a dozen drinkers in the bar, building up ammunition against the day's coming thirst. Two of them were young men; the others looked like pensioners. They all turned towards him as he came in the door and all instantly froze. They never miss, he thought, they have an unerring nose for a cop.

Malone said to the middle-aged man behind the counter, 'You the owner?'

'Nah.' He was bald and red-faced and had Irish written all over him; the Irish had once been very strong in this area. 'They're upstairs. Mr and Mrs Brigham. You want 'em?'

'Don't bother, I'll see them. Which way?'

The barman nodded towards a door and Malone moved towards it. Then he paused and said softly to the nearest drinker to him, a grey-haired man in a T-shirt that advertised the Bicentennial, shorts and thongs. 'Get your mates out of the bar. No fuss, just do it as quietly as you can.'

The man frowned. 'Jesus, what's up?'

'Go on,' said Malone. 'No fuss, as quietly as you can. Out the back way.'

The man swallowed the last of his beer, got up from his stool and jerked his head at the other men. One of them said, 'What's the matter, Bert, you want us to help you splash your foot?'

The others laughed, but the grey-haired man said softly, 'Come on!' The other men looked at Malone, then they got up and followed the grey-haired man. Malone noticed that they all took their beer glasses with them: they weren't going to waste their money. The barman looked at Malone and the latter nodded towards the rear door. The barman hesitated, then followed the drinkers.

Malone waited a moment, then took another deep breath, took out his gun and stepped through the inner door into the private hallway. A flight of stairs led to the upper floor. Coming down it was a grey-haired middle-aged woman carrying a brief-case and behind her, holding a gun to her head, was the blond man with glasses whom Malone had seen last night at Central Station.

'Good morning, Inspector. Don't try anything or I shall kill Mrs Brigham. Drop your gun.' Malone hesitated, then dropped the Smith and Wesson on the floor. 'Put your hands above your head.'

Malone put up his hands. 'Miguel Seville?'

Seville gave a half-smile. 'If you like. Names don't matter now.'

Mrs Brigham looked on the point of collapse; she stared at Malone with terrified eyes. 'Don't let him shoot me, please . . .'

Malone shook his head. 'I'm not going to do anything foolish, Mrs Brigham. What do you want, Seville?'

'You have quite a force out there, Inspector. I'll need you and Mrs Brigham to get me through it.'

'You'll never make it, not all the way.'

'I've been in this situation before, Inspector. Luck falls both ways. It isn't always on your side.'

Malone looked at the landlady. 'Where's Mr Brigham?'

'Upstairs. He – he hit him with that gun.' She was terrified, but she was not going to collapse after all. Malone had seen her type before, the resourceful woman who knew how to handle drunks and hoodlums. She had just never met a cold-blooded killer before. 'He could be dead . . .'

'He's not,' Seville told Malone. 'He's unconscious but he's not dead.'

'You've killed enough already,' said Malone. 'Don't add to the score.'

'That's up to you, Inspector.' He reached down quickly, picked up Malone's gun and put it in his pocket. 'Now we'll go out and get into Mrs Brigham's car – it's the big white one right outside that door there. She has the keys to it and she'll drive. If your men attempt to stop us, one of you will die. Possibly both,' he added as if as an afterthought. 'You can give them that message as soon as we step out into the open.'

Malone nodded. He knew there would be an SWOS man coming in from the rear of the hotel; he could only hope there would be no gunfire. If Seville was worried, there was no sign of it. He was cool and in command of the situation; for the moment at least. And that, Malone knew, was what counted: the moment. He and Mrs Brigham were only going to live from moment to moment and that was how the game would have to be played.

Malone opened the door from the hallway out into the street. He stepped out into the heat of the morning, his hands above his head. Seville and Mrs Brigham remained inside the doorway.

'Tell them, Inspector.'

Malone had to clear his throat before he could shout. 'Sergeant Clements!'

'Here, Inspector.' Clements stood up from where he had been crouched behind a car across the street. He had no gun and kept his hands in clear view in front of him. 'What's happening?'

'He has me and the landlady – she's right behind me. He wants clear passage out of here or we both get it in the head.' Behind him he heard Mrs Brigham make a whimpering noise. 'Tell everyone to back off and let us through. We're going in Mrs Brigham's car.'

'Tell them no one is to follow us,' said Seville behind him.

'He says no one is to follow us,' Malone shouted.

He imagined he could see the frustration and bewilderment in Russ Clements' face at that instruction. Then: 'Okay. Tell him he can take you through.'

At once Seville pushed Mrs Brigham through the doorway and stepped out after her. He turned the gun on Malone, standing close to him, while the landlady, after some fumbling, unlocked the car and opened the two kerbside doors. Malone could see several rifles aimed at Seville, but the terrorist was standing too close to him for the marksmen to take the risk of firing. Too, Seville's gun was held at the back of his neck.

Seville motioned to Mrs Brigham to get into the driver's seat, then he pushed Malone into the rear seat and quickly followed him, slamming the door closed after him.

'Give me my brief-case,' he said and Mrs Brigham passed over the case. He put it on the seat between him and Malone and leaned back in the corner, the gun pointing at Malone's chest.

'Both of you put on your seat-belts.' He smiled at Malone. 'That's the law, isn't it. A fifty dollar fine or something.'

'I take it you're not going to put yours on.' Keep 'em talking: he had learned that drill from several encounters with psychopaths. Though he doubted that Seville was a psychopath.

'I don't think so, Inspector. I hate restrictions of any sort. Drive, Mrs Brigham. Straight up the street, then towards the city when you get to the main road. And don't act foolish or smart. I shall kill you both if I have to.'

Mrs Brigham started the engine, forgot to put the car in Drive and revved it up. She made another whimpering sound, jerked the gear lever into the right notch, and the car lurched forward.

'Faster!' said Seville, who now they were moving seemed more tense.

Mrs Brigham speeded up the car. She was a good driver, but fear had affected her judgement; she almost collided with one of the police cars at the end of the street as it was a little slow getting out of the way. Malone, sitting back in his own corner of the rear seat, caught a glimpse of the SWOS men swinging their guns round to cover the big white Ford LTD as it swept by them. *For Christ's sake don't fire!* Then they had swung left out of the street into the main road, swinging into the stream of traffic and causing two cars to side-swipe each other. There was an angry chorus of horns and the screech of brakes and tyres, then the Ford was in the main stream of the city-bound traffic and moving easily with it.

'Don't pull up for any red lights,' said Seville. 'Get up to the head of this line and just keep going.'

'I can't get up any further – they won't move over!' Malone could see Mrs Brigham's nervous hands gripping the steering-

121

wheel; her knuckles were white. 'You don't know what Sydney drivers are like!'

'Blow your horn!' Seville was growing angry.

Mrs Brigham did that, but the car up ahead of her, an old model purple Holden, did not move over. A bare tattooed arm came out of the driver's side and the white Ford got a two-fingered salute. Despite their predicament Malone had to grin.

'You'd better be patient, Seville. I've been driving for twenty-five years and no Aussie driver has ever pulled over for me yet.'

Seville had sat forward as if he intended to fire a shot at the car ahead. He looked at Malone, then he nodded and sat back. He looked slightly less cool than he had back in the hotel hallway. He was wearing grey slacks, a navy-blue blazer and a plain blue shirt; the front of the shirt suddenly showed sweat stains, but he made no effort to loosen the tie he wore. But he did say, 'Turn on the air-conditioning, Mrs Brigham.'

She did so, her nervous fingers switching it on full blast. She fiddled with it again, conscious of Seville watching her suspiciously, then the unit settled down. She went back to steering, keeping close on the tail of the Holden in front.

'You're a nation of fools, Inspector,' said Seville.

'Because we're road-hogs? Or because we took in the Timoris?'

'Keep your eye on the road, Mrs Brigham!' The landlady had looked at them in the driving-mirror. 'No, Inspector, you're just fools in general. I'll be glad to leave here.'

'You think you'll get away?'

'I think so. I have before – not from you but from much better police forces.' Then he snapped at Mrs Brigham: 'Why are you slowing down?'

She had taken her foot off the accelerator. 'There's a red light up ahead.'

'Swing over the dividing strip. Go on – swing over! Go through the light!'

Mrs Brigham hesitated, glanced at Malone in the driving-mirror. He nodded, braced himself for the bump as she swung the car up over the concrete dividing strip on to the wrong side of the road. There was no sign of any oncoming traffic; the cars

122

coming the other way were halted at the traffic lights. Then a car came round the corner on the green light. Malone flinched, leaning in against his seat-belt as the two cars somehow managed to avoid crashing head-on; they scraped against each other, but Mrs Brigham kept the Ford going straight ahead. They went across the intersection right under the nose of a tourist coach and then swung back on to the correct side of the road with a clear path ahead of them.

Malone felt the sweat break on him and he let out a loud gasp. If there was a TV news helicopter following them and Maureen saw this tonight, he could already hear her cry: 'Great! Just like *Miami Vice!*' Except that he might not be there to hear her say it.

'I can't go on!' Mrs Brigham was trembling and the car was starting to slow.

'You had better keep going, Mrs Brigham.' Seville put the gun against Malone's neck; the latter noticed he had been smart enough not to put it against the landlady's. He had also noticed it was a short-barrel Smith and Wesson and he guessed it was the one that had been missing last night from the holster of the murdered policeman. 'If you don't, I'll kill Inspector Malone. Just steady yourself and keep going.'

Somehow Mrs Brigham regained control of herself. Malone could only catch glimpses of her in the driving-mirror; she seemed to be all terrified eyes. The sides and back of her grey head were dark with sweat and he could see her skin shining with it above the low-backed sun-dress she wore. He knew he was helpless to overcome Seville, but he determined he would do his best to see that nothing happened to the woman.

He wanted to lean back and look up through the rear window to see if any police helicopter was following them; he knew that Russ Clements would have called for aerial surveillance as soon as the big Ford had swung out of the side street into the main road. But if he tried to catch sight of the helicopter, if it was there above them, it would only alert Seville to their being followed. Malone knew, and Seville probably did too, that they *were* being followed; somewhere back in the traffic the police cars would have taken up the chase. But to protect Malone and

123

the landlady they would be keeping well back out of sight, guided only by the helicopter.

They went through two more red lights, horn blasting, missing one car only by inches. Then they were on the Western Distributor, speeding along the expressway above the Darling Harbour complex; below them Malone could see the beginning of the holiday crowd amongst the markets and diversions down there. The business district of the city loomed up ahead of them.

'Which way?' Mrs Brigham said. She seemed a little calmer now, as if, having got this far safely, she felt she would survive.

'Up into the city.'

Mrs Brigham curved the car right off the expressway and up into Market Street. At the first traffic lights Seville suddenly said, 'Left!' and she swung the car abruptly into Kent Street.

Malone was watching the terrorist. There was tension now in the olive-skinned face under the blond hair. He had taken off his steel-rimmed spectacles; he looked younger and a little vulnerable without them. But Malone knew the vulnerability was an illusion. This man had not survived so long on luck. He was formidable and dangerous and, though he might be worried now, he was not going to crack.

Malone glanced at the combination-lock brief-case on the seat between them, wondering if he could snatch it and throw it at Seville before the latter could shoot either him or Mrs Brigham; then he decided against such an action: he was not going to risk the landlady's life. He wondered what was in the brief-case. Another gun? Explosives?

'Did you get a gun from Dallas Pinjarri?' he said.

'Has he said he gave me one?' That was a slip and Malone saw that Seville knew it was; there was a momentary twitch of the full-lipped mouth. 'Who is Mr – Pinjarri, did you say?'

'You know him, Seville. He'll tell us eventually if he gave you a gun.'

'You torture prisoners? Just like they used to do in Argentina?' He was too loose in his talk; he was nervous and angry because of it. He glanced up ahead, then sat up straight. 'In there – follow that car into the parking station!'

Mrs Brigham slowed the car, swung into the Kent Street

124

parking station. A blue Honda Accord was going in ahead of them. It pulled up at the barrier, the driver leaned out and took a ticket and then the car climbed the ramp to the upper floors. Mrs Brigham took a ticket and followed the Honda. She was driving steadily now, but Malone could see that she could not last much longer. After this the drunks and hooligans in her pub would be no threat at all.

The Honda swung into a vacant space on the second floor. 'Pull up!' said Seville.

Mrs Brigham jerked the Ford to a halt. Seville sat a moment till a man and a woman got out of the Honda, then he picked up his brief-case, opened the door and slid out, the gun still on Malone. He spoke to Mrs Brigham without looking at her.

'Drive on up to the top floor – don't stop! If you do, I'll shoot those people over there by that car. Goodbye, Inspector.'

Malone made his own slip; he could not resist it: 'We'll get you, Seville!'

The gun came up, was pointed straight at his face. He shut his eyes, knowing he was going to get the bullet right between them; he was suddenly sick and deathly afraid. There was a loud bang and he flinched, almost fainting. But nothing hit him; it was the car door being slammed. He opened his eyes and saw Seville, smiling, backing off.

Mrs Brigham sent the Ford up the ramp ahead of them, tyres squealing as she drove too fast. Malone looked back through the rear window and saw Seville walk across to the two people standing transfixed by the blue Honda and raise his gun. Then the Ford had gone round a curve in the ramp and Mrs Brigham suddenly fell forward on to the steering-wheel. Fortunately her foot had slipped off the accelerator. The car lurched to one side, hit a row of parked cars, bounced back to the other side and hit the cars there, then slewed round and crashed into a pillar.

Malone, bruised and chafed, dazed and sick in the pit of his stomach, undid his seat-belt. He reached over and gently lifted Mrs Brigham's head from the steering-wheel. There was blood on her face, but she was breathing. Then he felt a terrible rage building up inside him and he knew that, sooner or later, unless he was stopped, he was going to kill Miguel Seville.

125

2

'So you lost him again,' said Commissioner Leeds.

'We never had him, sir. He had us, me and Mrs Brigham.' But Malone knew that the Commissioner was right.

'Scobie, let's face it, he's made a laughing-stock of us. What do you think, Harry?'

Chief Superintendent Danforth was a member of the old school, a Thumper Murphy in plainclothes. He had risen on seniority, not merit, and he was constantly afraid of being made to look foolish by the younger, better educated men under him. He did not like Malone, whom he thought of as a smart-arse, though a quiet one; but he knew that the Commissioner had the highest regard for Malone, so he was not going to make waves. He shifted his bulk in his chair, ran a beefy hand over his short-back-and-sides and lifted his face to the ceiling as if thinking. He had never been a thoughtful man, but since his position now called for little action he had had to find a substitute for it. So he was always running his hand over his head and looking at the ceiling.

'I wouldn't say that,' he said at last.

Leeds hid his irritation, looked at Assistant Commissioner Zanuch. 'Bill?'

Zanuch was a tall handsome man, always as well dressed as Leeds, a self-nominated ladies' man whose chosen duty was to make up for the male chauvinism of most policemen. He was vain, ambitious and everyone tipped him as Leeds' successor. He had also been a brilliant investigator in the field that had been his speciality, fraud. He knew nothing about homicide or terrorism, but ignorance of a subject had never deterred him. He had supreme confidence in his ability to be knowledgeable about any subject in the minimum of time. He was known in the Department as the Speed Reader.

'I think I should take charge, John. This case is too big now for the usual set-up. Harry can work under me.'

Malone sat quiet, feeling himself being shoved out of the room and off the case. He could feel the resentment growing

126

in him, but now was no time to be blunt. Leeds sensed his mood and glanced at him.

'Do you want to be taken off it?'

'No, sir.' Malone had to stop himself from snapping the answer.

'Your record's not good on this one up till now,' said Zanuch, and Danforth nodded almost too emphatically. 'You've let Seville get away twice.'

We've already made that point. 'Yes, sir. But I don't think any of us have come up against a feller like this one. He's the coolest I've ever come across.'

'He's certainly that,' said Leeds; and Malone was relieved to see that the Commissioner was still on his side. 'When he took that Honda from those two people, he took not only the car keys but the parking ticket. Then he drove down to the exit barrier, paid the attendant and just out and away. You'd have expected him to tear down the ramp and crash his way through the barrier.'

'I still don't understand why the chopper didn't pick him up when he came out of the parking station,' said Danforth, feeling he had to contribute something.

'I've seen the preliminary report,' said Zanuch, who would have read it in five seconds flat. 'The chopper was looking for a white Ford. The blue Honda came out on the heels of another car, a fawn one that they didn't identify in the report. They watched the fawn car go up King Street, but the Honda just kept going right along Kent Street towards the Bridge. They lost it because they were still waiting for the Ford to come out of the parking station. Or for Seville to come out on foot.'

'How's the woman, Mrs Brigham?' Leeds said.

'She's okay,' said Malone. 'She fainted when Seville left us, but she came round pretty quickly. She may not sleep for a night or two.'

'Her husband all right?'

'Concussed, but that's all.'

'Have you talked to your wife?'

'Yes, sir. She heard about it on the radio – they were on the air as soon as Seville put me and Mrs Brigham in the car. They

127

didn't mention my name, but my wife knew who was in the car.'

He had spoken to Lisa as soon as he had been brought here to Administration Headquarters. Clements and the other police, guided by the police helicopter, had arrived at the parking station less than two minutes after the white Ford had disappeared into it; the police convoy had come into Kent Street as Seville in the blue Honda had driven out of the far end of it. The SWOS men had been the first up the ramp, but by then Malone was out of the Ford and helping the recovered Mrs Brigham out of the car. Clements had appeared immediately behind the SWOS men, out of breath, all anger and worry.

'Jesus! Scobie – are you all right? Where is the bastard?'

He had looked on the point of having a stroke and Malone had put a hand on his arm to quieten him. 'I'm okay, Russ. Get someone to look after Mrs Brigham – she's still pretty shaky. Get an ambulance up here.'

'I don't want an ambulance! Just get me home, so's I can see how my husband is!' She was ready for the drunks and louts again; but Malone could see that, behind the determination to be herself again, there was still fear and shock. 'Just get me home, please!'

Andy Graham had come up and taken her away. Then Clements had looked at Malone. 'You sure you're okay?'

'No, I'm not – but keep it to yourself. I was scared. He'd have killed us, Russ, if you'd got too close.'

Clements nodded. 'I guessed that. I had a bit of trouble holding some of our guys back, especially that SWOS sergeant. I called for the chopper and they were on the job before you'd reached Pyrmont. They were already in the air, watching traffic out on the harbour . . . Where did the bastard go?'

Five minutes later Andy Graham came up the ramp again. 'You're wanted at the Commissioner's office, Inspector.'

'Oh shit,' said Clements.

'I think I'm going to be in it,' said Malone.

But when he reached Admin Headquarters in College Street he did not immediately go up to the Commissioner's office. A sympathetic sergeant took him into an office, gestured at the phone on a desk, went out and closed the door behind him.

Lisa must have been standing by the phone waiting for him to call. 'Oh God, you're all right? Truly?' She sounded on the point of breaking down, but he knew that wouldn't happen, not if the children were with her. They were: 'Okay, kids, outside! Out in the pool. It's Daddy.'

'Is he going to be on TV again tonight?' That was Maureen, faint in the background but with her priorities right.

'Oh, I'll be there all right, if in name only.'

'What?' Lisa had turned away to shout again at the children. Then she came back on the line, her voice soft, the edges of it fretted with the fear she had felt over the last hour. 'I tried not to listen – they were broadcasting it as if it were some sort of road race – they didn't say your name, but I *knew* it was you – a senior police officer –'

'Easy, darling. I'm okay – *really*. It was worse for the woman I was with – she didn't know whether her husband was dead or alive –'

'I know how she felt.' Then she laughed; but he felt it was an effort, not any mirth she felt. 'You have a knack of saying the right thing – you can really put a girl at ease –'

'Sorry.' But he laughed, though it was an effort for him, too. He could imagine her anguish of the past hour and he felt a tremendous guilt that he had brought it on her. They never mentioned guilt at the police academy; that was something for the crims to feel. They taught you duty, responsibility to the community, even self-preservation; how you felt about your family in relation to these priorities was, well, a family problem. If something happened to you, certainly they did something for the family: sympathy, the official funeral with all the trappings, the support afterwards. But it was all too late then. . . 'I can't promise, but if I can get home by seven, I'll take you all out to dinner tonight. Book a table for seven-thirty at Eliza's.' He'd show her that her father wasn't the only one with money to splash around.

'*Eliza's?*' She laughed again; this time it sounded more like the old Lisa. 'He did whack you, didn't he? You're light-headed –'

'I'll call you at six-thirty, let you know how I'm going.'

'Come home now, tell them to shove their murders and Mr Seville, too.'

'I wish I could. The Commissioner is waiting for me upstairs. I love you.'

He hung up and stood staring at the wall in front of him. When his eyes focused he saw he was gazing at an old traffic safety campaign poster: Take It Easy. He would try, but it wasn't going to be easy.

Now he was in the Commissioner's office listening to Bill Zanuch tell it how it was going to be: 'Situation-wise, we have to establish the impression that we are still in command. We have a crime situation that is unprecedented in this country . . .'

Christ, thought Malone, why don't I just retire here and now? Then in his mind's eye he saw Seville sitting next to him on the rear seat of the big Ford, saw the arrogant challenge in the cool stare of the man and he knew he could not retire, or even retreat, till he saw that face again, either dead or cowed by capture. He would have to put up with Assistant Commissioner Zanuch and Chief Superintendent Danforth. He glanced covertly at Commissioner Leeds and the latter caught his eye, seemed to read what was in his mind.

'Inspector Malone,' Leeds said, interrupting Zanuch's flow, 'will still be in charge of the leg-work.'

'I think he should be relieved,' said Danforth, shifting his bulk again; he was one of those big, overweight men whose bones somehow seem to discomfort them even through all the flesh. 'He's had enough. I'll put someone fresh on it –'

'No.' Leeds' voice had a clipped rasp to it. 'Inspector Malone stays on it. He has a score to settle, I think.'

Danforth looked at Malone as if *he* had a score to settle, then back at the Commissioner. 'Of course. A good incentive – I'd feel the same way myself . . .' If he did, it would soon evaporate: his laziness was legendary.

'Report direct to me, Inspector,' said Zanuch; and suddenly it was Danforth who was swept out of the room, out of the case. The big man looked angry and uncomfortable, like a newly castrated bull; but there was no bellowing from him, just a big fat silence. 'What's your first move?'

It was going to take Malone a little time to get used to

130

Zanuch's gung-ho efficiency; or was it just the *image* of efficiency? 'Sergeant Clements from Homicide has gone back to the pub where Seville was staying. He left his luggage behind – there may be something in that. In the meantime I have a meeting in my office in –' he looked at his watch '– in twenty minutes with a solicitor and a banker who may be able to help.'

'In what way?'

'Their names were in a book we picked up after the first murder, the Masutir one. I think one way of stopping Seville might be to find out who is employing him.'

'You think someone *is* employing him?' Either Zanuch hadn't read all the reports on all the cases or the speed reading had missed that line.

'I'm sure of it, sir.'

'Good. Keep me informed.'

Zanuch stayed behind with the Commissioner as Malone and Danforth walked out. As soon as the door was closed behind them Danforth said, 'You ought to think twice about going off this, Scobie. If you flop again, it's not going to do your career any good.'

'It hasn't done it much good so far. I've got to stick with it, try and make up for my mistakes.'

'The Dutchman's not too happy with the way things are going.'

'The Dutchman? Vanderberg? What's he got to do with it?'

'He's the Premier, for crissakes.' Danforth, like a lot of slow-thinking men, could be annoyed by the slow thinking of others.

'Has he been talking to you?'

'Not him personally. One of his minders was on to me. They want it all cleared up before tomorrow.'

Malone laughed, hardly believing what he was hearing. Yet he knew that anything was credible in this State's politics. Lisa, better educated than he, had said that Machiavelli would have had trouble holding his own amongst the local politicians. He would have been just another struggling ethnic.

'Harry, it could take us weeks, *months,* to get to the bottom of this. Even if we get Seville, it's not going to be the end of

131

it. There's an accessory before the fact, someone who's paying him to try and kill Timori.'

'Does it matter whether we get them?' Danforth did not like complicated cases, never had.

'I'll bet it does to The Dutchman.'

He had met the Premier only once, at a police function where he had won a commendation. Two minutes' chat with Vanderberg and half an hour of watching him in action had only confirmed what he had heard and read about The Dutchman. The little man was a manipulator, his smile as untrustworthy as his soul, or vice versa, the sort who gave politics a bad name but whose natural field could only be politics.

'I'm having a drink with the minder this evening.' Danforth had spent his whole career having drinks: with political minders, informers, criminals; his big belly was testimony to his search for clues. Or so he liked to think. 'What'll I tell him?'

'That we're doing our best, time will tell.'

'That's a political answer.' He had occasional moments of shrewdness.

'Then he'll understand it.'

Malone left him on that; Danforth was the sort of superior officer you could walk away from without being dismissed. There weren't many like him left in the force, the bulls of the past – 'bulls' had once been a slang term for detectives, but it was now out of fashion. The worst of them had gone, the ones more corrupt than the criminals they had chased; but Danforth was corrupt only in small ways, not worth the disgrace he would bring on the force if he were fired. So he survived, a chair-warmer, kept out of harm's way so that he could cause no harm. Though Malone wondered why one of The Dutchman's minders, all of them shrewd men, should bother with someone like Danforth.

Clements was back from the pub in Rozelle and was waiting with three men when Malone got back to Homicide. 'This is Mr Quirke and Mr Tidey. And, of course, Mr Sun.'

Malone hadn't expected the Chinese, but he showed no surprise. 'Sorry I'm late.'

'No, no, Inspector, we're early.' Quirke, the solicitor, was a man with a pear-shaped body and a pear-shaped face, his head topped by a shock of prematurely white hair that grew up and outwards; he had bright blue eyes and a bright sincere smile, all three of them dimmed at the moment by apprehension. 'Jim and I are only too glad to help, if we can.'

'And you too, Mr Sun?' said Malone.

'Of course he is,' said Tidey, the banker, a roly-poly man with a bald head and rimless glasses that he seemed to be able to angle so that the light fell on them and obscured his eyes. 'We're here to advise him.'

Or the other way round, thought Malone. He looked at Clements. 'Did you find anything out at Rozelle, Russ?'

'Nothing that will help us here.' Clements nodded his head at the three men, treating them as if they didn't speak English.

Malone nodded, smiling inwardly at Clements' contempt for the lawyer, the merchant banker and the Timoris' aide. 'Righto, shall we start? Mr Quirke, how many times did Mr Masutir visit you in the past eight months?'

'Mr Masutir?'

'The dead man, the one shot on Friday night,' said Malone patiently. 'You haven't forgotten him already?'

'Oh no, no. I know whom you mean.' *Whom:* Quirke was precise about his grammar, if a little imprecise about his clients. 'An inoffensive little man. Not one you'd expect to be shot.'

'I wouldn't know. I only met him when he was dead.' Malone guessed these men needed to be shaken up. He saw them both shift uncomfortably, but Sun showed no reaction at all. 'How many times did he visit you?'

Quirke hesitated, looked at Tidey as if for confirmation. 'Seven or eight? Yes. I could check in my diary.'

'Do that, Mr Quirke. Why did he pay you so many visits? What was their purpose?'

'Inspector, what's *your* purpose?' said Tidey. He had a rich roly-poly voice that went with his build; the words fell out like over-ripe plums. 'The purpose of your questions?'

'Mr Tidey –' Malone's own words sounded in his ears like dried prunes. 'We're investigating a murder – three, in fact. You've read in the papers that our principal suspect is a man named Seville – we think he is after Mr Sun's boss, President

133

Timori.' He looked at Sun, but there was still no expression on the Chinese's face. *Talk about the inscrutable Oriental!* 'Seville isn't acting on his own account – someone is paying him. Mr Masutir may be a lead to whoever that is.'

'I take it we're not suspects?' Several sour plums were dropped.

Malone smiled. 'Not at all, Mr Tidey. Not if you co-operate.'

'In what way?'

'What did Mr Masutir want with you?'

This time Quirke and Tidey looked at Sun. The latter didn't rush to reply and Malone said drily, 'I think it's your turn to advise them, Mr Sun.'

Sun still took his time, then at last he said, 'Mr Masutir was looking into investments here in Australia.'

'Who for?'

'Madame Timori.' For a moment Sun didn't look quite so inscrutable.

Malone looked back at Tidey and Quirke. 'I take it you invested her money for her? In the stock market, property or what?'

'Do we have to answer these questions?' said Quirke.

'No. But I can refer it all to the Corporate Affairs Commission and they might ask even more questions than me. I'll have access to their report. I'm just trying to save you time. And maybe some embarrassment.'

Glances were exchanged again, like surreptitious notes. Then Tidey said, 'We set up several companies. We bought property –' He named two of the top commercial buildings in the city. 'A cattle stud and a horse stud and a sheep station. We also bought substantial parcels of shares in blue chip companies.'

'Does Madame Timori have any partners in the investments?'

Quirke and Tidey glanced at Sun. Again he took his time, then he said slowly, 'Myself, in a small way – five per cent. Mr Tidey and Mr Quirke, one per cent each. And Mr Russell Hickbed.'

'How much does Mr Hickbed hold?'

'Twenty per cent.'

'No other partners?'

134

Again there was the hesitation; then: 'No.'

'President Timori has no holding in the investment?' He put that question to Quirke and Tidey.

Both of them looked flustered. Then Tidey said, 'Well, no-o. Not as far as we know. We don't know anything of the arrangements between the President and Mrs Timori. It could be her own money or it could be their joint wealth . . .'

'From what I read in the papers, it's Palucca's money.' He looked back at Sun, but, as he expected, there was no reaction from the Chinese.

'That's an insult to our client, Inspector,' said Tidey, all ripe plums again.

'Yes, I suppose it is. How much was invested overall?' It was none of his business, but he knew Corporate Affairs would ask that question.

'Seven hundred million dollars,' said Quirke, who seemed keener to answer questions than the other two.

It was Malone's turn to look inscrutable; he almost tore every muscle in his face trying to be so. 'And you say President Timori has no interest in all this?'

'Of course he has.' Sun had suddenly decided to volunteer an answer, as if the questions, if allowed to go on, might cut too close to the bone. It was obvious that he regarded Malone, and even Clements, as the enemy; nor did he have much time for Quirke and Tidey. Racism is not a one-way street, an obvious fact often overlooked. 'He and Madame Timori share everything. But she is the business brain and he allows her to handle all their affairs. The President knows about the investments here and approves of them.'

'Who else knows about them?'

'What do you mean?' Quirke's bright smile had disappeared completely.

'I told you, I'm looking for whoever might be employing this man Seville to kill President Timori. People kill for money. Sergeant Clements and I have seen plenty of that.' He looked at Clements, who was sitting quietly in the background taking notes. 'We're not sure that the attempted assassination of the President was a purely political act.'

'Does that mean we *are* suspects?' said Tidey.

135

'Not necessarily, Mr Tidey. Let's say we hope you'll help us with our enquiries.'

'They say that all the time,' Quirke, the lawyer, explained to Sun, who nodded as if he had heard it all before.

'I understand you've just spent some time in the company of this man Seville,' said Tidey, making it sound as if Malone had had tea with the terrorist. 'Did you ask him who was paying him?'

I should have, but I didn't. 'He was holding a gun at my head. Would you ask him a question like that if he was holding one at your head?'

'I wouldn't,' said Clements and fixed Tidey with a look that seemed to shrink the roly-poly banker.

'How much of this interview is confidential?' said Quirke. The bottom seemed to be falling out of his pear-shaped face; he looked almost ridiculously lugubrious now, like a bad actor in a horror film. 'We shouldn't be at odds on something like this.'

'I can't promise anything. A report on it will go to my superiors.' *Where it will be speed-read and you'll be up before Assistant Commissioner Zanuch before you can get your second breath and all your second-thought answers ready.*

'There are several important personages who know about the investments,' said Quirke reluctantly, and a flash of annoyance crossed Sun's face.

'You mean several politicians?' said Malone, and Quirke nodded. 'Federal or State?'

'We'd rather not name them,' said Tidey, voice all at once flat. He tilted his head and his glasses were suddenly opaque.

'I can guess a name or two. But maybe I'd better leave that to my superiors.' *Keep them worried,* he thought. Maybe Quirke and Tidey would come back with more information when they'd had time to go away and think about their association with Madame Timori. There would, however, be nothing forthcoming from Sun, not unless he was put on the rack and that, unfortunately, was not part of the New South Wales Police Force's equipment. Civilization had a lot to answer for. 'Righto, gentlemen, you can go. But I'd like a list, within twenty-four hours, of all the investments and companies, if any, that you've

136

registered in the partnership's name, plus nominees, if you have used any.'

'I don't think we're at liberty to disclose those without our clients' permission.' Tidey made one last try at bluster, dropped a few more plum notes.

'Mr Tidey, you know better than that. I can get it all from Corporate Affairs. But I thought you wanted to leave them out of it, for the time being anyway?'

'Of course, of course,' said Quirke, butting in. 'You'll have the list, Inspector. You'll be working tomorrow, the Big Day?'

'We never stop,' said Malone and grinned at Clements. 'Do we, Sergeant?'

'Never,' said Clements, standing up and snapping his notebook shut. 'Who knows, we may have Mr Seville by tomorrow and then he'll tell us everything.'

'Do you think so, Mr Sun?' said Malone.

'I don't know how an assassin's mind works, Inspector. I've never met one. We're a gentle people in Palucca.'

'Yes, you told me that before. But somehow you've been responsible for a lot of violence here in Sydney since you arrived.'

Sun had no answer to that; his face closed up again. The three men left abruptly, only Quirke managing a brief smile of farewell. Malone slumped back in his chair and looked at Clements.

'We've got the Speed Reader on our back. He's in charge now.'

Clements swore and sat down heavily, as if everything was all at once too much for him. He sat in silence for a few moments, biting his lip, then he looked up, took out his notebook again.

'I didn't get much out of the pub at Rozelle. The Brighams are okay – the old man's got a bit of a sore head, that's all. Seville kept to himself, never went down to the bar for a drink. He had two suitcases, but there was nothing in them to tell us anything about him, except he seems to have bought all his clothes in Beirut. We'll get nothing out of anyone there, you can bet on it. He took everything that might identify him with him in that brief-case. We got some more fingerprints, but they mean nothing, now we know who he is.'

'He's still looking for Dallas Pinjarri. I'll bet my neck that Dallas had a gun in that bag he was carrying when you tailed him. Concentrate on finding Dallas. Go back to Redfern and see if Jack Rimmer can help, tell him I sent you and I'll owe him if he can give us a lead on Dallas.'

'They don't like me out in Redfern.'

'Now's your chance to alter your image.'

'What are you going to do?'

'I'm going out to Point Piper to see the Timoris again. I'll let you know what life's like out there amongst the silvertails.'

3

Life amongst the silvertails was not going well.

'General Paturi's arrived here, did you know that?' said Russell Hickbed. 'He got into Sydney last night on a Garuda flight and went straight on down to Canberra. Phil's just been on the line to me.'

'Has he seen Philip?' said President Timori.

'Not yet. Phil's doing his best to dodge him, says his engagement book is full. He went down to Canberra first thing this morning and he's due back tonight for the Bicentennial Ball.'

'Have we been invited to that?' said Madame Timori, who loved every social occasion except a funeral.

'I don't think so. Come off it, Delvina. You should be lying low, keeping your head down.' Hickbed loathed social occasions, but only because they required social graces.

'Have you been invited?'

'Yes.'

'Are you going?'

'At a time like this?'

'We can't remain cooped up here for ever,' said Timori mildly. The Hickbed mansion and grounds were bigger than Kirribilli House but they were like a chicken-run compared to the palace back home. He was a sentimentalist, but only for the richest of memories. 'We have to come out in the open sooner or later.'

'Not tonight, not yet.' Hickbed was wishing his guests had gone elsewhere. Canberra, preferably: he had suggested that to Phil Norval when he had spoken to him this morning. Norval's reply had been more like a back-bencher's than a Prime Minister's, a vulgarity that would have had him banned from the air had he still been a TV star. 'You could go out to Kootapatamba.'

Kootapatamba was the 100,000-acre sheep station that their partnership had bought in western New South Wales. 'We don't want to be *that* much in the open,' said Madame Timori. 'Out there amongst all those sheep and flies and those bush people. Abdul would die of boredom.'

'Better that than a hole in the head,' said Timori, who knew nothing of sheep, flies or bush people, whoever they were. He turned as Sun Lee came out on to the terrace where they sat. 'You look worried, Sun.'

Hickbed looked at the expressionless Chinese, but could see nothing; Abdul must have X-ray vision. 'Things are going from bad to worse, Your Excellency. I have just spent an uncomfortable half-hour with that Inspector Malone. I and Mr Tidey and Mr Quirke. They told me afterwards that a great deal of your affairs may become public in a day or two. As soon as the celebrations are over, the media will be looking to stir things up.'

'It's public enough already, isn't it?' said Hickbed, steaming up his glasses in the morning heat. He took them off and wiped them. 'The bloody newspapers are trying to out-do each other in guessing games.'

'Conjecture, just guesses, as you say,' said Madame Timori. 'Conjecture never hurt anyone.' She had become regal, she had forgotten how vulnerable the common herd could be. Hickbed could have told her, but refrained.

'I don't mean the newspapers will cause the trouble,' said Sun. 'They will just broadcast it. We have to worry about a government body they have here, something called the Corporate Affairs Commission.'

'Bloody busybodies,' said Hickbed, who had run up against the Commission several times.

'That's what democracy is, a nest of busybodies,' said Timori, and was pleased he had never fallen for it. The generals back in Bunda would learn their lesson. He decided he might wait a month or two before he attempted to go back; he would let the rebels stew in democracy, a real mess. 'How much shall we have to tell them?'

'They are only concerned with what we have set up here in Australia. Mr Quirke tells me everything is legal. It is just the amounts we have invested that will cause comment – Australians are always interested in money, especially large amounts. It will give you and Madame Timori bad publicity.'

'Will it be made public?' said Madame Timori, who had never avoided publicity.

'As I understand it, no. But as I also understand it, Australia is what they call a leaky place – whatever that means.'

'It means government departments are full of holes,' said Hickbed. 'The media seem able to get any information they want.'

'I'd shoot anyone who did that in Palucca,' said Timori, who had indeed done that on two occasions. 'Can't the Prime Minister put a stop to something like that?'

'Not by shooting them. Anyhow, Corporate Affairs is a State thing.' Hickbed could see the leaks ahead and the mud forming. 'Premier Vanderberg isn't on your side, I've told you that.'

'Perhaps we should seduce Mr Vanderberg,' said Madame Timori.

Timori smiled at his wife. 'I saw a picture of the gentleman, darling. I don't think he would know what seduction is, not as a victim anyway.'

'I mean with money. Everyone can be seduced by money, even the rich.' Seduced by it herself, she knew its powers. She was not carrying the bag of emeralds this morning; she had, reluctantly, entrusted them to the security of Hickbed's safe. She felt penniless without them.

'Not The Dutchman,' said Hickbed. 'I tried it once. He's not interested in money. Just power and spite, that's all. If he could

140

topple Phil Norval from the Prime Ministership, he'd think of himself as the richest bastard in the world.'

'Perhaps we could help him topple Philip,' said Madame Timori. 'He's been no help to us so far.'

All three men, even Sun Lee, looked at her in astonishment. Then Hickbed said, 'But he's our little mate! For crissake, Delvina, what are you saying? Without him you wouldn't be here!'

'True. But what has he done for us since we arrived? We could approach Mr Vanderberg and suggest a quid pro quo.'

Before the men could respond, the Hickbed housemaid, an Asiatic, appeared. 'There is an Inspector Malone . . .'

'Oh Christ,' said Hickbed, whose only communication with the Lord was in expletives. 'Do we see him or don't we?'

'Tell him to go away,' said Madame Timori.

'Can one do that in Australia?' said the President. 'Just like back in the palace in Bunda?' He looked at Sun and smiled. The latter smiled in reply, but it was as if he were trying to express himself in a foreign gesture. 'Let's see him. Otherwise how shall we know how close they are to catching Seville? Remember, it is my head that is in Mr Seville's sights.'

Inside the house Malone was examining what he could see from the big entrance hall. A curving staircase led to the upper floor: Lisa dreamed of having a curving staircase, but it was difficult to fit such a feature into a one-storeyed house that would fit into this one six times over. The black-and-white tessellated floor was matched by the black-and-white abstract paintings on the walls; Malone would not have guessed that Hickbed was a lover of abstract art, but perhaps they reminded him of profit-and-loss graphs. Through an archway he could see an ornate drawing-room where the carpet looked so thick that the sheep might be lying there crushed with the virgin wool still on their backs. Lisa would love all this, and he wondered how he could suddenly build the fortune to buy it.

Nagler, whom he had met out in the driveway, had been equally impressed by the house and the way Hickbed lived. 'I have an uncle who used to live like this in Hungary.'

'What does he do now?'

'He lives like it in Melbourne. Made his money in property.

141

Every year he sends me a Christmas box, thinks it's the Christian thing to do. Being a Hungarian, he always asks for a receipt.' Nagler had looked up at the big house. 'I doubt very much if Mr Hickbed has ever done a Christian thing in his life. But that's just a Jewish thought.'

'You're not happy here, Joe.'

Nagler nodded. 'All of them are a bunch I despise.' All his wry humour had abruptly disappeared. 'I don't think I'd mind if this guy Seville wiped out the lot of them.'

'What's security like here? Easy?' The narrow street outside was jammed with a small crowd of demonstrators, media cars and vans and two police cars. There were no locals: public curiosity was something the Point Piper natives would never descend to. Curtains occasionally moved at windows, but that could have been the breeze of gossip disturbing them. Gossip was a permitted indulgence.

'Bloody difficult. Look around you.'

There were several large blocks of flats nearby and on the high side of the street there were big houses that overlooked the Hickbed mansion. It would be difficult to police every square foot of the surrounding properties, especially at night and more especially if the owners refused access. Which they were more than likely to do, since President Timori and his upstart consort were such unwelcome neighbours.

'I'm glad it's your problem, not mine.' Then he had an idea that had been niggling at him ever since he had interviewed Tidey and Quirke: 'Joe, what's your contact like with ASIO?'

'What've you got in mind?' Nagler at once was suspicious, but he smiled.

'Do they ever tap the phones at Kirribilli House when visitors are staying there?'

'I could ask them, but that doesn't say they'll tell me. What do you want to know?'

'What overseas calls went out of Kirribilli while the Timoris were there and where the calls went to. You can tell the spooks I'm trying to find out who's paying Seville.'

'Okay, I'll try, but don't hold your breath. How are you going on Seville?'

'No good so far.' He knew Nagler would understand. They

142

both had too much experience to believe that mistakes were never made. 'But I hope I don't have to explain why to the Timoris. You heard about what happened to me this morning?'

Nagler nodded. 'I didn't like to bring it up.'

Now Malone was in the house and the housemaid was coming towards him. 'Mr Hickbed will see you, sir.'

Malone followed her out to the back of the house, taking in everything he passed; Lisa would grill him tonight when she learned he had been here. He stepped out on to the terrace, saw them all dressed for the morning's heat and asked if he might remove his jacket. He figured this meeting, no matter how short, was going to be hot anyway.

'Of course,' said Madame Timori, assuming (or presuming) the role of hostess. 'You must be at boiling point, if only from frustration. Mr Hickbed heard on the radio about your adventure with that dreadful terrorist, what's-his-name.'

What's-his-name: so casual, as if Seville meant nothing in their lives. 'Yes. We talked about you and the President. But he didn't tell me who was employing him or why he wanted to kill the President.'

'A pity,' said Timori. 'One should always know the reasons for one's murder.'

Hickbed wasn't interested in what's-his-name: 'We're surprised to see you so soon. Mr Sun has told us about your interview with Mr Tidey and Mr Quirke. You've over-stepped the mark. That's for Corporate Affairs, not the police.'

'Oh, I explained that to them, Mr Hickbed. They chose to talk to me.' He looked at Timori. 'Before I came in, sir, I spoke to Sergeant Kenthurst out in the street –'

'Who?' Being a dictator and not a politician he had never had to bother about remembering names.

'The officer in charge of the Federal Police, the ones who are guarding you. I don't have the personnel, so they and Special Branch are going to interview every one of your staff individually –'

'Grill them, you mean?' Delvina Timori knew how the police worked; or anyway, the Paluccan police. She had herself given orders. Not all Paluccans, as Sun had claimed, were gentle. 'What if we refuse to allow such a thing?'

'I don't think the courts would allow you to claim diplomatic immunity for all of them, Madame. And it wouldn't be good public relations.' He could feel himself getting hot and it wasn't all due to the morning sun. He looked back at Timori. 'I'm sure you'll see it's better to co-operate, Mr President.'

'Of course. You're determined to save my life, aren't you, Inspector?'

'If it's possible, sir,' said Malone, not offering him too much hope, and hoping Joe Nagler could not hear him. He hated the man for his policies and his corruption, but could not help liking him for his stoical humour.

'Who do you start with?' said Delvina, feeling she was losing command.

'Mr Sun,' said Malone and looked directly at the Chinese.

'But you've already interrogated him, haven't you?'

'Not really.' Malone smiled, as if implying there were whips and blackjacks and worse in the closet.

Timori said, 'I'm sure Mr Sun will co-operate. There is an explanation for everything that's troubling you. Except, of course, who is paying to have me killed. I don't think Mr Sun will be able to help you there.'

'Who else is going to be interviewed?' said Hickbed.

'You,' said Malone, glad of the opening. 'I'll be doing that.'

'When?' Hickbed didn't like being besieged at any time, least of all on his own territory. BHP, the nation's largest corporation, had once tried to take him over and had finished up so badly bruised from its efforts that it had stayed away from him ever since. A mere police inspector could be crushed into a powder.

'Now would be as good a time as any.'

Hickbed took off his glasses; they had steamed up again. He made a noise like a wild boar grunting in the scrub; but he was dressed in Italian linen amongst the camellias and azalea bushes and the effect wasn't quite the same. 'I'll make up my own mind about that.'

Delvina, dressed in the best Chinese silk and as smooth, rose from her chair. 'Inspector, would you come for a walk with me?'

Malone raised his eyebrows, looked at Timori. Did you ask permission of an ex-President to go for a walk with his wife?

But Delvina had never asked permission of her husband for anything. She just walked away without a backward glance. Malone looked again at Timori, who smiled and nodded, then he followed Delvina.

She led him down steps on to a lower terrace, stood against the white stone balustrade with a statue of Aphrodite smiling conspiratorially over her shoulder. Malone knew nothing of Greek goddesses, but this one looked a shrewd sister to Delvina. The sculptor had been cynical rather than romantic.

'May I call you Scobie?' She was wearing a musky perfume that Malone could smell above that of the roses in the big stone urns along the terrace. She smiled at him, no longer the imperious wife of a President.

Malone, too, smiled. 'Go ahead. May I call you Delvina?'

'No. I have my position to keep up.'

'I have mine, too. But go ahead – Scobie will do.' He laid his jacket over the balustrade, thought about taking off his tie and decided against it. There was danger in being too relaxed around Delvina Timori.

'We're in a delicate situation,' she said. 'And a dangerous one, too. I know we're not popular here, but Australians don't understand how things have to be run in Palucca.'

'What about the Americans and the British and the French? They don't seem to understand, either.'

'Till you've lived there, you don't understand. I didn't, not till I'd been there two or three years. My husband is what I suppose the ignorant would call a dictator, but some countries need a man like him. Palucca does. So does Australia,' she added, as if waiting for Abdul to be asked. 'We are doing our best to see he returns to Palucca.'

'Who's we?'

'Me,' she said. 'I was using the royal plural.'

'It suits you,' he said with a grin.

She had the grace to smile; she wasn't all poison and steel. Then she was sober-faced again. A pity, he thought: she looked almost beautiful when she smiled. 'Scobie, what's the point of all this investigation? We'll be gone from here in a couple of weeks. Either back to Palucca or to Europe – we shan't stay here.'

145

'Why not?'

'Well, I mean, who would?'

She sounded like the expatriate snobs he had met on his one trip to London. He looked out at the harbour, a painting come alive by magic. The yachts were out again in force this morning, a chorus of gay notes swelling before the rising breeze. The tall ships, which had come from all over the world for the Bicentennial, were anchored in various bays for tomorrow's sail past; he could see them, their masts and spars like symbols from the past, riding majestically above the smaller craft. He looked along at the mansions on this point, then across at the distant shore and the green oasis of Taronga Zoo. This was silvertail territory and those out on the harbour in the boats, big and small, weren't short of a quid; but tomorrow wouldn't be celebrated by the silvertails alone. People would be coming in from all over the city, from the bush too, the poor as well as the rich, and all of them, even if a little unsure of the history they would be commemorating, would be loud in their pride in what they had. Everyone, that is, but Dallas Pinjarri and Jack Rimmer and what Jack called the tribe, but he doubted if Delvina had ever given them a thought anyway.

'I think I would,' he said quietly.

'A real Aussie?' she said, but managed not to sneer.

He nodded. 'Get on with it, Delvina. You're going somewhere in a couple of weeks . . .?'

For a moment she looked as if she might spit at him, something she might have done in Bunda but not in Point Piper. 'That's my point. We'll be gone and everyone will soon forget the fuss.'

'The fuss about Mr Masutir? And the old lady over at Kirribilli and the young policeman who was killed last night? I don't think I'll forget it.'

'Of course *we* shan't forget them. We're *involved*, you and us. But the public – do you think they remember those sort of things? They get all their news from TV and nobody remembers that. They'll even forget all this, what's going to happen tomorrow.' She gestured at the harbour.

'Not if they're here to *see* it. If they see it on TV, maybe yes. But not if they're here. I hope to bring my kids to see it and I

146

hope they'll remember it for the rest of their lives . . . You forget one thing. No one's going to forget you and the President too easily.' He looked up towards the house. Timori and Hickbed were still on the top terrace, gazing down at them. 'You could bring down the Federal Government. Someone's working on that right now.'

'Who?'

'The State Premier.'

'How do you know?'

'I don't. But I'd lay money on it and I'm not a betting man.'

'How much do you earn?'

He smiled sourly and shook his head. 'Don't try that one, Delvina. I'm squeaky clean, always have been.'

'No, how much do you earn?'

'Forty-two thousand a year, plus a few perks. A week's dress allowance for you, so my wife tells me.'

'Newspaper exaggeration. I get a discount.' Charges of extravagance never worried her; life should be an expensive dream. She put her hand on Aphrodite's naked buttock, as if to emphasize her own penurious nakedness. 'It's not much, is it?'

'It's more than you ever earned as a dancer.'

'Dancing was just a means to an end.' She looked around her, hoping this was not the end. She had met Malone only twice back in the old days of the dancing company; he had been on the Fraud Squad then and had come investigating a secretary who had been choreographing the books. They had never talked like this, but there had not been a situation like this. 'I could give you a hundred thousand dollars.'

'No.'

'Two hundred thousand.'

'I could arrest you – well, no I guess I couldn't. Did the President know you were going to try and bribe me?'

'No, it was a spur of the moment thing.' But he was sure she never did anything on the spur of the moment. Her emergency plans were as calculated as her ambitions. 'Forget it, Inspector.'

'Yes, Madame Timori.' He picked up his jacket from the balustrade. 'Are you worried for the President's safety?'

147

'Of course I am!' She was regal again: having tried the common touch she had, being common, recognized it had its limitations. 'How dare you suggest I'm not!'

'I didn't suggest anything. If he is killed, will the generals let you go back to Palucca?'

'Probably not. I don't know. Why?'

'Nothing,' he said, trying to look enigmatic. He felt he had regained a little of the initiative from her, though he was still not sure of the direction in which to head.

For the moment they headed back up the steps to the top terrace and the house. Timori watched them till they were only a few feet from him, his face as inscrutable as Sun's standing just behind him. Then he smiled. 'So what arrangements have you come to?'

'None, sir,' said Malone.

Timori pursed his lips. He had been sure the offer of the bribe would be accepted; Delvina had discussed it with him as an emergency ploy. He was nonplussed when he was faced with honesty, especially from a policeman. Dictators, in many ways, are uneducated in the ways of the world. 'So the investigation goes on? And all the muck-raking?'

Malone was surprised at the bitterness in Timori's voice. He had thought the ex-President was resigned to his future, to exile, to the opprobrium. 'I won't be muck-raking, Mr President, not unless it's necessary, to find out who's paying Seville.'

'Damn Seville! Who cares about him?'

'I thought you did, sir.'

Timori stared at him. In Palucca, Malone thought, my head would be off within the next hour. There was no mistaking the rage in the ex-President's dark face; then all at once the rage drained out of it and something else replaced it. It was a moment before Malone recognized it as fear.

'You may go, Inspector.' He turned and walked away to the end of the terrace and stood staring out at the harbour. Delvina hesitated, then she gave Malone an angry look and followed her husband. She took his hand and they stood close together, gazing north, towards Palucca. It was only by accident they were looking in that direction: neither of them had the slightest idea about the points of the compass. When Abdul prayed each

148

day it was Sun, the Buddhist, who always had to point him towards Mecca.

'You've over-stepped the mark again, Inspector,' said Hickbed. 'We'll have your head for this.'

Then the housemaid appeared. 'Inspector Malone? You're wanted on the telephone.'

Saved by Russ Clements: Malone knew it would be him. He followed the girl into the house. 'Are you Vietnamese? Or Filipino?'

'No, sir. I'm from Palucca. I work for Mr Hickbed two years.'

He might have known. 'What did you think of Madame Timori when you were there?'

She was not embarrassed by the question. 'Oh, she was wonderful, sir. She called herself the Mother of the Poor.'

'And was she?'

'Was she what, sir?'

'Mother of the Poor.'

The girl had her first doubt; she frowned. 'Oh, I think so. There's the telephone, sir.'

She went away towards the back of the house, shaking her head at foreign policemen who asked stupid questions. Malone picked up the phone. 'Yes?'

'Inspector Malone? Scobie, this is Russ. We picked up Dallas Pinjarri. But no gun.'

4

'General Paturi's on the doorstep,' said Neil Kissing, the Foreign Minister. 'Or anyway, his embassy's doorstep. You'll have to see him.'

'*You* see him,' said Philip Norval. 'He's not a Head of State. Or is he? How do these juntas divvy up their status?'

'*I'm* not seeing him, not on my own. He's your baby, not mine. He wouldn't be here if you hadn't invited Timori! He'd be in Washington or somewhere, worrying the guts out of them.'

Kissing had been in politics for twenty-five years. He was now in his mid-fifties, a bluff, curly-haired man who came from a working-class background. He had deserted his father's party, the Labour Party, because of the in-fighting that always seemed to be going on; he had joined the Liberal Party and been stabbed in the back so many times he had become known as the Dartboard. The deepest wound had been inflicted when Norval and his backers had manipulated the numbers and, after years of striving, he had been defeated for the Prime Ministership. He had been given Foreign Affairs as compensation and he had worked brilliantly in the post; the fact that the Big Powers, and even the Small Powers of Europe, took little notice of Australian policies did not count. The nation's voice, if only a bleat in the corridors of world power, was a triumphant shout in the nation's newspapers: Kissing's minders saw to that. He was biding his time, certain that he would be Prime Minister before he had to draw his superannuation.

'I'm not carrying the can for you this time, Phil. You handle these buggers on your own. I'm having enough trouble with Suharto in Indonesia. And with Singapore.'

Sometimes he wished Australia was elsewhere on the world map. Say where Sicily now was: shrunken, of course, to fit into the Mediterranean, but that wouldn't matter. There was so much of the country that could be discarded. The whole middle third of it, which was just so much desert; Tasmania, which was always being left off maps anyway, even by Australian cartographers; he'd wipe off Queensland, too, which wanted to secede, or so it was said. It would be a pleasure to have to deal with the Europeans instead of the Asians; he would still get the dirty end of the stick, but the Europeans were less touchy about abuse. They expected that from the relics of their empires.

Phil Norval smoothed down his hair. He had just had his personal barber attend to it; the blondness had been touched up a little so that it would catch the light in tomorrow's cameras. Tonight, too, he would be at the Bicentennial Ball and he wanted to look his best for that. His suntanned handsomeness always looked good at night and he would look particularly good beside Anita, who was fair-complexioned and, more importantly, short. He had never forgotten how, on a visit to Europe, he had been photographed alongside the six-foot-two

150

wife of a Scandinavian Prime Minister. He had looked like her page-boy.

He was feeling depressed and worried, not a common state of mind for him; he was famous for always being buoyant and smiling through any disaster, natural or political. He had had an uncanny knack for being able to shrug off the blame for any of his government's mistakes; he had chosen (with much advice from Hickbed and the kitchen cabinet) a Cabinet whose ministers, willingly or unwillingly, had always been able to carry the can. Now they were deserting him. None of them, with the exception of Kissing, was in Canberra and though he had sent for them, none of them had responded. They were, his minders had been told by their minders, celebrating the Bicentennial in their electorates, as all good ministers were expected to. They would come back to Canberra in the event of war or his own death, but that was all.

'What does Paturi want? Does he want us to hand over Timori?'

'I don't think so. The last thing they want is any sort of political trial – they might have to shoot Timori. They wouldn't want to do that in public. No, Paturi wants us to say we'll freeze all the Timori holdings here in Australia and return them to Palucca.'

'That could take years!'

'Maybe. Even if it does, it's the appearance of things. The generals would be seen to be *doing* things, they won't lose face. Neither shall we.' Losing face had never worried Kissing, he had become used to it. It was bums on seats, on a chair in the Cabinet room or here in the Prime Minister's residence, that counted.

They were in Norval's study in The Lodge. It was not a large room, not as big as his study in his own home back in Sydney. It had been decorated by Anita Norval in what one critic from a women's magazine had described as Network Moderne or Commercial TV Chic. The Lodge, it seemed, was continually being redecorated as each new tenant moved in; the taxpayers, it was said, only voted to re-elect an incumbent to save some of their own money. The study was in bright colours, the studio for an up-market TV host. The paintings on the wall were modern but not abstract, the carpet and the drapes were of best

151

merino wool, the desk and chairs and table of the best native timber. There was only a small bookshelf, but Anita knew camouflage could be taken too far.

'Timori will never forgive me if I see Paturi.'

'Does that matter? Nobody ever looks for forgiveness in foreign affairs – I've never met a foreign minister who could even spell absolution. Except maybe the Vatican's and he'd keep his fingers crossed while he gave it to you.'

'What do I tell Paturi then?' He was lost without his advisers. He had come down to Canberra only for a couple of hours and had told them there was no need for them to accompany him. He had been attracted to politics by the theatrics of it; he was still ill at ease with the problems. He had no burning beliefs; his conservatism was simple-minded. His minders acted as his conscience, which meant it was best that they had none of their own. 'He's sure to want a quick answer.'

'Agree to whatever he asks – that is, unless he asks for Timori. Much as I'd like to, I don't think we can hand *him* back. But the six or seven hundred million that's rumoured to be here –'

'We can't hand that back! We'll have the pensioners and the education gang and the bloody social workers on our back –'

'They're all supposed to be small *l* liberals – they're not supposed to be on Timori's side. In any case, we don't physically hand it back.' He wondered who took care of Norval's finances; it must be Anita or a good agent. 'We just persuade him to leave the holdings here, but we change them into the name of the new government. Or their nominees.'

'Who'll they be?'

'Him and his mates, possibly. We don't know yet how honest they all are.'

Norval sighed; the demands of office were sometimes too much. 'Okay, I'll see him. But you stay with me, just in case.'

'Just in case what?' But Kissing smiled, went to the door and told the secretary on duty to phone General Paturi and tell him the Prime Minister would see him.

General Paturi arrived ten minutes later; he must have been poised on one foot waiting for the call. He had had the good sense to wear mufti; his embassy had told him that Australians,

especially politicians, were always uncomfortable in the presence of uniforms. He was a small man with sleek black hair
and skin much darker than his ex-President's. He came from
an up-country family that had given up head-hunting only after
the turn of the century when his grandfather had come back
from a Dutch-paid trip to Europe and reported that heads had
no value in the outside world and were not considered trophies
unless they wore a crown. In his own language Paturi talked a
blue streak, most of it in blue words, but he was hesitant and
circumspect in English.

'Mr Prime Minister, you do me an honour. You too, Mr
Kissing.'

'It's a pleasure to meet you, General.' Norval had spent all
his adult life practising social lies. But he decided to be blunt:
'What can we do for you?'

Paturi was a career military man, but he was accustomed to
circumlocution: it had gone with the climate in Palucca. He
blinked, then decided to be blunt in return: 'It would please us
if you kicked out our ex-President.'

'We're trying to find somewhere for him to retire to. But as
you understand, it isn't easy. You wouldn't take him back?' He
smiled to show he was joking.

Paturi was not used to joking in serious matters; he looked
affronted. 'Never! Our people would never have him back –'

'Of course not,' said Kissing, feeling a little diplomacy was
needed.

'It is a pity the assassination attempt wasn't successful.' Paturi
was not going to waste any more time in diplomacy or niceties.

'That's pretty brutal, isn't it?' said Norval. After all, Abdul
Timori was supposed to be a friend.

'I'm a military man, Mr Prime Minister.' Perhaps he should
have worn his uniform with the double row of ribbons, all won
without honours but not dishonourably. 'Brutal solutions are
sometimes the best.'

'That sounds like a military solution.'

'It is.' If he hadn't fought a war, he at least knew what a gun
was for.

'Do you know who might be trying to have him assassinated?'
said Kissing.

'Yes,' said Paturi. 'Himself.'

'Himself?' Norval almost fell out of his chair; even Kissing was shocked at such a suggestion. But then neither of them understood the Asian mind. 'Timori *himself*?'

'He's a cunning man, Prime Minister, as cunning as a serpent. He could have arranged it so that it looked as if he was the one to be killed. Instead poor Mr Masutir got the bullet.'

'Got the bullet. A pretty drastic way of being fired.' Norval looked at Kissing and smiled; he could never resist a joke, in poor taste or otherwise. Kissing did not smile back.

'What would it achieve, General?' he said.

'Sympathy.'

'Not here, General. Most Australians are sorry the assassin missed.'

Paturi raised his eyebrows. He had been told most Australians were good sports, whatever that meant. 'Back in Palucca there would be sympathy in some quarters. I have to confess, not everyone was glad to see him leave. There are many ignorant people in our country who believed everything he and Madame Timori told them. We have to educate them,' he said and made it sound like a gigantic task.

Kissing knew what he meant: even the voters here needed educating. 'If what you say is true, maybe you should talk to him, come to a compromise.'

Paturi shook his head emphatically. 'We could never trust him, Mr Kissing. Nor that woman –' The disgust in his voice was like a dry retch. 'She is the one we'd never have back. She is worse than he is. She is a foreigner, too.'

The two foreigners nodded. Norval said, 'So what do you want?'

'All their assets in this country frozen. I am here to talk with lawyers. Once we have established what is held, we shall claim it. Then we shall sell all of it to you.'

'Us?'

'The Australian government. We shall sell you all the holdings, whatever they are, and you will give us the money. I have read in the newspapers that there may be seven hundred million dollars' worth held here. It is not much to a wealthy country like Australia. Petty cash, I think you call it.'

154

'General Paturi,' said Norval, 'this isn't some quiz show.'

'Excuse me, Prime Minister?'

'What the Prime Minister means,' said Kissing, who wished Norval would forget what he had once been, 'is that this isn't some sort of prize money we can hand out. The government can't buy the Timori holdings – for one thing, we don't believe in the government owning anything. We can possibly freeze the assets, I don't know the drill on that, but we could never *buy* them. You'll have to find your own buyers.'

'It would be much simpler –' Life in a democracy was complicated: he did not look forward to the future back home.

'Of course it would,' said Norval, who saw the opportunity for another joke, but resisted it; to Kissing's relief. 'But that's not the way we work here. Leave it with us, General. I'll get our Attorney-General or whoever to look at it.' He stood up, put out his hand. 'I'm sorry. I have my plane waiting to take me back to Sydney in half an hour.'

General Paturi was not used to being dismissed so abruptly, but he swallowed his resentment. 'I, too, am going back to Sydney. Perhaps –?'

Norval was deliberately slow; but Kissing was quick as a fox: 'Of course! The Prime Minister will be glad to give you a lift. It will give you the opportunity to get to know each other better for the future.'

'Will you be coming, Mr Kissing?'

'Alas, no. A pity. The celebrations, you know – I have to go back to my electorate, not fifty miles from here.' He grinned at Norval, having stabbed him in the back. 'You should get an electorate closer to Canberra, Phil.'

Norval, not normally a vicious man, gave him a look that would have severed his head from his body had looks been steel.

'I understand there is a Bicentennial Ball this evening,' said General Paturi on their way out of the study. 'I have been invited.'

'Who by?' Norval missed his step in surprise.

'I have never met the gentleman. The invitation came to the embassy by telephone. From the Premier of New South Wales, Mr Vanderberg.'

Behind them Kissing had a sudden fit of diplomatic coughing.

155

SIX

1

Seville pulled the blue Honda Accord into the kerb in the quiet suburban street. He had arrived here almost like something caught on a wayward breeze; he only knew he was in the municipality of Randwick because a council street sign told him so. He did not know he was only half a dozen blocks from the street where Malone lived, but he would not have been surprised if someone had told him so. Accidents of geography no longer amazed him, coincidence was part of the pattern of life.

When he had driven out of the city parking station he had known he would have to dump the stolen Honda as soon as possible. Though he had immediately headed north towards the Harbour Bridge, he had soon turned east and driven through the central business district of the city. Before long he had picked up what seemed to be a main stream of traffic. It had taken him through some inner city streets, where the houses were crowded together without front yards and the doors of some stood wide open like dark mouths gasping for breath in the hot morning. Then he was driving down a wide tree-lined avenue past what looked like a huge sports complex. A cricket Test was taking place there, but it meant nothing to him.

The Sydney Cricket Ground was no mecca for him; no cricket ground anywhere in the world tempted him. His father, the Englishman twice removed by birth from England (the family name had been Saville till his mother, the Argentinian, had changed it after his father's death), had done his best to teach his only son a love of the game; as a boy he had been taken each weekend by his father to the Hurlingham club and made to watch while his father played, usually badly. All he could remember from those hated weekends was the ignominy of watching his father fail week after week ('Jolly hard luck, old chap, better luck next week') and the once confided secret regret by his father that he had never scored a century. The old man was dead now, buried in the mausoleum in Recoletta, remembered for his decency, his love of things English and his disappointment that his son, the natural athlete, had never wanted to take advantage of his prowess. For his father's sake he had played the game at St George's School in Buenos Aires, always scoring well but never a century; twice he had been within sight of the hundred runs and twice he had got himself out deliberately. He had never attempted to analyse, because he had not wanted to know, whether he had committed cricket suicide to spite his father or out of respect for him. His father had tried so hard to be as English as possible, but there had been the *machismo* streak in him and he might have felt more hurt than pride if his son had achieved something that he had longed for and to which he had never got even close.

Seville drove on past the Cricket Ground, passed a racecourse on his right and climbed a ridge to a shopping centre. There, at some traffic lights, he turned left and went looking for a quiet street where he could leave the car. But first he had to look for a house with a *For Sale* sign on it. He found such a house, had driven past it a couple of times, then driven on another mile or so to abandon the car.

He got out of the Honda and locked it. Then, carrying his brief-case he walked back to the vacant house. He made sure no one was watching him; there was no one in the front gardens of the surrounding houses. They were all solid one-storey dwellings with orange-red tiled roofs, built in the 1920s: unpretentious, boasting nothing of their owners' ambitions, if indeed they had any. Music was blaring from a radio in the house immediately opposite, but the houses on either side of the house for sale had their windows closed and their blinds drawn.

He opened the front gate, walked across the narrow neglected lawn and round to the back of the house. He opened the brief-case; it was a small portable tool-shed. He had refined the case over the years, eliminating some equipment, adding other items. He took out a small leather wallet and in thirty seconds had opened the back door and was stepping into a back veranda that had been glassed in and converted into a room.

157

He went further inside and found the bathroom. He clicked on the light switch, but there was no electricity. The bathroom was dimly lit by sunlight through the narrow frosted window, but he would have to put up with that. He relieved himself, feeling both mental and physical relief as the fluid ran out of him. He was surprised and upset at how tense he had become.

Then he got to work. He propped up his remaining passport, the mark of his last emergency identity, and compared the photograph in it with the face that looked back at him from the dusty mirror over the bathroom sink. He had to change from the blond Michel Gideon to the dark-haired Martin Dijon, a French national born in Belfort. He took out the hair dye and the rubber gloves.

An hour later his hair was dark brown and dry. He brushed it and a sheen appeared on it, making it look more natural; it did not have that dull look he had noticed on the badly dyed hair of some men and women. He took a shower, relieved that at least the house's water had not been cut off, then got back into the clothes he had been wearing. He was fastidious about cleanliness and he regretted he had not been able to bring some clothes with him when he had left the pub in Rozelle. He should have at least put a clean shirt and underwear in his brief-case.

There had not, however, been time. It was only by chance that he had glanced out of his bedroom window and seen the police cars coming down the street. At the same moment there had been a knock on his door and he had opened it to be confronted by Mr and Mrs Brigham. He was not to know that, friendly people that they were, they had come up to ask him to have dinner with them that evening. He had panicked again when Brigham, a hearty man who had no sense of his own privacy and valued no one else's, had pushed uninvited into the bedroom. Seville had picked up the policeman's gun from where it had been lying on the bed and hit the landlord with it. Brigham had gone down with a loud moan and Mrs Brigham had opened her mouth to scream. He had warned her not to and she had shut her mouth so hard he had heard her teeth click. Then he had grabbed up the brief-case and, prodding her with the gun, gone down the stairs. At the bottom they had met Inspector Malone.

During their ride in the white Ford he had begun to respect the police officer. If Australians could be said to have dignity, something he doubted, then Malone had it; not a European dignity, or the arrogant South American kind, but a native self-respect that had nothing to do with anyone else's opinion. There was intelligence there, too: he must make no mistake in under-estimating it. This Sydney policeman might not have the sophistication of some of those senior officers he had come up against overseas, but he was no fool. He would remain out of Inspector Malone's way for the rest of his stay in Sydney.

He picked up the brief-case, into which he had re-packed the rubber gloves and the hair dye, put his navy-blue blazer over his arm and left the house. He had to find Dallas Pinjarri before the police found him. If he could not pick up the rifle from Pinjarri, he would have to examine the risk of breaking into some gun shop and stealing a weapon. He longed for the convenience of Beirut or Damascus or even Milan or Paris, where he had so many contacts and any sort of weapon, from a knife to a bazooka, was readily available.

He was beginning to regret he had accepted this commission. The money had been the temptation; he wondered if, in his youth, he would have come all this way out of political belief. Now he was approaching middle age he was beginning to doubt that he had indeed ever had any political beliefs. He had despised his mother and his sisters and their friends: *their* beliefs, political and social, had ossified into stony attitudes that nothing could chip. He had sometimes sat watching them at dinner parties and tea parties (his mother, introduced to it by his father, had had tea at four every afternoon) and compared them with the stone and marble busts on the mausoleums in the cemetery in Recoletta, where his ancestors, one of them a general, another an admiral, lay in their extravagantly built crypts. He had had the proper background: St George's School, university, working in the family law firm, vacationing on the family *estancia*. He had escorted girls from the right families, made love to two or three of them. His life had been laid out for him, like an old well-travelled road where all the bends and dips were known and no ambushes could possibly occur. Then he had heard about the Tupamaros and the future they wanted for Argentina.

He had joined them to escape the dullness of what faced him. He had told himself and them that he believed in their aims; only later had he admitted, but only to himself, that it was their methods that appealed to him. There had been excitement such as he had never before experienced: the risks were like a drug, though even then he had gained a reputation for being ice-cool under all circumstances. He had left the Tupamaros eight years ago; or rather, they had expelled him. They had realized he was in the battle for his own ends, a mercenary whose only pay, then, had been self-satisfaction; he had not cared at all about the wider aims against the junta and its oppressive rule. He had moved to Europe and the Middle East, joined other factions, gained an international reputation for his planning and his daring; but he had always been in the shadow of Carlos, the Venezuelan, and Abu Nidal, the Palestinian. During the Falklands war he had sardonically thought of offering his services to the British; his father, had he been alive, would have been torn apart by conflicting loyalties. But the British, decent as always, would never have employed a terrorist, at least not in a war they knew they could not lose.

He was a complex man, too much so to encourage close friendships, and he had begun to feel lonely. The excitement of the risks had lasted till a year or two ago and then it had begun to fade. It was then that he had begun to think about retirement.

The successful completion of this job and the claiming of the full payment of a million dollars had now become the ultimate ambition. He had never wanted anything so much before, if indeed he had ever really wanted anything at all. Life had been a day-to-day affair, well planned only in regard to the task in hand: he hated sloppy execution. There had been no final aim, for any cause or for himself. But *this* was different.

He walked back to the shopping centre on top of the Randwick ridge and found a phone-box. He dialled Dallas Pinjarri's number, waited while it rang and rang; he was about to hang up and then the receiver was lifted. The voice on the other end was breathless, as if its owner had been running.

'Yeah? That you, Dallas?'

'No. I wanted to speak to Dallas. He's not there?'

'Who's that?'

'A friend of his. Who are you?'

'It's none of your business, mate.' The voice was youthful, a boy's; but it had all of Dallas Pinjarri's belligerence. 'What you want him for?'

The voice was too young to be a policeman's; Seville took a risk. 'He has a package for me.'

'Oh.' There was silence for half a minute; Seville guessed a hand had been put over the mouthpiece. Then: 'Dallas has been taken away by the pigs.'

'I'm sorry to hear that. Did the police take the package?'

Again the hand must have been placed over the mouthpiece. Seville wondered who was there at the other end with the boy. Then the hand was taken away: 'No, they didn't. Are you Mr Gideon?'

Seville hesitated, then said, 'Yes. Are you the boy who met me at the Entertainment Centre the other night?'

'Yeah.'

'Do you have the package?'

Again there was a silent consultation at the other end of the phone. Seville wished the boy would get off the line and let whoever was in charge take over. But perhaps there was no one in charge. He remembered his encounters with the Aboriginal radicals on his last visit: there had been half a dozen leaders, but no one in charge. Maybe that was the tribal system; he did not know. He had never believed in anarchy: that was only a fools' empire.

The boy came back on the line. 'Yeah, we got it. Not here. We got it somewhere else. Dallas said you were paying five thousand bucks for it.' The boy said the amount as if he didn't quite believe anyone would pay that much for any-thing.

'That's correct. A thousand dollars down and the rest will be paid by bank draft.'

'Yeah, that's what he said. Well, you still want it?'

'Yes, I do. As soon as possible.' So that I can get the job done and be gone from here as soon as possible.

'You wanna come here and pick it up?'

'Where's here?'

'Redfern. Wonga Street.'

'Is that where the police picked up Mr Pinjarri?'

'Yeah, why?'

'No thanks.' They really were naïve. 'Choose somewhere else. Somewhere where there will be a crowd.'

Another consultation, this time without the hand over the phone: there seemed to be half a dozen voices offering suggestions. Then the boy was on the line again: 'How about The Rocks, down by the harbour? I'll be waiting on the corner of Argyle Street in an hour, okay? Bring the thousand bucks.'

'Argyle Street. And no tricks, young man, or you'll be a dead young man.' Seville did not like melodramatic threats, but he had found, with the young Arabs he had had to work with, that melodrama seemed to accentuate the seriousness of a situation in their eyes.

The young Aborigine wasn't impressed: he had been too long amongst the phlegmatic whites or had a sense of Aboriginal fatalism. 'Yeah? Well, we'll see about that. You be there, mate. I ain't gunna hang around with that package too bloody long.'

Seville came out of the phone-box, looked around for a taxi, but there was none in sight. He had to wait ten minutes before one came along; impatience began to put him on edge again. 'American Express head office.'

'Where's that, mate?' The driver was an Asiatic.

'I haven't the faintest idea. It's your job to find it and take me there.'

The driver looked at him in the driving-mirror. This bloody foreigner hadn't got into the front seat with him, like any democratic Aussie would do; he was so bloody uppity, he was sitting in the back and giving instructions. 'Don't talk to me like that, mate, or you can get out and walk.'

Seville put his hand on the brief-case; he could almost feel the metal of the two guns through the leather. 'Perhaps you'd like me to report you to the police?'

Then to his horror he saw the police patrol car coming up

162

the street towards them. The driver saw it, too. He looked at Seville again in the mirror, looked at the police car; then he put the taxi into gear and took off as if the police might arrest him for loitering. 'Slow down,' said Seville, recovering. 'You don't want to be arrested for speeding. Pull up at the next phone-box and we'll check the address of American Express in the phone-book.'

When they pulled in at the first phone-box they came to, the phone-book, naturally, was missing half its pages. They had to pull up at two other boxes before Seville found the address he wanted. Another five minutes brought them to American Express headquarters in the heart of the city.

'I can't wait here,' said the driver.

Seville got out and paid the exact fare, something he normally never did; he had never been a lavish tipper, because that only brought attention to oneself; but he had always been generous. He handed over the cash and waited for the abuse. But the driver, working in Sydney, had become accustomed to no tipping. Australians, he knew, were the lousiest bastards on earth. He was just surprised that the foreign bastards were picking up the habit. It was just as well there were so many Americans in town or he mightn't have had any pickings at all.

'I hope you get your cheques cashed,' he said. 'You look as if you need it.'

'Thank you,' said Seville.

'Up yours,' said the driver with Oriental politeness and drove off.

Seville put on his blazer and went into American Express. There was a line in front of each of the two cashiers' desks and it took twenty minutes for him to reach the counter. He produced his Dijon passport and his traveller's cheques. The girl behind the counter gave him an American Express smile, then threw cold water on him.

'I'm sorry, sir, our limit for the moment is five hundred dollars. We've had a terrific run on our cash. If you could come back later?'

'You couldn't make an exception?' He gave her his most charming smile.

She had had a surfeit of charming smiles. 'I'm sorry, sir. Later, for sure. But five hundred dollars for now.'

He settled for that and left the office. He looked at his watch, then for a taxi; but all the taxis going past were engaged. He asked the way to The Rocks, then headed north towards the harbour. He passed the Regent Hotel, went in and tried to cash more cheques; but the hotel was cashing cheques only for guests. He went on, feeling the heat now as he hurried. He saw the boy waiting on the corner of Argyle Street, but he walked on past him, knowing the boy would not recognize him. He crossed to the opposite side of the wide main street, which a sign told him was George Street North; he always liked to know exactly where he was. He stood there and watched the boy.

He was waiting anxiously, carrying a canvas bag, on the corner of Argyle Street. Seville watched him for several minutes. The boy seemed nervous, but there was no sign that he was accompanied by anyone, certainly not by any Aborigines. At last Seville decided he had to come out into the open. He surreptitiously took one of the Smith and Wessons out of the brief-case and slipped it into his blazer pocket. Then he crossed the road towards the waiting boy.

The boy had chosen the spot well; or had it chosen for him. The Rocks, a restored early settlement area, was crowded with tourists and holiday-makers. The nineteenth-century shops were full of people buying reminders of the country's history; there were many genuine home-made articles, but there were plates made in Korea and Taiwan that were decorated with pictures of Captain Cook landing at Botany Bay. Glassware, pottery and leatherware celebrated the Bicentennial; T-shirts proclaimed *My Dad Was A Convict* or *My Granny Was the Darling of The First Fleet*. Nobody seemed to be taking any notice of the light-skinned Aboriginal boy holding tightly to the canvas bag. If he looked nervous and sullen, that was not their concern. If the bloody Abos didn't want to enjoy the celebrations, bugger 'em.

The boy was standing against the wall of a hotel, a pub where he was surrounded by drinkers standing in the hot sun so that they could maintain their thirst for more beer. Seville was half-way across the wide main road when he saw the sign above

164

the building on the corner opposite the hotel: *Police.* He pulled up sharply and was almost run down by a car; there was a shriek of brakes that was almost like the shout of someone pointing a finger at him. *There he is!* Panic flashed through him again, but he brought it swiftly under control. He continued, his hand now in his pocket clutching the gun.

Seville caught the boy's eye, jerked his head and kept walking up the hill of Argyle Street. He didn't look back to see if the boy was following him; he was looking covertly across at the police station. It was an old building, looked as if it might once have been a bank; it was discreet, as if the police did not want to frighten off the tourists. As far as he could see there were no faces at the windows, no guns showing. He kept walking, the crowd flowing up and down on either side of him like a moving protective wall.

He turned into a side street and a moment later the boy caught up with him. The boy, peering at him cautiously, said, 'Are you Mr Gideon? You look different –'

Seville said angrily, 'Are you trying to set me up? Why did you choose to meet me right opposite a police station?'

'I didn't know, but. Honest –' The boy's face was glistening with sweat; he was afraid, more than just nervous. 'I never been down here before – one of the other guys, he suggested it –'

Seville was watching the corner, waiting for the police SWOS men in their flak jackets and with their automatic weapons to come plunging round it. But all that came round it was a crocodile of very young children, twenty or thirty four-year-olds, all holding on to a rope and led by a pretty young girl who looked hot and harassed and obviously wishing she had chosen another day and a few more years to introduce the children to their heritage.

'You got the money?' said the boy and held out the canvas bag, plainly wanting to be rid of the rifle it contained.

'I have only five hundred dollars in cash. I'll have to give you the rest in traveller's cheques.'

The boy stopped, at a loss. 'Nah, nah. I dunno nothing about cheques. What's a traveller's cheque?' Why should he know? thought Seville. He has probably never travelled more than a hundred miles in his life. He was a city Aborigine, not a bush nomad and certainly not one who could afford traveller's cheques. 'Cash or nothing, mate, that was what I was told to ask for.'

'I don't have the cash! I can't get it for you right now –' Seville could feel his temper rising. He began to wonder what else could go wrong. He had always thought that Ireland or Italy was where Murphy's Law worked best, or worst: Australia seemed just as bad.

The long line of children was almost on them, the bright sunburned faces looking curiously at the two men arguing. They were a mixed bunch: freckled Anglo-Saxon faces, dark-eyed Mediterranean ones, two or three Orientals: only their voices were Australian, flat-vowelled and quick. Then the girl supervising them, looking back to make sure she had not lost any of her charges, suddenly stumbled and fell into Seville.

Instantly all the children yelled with glee. 'Watch the hole, Charleeeeeeen!'

It was obviously an old joke to them. They fell about with mirth, running round Charleen, Seville and the young boy, trapping them loosely with the long rope. Again Seville felt panic; he winced as the girl fell against the gun in his pocket, bumping it against his hip bone. He pushed her away, looked wildly at the children; he waited for their fathers and uncles, the SWOS men, to come round the corner. But nothing happened.

The girl straightened up, face red with embarrassment. She apologized to Seville and the young boy, got the young children once more into a semblance of a straight line. Clutching their rope, their umbilical cord, they went on up the street, still giggling and laughing, still chanting, 'Watch the hole, Charleeeeeeen!'

Seville mopped his face with a handkerchief. He and the boy were standing outside an old stone house: a plaque said it had been built in 1830. The sun bounced back from the pale beige stone, throwing glare and heat; they could have been standing outside a furnace. Seville suddenly wondered if the dye in his hair was starting to run; he could feel something trickling down his forehead and temples. He took out his handkerchief, wiped his temple; the handkerchief came away unstained. The boy was staring at him.

'What's the matter?'

'I didn't recognize you when you went past me back there. You don't look nothing like you did the other night. I recognized your walk, but.'

'My walk?'

'Yeah, you sorta roll. Like a sailor. It's a nice dye job, but. You trying to be an Abo?' The boy grinned; his fear was diminishing. 'Okay, what about the money?'

'Dallas was going to trust me. Why can't you?'

'Dallas is Dallas. I'm just me, just the messenger boy.' His modesty was genuine; there was no attempt to build himself up. 'Geez, I dunno, Mr Gideon. I don't wanna hang on to this –' He swung the bag forward. 'Even Dallas wanted to get rid of it soon's he could, he told us that.'

'Look –' Seville produced the money. Then he explained the procedure for cashing the traveller's cheques. 'I countersign them here and I'll make them out to Dallas Pinjarri. All he has to do is take them to American Express or any bank and they'll cash them for him.'

'Geez, I dunno . . .' He was out of his depth. 'You sure they're fair dinkum?'

Fair dinkum: more Aboriginal dialect? 'I don't know. What's that?'

'Okay. On the level.' Seville nodded and the boy hesitated a while longer. Then: 'Okay, sign 'em. But Christ help you if you're pulling a swifty. Dallas can be pretty bloody dangerous.'

'I'm sure he can,' said Seville and, using his brief-case as a desk, he signed five one-hundred-dollar cheques. He signed the name Gideon because he did not want to confuse the boy further.

He handed over the cash and the cheques and the boy gave him the canvas bag. He zipped it open and felt the cloth-wrapped dismantled rifle inside it; he also felt the two boxes of ammunition and the cloth-wrapped telescopic sight. People were passing them and he tried to look like a man checking he had brought his picnic lunch. He zipped up the bag and nodded.

167

'Thank Dallas for me. Tell him I shan't be seeing him again, but good luck with his cause.'

'His what?'

'Never mind.' It would be cruel to joke about Pinjarri's cause; he had never joked about other hopeless ambitions. He had read that some land had been given back to the Aborigines, but the whites' patience had grown thin, their sense of guilt not equalling their need for profits. 'Good luck to you, too. Don't lose the money or the cheques.'

He left him then, going up the side street through the increasing crowd which was now looking hot and already beginning to sound irritated. Mothers were snapping at their children, though the day was less than half over, and fathers could be heard complaining that they should have stayed home in the pool. 'Why'd we have to come today in this heat? It's all gunna be here for another coupla hundred years. If it ain't, it ain't worth coming all this way to see.'

Seville turned down towards Circular Quay, passed the ferry wharves and saw the sign: *Harbour Cruises*. He crossed to a man standing at a turnstile. 'Does the cruise go past Point Piper?'

'You live there, mate, or you wanna see how the other half lives?'

'I want to see how the other half lives.'

'Then this is your cruise, mate. We cater for the battlers of the world. It goes right past Point Piper and the silvertails. If you're lucky you might catch sight of President Timori and his missus. They've just moved in there.'

Seville bought a ticket and went aboard the big cruising ferry, going on up to the open upper deck and sitting by the rail with the canvas bag and his brief-case between his legs. He had taken the Smith and Wesson from his pocket and put it back in the brief-case. He sat there on the upper deck, complete with weapons, ready for the sight-seeing cruise and particularly the sight of the house where Abdul Timori was sheltering.

A family of five squeezed into the seats beside him. The father, an overweight man in his forties in sports shirt, shorts and long socks, glanced at Seville and grinned as he took off his straw hat and wiped his red face with an already soggy

168

handkerchief. 'Man wants his head read. I coulda stayed home, sunk some tinnies and had a good rest-up.'

It was all double-Dutch to Seville, but he nodded pleasantly in reply. Beyond the man his three children, all under twelve, were pestering their mother for money to buy ice-cream or lollies or Cokes. The mother, who might have been plumply pretty when she had started out in the early morning but now looked like a wet rag doll, resignedly took money from her handbag and waved the children away. 'You'll send me broke!'

'Kids!' said their father. He was one of life's battlers, someone who would never make it to Point Piper. 'I hope they bloody fall overboard!'

'You'd be the first to jump in after 'em,' said their mother.

'Only because Gloriette is wearing me best shirt.' He looked again at Seville, friendliness exuding out of every sweat-opened pore. 'You a visitor? Where you from?'

'France,' said Seville, fitting into Martin Dijon.

The man leaned towards him confidentially. 'I wouldn't broadcast that if I was you. The French ain't too popular with us. But welcome to Aussie, anyway.'

'Thank you,' said Seville, wondering if he would be any more popular if he'd said he was Argentinian. He pressed his heels harder against the bag between them.

The ferry eased away from the wharf, went out into the mainstream and passed the Opera House, an operatic extravaganza in itself; from the north he thought it looked like a school of giant sharks rising to swallow whatever sailed past it. He listened with only half an ear to the amplified descriptions of what could be seen. They sailed close to two of the tall ships and there were excited *oohs* and *ahs* and *Geez, look at that!* from the crowd on board the cruise ferry. Seville looked at the sailing ships, saw that one of them was a training ship from Argentina, one he had seen dozens of times on the River Plate; homesickness all at once hit him like a dizzy spell from the heat. He clutched at the rail.

'You all right?' said the man solicitously. He turned to one of the children who had come back, the eldest girl. 'Gloriette, go and get the gentleman a drink, a bitter lemon or something. Quick!'

'I'm all right,' said Seville. 'Really –'

'It's the heat. If you're not used to it . . . The wife's not, and she was born here. She gets the hot flushes . . .'

'Charlie!' His wife had a hot flush of embarrassment.

Gloriette came back with a bottle of bitter lemon and Seville took it and drank from it. He was surprised at how grateful he felt towards this family; he was not accustomed to ordinary emotions. He gave them all a smile and they all smiled back, welcoming him to Sydney.

The ferry sailed on, then the guide's voice said over the loudspeakers: 'And now we're approaching Point Piper. That big white house up there, that's where President Timori, from Palucca, is staying. It belongs to Mr Russell Hickbed, one of Australia's richest men. If you like to pass around the hat, we can buy it for seven or eight million . . .'

The man beside Seville took out a pair of binoculars and scanned the rich territory on the narrow point. 'Boy, would I like to live up there!'

'There isn't any Leagues club around here,' said the wife.

'I'd build me own.' He turned to Seville, offered him the glasses. 'Care to have a look? I suppose you got places like that along the Riviera?'

Seville took the glasses, focused them on the Hickbed mansion. His luck could not have been better: a small group was standing on the top terrace, the Timoris amongst them. Then he saw the woman, Madame Timori, walk away and go down to a lower terrace, followed by one of the men. He gave a small cough of surprise when he recognized Inspector Malone.

'See someone you know?' said the man beside him.

Seville smiled at him. 'I don't have that sort of friends.'

'Me, neither. The only silvertails I know, I read about in the papers. As for that guy Timori – who'd wanna be a friend of his?'

'I agree,' said Seville, and looked back at his intended target. Then he scanned the surrounding houses and blocks of apartments. At last he saw what he wanted. Then he looked back at Timori, now standing alone at the end of the top terrace, a perfect target at no more than three hundred metres. He would kill him tonight, from an even shorter distance.

He handed the glasses back to the man beside him. 'Perhaps I could buy you and your family lunch?'

'Thanks a lot, but nah. We brought it with us. Shirl, give the gentleman a sandwich. I got some tinnies in the esky. Be glad to have you join us.' He opened a portable ice-box and took out two cans of beer. 'Foster's, mate, best beer in the world. Or do you drink wine, being a Frenchman?'

'No, I drink beer.' But not often; he couldn't stand the awful stuff that was brewed in Damascus. 'Thank you, Mr –?'

'Charlie McGinn. Charlie will do.'

'Martin Dijon.'

'Well, here's to you, Marty.' He raised his beer can, then took a last look back at silvertail territory. 'That Timori, bastards like him, they're a blot on the bloody landscape. It's a pity that guy the other night missed him. There you are, chicken and salad. It ain't gourmet stuff, but I suppose even you French don't have that all the time.'

Seville took the sandwich and bit into it; it tasted good and filling. For the first time he was beginning to enjoy Australia and the Australians.

He looked back at Point Piper, at the big white mansion fading into the glare. The figure was still there at the end of the top terrace, but it was hazy, like a figure about to be washed out of a landscape.

2

'You heard about the bushfires,' said Clements as he and Malone walked towards Homicide's interrogation room. 'They're everybloodywhere. Terrey Hills, Heathcote, up the Blue Mountains. Poor buggers, they'll have nothing to celebrate tomorrow.'

Malone hadn't listened to any news all day; he hadn't wanted to hear any references to his shame this morning. No policeman likes being taken as a hostage; it is like being stripped naked in public. 'I'm sorry for them. But what do you think we've got to celebrate?'

171

'Nothing.' Clements bit his lip. 'Have you heard the cricket score?'

'Don't tell me.'

'We're a hundred and twenty for six. We're in dire straits.' He opened the door into the interrogation room.

Pinjarri was there with Jack Rimmer and a bearded young white man whom Malone recognized as Ray Cassell, from the Aboriginal Legal Service. In the past Malone had found him a pain in the neck: like all converts, he was more devout to the faith, more black than any black. He opened up with all guns at once.

'You've got no right bringing Dallas in here – he's done nothing – this is nothing more or less than racism –'

'What tribe are you from?' said Malone, then shook hands with Jack Rimmer. 'G'day, Jack. Nice of you to come. Hello, Dallas.'

Pinjarri just grunted, looked at Cassell to provide the ammunition. The lawyer obliged: 'I repeat, you have no right to bring him in –'

'Mr Cassell,' said Malone patiently, 'I'm trying to keep Dallas out of trouble, not pour it all over him. Ask Jack here. Dallas is getting himself into deeper crap than he's ever been in – he just doesn't know what's happening –'

'That's fucking right,' said Pinjarri. 'I don't fucking know what's fucking happening.'

Jack Rimmer said quietly in his gravelly voice, 'Tell us about it, Inspector.'

Malone was glad of the older man's presence; he knew he would have got nowhere if he had had to deal with the two younger men alone. 'This bloke Seville, the terrorist –'

'So called,' said Cassell.

'Okay, this *alleged* terrorist is trying to kill President Timori –'

'How do you know?' said Cassell. 'Or is this another alleged offence?'

Malone looked at Rimmer. 'Why don't you take him outside and point the bone at him, Jack?'

Rimmer grinned. 'Go on, Scobie. Shut up for a while, Ray.'

Malone continued: 'I spent twenty minutes with Seville this

morning, at gun point. He's going to kill Timori, make no mistake about it. He has a hand-piece, two in fact – mine's one of them,' he admitted, and could have torn Cassell's beard out by the roots when the latter smiled. 'We don't think he'll want to use those to kill Timori – he'll want to do it from a distance, with a high-powered rifle. We think Dallas has been trying to supply him with that rifle. If he has already done so, or if he does so when we let him go, he's going to go down the gurgler.' He looked straight at Pinjarri. 'You'll never get out of jail, Dallas. This is political. They'll throw the book at you.'

'You want to help him?' said Rimmer.

'I wouldn't be sitting here talking to him if I didn't.' Malone turned back to Pinjarri. 'Dallas, we know you had a gun to give him. He told me that this morning.' A little lying was part of the tools of his trade. Cassell, like a good lawyer, made a scoffing noise, but Malone took no notice of him. 'Tell us where the gun is and you're free. Otherwise . . .'

'Don't say anything, Dallas,' said Cassell. 'You're free as it is.'

Malone looked at Rimmer. 'What's your advice to him?'

Rimmer looked like a man who was resigned to his advice being ignored, especially by the young. Finally he said, 'I think you better tell him, Dallas. You go up before the beak again, you're gunna be a three-time loser. You'll cop the maximum.'

Pinjarri sat slumped in his chair, sullen as a young buffalo. He was picking at a fingernail, stopping every now and then to open and shut his hand, as if he were suffering from cramp. Malone recognized the nerves that were possessing the young Aborigine and he waited, knowing it was only a matter of time.

'Don't trust 'em,' said Cassell.

Clements looked ready to hit the young lawyer, but Malone glanced at him and shook his head. Cassell was unimportant. Pinjarri was going to make his own decision.

He shifted restlessly in his chair, then abruptly sat up. 'Okay, I'll talk if you don't take nothing down, okay?'

Malone nodded to Clements, who reluctantly put away his notebook. 'Go ahead, Dallas. Has he got the gun yet?'

'No. He come to me and offered me five thousand bucks to get him a rifle and a 'scope. I took it to him last night, but youse blokes turned up before I could give it to him – I mean, at Central. I ain't seen him since.'

'Where is it? At your place in Redfern?'

'It's in Redfern, but it ain't at my place. Someone is looking after it for me. You won't bust them, will you?'

'No. If we get the gun, nobody's going to be busted. What sort of gun is it?'

'A Sako .270.'

Malone looked at Clements, the gun expert. The latter said, 'It would do the job. The 'roo shooters use it a lot. If he could get within three hundred metres, Timori would be a dead 'roo.'

'Or a dead man. You ever been an accessory to a murder before, Dallas?'

'Christ, no! You told me there'd be no fucking bust –'

'There won't be. Righto, let's go and pick up the gun.'

'I'm coming, too,' said Cassell, but was no longer as belligerent.

'Sure,' said Malone. 'You got your own transport? We never give lawyers a lift in police vehicles. It's just a prejudice on our part.'

'What about me?' said Rimmer, grinning.

'Social workers are just as bad, Jack. But we'll make an exception for you.'

They went downstairs and got into the police car, with Clements behind the wheel, Rimmer beside him and Malone and Pinjarri in the back seat. They drove out of the cool of the garage into the furnace heat of the day and Clements switched on the air-conditioning. 'Do you Abos feel the heat?'

'All the time,' said Rimmer, grinning again. 'You guys never let up on us.'

Pinjarri suddenly laughed, a surprisingly healthy sound; then the two white men joined in. The good mood lasted till they turned into the narrow street in Redfern where Pinjarri directed them. The street was deserted, everyone having retreated from the heat, but as soon as the unmarked police car entered the street Aborigines appeared at the front doors of the shabby terrace houses.

'How do you know we're coming?' said Clements.

Rimmer tapped his nose. 'There's a certain smell. No offence.

It's like back home in the mulga where I come from. We could always smell the wild donkeys and the wild camels and the buffalo.'

'You mean we're just bloody wildlife down here?'

Rimmer grinned once more. 'No offence.' Then he noticed where they had pulled up. He looked back at Pinjarri, no longer grinning. 'Here? You left it with young Albert?'

'Not just with him,' said Pinjarri sheepishly.

'Jesus,' said Rimmer despairingly, looking out at the house, shabbier than the rest, its windows blocked with a sheet of galvanized iron, its front door black from fire. Whoever lives in there, thought Malone, is at the bottom of the heap.

A young boy stood in the open doorway staring out at the police car. His blunt-featured face was a mixture of fear and belligerence; it was difficult to know whether he was going to come out fighting or flee for his life. He peered into the car, saw Pinjarri and suddenly looked as if he might weep.

'Go easy with the lad, Scobie,' said Rimmer. 'This kid's been in trouble since he was nine years old. His old lady's a wino and Christ knows where his dadda is. I thought I had him straightened out –' He looked back at Pinjarri. 'I dunno why I bother with you, Dallas.'

Pinjarri said nothing. Then Malone got out of the car and motioned for the young Aborigine to follow him. As they did so, Cassell pulled in behind the police car in a shabby, gasping Toyota. He got out, but then stood irresolute in the middle of the pavement, saying nothing. By now a dozen Aborigines had congregated, muttering amongst themselves and one or two of them offering to support Pinjarri.

'Tell 'em there's no trouble,' said Malone. 'It's just business between you and me.'

Pinjarri passed the message on. Then, as if wanting to get everything over and done with, he abruptly pushed the boy Albert ahead of him and went into the house. Malone motioned to Clements and Rimmer to remain in the police car. After a moment's hesitation and a challenging look from Malone, Cassell decided to stay in the street.

The house stank, a mixture of smells that Malone didn't care to analyse. A woman's drunken voice shouted from upstairs,

175

but no one took any notice of her. Pinjarri led the way out to the kitchen at the rear; even he looked with disgust at the condition of it. Dirty pots and pans were in the sink, on the blackened stove, even on the floor; food was caked in them like mud. The remains of what looked like several meals were on the table, which was covered with stained and torn newspapers. Empty wine flagons were piled in a corner like discarded fishing lamps and a mangy mongrel dog was curled up in a filthy piece of sacking. The floor and the walls were dirty and grease-marked; the ceiling looked just as bad. There was a smell that made Malone, a fastidiously clean man, want to retch. Jesus Christ, he thought, Happy Australia Day! He wouldn't describe this place to Lisa tonight. This was a house of hopeless, busted lives and he knew there was nothing he or any other police officer could do about it.

'Where's the gun, Albert?' said Pinjarri. The boy just looked at him, as if bewildered by this invasion, and Pinjarri went on, 'It's okay, mate. Nothing's gunna happen. I'm handing over the gun to the Inspector here. Where is it?'

'Geez, Dallas –' The boy looked ready to run. He backed up against half a dozen banners, rolled tightly round their poles, standing against a wall. The calico of the banners looked new: Malone guessed they were to be used tomorrow in some demonstration. 'I didn't know – he rung up – we was at the other place, you know –'

There would be no phone in this house, Malone knew; he doubted if even the electricity was still connected. 'What other place?'

'No,' said Pinjarri, 'leave 'em out of it. Where's the gun, Albie?'

The boy gulped. 'I give it to him this morning. Geez, Dallas, I thought I was doing the right thing, you know? Here, here's the cash and the cheques –'

Pinjarri looked at Malone; he couldn't disguise the triumph in his dark eyes, but Malone chose to ignore it. Standing here in the midst of all this defeat and degradation, he couldn't bring himself to resent the Aborigine's exultation, silent as it was. Or perhaps, he thought with horror, I'm glad Seville has the means of getting rid of Timori. This case was upsetting all his

176

sense of values. Pretty soon they would smell like this house.

'How much did he pay you?' he said to the boy.

'A thousand bucks.' Albert held out the fifty-dollar notes and the traveller's cheques. His hand was shaking, as if so much money, more than he had ever held in his short life, was too much for it.

Malone looked at the signature on the cheques: M. Gideon. 'You sure it was him? A blond man with steel-rimmed glasses, a bit shorter than me?'

'That was how he looked the other night when I seen him, last Sat'day night. But he didn't look like that this morning.'

'How did he look?'

'He had dark-brown hair, about your colour.'

'A dye job or a wig?'

'I dunno. A dye job, I think.'

'How'd you recognize him?'

'I didn't, at first. It was only his walk – he walks like a sailor. You know, he rolls a bit.' He wobbled his shoulders up and down.

'Did he say anything to you? Where he was going, anything like that?' He didn't expect a professional like Seville would say a word about where he was going or what he intended to do, but the questions had to be asked. He had made mistakes in the past by not asking the obvious.

'Nah, nothing. He just give me the money, took the bag and buzzed off.'

Malone looked at Pinjarri. 'You said five thousand? When's he going to pay you the rest?'

'He said he'd send a bank draft.'

'Where from?'

'I dunno. I just trusted him – I had to. He said he didn't have the ready cash.'

That meant Seville could be running short of money. Malone handed the money and the cheques to Pinjarri, who looked at them in surprise.

'I don't think you'll ever get the bank draft, Dallas. We'll have him locked up before then.'

Pinjarri was looking at the money in the same way the boy had, as if he didn't believe it was real. But for a different reason. 'You mean we can keep this? You're not gunna confiscate it?'

177

'I never even saw it, Dallas. Just don't use it to blow up us honkies. Give it to Jack Rimmer and see if he can do something about things like this.' He looked around the kitchen. The money might never even get to Jack Rimmer, but that was a gamble Malone was taking. He already had Rimmer's goodwill; now he was trying to buy Pinjarri's. It was a bribe, just like the one Delvina had offered him; but he hoped it would do more good. The irony was that he was using a terrorist's money. 'Stay out of trouble, both of you.'

As he moved out of the kitchen he stopped by the rolled-up banners and unrolled one a few feet. Big letters said: GIVE US . . . He unrolled it no further. 'When's the demo?'

'Tomorrow,' said Pinjarri.

'Nobody will be paying any attention, not tomorrow. But good luck.'

He went down the hallway and out of the house. The mongrel, listlessly raising itself from its bed, barked after him; the whining wino's voice shouted an obscenity from upstairs. He stepped out into the street, glad of the hot dry air that scoured the smell of the house from his nostrils.

'You're not busting them?' said Cassell.

'I told you there wasn't going to be one. You should trust us coppers more.'

Rimmer got out of the police car as Malone opened the door. 'Everything all right?'

'Yes, Jack. Go in and see Dallas and that kid. Try and get the kid out of that house.'

'I told you, I been trying since he was nine years old. He won't leave it till his mumma drinks herself to death. You'll never understand us, Scobie.'

'You're wrong, Jack. I do understand. I just can't do a bloody thing about it. Hooroo.' He got into the car and slammed the door. 'Get me out of here, Russ, before I start swearing.'

3

To the north, west and south of the city the sky was brown with smoke. The bushfires had been raging all day and all thoughts of celebration had been burnt out in the fringe suburbs. The professional and the volunteer firefighters, who had been told to stand by in case the celebration fireworks got out of hand, were now fighting something fiercer and more horrifying. Almost every year they faced this hazard, a seasonal peril of a country where the bush could turn tinder-dry almost in a week; it had been so since time immemorial, long before the white man with his carelessness and the fire-bug with his insanity had come to this great brown continent. This year, like nature's protest at the anniversary of its rape, the fires were the worst in living memory.

Hans Vanderberg came into his office in the State Office Block sweat-stained, smoke-begrimed and angry. He went into his washroom, washed his face and, still wearing his creased and sweaty shirt, came back and slumped down in his chair behind his desk. He had clean shirts in a drawer in his washroom, but if he was photographed when he left the office he knew the value of looking like a Premier who had just been sharing the worst with his voters. Most of those living in the fire-ravaged areas, poor buggers, were Labour voters.

'I've just been out assessing the damage. Oh, my word, it's terrible.' Besides being Premier, he held the portfolios of Police and of Local Services. It was sometimes said that he secretly held all the other portfolios in the State Cabinet, since he usually announced every new project, no matter what the field, and all the respective ministers got was the blame when something went wrong. But he knew whom the voters would rather listen to. 'Bloody millions of dollars. It's a bugger of a fire that doesn't blow anyone any good.'

'True,' said Ladbroke, wondering if he would have to translate that for the media before the day was out.

'What's happening with the Timoris?' said The Dutchman, suddenly changing tack.

'They're still safe,' said John Leeds. 'But that fellow Seville is still loose.'

'That was bad, him kidnapping your bloke Malone. My word, yes.'

'Yes,' said Leeds, making a short word sound even shorter.

Vanderberg looked at Assistant Commissioner Zanuch. 'You

179

in charge now? Otherwise you wouldn't be here, right? What're you going to do?'

'I'm using every available man, Mr Premier. Unfortunately there are not that many available. They're all on special duty for the celebrations. All the senior men, superintendents and above, are on that.'

'We've got to protect the public. They dunno how to look after themselves – they expect us to do it for them. If something goes wrong and someone gets hurt, they're gunna complain we didn't have enough crowd control. It's the welfare state mentality.' Then he realized what he, a socialist Premier, had just said. 'Did I say that?'

'No,' said Ladbroke.

Vanderberg swung his chair right round in a circle, getting only a quick glance out of the window at his back. He was edgy this morning; not nervous, but quickened by crisis. He would never be overwhelmed by events, but he could not remember such a conjunction of events as had happened this weekend.

'We've got to get this feller Seville out in the open. How're we gunna do that?'

'If we bring him out in the open,' said Leeds, 'some of the public may get hurt.'

'That would depend where he came out,' said Zanuch, risking his Commissioner's wrath. He had never had a direct audience of the Premier and he wanted to impress. After all, when it came time for Leeds to retire, it would be the Premier, the Minister for Police, who would appoint his successor. 'If we chose the right place –'

'Such as?' said Leeds and put paid to that suggestion. 'We can't risk any bizarre scheme, Hans. We have to play it safe.'

'Bizarre? I was just going to suggest something bizarre. I have a pension for the bizarre, haven't I, Laddy?'

'You certainly have,' said Ladbroke with heartfelt conviction.

Encouraged (if he needed it), Vanderberg went on, 'I'm going to invite the Timoris to the Bicentennial Ball tonight. That should bring Seville out into the open.'

'Yes,' said Zanuch. 'That would give us ideal access to him. Tactics-wise –'

180

Leeds was aghast, but managed to look calm. 'I couldn't promise to protect the public. Some of this State's most prominent citizens, including you and me, Hans, might get in the way of the shooting.'

'I wouldn't be within a bull's roar of them. If the voters saw me sitting with them, they'd never vote for me again. No, they can sit at a table near the PM. Or with him.'

'But you'd be their host, if you invited them. You'd at least have to greet them when they arrived. You're the host anyway tonight – it's not a Federal do.'

'John, the easiest thing in the world in politics is to shove your responsibilities on to someone else. What d'you think I've got a Deputy Premier for?'

Deputy Premiers were expendable, by a bullet or any other means. 'I'm still against the idea, Hans. How do you think all the guests at the ball are going to enjoy themselves if they see a couple of dozen police officers stationed around the ballroom with their guns bulging out of their dinner jackets? We'll need the Tactical Response squad and the SWOS men. They'll be wearing flak jackets with bow ties.'

Even The Dutchman had to grin at the picture. 'All right, all right, it's too dangerous. But I was looking forward to it. I've got this General Paturi coming. Him and the Timoris together – that'd be quite something. Like putting a mongoose and a couple of rats in the one bag.' He dreamed for a moment, which even the most pragmatic of politicians sometimes do. Then he came back to the practical: 'All right, no Timoris at the ball. So how do you catch this feller Seville?'

'Just dogged foot-slogging,' said Leeds, 'and luck.'

'Just like politics,' said Zanuch and got a glare from Vanderberg that set his promotion back about three places.

The Premier then dismissed them just by saying, 'Well, g'day,' and getting up and going into his washroom. Ladbroke escorted the two police officers out of the room, whispering apologies for his boss's abruptness. Then he went back in and waited till Vanderberg came out of the washroom zipping up his fly.

'Do you think Gorbachev has trouble with his coppers like I have with mine?'

'Probably not,' said Ladbroke, but didn't explain the reasons why he thought so. 'What sort of release do you want me to put out on the bushfires?'

'Make it compassionate. Say we'll appropriate so much money to a disaster fund, but don't say any figures. I dunno how much these bloody celebrations are going to cost us.'

Ladbroke jotted down a note: *A substantial appropriation.* Political appropriations were like twenty-first birthday presents: most of them were forgotten after the thank-yous were said. 'What about Paturi? Do we send a car for him?'

'We'd better. Put him at my table – find out if he's bringing a woman with him. If he's not, ring up Mrs –' He named a well-known society matron who was equally well-known as a free-loader.

'She's already on someone else's list.'

'All right, let him come on his own. How's the dirt-digging going on the Timoris?'

'Inspector Malone had a session this morning with Tidey and Quirke, their banker and lawyer. And Timori's private secretary, that Chinese guy, Sun Lee.'

Vanderberg grinned appreciatively. 'How do you find out these things?'

Ladbroke grinned in reply. 'I do favours for people, they do favours for me.'

'You oughta go into politics. How'd you like my job?'

'I have my eye on it. Say in about ten years' time.'

Vanderberg nodded, knowing he was safe. 'Get me that feller Malone. But tell him I don't want his boss to know. I think it's about time we started running this case ourselves. It's too good to leave in the hands of the police.'

4

'I was looking forward to dinner at Eliza's,' said Claire, the connoisseur of expensive restaurants.

'I told you, darling,' said her mother, 'Eliza's was booked out. I mentioned your father's name, but they weren't impressed.'

'That's because they didn't see him on TV,' said Maureen,

the ratings guide. 'They should of been looking. We'd of got a special table. With a spotlight, prob'ly.'

'I couldn't see you,' said Tom. 'You were in that white car all the time.'

'The best place,' said Malone. 'I don't like the spotlight. Now what do you want? A cheeseburger or a Double Mac?'

'Both,' said Tom. 'What's for dessert?'

'Oh God,' said Claire, 'just as well we didn't take him to Eliza's. He's a real pig.'

'No, Daddy's a pig,' said Maureen. 'That's what they call a policeman on TV.'

'With kids like you, who needs crims?' Then Malone looked at Lisa, cool and beautiful on a night when every other mother in this McDonald's looked as if she had just come straight out of the kitchen. In these wrong circumstances, he suddenly longed to take her away somewhere for a second honeymoon. 'I'm sorry, I wish we could have got into Eliza's. Did you try anywhere else? Pegrums'? Prunier's?'

She smiled, knowing his credit card would have gone limp if he had taken them all to Prunier's. 'Everywhere. They're all booked out – even TV stars like you can't get in. I doubt very much if Sonny Crockett could get a table. I don't mind.' She looked around the big crowded restaurant. 'I've always liked McDonald's. It's sort of – of –'

'Lower class,' said Claire, who had just been introduced by her mother to Jane Austen.

'Shut up and enjoy yourself,' said Malone; but he couldn't blame his elder daughter for being disappointed. He had promised them all a superior evening; instead he had brought them to this McDonald's where they ate every Thursday night after they had done the week's grocery shopping. He hated letting them down and he knew it happened too often. He looked across at Lisa, and said, 'I'll take my holidays when this is over and you can plan what you like for every day.'

She smiled a policeman's wife's smile: that is, it was cynically sceptical, like a defence lawyer's. 'A promise?'

'A promise. Now what does everyone want?'

He went up to the counter, taking Maureen with him, and they came back with two loaded trays. He and Lisa had finished their hamburgers and were sucking on their thick shakes when Lisa put her hand across the table and took his.

'I love you,' she said.

'Erk!' said Tom, but the two girls looked on with shy pleasure.

'I don't know why,' said Malone.

'Because you're *decent*.'

'Yes,' said Claire. 'That's what you are. Decent. You're a pain in the neck when you're bad-tempered, but you're nice and decent.'

'What's decent?' mumbled Tom, mouth full of ice-cream.

'Whatever Daddy is, is decent,' said Lisa. 'And don't any of you forget it.'

'What's Mummy?' said Maureen, suddenly a defender of equal rights.

Malone looked at his wife. 'Lovely. That's all – lovely.'

She gave him a smile that turned his heart over. Then one of the McDonald's boys, who knew them as regulars, came to the table. 'Mr Malone, you're wanted on the phone.'

Lisa's face clouded. 'You didn't tell me you'd given them this number.'

'I had to, darl. I'm on this Seville case round the clock, you know that.'

'Just as well we didn't go to Eliza's – I'd have been stuck with the bill.'

He had let them, and particularly her, down again. The food in his stomach suddenly seemed to turn sour. He got up and went behind the counter and picked up the phone. Clements was on the line.

'Sorry, Scobie. But Zanuch has called us all in. Get into your monkey suit – we're all going to the Bicentennial Ball.'

'What the hell for?'

'Christ knows. General Paturi, this guy from Palucca, is going to be there with The Dutchman. Zanuch evidently thinks Seville might try to gate-crash, looking for the Timoris.'

'Are they going to be there?'

'Not as far as I know. But I've given up guessing on this case. Oh, another thing. Joe Nagler called. He's got that information from ASIO. They'd been tapping Kirribilli House while the Timoris were there. There were two calls to Beirut. Joe has got copies of the tapes, but it's all under the lap. Officially they don't exist.'

'What time are we expected at the ball?'

'Nine o'clock. Oh, don't bring Lisa. Zanuch said no women. We're supposed to dance with each other.'

He laughed; but Malone couldn't. He said miserably, 'Okay, I'll be there. But Lisa and the kids are going to boil me in oil.'

'I know,' said Clements sympathetically. 'It's times like these when I'm glad I'm not married. The rest of the time I envy you.' He hung up abruptly, as if embarrassed by his sentiment.

Malone went back to their table and explained the situation.

'You're going to the Bicentennial Ball without me?' said Lisa. 'The biggest function in two hundred years and you're taking Russ Clements, not me? Did we say he was decent, kids?'

'He's not any more,' said Claire.

'Is it going to be on TV?' said Maureen.

'Can I have another ice-cream?' said Tom.

Malone looked mournfully across at Lisa. 'I wish I could take you. But –'

'But what?'

He shook his head and Claire said, 'He doesn't want to tell you in front of the children. He's going with another woman. A police lady, I expect.'

'Is that so?' said Lisa.

'I told you, I'm going with Russ Clements. He's a good sort, but we don't hold hands.'

Then Lisa, whose immediate disappointment had slowed her reflexes, caught on. She reached across and put her hand on his. 'It can't be helped. But be careful, darling. Be careful.'

'Is he decent again?' said Tom.

'Yes.'

Why do I love them all so much? He knew, however, that it was a stupid question.

SEVEN

1

The Bicentennial Ball was being held in the Exhibition Centre in the middle of the Darling Harbour complex, a monument of festival gardens, tourist markets and various halls that Hans Vanderberg had built for himself. His name was on various foundation stones, like that of a graffiti artist given his head. The Exhibition Centre was a huge hall, more than two football fields long, and was ideal for the occasion, the biggest social event ever held in the State. Several of the biggest hotels had lobbied for the function, but their ballrooms, like tight jeans, were not large enough.

The tickets were fifty dollars a head and they had been distributed evenly across the social scale; a small percentage had been set aside as free, so that the very bottom of the scale could be represented. Dress ranged from white tie and tails and ball-gowns to T-shirts and jeans; nobody was excluded because they couldn't afford to dress up. Four bands had been engaged and the music ranged from hard rock through country and western to schmaltz waltz. The only time the music was common was when the four bands simultaneously played 'Advance Australia Fair'. A forgetful cornetist in the old-time band then went into the first bars of 'God Save the Queen', but found he was playing solo and only those at the Returned Servicemen's table were standing to attention. He gurgled away into silence. Four thousand dinki-di Aussies weren't going to waste their night celebrating their ties to Britain, especially those natives with names like Castellari, Stefanopoulos, Pilsudski, Jagonovich and Van Trung.

Bunting covered the upper reaches of the huge hall; flags hung like green-and-gold guillotines above the heads of the dancers. Five thousand bottles of wine and champagne were on hand, five hundred gallons of beer, seven tons of food: another miracle of loaves and fishes would not be needed tonight, as the Cardinal, an honoured guest, remarked to his host. Five hundred waiters and waitresses and twenty-five *maîtres d'* whizzed amongst the tables, doing their best to look happy in what they were doing and, for the most part, failing miserably. There would be no tips tonight.

Philip and Anita Norval arrived to a fanfare from one of the bands; the other three, being unionists intent on their work practices, had chosen that moment to knock off for a smoke-o. There was not a better-looking pair in the whole huge hall than the PM and his wife; he handsome in white tie and tails, she beautiful in a green and gold gown by Mel Clifford, one of the nation's top designers. They walked from one end of the vast indoor field to the other, acknowledging the applause; the Prime Minister, heady with the occasion, turned to retrace his steps, but Anita, already footsore, grabbed his arm and guided him to their table. A Labour voter from the western suburbs remarked that if Anita had not been with the PM, he would have worn his jogging shoes and done a dozen laps. A few boos were heard, but Norval had a politician's ear, selectively deaf.

The host for the night, Hans Vanderberg, was already at his table with his wife, a homely soul famous for her pavlova cakes, her pot plants and her potted wisdom. She had once remarked that egalitarianism only worked when it had an elite to run it, an opinion that had brought a demand that she be expelled from the Labour Party. She had sent the man a kiwi fruit pavlova, a pot plant and a note saying she had never belonged to the Party; he had withdrawn the motion. The Dutchman was in black tie and a dinner jacket, aware that in mixed political company one could take dressing up too far. Gertrude, his wife, was in plain pink, not a designer's gown but something run up by her local dressmaker and looking none the less attractive for that. She had never been beautiful and she had the sense to accept the advice her mirror gave her and not try for the unattainable.

It was still too early in the evening for any mixing of the classes. The silvertails stayed at their tables or danced with each other; the poorer voters did the same. Occasionally one couple would bump into another on one of the dance floors and there would be an exchange of smiles such as one might get across the Russian–Chinese border. Relations would warm up as the night went on, but for the moment everyone seemed afraid of being rebuffed. The Stefanopouloses and the Gore-Hills hadn't yet run up the Southern Cross and saluted it together.

General Paturi had arrived in full dress uniform and looked out of place, as if he had been bound for a fancy dress ball and had got off at the wrong hall. He was sitting at the Premier's table, lost and embarrassed; he had nothing in common with either The Dutchman or his wife. He had brought no female partner with him; he could not dance, so he did not ask Mrs Vanderberg if she would like to go out on the floor. The music deafened him and the dancing looked obscene and insane. So he sat at the table and nodded while Mrs Vanderberg tried to explain, across him, the method of making a pavlova cake to the wife of the Minister for Water Resources. When the Norvals arrived and made their progress up the middle of the hall he stood up and saluted.

'Sit down, General!' snapped Vanderberg, horrified at such homage to the enemy.

Paturi slumped back in his seat. 'You don't salute your leader?'

'Only when we're burying him. Did you salute President Timori every time he appeared?'

'Of course. He insisted on it. Or rather, Madame Timori did.'

The American ambassador passed by, avoiding Paturi's eye. The Dutchman, grinning maliciously, called out an invitation to join them, but the ambassador was too quick. Diplomacy is as much acts of omission as of commission.

'Did you get to the Prime Minister today?' Vanderberg said to Paturi. 'What did you talk about?'

Paturi was not altogether a fool in politics. 'I think you must ask him, Mr Premier.'

'No politics tonight,' said Gertrude, turning away from the subject of pavlovas. It was a night for enjoyment, for gossip, one of the best enjoyments: 'What is Madame Timori like?'

'Evil,' said General Paturi, who had no small talk and so tended to turn conversations into large silences.

'Oh no,' said Mrs Water Resources, a feminist and not to be silenced. 'Women are always less evil than men. Isn't that so, Gert?'

'Of course,' said Gertrude Vanderberg and looked at her husband for corroboration and as proof. She had no illusions about him. She loved him, but sometimes it was a strain.

'Speak of the she-devil,' said the Premier and couldn't believe his luck.

There had been a break in the music and the dance floors had begun to clear. Slowly at first and now all at once quickly, as if all the dancers had decided the spotlight should not be shared, least of all by them. They paused on the edge of the dance floors and all heads turned in the same direction.

Delvina Timori had entered on the arm of Russell Hickbed. She was dressed in a shimmering gold gown that clung to her body so that she looked as if she had been sprayed with gold-leaf, like one of the statues in the palace in Bunda. She wore a single large emerald, bigger than anything anyone in the hall had ever seen, on a heavy gold chain round her neck. Her dark hair was adorned with a thin gold tiara. On her wrist was a thick gold bracelet set with emeralds and the one ring she wore was also set with an emerald. She had been careful to show restraint.

'Green and gold,' said Gertrude. 'Is she turning out for the Olympics? Where are you going, sweetheart?'

'I can't miss this,' said her husband, moving out of his blocks like an Olympic sprinter. 'I'm going to introduce her to Phil Norval.'

'Wait till she comes up against Anita,' said Mrs Water Resources. 'She's going to make Anita's little green-and-gold number look like last year's gym suit.'

Hickbed, aware of the sensation they were causing and unexpectedly revelling in it, marched up the middle of the hall with Delvina gliding along beside him. There was no applause, no booing, nothing but silence from four thousand guests; it is a phenomenon of science that silence is magnified by the number who create it. Hickbed had stood in the deserts of central Australia at night during an inspection of one of his mineral holdings; the silence then had been a thunderstorm compared to this. It was difficult to tell whether the utter quiet was hostile, appreciative, curious or just plain amazed at something so totally unexpected. Perhaps it was just a silent cheer for a local girl who had made good, in a bad way. The cutting down of her as a tall poppy, a national sport, would come later in the night.

There were two vacant places at the Prime Minister's table. They had been reserved for Hickbed and one of his current mistresses. The lady in question had been unceremoniously dumped for the evening and was now in bed in Double Bay with a migraine that would get worse when she tried to explain why a substitute had been called in for tonight's game. It would do nothing for her reputation that she had been supplanted by Madame Timori, a higher-priced whore.

Vanderberg caught up with Hickbed and Delvina when they were still some distance from the Norvals' table. 'Madame Timori, welcome to our ball. I'm Hans Vanderberg, the host for tonight. G'day, Russell.'

'Hello, Hans,' said Russell Hickbed, willing to be friends with anyone tonight. 'I thought Madame Timori would like to join in our little celebration. After all, she is half-Australian.'

'I'd like to think of myself as all-Australian this evening,' said Delvina, making herself sound like a football fullback. She smiled at Vanderberg and he smiled back, not taken in.

'Where is the President?' he said.

'Matters of state,' said Delvina, and The Dutchman, still in power, wondered what matters of state could occupy a man so out of power as Timori.

'We also thought it would be asking for trouble,' said Hickbed, who sometimes could not help telling the truth. 'That guy Seville is still on the loose.'

'He might even be here,' said Vanderberg and looked around with an ugly grimace of hope. 'Well, let me escort you to your table.'

'Do you need to do that?' said Delvina, who had decided she did not like The Dutchman. 'Isn't it beneath your dignity as Premier?'

190

Vanderberg took no notice of the insult. 'Dignity never won any votes, not here in Australia. You'd have learned that if you'd had honest elections back in Palucca. Ah, here we are. Phil, Anita – here are your guests. Everybody smile!'

Photographers had appeared like mosquitoes around a swamp. Lights flashed and so did teeth; the smiles in tomorrow's papers would look like a tossed box of cutlery. Vanderberg shook hands with everyone and then paused in front of Norval.

'Get 'em out of Sydney as soon's you can, Phil,' he said quietly and threateningly, but smiling as he said it, aware of the photographer behind them. Next day the caption under the photograph would read: *The Prime Minister and the Premier exchange a joke at last night's ball.* 'You're over-working my police force.'

'Too bad, Hans,' said Norval, more than matching Vanderberg's smile. 'You shouldn't have made Sydney the best city in Australia. Isn't that what you claim?'

'If Timori finishes up as a corpse, it won't do you any good, whether he's in Sydney or Oodnadatta. Get him out. Get your friend in Washington to take him.'

'I'm doing my best,' said Norval, suddenly backing down.

'Do better,' said The Dutchman. 'And don't sit too close to the whore. That assassin may be gunning for her, too.'

He smiled at everyone at the table, then went back down the long hall, walking alone down the wide space of the empty dance floors, king for the night.

2

Malone and Clements, both in dinner jackets, had met at Homicide where Clements produced copies of the ASIO tapes. 'These are strictly unofficial, Scobie. We can't use them for anything, not as evidence, nothing like that.'

'Two calls to Beirut? Were they ISD calls?'

'Yes, but all calls out of Kirribilli House are monitored, anyway, through a central switchboard. They're not taped, just a record kept of where the calls are to.'

191

'Did you get the numbers?'

'The same number each time. Beirut 232-3344.'

'Righto, let's have a listen.'

Malone at once recognized the voice at the Australian end. 'That's Sun Lee!'

The tapes were clear, though at times the voice in Beirut faded a little:

Sun: 'Mr Zaid, we spoke the other day about a certain matter in Palucca.'

Zaid: 'Ah yes, sir. I gather from the news that the target is no longer in Palucca.'

Sun: 'No, he is here in Sydney. Can you get in touch with your client?'

Zaid: 'I'm afraid not. I don't know where he is.'

The rest of the first tape was inconsequential, although Sun sounded as if he were upset. The second tape, like the first, was short, as if Sun were trying to sneak the call in without being overheard:

Sun: 'Mr Zaid, I am calling again from Sydney.'

Zaid: 'Good evening, sir. Has my client turned up in Sydney?'

Sun: 'Yes. He has made a terrible mistake. He killed the wrong man.' There was silence for a moment. 'Mr Zaid? Are you there?'

Zaid: 'I am here. That's most unfortunate. It is not like my client – he is usually so reliable. Are you sure it is him?'

Sun: 'The police have identified him, though they have no proof.'

Zaid: 'What do you want me to do?'

Sun: 'Is he likely to be contacting you?'

Zaid: 'It is very unlikely. I am just his agent, not his control. What did you want me to tell him?'

Sun: 'I shall call you again.'

The second tape ended abruptly there. Clements said, 'Sun hung up. ASIO thinks he was interrupted by someone. I'm a bit surprised he made the calls from Kirribilli House.'

'I've got the feeling he doesn't think much of us out here, that we're just a mob of innocents. Maybe he thinks we don't know how to tap a phone. The Chinese are a superior lot of bastards.'

'I've noticed that, even in Chinese restaurants. When the waiters take my order I feel I'm in a dole queue.'

Having worked off their dislike of Chinese superiority, Malone turned to the Australian security service, another superior lot. 'Do ASIO want these tapes back?'

Clements nodded. 'Joe Nagler promised them back. You want me to do the dirty and copy them?'

'Better not. That might mean having to hand them over to Zanuch. The less he can interfere, the better.' It was no way to talk about an Assistant Commissioner to a junior officer, but he knew that he and Russ Clements had the same opinion of Zanuch and he knew, too, that Clements could keep his mouth shut.

'What will ASIO do with them?'

'Probably sit on them. If these tapes are unofficial, that means the PM would hit the roof if he knew one of his phones had been tapped. He wouldn't want the civil liberties people laughing at him. They're dead against phone taps of any sort and they'd make a great propaganda joke out of it if it ever came out that the PM's guests were being listened to.'

'I guess so.' Clements bounced the tapes in his hand, wishing he could drop them into his murder box; then reluctantly he put them away in his desk and locked the drawer. 'There's one other thing, Scobie –'

Malone noticed his hesitancy. 'Yes?'

'They found that blue Honda that Seville pinched. Out in Randwick, about half a dozen streets away from your place.'

Malone felt a tightening of his nerves. 'Any sight of him?'

'None. We checked the neighbours – no one saw him. Scobie, just in case –' Again he hesitated. 'I asked the boys out at Randwick to keep an eye on your place. They're going to drop by there every half hour or so.'

'They're not going to drop in on Lisa? I don't want her scared stiff.'

'No, they'll just cruise by, keep an eye skinned. If Seville's watching your place, maybe it'll scare him off. I didn't know whether to tell you . . .'

Malone put a hand on Clements' arm. He was not given to affectionate gestures; he belonged to the old school of men who didn't throw their arms round each other. In that he was like his father: Con had been heard to remark that he was glad his son had retired from cricket before all the kissing and hugging poofters had invaded the game. But Malone was not afraid of sentiment and emotion.

'Thanks, Russ. If anything happened to her and the kids . . .'

'I know how you feel,' said Clements, the bachelor.

Before they left Homicide, Malone rang Lisa at home. He felt weak with relief when her calm, confident voice came on the wire. He sat down heavily in his chair. 'I – I just wanted to say I'm sorry I spoiled the evening.'

'Sometimes I could kill you,' she said. 'Or anyway the Police Department. But you're forgiven. What about tomorrow?'

'What about it?' He was losing track of the days.

'Scobie –' She usually called him *darling* or *sweetheart:* when she called him by name she was annoyed. 'You promised to take us all out on a tug. Have you forgotten that?'

He had not forgotten; at least not till the last hour or so. It had been at the back of his mind for the past three days. He had arranged weeks ago with a tug-boat captain, for whom he had done some legitimate favours, for Lisa and the children to accompany the captain's own family and friends out on the harbour to see the sail-past of the tall ships. With the enthusiasm that fathers feel for what they think their children should enjoy, he had hoped it would be the highlight of the year for them, something they would remember all their lives.

'It's all fixed,' he said, hoping the tug wouldn't sink at its berth overnight; it would run true to his current luck if it did. 'We have to be down at the wharf at nine o'clock.'

'You too?'

'Of course,' he said and tried to sound confident. 'I should be home by midnight at the latest. Keep the bed warm.'

'In this heat? I hope you break a leg while you're dancing with Russ Clements.' Then she said, 'I still love you.'

'What was that noise in the background?'

'It was Tom saying Erk! Enjoy the ball, darling. Give my love to Mr Zanuch, the bastard.'

'I hope your son didn't hear you say that. I love you, too.'

'Did I hear a noise in the background?'

194

'It was Russ saying Erk!' He hung up and grinned at Clements. The latter grinned back, saying nothing but saying a lot. Some day he would do something about the occasional loneliness he felt.

Malone was quiet on the way to the Exhibition Centre. It might be just sheer chance that Seville had dumped the stolen car in Randwick, nonetheless he was worried. He had always managed to keep his family life separate from his police work; despite the number of criminals he had brought to justice, none of them had ever threatened his family. If Seville was not caught within the next twelve hours, he would move Lisa and the children to her parents' home. They were not going to become part of the stakes in this case.

A special section had been set apart in the parking area for police cars; Malone was surprised at the number there. Zanuch, as usual, had over-reacted.

'Well, we're among the usual company,' said Clements. 'Look who's here.'

Malone looked at the two groups of guests going in ahead of them. One of them was led by the biggest criminal in Sydney, a man as notorious for never having gone to jail as for the crimes that should have sent him there; he was a worthy descendant of the more evil convicts who had helped found the colony and therefore deserved to be here to celebrate. The second group was led by the city's most famous madam, giving her girls a night off their backs and a glimpse of their clients with their wives. All the city's minority groups had been catered for and made welcome.

Assistant Commissioner Zanuch, handsome as a male model in his expensive dinner suit, was waiting for them in the foyer. He seemed surprised that his two junior officers looked as good as they did. Even the beefy, usually rumpled Clements appeared to have been slimmed down and run over by a steam-iron.

'No one would ever know . . .'

'That we're coppers, sir?' said Malone. 'The shoulder holster makes my jacket a bit tight. My gun would have stuck out more if I'd worn it on my hip.'

'You won't be doing any dancing, so no one will notice.'

'Why are we here?'

'General Paturi is here, at the Premier's table.' Zanuch turned away for a moment to acknowledge greetings from two politicians and their wives; as he turned back he then nodded his head and flashed a smile at three businessmen and their womenfolk. He knows everyone, thought Malone: he was his own PR department, his eye always on the right connection, the main chance. 'I've put him down as one of the chief suspects.'

It took Malone a moment to follow his chief's thinking. Then he caught on. 'You think he could be the one employing Seville?'

'Of course. It's too much of a coincidence that he arrives here just after the assassination attempt fails. He and his fellow generals have the most to gain with the death of Timori. He's the logical suspect. What are *they* doing here?'

A group of homosexuals had just come in. They looked no different from any of the other men, except for a superfluity of thick moustaches and short-cropped hair; they might have been a team of footballers having a stag night out, except that some of them were holding hands, something footballers might do on the field but never off it.

'Sydney's the gay capital of the country,' said Clements, who had been a poofter-basher in his youth but now was tolerant of them. 'The ball committee said everyone had to be represented.'

'Disgusting,' said Zanuch. 'They should all be locked up. Is he smiling at you, Malone?'

One of the men, recognizing Malone, had smiled and waved a greeting. 'Yes, sir. He's one of ours, on the Vice Squad. Are we expected to tail General Paturi?'

Zanuch glared at Malone, as if he suspected the latter was pulling his leg; but he decided to risk his leg no further. 'Yes, keep an eye on him. And Seville himself might turn up here. They have to make contact again some time, one assumes.'

Malone held his tongue. He and Clements, it seemed, had been called in on a job that any junior detective constable could have done. Zanuch noticed his silence.

'Something wrong, Inspector?'

But then a party of eight came into the foyer, all fluting vowels, too-wide smiles and three-thousand-dollar gowns, making their own loud entrance into the third century of the country. Malone recognized the women if not the men: they were the queen bees of the charity balls. But tonight's affair was not a charity ball and The Dutchman, with his malice towards those who would never vote for him, had seen to it that they had all been placed at the one table. The queen bees were sharing the one hive tonight and they were buzzing loudly to show everyone that they did not care. Zanuch left Malone and Clements, went across to the group and bowed low over the hands of the women.

Clements looked at Malone in disgust. 'Thank Christ I'm not ambitious!'

'Let's go inside before he gets our backs up any further.'

They went into the crowded auditorium, keeping to the walls, not sure what they were supposed to be looking for, even less sure what they would do if they found it. Surely Seville wouldn't come here? Malone thought. Then he saw Delvina Timori sitting at the table at the far end of the room.

Delvina was having her best evening since arriving back in Australia. She delighted in other people's discomfort; her malice, unlike Vanderberg's, was almost juvenile. A good many of the people here at the ball, including those at this table, would not have entertained her back in the old days of the dance company. Besides *la crème* of the natives, there were foreign dignitaries at the neighbouring tables: ambassadors, foreign ministers, even an African chief who had been invited on the mistaken assumption that he still amounted to something in his own country. There were no Heads of State. So that Delvina, who had studied protocol as other women study diet charts, knew that she out-ranked them all. As the wife of a President, an ex-President maybe but one still recognized, if only because of slackness or indifference, by most governments, she knew who belonged to the common herd and who did not.

Anita Norval was one of those who belonged, though no one had ever thought of her as common. Delvina leaned towards her, her smile like a knife in honey. 'You'll never have a bigger night, will you, Anita?'

Anita was equal to the jibe. 'I suppose it's bigger than your last night in the palace in Bunda. What's it like when the bailiffs move in? Especially with tanks?'

Everyone at the table leaned forward as if grace were being said; ears stood out like satellite dishes. They all despised Delvina, but they would have fought, with tanks if necessary, if anyone had suggested they should move from this table.

Delvina did not disappoint them. 'Unless you've lived dangerously, Anita, I couldn't describe it to you. But you've always played it safe, haven't you? Both of you.' She smiled at Philip Norval across the table. 'I suppose one has to when one has to pander to the voters. We never had to do that in Palucca.'

All the voters around the table looked at the chief panderer. Norval, for the second time that day, wished someone dead; but he knew it would take more than a steely glare to kill Delvina. There had been times when he could not resist jumping into her bed. She had taught him that the *Kama Sutra*, which he had read as a schoolboy, was actually only a nursery primer; he had learned things from her that were never mentioned on quiz shows. Then he had become conscience-stricken, a condition that goes with loss of potency; he had always loved Anita and still did, and he had been relieved when Delvina had moved on to foreign fields and foreign beds. But the allure of her still remained, like a musky scent that no amount of Persil can wash out of old sheets. And he knew that Anita knew it. Women have a nose for such things.

He was saved from replying by Russell Hickbed, who decided the baiting had gone far enough. He had protested at first when Delvina had suggested he should bring her to the ball; then, though he had little or no humour in him, he had seen the chance of some comedy. And of sensation, a ploy to which he was no stranger. Delvina had that effect on men: she raised them above themselves, though not in moral terms.

Hickbed said, 'President Timori sent his respects to you, Anita. He is a great admirer of yours.'

'Really?' said Anita, who had never spoken to the ex-President. 'Philip has never told me so.'

'I must have forgotten,' said the Prime Minister, who couldn't remember having an unhappier night; this was worse than the

198

night he had beaten Neil Kissing by only one vote for the Party's leadership. A waitress put something down in front of him and he looked at it. 'What's this?'

'Pumpkin pavlova, sir,' said the waitress. 'The Premier's wife, Mrs Vanderberg, made it specially for you.'

Norval looked down the long hall. In the far distance Gertrude Vanderberg was fluttering her fingers at him, smiling brightly and nodding. He knew there was no spite in the old duck; in fact, on the rare occasions that they had met he had liked her. He bit into the pumpkin pavlova, was surprised that he liked it and waved a hand in acknowledgement to Gertrude.

'Any taste of arsenic?' whispered Anita.

'Not that I've noticed.'

'Pity,' she said.

Delvina had been looking around the auditorium, basking in the unabashed stares of the thousands as if it were the sun in her private garden in the palace in Bunda. If the more radical of the guests were hating her, it was water off a swan's back; she just arched her neck and looked more regal, or what she thought was regal.

'Let's dance, Russell.'

He shook his head. 'I can't dance. I'm not going to make a fool of myself out there on the floor. Ask Phil – he thinks he's Fred Astaire.'

She was tempted to ask Norval to take her out on the floor, but Anita had overheard Hickbed's suggestion and was already rising to grab her husband. Then Delvina saw Inspector Malone standing against a decorated pillar, looking manly and almost handsome, certainly better than he had looked this morning.

The band on this particular dance floor had just struck up a modern waltz; they were under instructions to cater to everyone up to their eighties, since several senior citizens were on the invitation list. Malone saw Delvina raise a hand and crook a finger at him. He was about to turn away and ignore the summons when Zanuch appeared beside him.

'Is that for you or me, Inspector? I've never met the lady.'

He sounded as if he were ready to crawl on hands and knees across the floor to the lady, and Malone encouraged him. 'I think she means you, sir.'

Zanuch put a finger to his chest, but Delvina shook her head and pointed to Malone. The Assistant Commissioner, the bruise to his ego already turning blue, looked at his junior officer. 'It's you, Inspector. Go ahead.'

'Do I have to? Isn't that what we call consorting with criminals?'

'It's an order, Inspector,' said Zanuch, another with little or no humour, and marched back to his table and his long-suffering wife.

Malone made his way to the Prime Minister's table, aware that everyone within fifty yards was staring at him; several couples already on the dance floor missed their step and there was a small pile-up near the dance band. Two of the girls at the brothel table waved to him, but he just kept going. Delvina stood up as he reached her.

'Of course, Inspector,' she said before he could say anything. She glanced at Anita and the other women. 'Inspector Malone asked me to dance with him years ago, but I was a professional then.'

'A professional what?' said Anita as she fitted herself into her husband's stiff arms.

Malone took Delvina into his arms, cautiously. 'What's going on, Madame? Don't start using me for any tricks.'

'You're a good dancer, very light on your feet.' They were not dancing close together, but she could detect the bulge of his gun in its shoulder-holster. 'Do you remember the old Mae West joke? Is that your gun or are you just glad to have me in your arms?'

'Cut it out, Delvina.' He was uncomfortable, but not sexually. He was conscious that, no matter how subtly, she was leading him in the dance. 'Where are we going? Not outside, I hope.'

'No, we're going down to pay our respects to General Paturi.'

Malone was aware of everyone they passed staring at them, some of them candidly, others giving themselves eye-strain in their efforts to be both polite and curious. Other couples on the floor peeled away from them as if he and Delvina were about to do a speciality routine; he would not have been surprised if the band had struck up one of the old Astaire—Rogers numbers. At the tables the diners, turning away from their Waltzing Matilda torte, a cake made in the shape of a bed-roll with marzipan straps, were observing their progress down the hall like guests watching a wedding march; short-legged diners and the short-sighted were standing up to get a better view. Malone could hear the questions: 'Who's the man? It's not President Timori, is it? He doesn't *look* foreign, does he?'

He wanted to dump Delvina, just let his arms drop and walk away from her. He had, however, been cured of his Australian male chauvinism by Lisa: he could not treat a woman as crudely as he sometimes treated men. On top of that she was leading him close to General Paturi, the reason, so Zanuch reasoned, he was here tonight. They went from dance floor to dance floor; the four bands were playing simultaneously and by now were playing the one number. Malone and Delvina waltzed a hundred and fifty yards, a marathon, and by the time they reached the Premier's table Malone could feel the sweat soaking his shirt. Delvina looked as if she had just glided through an ice-works.

She eased herself out of Malone's arms. 'Mr Premier, I haven't met your charming wife. I've heard so much about you, Mrs Vanderberg.'

Gertrude Vanderberg, in thirty-five years in politics with The Dutchman, had met all types; the richest whore in the world, as she thought of Delvina, was just another type. 'Madame Timori, I'm so glad you're enjoying our little soirée.'

Malone grinned inwardly. He didn't know whether Gertrude Vanderberg could speak French, but her pronunciation of the one word had sounded perfect to him, even though her tongue had been in her cheek.

'A lovely understatement,' said Delvina, recognizing that this homely old cow was as shrewd as the equally homely old goat sitting beside her. Then she looked at Paturi. 'General, what a surprise to see you here! Are you planning a coup here in Sydney, too?'

Even Vanderberg had to chuckle at that. But Paturi just sat stone-faced; in ten years of dealing with Madame Timori he had never scored a point. Not until the coup of last week, and he was still getting adjusted to that.

'I have nothing to say,' he said, which was the truth.

'Oh, you haven't met Inspector Malone.' She waved her hand at Malone as if he were a prize possession. 'He is in charge of the police trying to find out who is trying to kill the President. I think he suspects you, General.'

There was a gasp from the wife of the Minister for Water Resources: it sounded like a pipe bursting. Everyone else at the table sat up in shock; all except The Dutchman, who continued to lounge in his chair as if he had heard all this, or something like it, before. Malone, aware that everyone was staring at him, kept his eye on Paturi.

The General said, 'You are mistaken, Inspector.'

'I hope I am, sir. But perhaps I may talk to you some other time? Tomorrow morning, maybe?'

Paturi just shook his head and Vanderberg said, 'The General has diplomatic immunity, Inspector. But maybe I can persuade him to talk off the record with you.' He was a master himself at talking off the record; that way he had torpedoed more opponents, in his own party and in the Opposition, than he could remember. 'Leave it with me.'

Paturi saw he was trapped. Being a general who had fought no wars, he knew no way to retreat. He just sat in stony silence. Delvina gave everyone at the table a regal smile, took Malone's arm and guided him back on to the dance floor. But now the music had stopped and they had to traverse the length of the hall past tables lined with stares. I'm dreaming this, Malone thought, I'm walking down here in a Maidenform bra and nothing else.

'You're not used to the limelight, are you?' said Delvina.

'That was something I told my kids just a couple of hours ago.'

'You have children? One never thinks of policemen having them.'

'You've read too many American detective novels. How did you know we have General Paturi on our list of suspects?'

'It's logical, isn't it? The assassination attempt fails, he arrives here a couple of days later. It's too much of a coincidence.' She was echoing Zanuch.

'Aren't you afraid you're on the hit list, too?'

'No. Well, yes, maybe.'

They had almost reached the Norvals' table. She had made her royal progress and the bystanders, even those who sneered at or hated her, would be sorry to see her go. Society, T-shirt as well as shirt-front, was tolerant of her tonight at this celebration of Australia making good. She was an Aussie who had made good, if by the worst possible means; if the outlaw Ned Kelly was a national saint, that was no sin. If footballers could become heroic by thuggery, they must give equal rights to a woman. It was the husbands who said that, not the wives.

'Will you arrest General Paturi if I'm shot?'

'We may. Or we may arrest Sun Lee. He's made some interesting phone calls to Beirut since he's been here. Did you know that? Good night, Madame. Thank you for the dance.'

He left her staring after him. He could have sworn that her eyes were glazed with fear.

3

Seville sat in the attic of the big house on the high side of the street from the Hickbed mansion. It was an old house, built at the turn of the century, all gables and balconies, the baronial castle of a family that was a household name in the State's history. Most of the rooms were now unused, their Victorian furniture covered with dust-sheets; only an elderly couple, the last of the family, still lived in the house.

Seville had come out here to Point Piper this afternoon, having deposited the canvas bag with the rifle and ammunition and his brief-case in a locker at Wynyard Station in the centre of the city. He had had confidence in his disguise; he had settled into the identity of Martin Dijon. He had used public transport to get here, getting off the bus at the beginning of the road that ran along the ridge and walking to the end of the point. This was not an area where people sat out on their front verandas; the front doors looked as if they might never be opened. No one tinkered with his car or washed it in these streets; no children played on the footpath. Some of the houses were striking advertisements of the wealth on this narrow point, but in the main anonymity was the name of the game. Conspicuous anonymity, perhaps, like the dark glass in celebrities' limousines, but at least a knee was bent to the wish.

The street where Russell Hickbed lived was not deserted. There, the demonstrators were still doing their picketing and at least one television crew was still staking out the house. A few spectators, outsiders, not locals, had arrived, but, having got there, looked as if they were not quite sure why they had come. Two police cars stood outside the Hickbed ornamental gates, which looked to be decorated with crossed dollar signs and three golden balls, the gamut of financial speculation. Seville, standing amongst the spectators, could see at least two uniformed policemen in the mansion grounds.

Then he had gone looking for the house he had observed through the glasses from the cruising ferry this morning. It was almost opposite the Hickbed house, on high ground held up by a sustaining stone wall. A curved driveway, beyond gates even bigger and more ornamental than Hickbed's, led up through gardens to the house. A sign on the gates said that the property was protected by Delphi Security Service.

Seville studied it without making himself too conspicuous. He decided that the line of sight from the attic windows in the gabled roof would give him a clear view into the Hickbed house. All he had to do was bide his time, come back this evening and hope that he could force entry into the house without too much commotion. He did not want to have to kill again unless it was absolutely necessary. It was, of course, necessary that he kill Timori.

He was back again at nine o'clock, this time with the canvas bag and his brief-case. He had again come by public transport; again he walked along Wolseley Road to the end of the point. But this time he cut up into a side street before reaching the street where Hickbed lived. He entered the side gate of a rambling stone-and-brick house; the gate said *Tradesmen's Entrance*, a relic of times past; but he was a tradesman and he smiled at the irony. He went down a side passage, treading quietly in his rubber-soled shoes, and through the sweet-smelling garden at the rear. He climbed the back wall and dropped down under the trees in the rear garden of the old gabled house. It was not fully dark, but he felt certain he would be difficult to see in the shadows under the thick camphor laurel trees.

The rear of the house was in darkness, but there were lights in the front rooms and upstairs. There was no flood-lighting in the gardens; whoever lived here kept advertising to a minimum; the grand old house itself was enough advertisement. Seville had no idea who lived in the house nor did he care. If he had to kill them, he would rather not know their names. Now that he had decided to retire, he wanted to discard memories, not go on collecting them. He smiled at the thought that perhaps, subconsciously, he was aspiring to his mother's sense of respectability.

As he had suspected, the grounds were being patrolled. He crouched down behind two large, thick camellia bushes as a policeman, cap off as he wiped his sweating forehead, strolled past. The officer, a young man, paused, then stepped into another clump of camellias farther along. A moment later Seville heard him relieving himself. Then he stepped out of the bushes and continued on his round.

Seville waited till he came by again. It took him six minutes to circle the grounds; he must have paused for a while at the front of the house. Seville waited and watched as the policeman did two more circuits: five minutes and seven minutes. It was not tight security, Seville noted, but perhaps the presence of the police was meant as no more than a deterrent. There was, he guessed, probably another officer at the front of the house.

As soon as the young policeman passed out of sight on his fourth round Seville made his move. He sprinted across the back lawn, stumbling as his knee almost gave way, and finished up on a wide back veranda that was half-enclosed by lattice-work. It took him three minutes to find the alarm system; it was as ancient as the house. Perhaps the Delphi Security Service was better at protecting oracles.

Then he heard the policeman coming back, this time accompanied by a colleague. He crouched down low, shielded by the lattice-work. He had zipped open the canvas bag and he had one hand on the Smith and Wesson that lay on top of the dismantled Sako rifle. The policemen paused almost opposite him and one said, 'Geez, I'd love a beer!'

They passed on and Seville went to work. He opened his brief-case and took out a small hand-drill. He drilled a hole in the alarm-box by the back door; he had to smile at the simple innocence of people who believed in such an antiquated safeguard; it would not have kept out a lapsed Boy Scout. He put the drill away in the case, methodical as always; then he took out a can of fast-setting foam and sprayed the foam into the hole. He wiped the nozzle of the can and put it back in the case and took out a Swiss army knife. Then he heard the footsteps again and he dropped back down behind the lattice-work.

The young policeman, alone this time, came by again. He paused, then walked across the lawn. Seville, watching him through the lattice-screen, saw him draw his pistol; then the beam from a torch he held probed the bushes along the back wall. A cat darted out of the bushes and the policeman gave a grunt, then laughed and switched off the torch. He continued on round the front of the house.

Seville stood up again, sure now that the foam had set and neutralized the bell in the alarm box. With the knife he slipped back the catch of the window into the kitchen. He put the knife back in the brief-case and snapped it shut. Brief-cases were the tool-bags of bankers, businessmen and diplomats: his carried just a few extra tools.

He slid over the sill and found himself in the large kitchen, the sort where in other days, when such human conveniences existed, the staff would have eaten. He could hear voices and music from inside the house: someone was looking at television. He went quietly along a narrow hallway that led into a wide entrance hall. He paused a moment, listening to the sounds coming out of a doorway to the left; the television set was in there. An old movie was playing; he heard a distinctive voice, Cary Grant's, say, 'Never trust anyone.' Seville nodded at the sentiment.

He went quickly and silently up the wide stairs that led to the upper floors. Some of the rooms were lit, but most of them were in darkness. He passed a huge bedroom; it was like peeping into a corner of a Victorian museum. A big brass-railed bed, two heavily stuffed armchairs, a full-length mirror on wheels: it was like a return visit to his grandmother's bedroom in the *estancia* near Bariloche. He went on past it, hurrying now, struck by some odd feeling he couldn't identify. Was it regret for the way his life had gone, or conscience, or just homesickness?

The question stayed with him as he climbed the narrow stairs into the attic. There he sat amidst the alluvia of other people's lives, things washed up from the life that had gone on in the house below: toys, a baby carriage, books, heavily-framed photographs, a gramophone and a pile of 78 rpm records. He sat down in an old leather chair and tried to drain himself of the feeling that had attacked him. Yet over the next hour his life of years ago kept coming back to him, as if this attic, indeed this house, was a museum where memory was endemic.

It was warm here in the attic and he had taken off his jacket. Far to the west there was a red glow in the sky: he guessed the bushfires were still burning. He had no interest in such disasters: they were for people who left themselves exposed to such hazards.

He had assembled the rifle, checked the telescopic sight: it was more than adequate for the job in view. He could see down across the street and the Hickbed front gardens into the Hickbed house; the range would be less than a hundred yards. He would have to move fast once he had fired the fatal shot, but he was confident that in the initial confusion after the shot he would have plenty of time to be gone. There was no organized fireworks display tonight, but out on the harbour the occasional rocket was being let off. The sound of the shot could, for a moment or two anyway, be mistaken for a firecracker.

The Hickbed grounds were flood-lit, the flowers and shrubs somehow drained of their colours so that they looked like clumps of bone coral. All the lights in the house were on; the drapes were drawn in the ground-floor rooms but not in the rooms above. He had been sitting there two hours, beginning to grow impatient, wondering if he had chosen the wrong side of the house to watch, when he saw Abdul Timori appear in one of the upper rooms.

He steadied the rifle and took aim.

207

Abdul Timori did not like his own company, but he had had to get used to it over the past week. He had always surrounded himself, even as a young man in Palucca and in Europe, with friends and hangers-on, he had never cared which, who would laugh at his jokes or keep him entertained. When he had married Delvina she had tried to weed out some of the hangers-on and he had let them go; he had objected when she had tried the same sorting out amongst his friends, or those he called his friends. He needed company, he had told her, and he had been adamant that he would not be deprived of it. He did not crave friendship, not after he became President: that, he realized, would be a weakness. But company, yes: he needed to be reassured, to see his position reflected in the faces of others.

He was now also afraid: something he had never been before. The coup had startled him by its success; he had been aware that it was being plotted, but he had never dreamed that it would succeed. The friends, the company he had craved, had abruptly deserted him, leaving the sinking captain for a ship they hoped would remain afloat. He had not feared for his life then, such revenge had long since died out in Palucca; or so he had thought. Then last Friday night's assassination attempt had brought him face to face with the ugly fact that someone actually wanted to kill him.

He had run through a gallery in his mind, at first quickly, then slowly, dropping off suspects along the way like the judge in some art competition. At least two of the generals in the junta would be capable of ordering a murder, if not of actually committing one: General Paturi, he was sure, would be one of them. There had been others in the gallery: Sun Lee, Russell Hickbed, even Philip Norval: he spared no one his suspicions. And there were, of course, the organizations that arranged termination, as he believed they called it: the CIA, the KGB, the various terrorist gangs, including those backed by the emergent fundamentalist Islamic groups that had spread from the Middle East. He was eclectic in his suspicions, the mark of a true dictator.

It was fear that had prompted him to say no when Delvina had suggested they should accompany Russell Hickbed to the Bicentennial Ball. Security there would, of necessity, be lax; he would, at some point in the evening, have to present himself as a perfect target, if the assassin should still be tracking him. And why go, anyway?

'We need to present ourselves more publicly,' said Delvina. 'Show we are not the dragons the newspapers are saying we are.'

'My dear, we *are* dragons. Or were.' He was having no late pangs of conscience; he knew what they had been. But he had been amazed at the freedom of the press here in Australia; it seemed it was allowed to criticize anyone, even the country's own leaders. Democracy could be taken to stupid lengths. 'No amount of public relations is going to change their image of us. Australians are simple-minded. They tolerate their corrupt politicians because they elect them and to condemn them would be a reflection on their own judgement. But they can't stand an honest dictator like myself. I'm not going to go to some ball and be jeered at.' He had had enough of that on the way to the airport in Bunda. 'We are not going.'

'*I'm* going.' She had no maid, because there was no accommodation for her in the Hickbed house; she began to lay out her own things. She chose carefully because she knew this might be her farewell performance in Australia.

'Darling, you've been jeered at before – I've read some of the critics' reviews of your dancing. You're used to it. I'm not.'

'You don't have to be nasty.'

She took out her jewel-box from a closet, put it on the end of the bed. It was no small box; it was almost the size of a butter-box, a jewel-case for a medieval caliph. It was made of thick teak bound with decorated iron straps; it was an effort for her to lift it on to the bed. When she opened the lid the light flashed on a king's ransom; if anyone was buying back kings these days. She looked at it, as always, with greedy delight.

'No, I don't have to be nasty. I'm surprised that I am. Perhaps

209

we have been seeing too much of each other since we left the palace. There was room enough there for us to avoid each other.' He looked around their bedroom, a large room by local standards, a cupboard by his. 'I don't know why I'm not suffering from claustrophobia.'

'I'll move out, find another bedroom.' She picked out a tiara, a necklace, a bracelet and a ring: tonight was emerald night.

'Please yourself. Perhaps Russell will share his with you. It's bigger than this.'

She went off in a huff, her tiara and her fifteen-thousand-dollar gown, intent on public relations even if her private relations were in need of repair.

Timori had watched Hickbed go off with her, glowing as if he had just been presented with an oil lease. He had had dinner alone and then gone into Hickbed's library and sat amidst the unread books and reviewed his life past and future. He did not consider the present, for he knew that for the moment he was helpless and at the mercy of the Australian police who were protecting him. Then he had come upstairs to the bedroom again.

He looked at the jewel-box still standing on the end of the bed, though Delvina had closed its lid and locked it again. It was only part of their treasure, petty cash in the form of diamonds, emeralds and other precious stones. He was a rich man, one of the world's richest, though not in the same bank as his neighbour, the Sultan of Brunei. At one time he had had ambitions for expansion; he had looked at territories that might come under his influence; he would be the Sultan of Spice, a heady title. But as soon as his ambitions became known they had been knocked on the head. Indonesian guns began to growl; the Sultan of Brunei tried to buy the entire British Army, which needed the money at the time; the Americans, worried enough by their losses in Vietnam, told him to be a good little dictator and stick to his own domain. So he had sacrificed his ambition for power and settled for plain greed, a more acceptable aim amongst the world powers.

Even if General Paturi succeeded in confiscating his Australian holdings, there were the assets in the United States, Canada, Europe and Hong Kong; there were also the cash and gold

210

and more gems in the bank in Switzerland. He would not be penniless, no matter where he finished up; but riches would not amount to much if he had to live in Paraguay or some Central African republic. He would settle for the French Riviera, where he had mis-spent a lot of his youth; or the Bahamas or the more respectable parts of California like Santa Barbara. But above all he wanted to return to Bunda, to the power and the palace that had once been his.

He patted the jewel-box, as if it were a talisman. Delvina might think of it as hers, but he was a Muslim. He still had the power in their marriage.

He sent for Sun Lee, who came in soft-footed as usual. Even on some of the marble floors in the palace in Bunda he had moved as silently as a ghost. The effect had never worried Timori before, but now it did.

'Why do you have to be so cat-footed, Sun? Are you sneaking up on me?'

'Why should I do that, Excellency? I am just naturally quiet, I suppose. It was the best attitude for a Chinese in Palucca.'

Timori couldn't remember his ever having referred to his race before. 'You thought I persecuted you?'

'Not you personally, Excellency. But the police and the bureaucrats – yes. I was fortunate to have your protection because of my position.'

'I couldn't do without you, Sun. What would you do if I were assassinated?'

'I've never considered the possibility.'

'Why not? That bullet on Friday night was close enough to be a probability.'

'I think you lead a charmed life.'

Timori smiled. 'I think you're a charming liar, Sun. If I divorced Madame Timori, would you stay with me or go with her?'

An eyebrow flickered; it was the only reaction. 'Are you going to divorce Madame?'

Timori sighed. 'Probably not. We've had enough publicity. I was just testing your loyalty. Tell me, Sun, about our investments.'

'Which ones, sir? Where?'

211

'World-wide. Don't let us confine ourselves. Sit down and tell me everything. And remember – your head may depend upon it.'

An hour later he dismissed Sun. He sat in a chair staring at the windows. The Paluccan housemaid had forgotten to draw the drapes and Timori left them as they were. There had been countless servants to perform those sort of chores in the palace; or perhaps he thought the curtains drew themselves. In any event he had too much on his mind this evening to look at the view the windows offered. One flood-lit garden looked like another: they had always been part of the security precautions in Timoro Palace.

He went to one of his bags and took out a gun, a Colt .45 automatic. He had never fired it in anger and he wondered if he would fire it tonight. He sat down in the chair again and the gun, somehow, gave him unexpected comfort. He began to feel a little less afraid and he again ran his hand over the jewel-box, as if luck lay there amongst the gems in the treasure chest.

5

Delvina Timori had suddenly grown bored with the ball and everyone attending it, especially those here at the Prime Minister's table. Insults are like sex: one needs exceptional stamina to keep up the standard. Anita Norval was now blatantly ignoring her. Philip Norval had suddenly developed a passionate interest in the Prime Minister of New Zealand, a lesbian lady who hoped the Australian PM, a woolly ram if ever she'd met one, didn't think she was double-gaited. Everyone else at the table, including Russell Hickbed, looked exhausted. Delvina looked at her watch: 10.40, still a young night. But it was time to go. She was not only bored, but disturbed. What had Scobie Malone been hinting at with his warning?

She stood up, nodding to Hickbed, who was relieved to get the command. Anita Norval turned round, all at once all smiling concern. 'You're not going! I meant to tell you – I love your dress! It fits so perfectly.' *Every nook and cranny.* 'What there is of it.'

'One dresses for the occasion. If there's no one to be impressed, one doesn't wear much. Good night. Thank you for a lovely evening. Enjoy yourselves.'

'We shall,' said Anita, voice silent under the band's 'Lay Your Love on Me', 'now you're leaving.'

Philip Norval turned away from the New Zealand PM, much to her relief, and gave Delvina as many teeth as he could show in a good night smile. This was to have been his Big Night before the Big Day tomorrow; Delvina, the bitch, had stolen it from him. Tomorrow night he would be on to Washington, telling Fegan he would be putting the Timoris on a plane and telling the pilot to keep flying till he saw a landing field with the Stars and Stripes fluttering above it.

Delvina had made an entrance; she was not going to leave without making an exit. With her hand resting lightly on Hickbed's arm, she made her way down the length of the hall, skirting the dance floors yet somehow managing to suggest she was in the centre of them. Some guests nodded to her, not out of friendliness but out of habit; they were the sort of spectators who always saw themselves as part of the action. On Judgement Day they would nod to God in the same familiar way.

Hans Vanderberg saw her go, but he did not rise to say good night. He just lolled in his chair and grinned at her and Hickbed. He had milked them of all they had to offer tonight; he could already see tomorrow's headlines. Beside him his wife did not look in Delvina's direction; she knew Madame Timori would not be looking at her. Nobody had ever snubbed Gertrude Vanderberg: she was always a glance or two ahead of them.

The Dutchman leaned across to John Leeds, who had just joined the Premier's table. 'I'd like to see Inspector Malone at eight o'clock tomorrow morning, John. Can you see to it?'

'It's unusual, Hans. Why don't you see Bill Zanuch? He's just over there – I'll call him, if you like.'

'I don't want to see Zanuch – I want to see Malone.'

'May I ask why?'

'Yes.' Vanderberg grinned. 'But you won't get an answer. Not for a day or two anyway.'

213

'Hans, he's one of *my* men. I could refuse to let you see him.'

'You wouldn't do that, John. Care for some of Gert's pump-kin pavlova? It's better than this cake they're serving.'

Malone, squeezed in at a wall table for two with Clements, a thundering rock band right above them, saw Delvina go and was relieved. Then he saw the Commissioner beckoning to him. He got up and made his way round the rocking dancers to the Premier's table. Here the decibels were much lower; just by leaning down he could hear Leeds' quiet voice.

'The Premier wants to see you in his office at eight tomorrow morning. You'd better go home and get some sleep.'

'What's it about, sir?'

Leeds looked at Vanderberg, who was watching them with a crocodile's eye. 'I'll leave him to tell you in the morning.'

'Does Mr Zanuch know I'm to be there?'

'I'll tell him. You go home and get a good night's sleep. You may have a busy day tomorrow.'

Not if I can help it. But Malone couldn't tell the Commissioner about his plans to take Lisa and his family out on the harbour. Leeds might understand and sympathize, but he was a police-man: duty came first.

Malone went back to Clements, who stood up from his half-eaten dinner, bellowed, 'Too much bloody noise!' and followed Malone out to the lobby. There Zanuch was waiting in ambush for them, as if he had expected them to sneak off early.

'Where are you going, Inspector?'

'Home, sir. The Commissioner's orders. I have to report to the Premier's office at eight in the morning.'

'What for? Why wasn't I told?'

Malone had no answer to either question.

Zanuch knew he had just been stripped of some of his authority by the Commissioner and, he had no doubt, the Premier. But he had to show he had some left: 'On your way home go out to Point Piper and see that Madame Timori has arrived safely.'

'Me, too, sir?' said Clements, eager to be gone.

'No, you stay and keep an eye on General Paturi. He is still our chief suspect. Stay with him till he goes home to the

Consulate. He may try to contact Seville – there he goes now! He's leaving now!'

General Paturi, bored almost to the point of sleep, deafened by what the Australians evidently thought was music, had had enough. It had not taken him long to realize that Premier Vanderberg was on his side; but to what effect and to what extent he did not know. He was ignorant of State and Federal politics in this country; it seemed to him, having lived under a virtual dictatorship all his adult life, that Australia was over-governed. But he understood jealousies and the animal instinct of the territorial imperative and he knew Premier Vanderberg would never do anything to help Prime Minister Norval. Instead, he might do an awful lot to help General Paturi and his colleagues.

But Paturi could suffer just so much in the cause of Paluccan democracy. He thanked The Dutchman, saluted him and Gertrude, and marched out of the huge hall while the nearest band, at full blast, belted out 'Papa, Don't Preach'.

Malone and Clements went their separate ways, each following his own quarry.

Delvina sat in the back of Hickbed's Rolls-Royce, well away from his tentatively groping hand. 'None of that, Russell. I had enough of that from the New Zealand PM.'

'You were the one who wanted to go to the ball.'

'I made a mistake.' She made few mistakes and rarely admitted them. 'The sooner we are out of Australia, the better. Even Upper Volta would be preferable to this.'

He had no idea where Upper Volta was; and she only knew because she had been studying atlases this past week, looking for havens. 'I'll try for Upper Volta, if you like.'

'You would,' she said witheringly.

'Don't get too nasty, Delvina, or I'll kick you and Abdul out of my house. I don't have to put up with your tantrums. Without me you'd have been out on your arse on some beach in Palucca, with all the Aussie hippies.'

'God forbid!'

They sat in sullen silence for the rest of the journey back to Point Piper. When they got out of the Rolls-Royce she strode into the house without saying good night, went up the curving

215

staircase and along to the main guest bedroom at the front of the house. She had been upset that she and Abdul had not been given Hickbed's own bedroom, with its magnificent view of the harbour, but Hickbed never stretched his hospitality too far. She flung open the door and marched in, in no mood for further argument with Abdul.

He was sitting in a chair facing the door, his hands folded in his lap.

'I've come to get my night things,' she said. 'I'm sleeping in another room.'

'With Russell?'

'No, not with Russell.' She snatched up her night-gown, then moved to the dressing-table to get her creams and lotions. She stopped, looking at him in the mirror, suddenly caught by his very still composure. 'What's the matter with you? Are you sick or something?'

'A little. I've been talking to Sun.'

'What about?' She turned round, one hand screwing up the night-gown.

'Just about everything. I know who's paying to have me murdered.' He stood up and for the first time she saw the gun in his hand.

'Who?'

He had moved away from the chair, stood with his back to the window, the yellow silk drapes framing him on either side. He lifted the gun and pointed it at her.

'You.'

Then, as he pulled the trigger of the Colt .45, the window glass behind him cracked and he stumbled forward. He fell across the foot of the bed, hitting his head hard on the iron-bound corner of the jewel-case, then he crashed on to the carpet.

EIGHT

1

When Malone got out to the car park from the Exhibition Centre he was accosted by Thumper Murphy, in uniform and a bad mood. ''Night, Scobie. Been enjoying yourself?'

'No.'

'Me, neither. I'm over here in charge of a detail looking after four thousand bludgers who should be paying for their own security. All the crims on my own turf must be having the time of their lives, breaking and entering and raping old ladies.' Then he said quietly, 'I hear you had a bad trot this morning with that bastard Seville.'

Who hadn't heard of it? Some deaf Laplander north of the Arctic Circle? 'I wouldn't want it to happen again.'

'I'm glad you got out of it okay.' Thumper Murphy was a man afraid of sentiment; somehow he managed to make his sympathy sound like abuse. 'Don't shove your neck out too far. No one'll ever appreciate it.'

Malone smiled and nodded, suddenly warmed by the rough old cop's support. He walked across to his car, his own Holden Commodore in which he and Clements had come to the ball, got in and manœuvred his way out of the packed car park. He took his time, in no mood to go tearing after Delvina Timori and Russell Hickbed. As Thumper had said, they should be paying for their own security.

He drove leisurely out to Point Piper. There was a lot of traffic and he just let himself be carried along with its current. At one point he found himself wishing Seville could end the situation by killing Timori; but of course the situation would not be ended nor would he have peace of mind. There had been times in the past when he had felt no regrets, indeed had felt satisfaction, at the murder of some vicious criminal or a

217

child molester or a brutal rapist; there had been just a simple atavistic sense of justice having been done. He had, however, never before wished for a man to be murdered; though he had, on one occasion, wanted to kill a man. That had been in New York on a trip he and Lisa had made before the children were born. They had won twelve thousand dollars in a State lottery and decided to blow half of it on a cheap world trip before they settled down to having a family. In New York Lisa had been kidnapped by a pair of Anarchists; her kidnapping had been accidental, since the Anarchists' real target had been the wife of the then Mayor of New York. Malone had spent an agonizing couple of days and when he had finally sighted the male kidnapper all thoughts of law and order had been wiped from his mind: he had wanted to kill the man. He had stopped being a policeman; he had become a desperate, avenging husband. Fortunately he had been caught in time, but he had never known such rage before or since.

He felt no rage about Seville or the Timoris, just frustration and a sour cynicism and disgust. If he felt any anger at all it was at the future his children faced, a world where corruption and greed were no longer capital sins.

He had just got out of the car in the narrow street in Point Piper when he heard the shot. At first he thought it was another firework rocket going up; he instinctively looked up towards the sky over the harbour. But the sky remained dark; then he knew there had been a shot. Perhaps two: he couldn't be sure. He ran towards the Hickbed mansion, was held up for a moment at the gates by a Federal policeman who didn't recognize him in his dinner suit. Then he was in the driveway, was joined by Joe Nagler who had come panting up from the waterfront.

'Where did that come from? Inside?'

'I think so – I dunno. Were there two shots?'

Kenthurst had now appeared; he looked as if he had been asleep somewhere. They banged on the front door and it was opened almost immediately by Hickbed.

'Upstairs – the front room!' He had lost his glasses or forgotten to put them on; his face was blank with shock. 'It's the President!'

Malone led the way upstairs at a run. The door to the front

218

bedroom was wide open; Sun Lee stood there with hand spread as if inviting them to come in. Delvina sat slumped on the big silk-covered bed. Abdul Timori lay face down on the yellow carpet, a gun clutched in his right hand and blood oozing from both the top and the side of his head. It was only later that Malone would remember that there was a remarkable silence in the room, that there was no sound at all out of Delvina or Sun and certainly none out of the seemingly dead Timori.

'Get the emergency unit!'

He dropped to his knees beside Timori as Kenthurst picked up the phone and dialled the Police Centre. Malone saw the extent of the two wounds on Timori's head and was certain the emergency unit was already too late; but when he felt the President's throat there seemed to be the faintest hint of a pulse there. He looked up at Nagler, who was bending over him anxiously.

'There's still a flicker there. But they'd better hurry!'

He took the Colt .45 from the President's hand, smelled the barrel, checked the magazine, then looked for a sign of the bullet that had been fired. Delvina saw what he was looking for and without a word pointed to the hole in the silk coverlet beside her on the bed.

He looked down at Timori lying face down on the floor, then he turned to the window and saw the bullet-hole and the star effect in the glass. He stepped to the window and looked out and up, saw the old house on the high ground on the opposite side of the street. He saw two uniformed police down in the front garden. He pulled up the window, careful not to shatter the glass.

'Get over into that house opposite – that's where the shot came from! Get on the blower to Centre – tell 'em I want SWOS or Tac Response here on the double! Move!' He turned back into the room, looked at Kenthurst. 'Bob, get things organized around here, will you, till my fellers turn up. Check the streets – we're looking for Seville. No description except that he's slim and dark and walks with a sailor's roll. I'll look after Madame Timori.'

Kenthurst went out on the run and Malone looked at Delvina. She had been sitting absolutely still, gazing at her unconscious husband; not staring but just gazing at him as if she were making some decision about what to do with his body. She looked up when she became aware that Malone was waiting on her.

He gestured towards the doorway. 'Let's go somewhere else, Madame. Sergeant Nagler will stay with the President.'

Sun Lee spoke for the first time. 'I shall stay, too.'

Delvina stood up, took another look at her husband, then went ahead of Malone out of the room. 'Downstairs,' he said, trying to make it sound like a suggestion rather than an order.

At the foot of the stairs Hickbed was waiting, his glasses restored, his arrogant air, though a little tattered, re-donned. 'Is he –?'

'Not yet,' said Malone. 'We'll have him on his way to hospital as soon as we can. Can we go in here?'

But he had already led the way into the huge living-room. It was not a room to offer comfort to the spirit: comfort for the bones and flesh, yes, but not for a grieving, frightened soul. It did not matter: Delvina looked neither grieving nor frightened. Her only sign of agitation was that when she sat down she asked Hickbed for a cigarette.

'The window cracked and Abdul just went down. I –' She drew on the cigarette, then blew out smoke. Most people Malone had interviewed did not blow out smoke, when agitated, in such a cool manner.

Malone, sitting on the edge of a deep, raw silk-covered chair, put the Colt .45 down between his feet. 'What was the President doing with this in his hand?'

Delvina stubbed out the cigarette, carefully and with no nervousness. 'He was trying to shoot me.'

She was sitting on a long couch and Hickbed was standing at the end of it, as if not sure whether he was wanted for the interview or not. Now he suddenly moved and sat down heavily. 'Jesus, Del, what are you saying? Don't take any notice of her, Inspector, she's upset by this terrible happening –'

'I'm upset, Russell, but I know what I'm saying. Abdul was trying to kill me.' She was still wearing her tiara and her jewellery, but now she began to take them off, as if she thought them inappropriate. She opened her legs just a little and put the treasure in her lap, a peasant's way of holding it.

'Why?' said Malone, watching her carefully.

'I'm not sure. Before I left for the ball he mentioned suicide – he wondered if it was worthwhile going on –'

She's lying, thought Malone. 'What did he say when you came home?'

'Nothing. Well yes, he said *you*.'

'You? Y-O-U?' She nodded. 'And that was all?'

'Yes. I don't know whether he intended to kill me and then commit suicide. Or –' She didn't finish the alternative. 'Then the gun went off and he fell. Or it must have gone off as he fell – that was how the bullet hit the bed. He hit his head an awful crack on my jewel-box –' She shuddered, as if the memory of that was worse than the thought of the bullet that had creased the top of his head.

'Did you go to the window to see what had happened?'

She shook her head. 'It was a moment or two before I realized what had happened. Then I couldn't move . . .'

Not much, thought Malone. There was the sound of approaching sirens out in the street. Malone got up, went out to the front door and saw the flashing blue lights of half a dozen police cars; then there was the sound of another siren and in a moment the emergency unit ambulance, red lights flashing, came in through the open gates. Lights had gone on in the surrounding houses and apartment blocks and a few people had gathered in the street. Point Piper could no longer contain its curiosity. Malone turned back into the house; he had asked Kenthurst to take charge and he did not want to interfere. Besides, he was certain that the clue to tonight's crisis was back in the Hickbed living-room.

He went back, walked in on Hickbed sitting close to Delvina and holding her hand. He dropped it as Malone walked in, but didn't move away from her. He looked more composed, more like his old aggressive self.

'I've advised Madame Timori to wait till I've contacted my lawyer –'

Then he stopped as the emergency medical team, led by Kenthurst, hurried in the front door and ran upstairs. Delvina gave them only a cursory glance, as if they were no more than a team come to clean the carpets.

221

Then she said, rising unhurriedly, gathering up her tiara and jewellery as if they were a fistful of vegetables she had been peeling, 'I think I should be upstairs with my husband while they are with him. If he dies . . .'

Malone waited for her to go on, but she didn't. He said, 'Would you ask Mr Sun to come down here?'

She nodded and left the room, gliding out with her dancer's walk, no hint of agitation showing. Hickbed looked after her. 'She's a remarkable woman.'

'Remarkable,' said Malone. 'I just wonder why she thinks her husband was about to kill her.'

'Maybe he was going to kill her and then commit suicide?'

'Do you think he's the suicidal type? He'd no more commit suicide than you would, Mr Hickbed. I mean that as a compliment,' he said straight-faced.

Then he turned, satisfied that he had lodged an arrow somewhere in Hickbed's armour, and saw Nagler beckoning to him from the entrance hall. He went out to him. 'How's His Nibs?'

'Still alive – barely. They're taking him into St Vincent's. I called Police Centre and they've been on to the Exhibition Centre. The Commissioner knows what's happened and I guess he's told the Premier and the PM. Are we still looking for Seville?'

'You got any other starters?'

Nagler shook his head and he and Malone went out to the front gates where Kenthurst was receiving a report from a uniformed sergeant. Kenthurst said, 'They've come up with nothing in the streets. He was in that house opposite all right, up in the attic.'

'Jesus!' said Malone. 'Were they your blokes or ours patrolling the house?'

'Yours,' said Kenthurst and somehow succeeded in not sounding smug.

'Have you got anyone out scouting for him around here?'

'As many as we can spare. The SWOS guys have arrived.'

'Tell them I want him alive.'

'Why? He's sure to start shooting if they find him.'

'I want to find out who's paying him.'

'Fair enough. I'll tell them to shoot for his legs. We'll find out how good they are in the dark.'

Malone and Nagler went back into the house. 'Joe, I'm going to stick with the Madame, if she goes to the hospital. You can bet Bill Zanuch will be here soon. He'll take over.'

'I think I'll go and jump in the harbour now.'

Malone grinned and patted his shoulder. 'Don't give up, Joe. *Shalom,* isn't that what you fellers say?'

'Not when Zanuch is around.'

Then he looked up the stairs as the medical team, moving carefully, came down with Timori on a stretcher. Malone saw that there was no sheet over the President's face and his instant reaction was one of disappointment; then he was ashamed of his feeling. As the stretcher was carried past him he looked down at the still face, a pale dirty grey now, and tried to forget who the man was. He was a *man*, a human being, and he should not die this way.

Delvina had done a quick change; it must have been her dancer's training. She was now in a simple dark-green day dress; she had even changed her shoes, was wearing plain black court ones. Her hair was drawn back in a chignon; she had removed her make-up and wore only pale lipstick. She was all ready to look the grieving widow, if it should be necessary. Sun Lee came down the stairs after her.

'I'd like you and Mr Hickbed to come to the hospital with us, Mr Sun.' Malone wanted to keep them all together. 'Perhaps we could all ride in your car, Mr Hickbed?'

'Is there any necessity for me to come along?' Hickbed had taken off his bow tie and loosened the neck of his dress shirt. He still looked aggressive and Malone waited for him to roll up his sleeves and bunch his fists.

He pulled off his own tie; when they got to the hospital he did not want to look like a *maître d'* ushering them in. 'I thought you'd want to accompany your friend the President?'

'I think you should, Russell,' said Delvina, and Malone sensed that she, too, wanted them all together. 'And you too, Mr Sun.'

She went out of the house, not looking back, the President's wife taking it for granted that she would be obeyed. Hickbed

223

for a moment lost his composure; he gestured helplessly. Then he focused on Malone and seemed to regain his strength.

'Don't overstep the mark, Inspector.'

'You've already warned me about that. I'll keep it in mind.' As he turned away he winked, on the blind side, to Nagler. 'If Russ Clements rings up, Joe, get him to ring me at the hospital.'

As soon as the Rolls-Royce pulled out of the gates Hickbed said, 'I thought you'd be out chasing that assassin Seville.'

'We're doing that.' Malone gestured to the half a dozen police cars and the two SWOS vans and the Tactical Response van. 'Our men know what to do. They don't need me riding herd on them.'

'Why are you riding herd on us?' said Delvina.

She was in the back seat between Hickbed and Sun. Malone was in the front seat beside the uniformed chauffeur, a young Paluccan, Malone guessed by his looks. The car was a Camargue and Malone could smell the rich leather, even imagined he could smell the walnut panelling. It was the sort of car that invited the use of all the senses and he knew he would never be riding in another one again. Tomorrow it would be back to the five-year-old Commodore and the vinyl and the smell of oil and the air-conditioning that blew cold in winter and hot in summer. He turned round, feeling the soft thick leather beneath his hand as he rested it on the back of the seat.

'Because I think one of you three is going to tell me more than Seville ever will. That is, if we catch him alive.'

'You don't think you'll catch him alive?' said Hickbed. 'You mean you'll shoot him down?' He sounded hopeful.

'I've met him, Mr Hickbed. You haven't. He's not the sort of man who will let anyone take him alive. Sometimes with crims like that there's no alternative but to shoot them down.'

He turned to face the front again, aware of a sudden nervousness in the chauffeur, as if the young Paluccan all at once saw the possibility of Seville riding up beside them and gunning them down. Malone grinned to himself, hoping the three of them in the back were also feeling scared. He was sure, though, that Delvina, if she was capable of fear, would never show it. She was, he decided, as cold-blooded as Seville.

They drew up outside the hospital. Timori had already been

224

taken inside; when the four of them got into Casualty, he was already on his way to Intensive Care. A nun led them through the bloody wounded who crowded the Casualty section on this busy night: the victims of road carnage, the drunks who had fallen on broken bottles, the drug addicts who had over-dosed, the woman with her throat wrapped in a bloody bandage. Malone had seen it all before, but he had to steel himself not to be upset by it. Hickbed looked nervous and disturbed; even Sun kept his eyes averted from some of the bloodier cases. Delvina sailed through it all as if through a late-night crowd of passengers at a bus station.

The nun opened a door, ushered them into a side room. She was a wizened little woman with a soft voice, a soft chin and eyes that Malone knew could harden into marbles if someone crossed her. He had met her before.

'Thanks, Sister. Let us know what happens, will you?'

'There'll be nothing for several hours, Inspector. Unless . . .'

Unless the President dies.

'Is there a phone I can use?'

She took him along to her office, a cubby-hole as neat as herself. She left him alone while he dialled home. Lisa was waiting for him. He told her what had happened to Timori, then said, 'I have no idea when I'll be home, darl.'

'What about tomorrow? You're not going to disappoint the kids again?'

'I'll call you at seven-thirty. But if I can't make it, there's no reason why you and the kids should miss it. Eric Mack will be expecting you. Just turn up at the wharf where I told you.'

'I'm beginning to hate you. Or anyway your job.'

'So am I. The job, anyway. I love you.'

'Sometimes I wonder.' There was a quick intake of her breath, then she said, 'No, I don't mean that. I know you do. Take care. Stay away from that man Seville.'

He hung up, stood for a moment while the effect of her settled down in him. He had never imagined that love could be felt as deeply as he felt it for her; it went beyond sex, companionship, respect. He knew, as he had discovered that time in New York, that he could kill to keep her.

He looked up the Hickbed number in a phone-book on the

225

nun's desk and was pleasantly surprised when he found it listed. Most rich men preferred unlisted numbers; Hickbed evidently liked to be available to the voice of the people, most of whom he despised and most of whom would abuse him if they took the trouble to call him. Malone dialled the number and Joe Nagler answered.

'Joe, is Russ Clements there?'

'He's just arrived. With our friend You-Know-Who. You want him?'

'Yes. Don't tell Zanuch I've called. Say it's your mother.'

Nagler chuckled and went away and a few moments later Russ Clements was on the line. 'Is he still alive, Scobie?'

'As far as I know. Did General Paturi get the news?'

'I don't know. If he did, he's locked himself away in the Consulate and giving no comment. If he's grinning in the morning, that'll shorten the odds that he had something to do with it.'

'Maybe. Listen, take Kenthurst outside and have a quiet word in his earhole. Tell him I want a tap on the Hickbed phone line – there may be a couple, an unlisted number, so check. The Feds can get a permit to tap easier than we can – tell him I want it kept quiet. Don't let Zanuch know.'

'What's going on?'

'You'll be the first to know, Russ, when *I* know. Any word on Seville?'

'None. Zanuch has ordered a watch on all airports, Central Railway and the bus stations. We'll get him sooner or later.'

'Sooner, I hope. If he hears Timori isn't dead, he may try again.'

2

Delvina Timori sat in the ante-room at St Vincent's Hospital, totally unconcerned about the shattered lives out in Casualty. Her own life was badly cracked, though not yet shattered. There was a glue-like quality to her that would never allow that to happen.

Her mother, whose own mother had begun life as a latex

226

gatherer in the British rubber plantations of Malaya, had been a formidable lady, one with as much tough bounce as rubber itself. She had been working as the cashier in a bar when she had met Delvina's father, a quiet, rather lonely RAAF sergeant who was married before he had quite realized what he was getting into. He had brought his bride back to Australia, where she had not been welcomed by the white Australian wives on the RAAF station, and sired a daughter on whom he had doted. But his life with Delvina's mother had not been happy; it had gone downhill from the day they had set foot back in Australia. When he had been killed in the air crash of another over-age RAAF bomber, it had been a release for both of them.

Delvina's mother had thought of returning to Malaysia, as it had now become, but decided against it. She was a stubborn woman; she would take on Australia and beat it. As the trickle of Asian immigration had increased, her foreign appearance had become less conspicuous; local men, more daring than their fathers and wanting to taste some foreign spice, had taken an interest in her. She had slept with some of them, taken money from some, but made no lasting liaison with any of them. She was not a whore nor did she think of herself as one; she acted out of revenge, getting her own back on the xenophobic RAAF wives who had so cruelly snubbed her. She trained her daughter to the same frame of mind.

Except that Delvina ignored the objective of revenge. Men, she decided, when she was no more than fourteen, were tools to be used. Since they made up 50 per cent of the world and had most of the power and wealth, they were the obvious means for her to rise above what the nuns at her school, conservatives all, still referred to as 'one's station in life'. She was eighteen when her mother died; she buried her with regret but not much love. Already she had discovered that she was not capable of love, though she did not bother to fathom why. Her mother, on her death-bed but still clear-eyed about the daughter she had raised, had said, 'Your heart is rubber. Use it.' Delvina had taken the advice to heart, rubber or not.

Now, many years and much success later, doing much better than the rubber industry was, she sat in this bare disinfectant-smelling room and pondered the possibility of the end of the

227

road. Or, at best, another, bumpier road. She was furious at
the possibility, but she showed none of her fury.

Hickbed, showing everything, including a partly unzipped
fly, was in a mixture of rage and fear. 'Christ Almighty, Delvina,
you've got to pull yourself together! Watch what you say in
front of that bastard Malone. He could bring everything down
on top of us! What did you mean, telling him Abdul was going
to kill you? Christ!'

'Do up your zip,' she said, like a wife whose patience was
running out. He looked down, then pulled up the zipper with
such force that he broke it. 'Get control of yourself, Russell.
We don't need to tell Malone anything.'

'You've told him enough already, for crissake!' He looked
at Sun sitting against the wall opposite them. The Chinese
looked tired, his skin a distinct yellow in the pitiless light of the
strictly functional room. A picture of the Sacred Heart hung
above his head like a falling bomb; Jesus appeared to be
looking elsewhere but at the three of them. 'Have you told him
anything, Sun?'

'No more than I told him yesterday with Mr Quirke and Mr
Tidey. I think Madame Timori is right – we should keep control
of ourselves.'

Hickbed glowered but said nothing; he did not like upstart
Chinks telling him how to act. He took off his glasses and
cleaned them for the second time since entering the room; he
seemed to be having difficulty in seeing things clearly. It was
the first time in years he had not been in charge of a situation
and he was worried.

A nurse in green overalls and cap, bouncy and cheerful, put
her head in the door. 'President Timori is going into surgery.
It may be a long wait.'

'What are his chances?' said Hickbed.

'We never give up,' she said cheerfully: she was the sort who
at Galilee General would have told John the Baptist's head not
to worry.

Then she left and Delvina and Hickbed looked at each other.
She said, 'He's going to die.'

'Maybe not. Don't start expecting the worst . . .' But he
looked as if he already knew the worst.

Delvina, even at the convent, had never had any faith in the efficacy of prayer; otherwise, she might have prayed for Abdul's death. She certainly *wished* for it. Otherwise there had been no point in paying so much money for Miguel Seville to kill him.

She had not thought of murder till the last week of the rebellion in Palucca, when she had realized their days in Timoro Palace were numbered. Abdul had continued to live in the illusion of his popularity, had been blind to the signs of growing strength in the opposition. She, however, had read the graffiti on the walls, seen the demonstrating crowds growing larger day by day. She had recognized that the end of their power was near and she had decided she would end their marriage. End it her way.

Abdul had wanted to end it two years ago, by clapping his hands and telling her to get lost. But she would have none of his Muslim ways; for a month she had reverted to Catholicism, at least in her attitude towards divorce. The crisis had passed, they had climbed back into bed again, but from then on each had known it would be only a matter of time before they would be separated for ever. Neither had ever really loved the other. Abdul was capable of love, but not lasting love; he did not have the stamina for it. Delvina was capable only of affection and even that was only superficial. Sex had satisfied them for some years, but it is only a part-time bond. A full day's sex is no pleasure for a man whose organs are wearing out, as Abdul's were. He had started to think of looking for a mothering wife, a role Delvina could no more play than she could that of a vestal virgin.

When she had married him, Abdul's wealth had been mainly concentrated in Palucca. It was she who had started putting together their overseas investments. Twice a year she had gone abroad, sometimes with him, sometimes with Sun Lee and the now-dead Mohammed Masutir. Occasionally she would meet Russell Hickbed in London or New York or Houston; occasionally she would go to bed with him, but only after the latest Timori investment had been sealed. When their holdings had passed the first billion-dollar mark, she had gone home to Bunda and made love to Abdul as if it were the first night of

229

their honeymoon, a memory that at the time had convinced him he had at last married the right wife. For some, money is an aphrodisiac. The itch generated by a gramme of crushed rhinoceros horn is but a baby's tickle compared to that whipped up by several kilos of dollar notes.

When she decided to kill Abdul it never crossed her mind that she should do the deed herself. She was shrewd enough not to think of employing a Paluccan; murderers were too close to home if they were part of the family, albeit the extended family of the voters. She turned for advice to Sun Lee, whom she never thought of as a Paluccan and who, she had learned from her own research, came of a family where murder was not unknown. Sun might not understand the meaning of loyalty, since no Paluccan, least of all Abdul, had ever taught him any. He did, however, know that he liked his bread to be buttered.

'We should get someone associated with a terrorist gang,' he advised.

He had not expressed any shock that his President, his own master, should be murdered. He was a long-sighted man when it came to the future and he could see no joy in being the messenger boy, which is all he would be, for an ex-President in exile. Once, a long time ago, he had seen a magazine which had featured a picture story on the exiled kings and royal pretenders who then lived in Estoril in Portugal. He had never seen such a lost, unhappy lot, their aimlessness clear even in the smudged faces of the newsprint photographs.

'That way it can be blamed on the more radical elements of our opposition. It will bring the Americans back on our side.'

Our side, *our* opposition: he was already to be trusted. 'Do you know someone to contact?'

He nodded. 'In Beirut there is an agent.' She didn't ask him how he knew such a thing; in their business dealings she had often been surprised at what he knew. 'If we could get Miguel Seville –'

'Who's he?'

Sun explained who Seville was: 'He might be expensive –'

'It doesn't matter, if he does the job properly.'

230

But she was shocked when Sun came back to her two days later and said the agent was demanding a million US dollars. 'But one could start a war for that!'

'I told the agent exactly that and all he did was laugh. They have no idea of the value of money in the Middle East.' *Not like we Chinese.* He didn't say it, but she nodded. 'Perhaps it is worth it, Madame? The stakes are high . . .'

Finally, after scouring her own sense of values with steel-wool, she agreed to the million-dollar fee. She was not averse to spending money, but, woman-like, she had never thought that murder came so expensively. She had always thought it was a bargain basement item.

She had been no happier when Sun Lee had added his own fee. 'I should want to be protected, Madame.'

'How much?'

'Five million US dollars. You will be one of the richest women in the world, Madame – you will be able to afford it. And you will have my undying loyalty.'

Neither of them smiled; the joke was too serious. 'All right, then. But only if the murder is successful.'

She had been angry when the first attempt to assassinate Abdul had only resulted in the unfortunate death of Mohammed Masutir. She had not regretted Masutir's death. He was a fussy little man who was always getting in the way; it was typical of him that he should end his life by getting in the way of a bullet intended for someone else. She had had Sun phone his contact in Beirut to complain, but there had been no satisfaction from the agent. She had, accordingly, stopped payment on the cheque for the down payment of $500,000 by the bank in Zurich on which it was drawn. Sun had called the agent again to tell him the full million dollars would be paid when the assassination was completed, but then and only then. The agent (whose name Sun had never told her and for which she had never asked) had not answered the call. Neither she nor Sun Lee knew, or ever would know, that Rah Zaid had been blown sky-high by a hundred-kilo car bomb placed outside his apartment by a Christian militia group acting with the best of Christian intentions. When the agent, after several more calls, could not be contacted, it occurred to her that Miguel

Seville might, unwittingly, murder Abdul for free. She had been buoyed by the thought.

Now, here in this small ante-room, she looked up as Malone came back. She did not like the detective, but she had come to respect him; or at least his authority. He was no fool.

'I've just spoken to one of the doctors. It's touch-and-go whether they can save the President. The bullet chipped the skull when it creased him, but it was when he hit the jewel-box that the damage was done. It caused something they call a –' He looked at his notebook. 'A sub-dural haemorrhage. There's intra-cerebral bleeding into the brain. He's going to be on the table for hours, they think. Perhaps we should go back to your house, Mr Hickbed? Some more police have arrived here – the Federals and a Special Branch man. They'll keep us informed.' He looked at Delvina. 'Unless you'd like to stay?'

She shook her head, stood up. 'I'll wait at home.'

'It would be better if you waited here,' said Hickbed.

She fixed him with a look. 'I am going home. The reporters will be here any minute –'

'They're already here,' said Malone.

'Then I am *not* waiting.'

In the Rolls-Royce going back to Point Piper there was no conversation. This time Delvina sat up front beside the chauffeur and she set the silence. Malone sat in the back, with Sun squeezed between him and Hickbed. He had spent happier times in the worn-out old Commodore, while Lisa drove and the kids fought and scrambled all over him.

At the Hickbed house he left the others and went looking for Nagler and Kenthurst. Delvina led the way into the house and went straight upstairs without saying good night. Then she came back on to the landing and looked down at Hickbed and Sun still standing in the entrance hall.

'I can't sleep in that room – there's blood on the carpet.'

'I'm surprised you noticed,' muttered Hickbed.

'What?'

'Nothing. I'll get the maid – she'll turn down the bed in another room.' On another night he would have been tempted to offer her his own bed, with him in it; but not tonight. He had become suddenly afraid of her, though he was not sure why.

Ten minutes later, face creamed, hands too, she was lying in bed in the smallest room she had slept in for years, one not much bigger than the one in which she had slept as a young girl in the semi-detached house in suburban Hurstville. She was determined, however, that she was not going to go backwards, not an inch nor a day. She would continue to use Russell Hickbed till she no longer needed him. He knew nothing of her plan to kill Abdul; he still thought it was engineered by one or all of the generals in Palucca. For the moment he was offering her a comfortable roof over her head and she would accept his hospitality till she was ready to leave this country she hated. But first she had to find a country that did not hate her.

She fell asleep lying on her back, the position in which she had begun her ascent in the world.

She was wakened half an hour later by Sun Lee knocking on her door. 'Madame? May I come in?'

She came awake at once, though for a moment or two she was not sure where she was. She switched on the light and looked at her watch: 1.15. She sat up, pulled her robe round her shoulders. 'Come in.'

Sun came in hesitantly, like a priest into a whore's room. Delvina smiled at his hesitancy, though she did not think of herself as a whore. 'I'm sorry to disturb you, Madame –'

'Is it the President?'

'No, there's no news of him yet.' He stood at the foot of the bed, keeping his eyes fixed firmly on her face, above the level where the hollow between her breasts showed through the half-open robe. 'Inspector Malone is arresting me –'

'*What?*'

'Yes.' She hadn't seen Malone standing outside the half-opened door. 'I'm holding him on suspicion of the attempted murder of President Timori.'

She had her wits about her now: 'But you know it's that man Seville!'

Malone nodded. 'He's the one pulling the trigger. But I'm charging Sun Lee with conspiracy, with being the one who's paying Seville.'

233

Seville had had Timori exactly in the centre of the cross-hatch of the telescopic sight. He hadn't hurried the shot; Timori had been as still as if posing as the target. His back had been to the window, one arm outstretched in front of him. Only as Seville pulled the trigger did he realize that Timori had been holding a gun.

He saw Timori go down and he knew the shot had been successful. He had quickly but without panic dismantled the rifle, stuffed it into the canvas bag, put on his jacket and left the attic. He steadied himself, telling himself he must not panic as he had at Kirribilli. The job was done and now all he had to do was quietly slip away.

He was halfway along the hallway to the kitchen when a phone on a small table right beside him rang. He jumped sideways with shock, hit the wall so hard he felt pain in his shoulder. He heard a voice say, 'I'll get it,' and an old woman appeared in the doorway to the room where the television set was still blaring. It seemed to him that she looked straight at him and he was ready at once for murder.

Then there was a banging on the front door and she turned away, repeating, 'I'll get it,' and tottered on frail legs towards the front door. Seville turned quickly and almost ran the rest of the way down the narrow hallway. He plunged into the dark kitchen, hit his hip on a corner of the big table in its centre and almost fell against the window. He didn't hesitate to see if there was any policeman at the back of the house; he pulled up the window and scrambled over the sill on to the back veranda. There was no sign of the young policeman: that must be he and his colleague pounding on the front door. Seville ran across the back lawn, hobbling a little with the pain in his hip. As he swung up and over the back wall he heard one of the policemen running up the gravel drive beside the house.

He dropped down from the wall, steadied himself and went down the side passage of the house at the rear. There were lights in two of the rooms. A window was open and he heard what sounded like a television commercial: 'AMP guarantees you security for life . . .' He went on down and let himself out of the *Tradesmen's Entrance*, his job done in a tradesman's-like way.

He needed a car now; public transport no longer would be safe. The police would be scouring these streets in just a few minutes. It took him only a minute to find the car he wanted, a nondescript brown Mazda. This was an area for more expensive cars, but most of those, he guessed, would be equipped with alarms. He opened the door of the Mazda in seconds, connected the ignition wires and drove away with the canvas bag and brief-case on the seat beside him and a feeling of a job well done. As he came down to the traffic lights on the main road and waited for them to turn green, two police cars, sirens screaming, came speeding up the main road and turned into the street where he waited. The lights turned green and he drove on. He would head for the airport and be on his way home before the news of Timori's death hit tomorrow's headlines.

Kingsford Smith airport was almost deserted when he arrived there. He parked the car in the near-empty car park. He took the Sako .270 out of the canvas bag and put it under the driver's seat; he then put the two police pistols under the passenger's seat. That left the canvas bag empty, but he would fill it with shirts and underwear when he got inside to one of the airport shops. He had his two return air tickets, one to Singapore and the other from Singapore to Damascus, and several hundred dollars' worth of traveller's cheques. And a million dollars waiting for him in his bank account in Zurich.

He went into the overseas terminal carrying the canvas bag and his brief-case and was shocked to see nobody about. It was as if it had been cleared because of a bomb alert; he had once caused the same effect at Rome airport. The airline counters were closed and so were the shops. The Departures and Arrivals boards were blank; the sky, it seemed, had been closed for the night. He saw two cleaners at the far end of the hall and he hurried towards them.

'What has happened to the planes?'

One woman was an Asian and the other a Turk: their English was barely basic. 'Eh? Planes? They finish.'

'You mean they aren't flying? The crews are on strike?' He had heard about the Australian fetish for strikes: it was a national occupation.

'Strike? Where?' The women downed their tools, ready to be called out: they were basic Australians.

Seville turned away in disgust, saw the security officer coming towards him and automatically reached for the gun that had been in his jacket pocket. But it wasn't there and he felt a surge of relief that he had left it in the car. He must see that he didn't panic.

'Something wrong, sir?' The security guard looked as wide as he was tall, able to block a whole crowd from advancing; he had a jovial face that he had tried to make stern with a thick dark moustache. 'Are you lost?'

'I think I must be,' said Seville, careful to be polite; he had been brought up to be polite and often in the past he had appreciated the camouflage of it. Men in uniform liked to be deferred to; it was one of the perks of the job. 'I was expecting to be able to catch a plane . . .'

'Where to?'

Anywhere out of Australia; or anyway Sydney. 'Singapore. I hadn't booked . . .'

'We have a curfew,' explained the guard; he looked as if he might shake his head at the ignorance of foreigners. 'No planes out of here after eleven p.m.'

'Why?'

'People under the flight paths can't sleep with the jets coming in over them all night. It's a civilized custom,' he added, as if he would like to be home asleep himself.

'No planes to anywhere? Melbourne? Perth?'

The guard shook his head. 'Nowhere. The first plane will be at six tomorrow morning, over at the interstate terminals. There'll be nothing out of here before nine.' He looked up at the blank indicators. 'Around nine, I think. I'm off duty by then.'

Do you live under a flight path? How do you sleep? But he was too polite to ask those questions. 'Then I shall have to come back in the morning.'

'There'll be plenty of planes then. You can go anywhere you

236

like.' He grinned behind the barricade of his moustache.

Seville went back out to the car park, cursing a city that stopped dead at night like a Syrian hill village. As he went out past the airline counters he saw a sign: Air New Zealand; and in small letters beneath it: Agents for Aerolineas Argentina. Suddenly he wanted to go home, to hear Spanish spoken, to walk in Palermo Park, even, maybe, to visit the big dark apartment in Recoletta where his mother sat with her needle-work, her snobbery and her prejudices, waiting to join her illustrious ancestors in the family mausoleum in the Recoletta cemetery, the only place where one could be properly buried according to one's station in death.

He took the rifle and the pistols from beneath the seat and put them back in the canvas bag. He was not sure why he did it; it was a form of housekeeping. He started up the car again and drove out of the airport and back towards the city. On the way he passed two police cars, lights flashing and sirens screaming, going in the opposite direction; it was a warning not to come back to the airport in the morning. Over to his left the outer city's lights lit up yellow clouds that could have been rain clouds or just smoke. As he drove he thought of Timori falling face down away from the window in the Hickbed house.

He had no remorse about taking the man's life. He had never felt remorse, not even when innocent people died in the bomb attacks he had organized. In any war there had to be casualties amongst the innocents; how many had been guilty amongst the casualties in London and Dresden and Hiroshima? There had been less of that when he had belonged to the Tupamaros; except for the police torture, that had been a simple, almost innocent war compared to those he had joined later. He had not examined the whys and wherefores of the Paluccan situation, but it was still a war of sorts. Any struggle for power was a war and he drew no distinctions.

He switched on the car radio, as much to keep himself awake as anything else. He was all at once bone tired, mentally as well as physically; he would sleep for a week when he got home to Damascus. The radio was playing some middle-of-the-night music, a group he hadn't heard in years: Dave Brubeck and his quartet. He knew the number, 'Things Ain't What They Used

237

to Be'. It brought back memories of his first year at university, when he and the varsity jazz club would sit far into the night playing Brubeck, Mulligan and the other Americans who excited them then. He began to hum the melody.

Then the music stopped and the announcer said, a little breathlessly: 'We've just had a news flash! President Timori, of Palucca, has just been shot! He's been admitted to St Vincent's Hospital, where he is in a critical condition. That's all we have at the moment. More later . . . Now back to Dave Brubeck . . .'

Seville snapped off the radio and thumped a hand hard on the steering-wheel. They were faking: the man was dead! He knew it – *dead!* He could not have missed: the back of the dark head had been squarely in the centre of his sight. The range had not been extreme, his aim had been steady, the bullet at that distance could not have failed to do the ultimate damage. They were faking, hiding the truth for some political reason.

But he would have to stay on in Sydney now to be sure. He had been consumed with pride in a job well done; which might not, now, have been done well or at all. Besides, there was the matter of the million dollars. He wondered if his client would pay pro rata, if Timori should survive and he could not get to him again. Half a million was better than no bread at all.

The city was quiet, though there were people in the streets, a good many of them drunk or at least merry. Some of them had been partying since the beginning of this long weekend; the weekend would end tomorrow, Tuesday, the last day of the second century of the founding of this colony. A few people, mostly young, looked as if they had been celebrating since the end of the first century; they leaned against lamp-posts and threw up their insides, their dignity with it. Australians, he decided, were the worst sort of drunks; but he thought with Latin prejudice. He had never seen, only read about, the English and Scottish football fans. Once again he wanted to be gone from this uncouth country as soon as possible. For one mad moment he wanted to take out the Sako and mow down all the drunks as a contribution to civilization. He had his standards.

He dare not go looking for a bed in a hotel, if any could be found. He had seen a headline in a weekend newspaper: NO

238

ROOM AT THE INN. He would stay in the car, let it be his hotel for the night. He drove through the midnight streets down towards the harbour, carefully negotiating the drunks, came out on to the waterfront and saw the Harbour Bridge towering above him like a giant Meccano set. Cars were parked end to end along the kerbs of the road that ran back under the bridge; he drove under the giant arch and along past a wharf which had been turned into restaurants and souvenir shops. The restaurants were still open, their owners having decided that tonight there would be enough business to warrant staying open all night. The crowds were gathering for tomorrow's sail-past, getting in early for the best view of the harbour. Cars were still arriving and, though Seville passed several parked police cars, he felt safe. No policeman would be looking for a stolen car in this confusion.

He drove on along the wharves, found no parking spot, turned round and drove back. As he passed back under the bridge a car pulled out in front of him on the waterfront side of the road. He swung into the vacant space at the kerb, bouncing one wheel up on the pavement and down again as he squeezed the Mazda in between a van and a BMW. He disconnected the ignition, letting the motor die, then looked up to see the burly policeman coming towards him. His hand went into the canvas bag.

The policeman stopped by the open window of the car, bent down. 'How lucky can you be, eh?' He grinned and walked on.

Seville leaned back in the seat, his body turning to jelly. He had felt like this only once before. He had flown from Tripoli in Libya to Tokyo, arriving worn out by jet lag, only to find that the Red Army group which had sent for him were expecting him to engage with them at once in the kidnapping of a Cabinet minister. Everything had gone wrong through no fault of his; the planning had not been right, the execution too hasty, his own tiredness too strong. He had collapsed after it, escaping only by the skin of his life, and he had never forgotten the experience. He was weak now and he lay for a few minutes trying to recover some muscle and bone. Then he realized he was also desperately hungry: he hadn't eaten anything since the sandwich on the cruise ferry.

He couldn't leave the car and go along to one of the restaurants; he had broken the lock on the driver's door and he did not want to leave the canvas bag with the guns in it in the car, not even in the boot. Then he saw the lighted van parked on the opposite side of the road, a line of ten or twelve people queued beside it. He got out of the Mazda and on unexpectedly weak legs, so that he staggered the first couple of steps, he crossed the road to the van. Five minutes later he came back with two meat pies and a carton of coffee that tasted as if it had been brewed in a dish-washing machine.

The burly policeman came back as he reached the car. 'Pies, eh? Best bloody meal there is. Enjoy it, sport.' He went on, handing out camaraderie as on other occasions he would hand out warrants.

Seville ate his supper, drank the coffee, then settled down for the night. The crowd had quietened down, sleeping on the pavement or in their cars or vans, storing up their energy for the Big Day tomorrow. Seville thought about Timori, wondered whether he was still alive or had died in the hospital; but he was too tired to care. Timori, dead or alive, could wait till tomorrow. He slept and dreamed: he was climbing the Perito Moreno glacier in Patagonia, but the ice kept breaking off beneath him, falling away with a loud crack into the lake below him while he leapt from one foot-hold to another on the towering blue-white wall.

He woke stiff and still tired, blinked at the sun coming straight in on him through the windscreen. He sat up, twisting his neck to take the crick out of it. He felt dirty and sweaty and wanted nothing more at the moment than a good soaking bath. Well, yes, there was *something* he wanted more than a bath or anything else: news of Timori. He connected the ignition wires again, then turned on the radio.

He was lucky: the on-the-hour news was just beginning: 'President Timori, of Palucca, who was shot last night in the home of Sydney businessman Russell Hickbed is still in intensive care in St Vincent's Hospital. After an operation lasting four-and-a-half hours, doctors say that his condition is still critical. Police are searching for his alleged assailant, Miguel Seville, who is believed to be still in Sydney . . .'

Seville switched off the radio, then disconnected the wires again. He sat for a moment staring out at the harbour, its waters just a golden lake under the rising sun. Small private boats and early morning ferries were dark moving shapes on the golden glare; the shells of the Opera House seemed about to take off into the yellow sky. He turned his head and looked back under the bridge and saw the yellow-brown pall of smoke spreading from the west. The bushfires evidently were still burning.

He got out of the car and stretched his limbs. He would have breakfast – the pie-van was still parked across the road – and then he would head out of Sydney for some other airport, there to catch a feeder plane that would connect with a plane for Singapore, Hong Kong, anywhere. He would settle for half a million dollars; he would leave Timori to the doctors. But it would always be a festering sore that he had not done the job properly.

He crossed the road to the pie-van, stood at the end of the queue that was even longer than last night's. He idly glanced up the grassy slope that run up from the roadway and under the bridge. It was already packed with spectators for today's big event; it seemed that most of them had been there all night. Then he saw the group of twenty or thirty Aborigines and the big calico sign, supported by two poles dug into the ground, that hung above them: GIVE US BACK OUR LAND!

Then he heard a shout and saw the Aboriginal boy stand up and point a finger at him. Dallas Pinjarri stood up beside the boy, opened his mouth and shouted something; but at that moment a train rumbled over the bridge high above their heads and the shout was lost in the rumble. Seville turned and ran back to the car.

4

'How is he?' said Philip Norval.

'Bad, very bad,' said Hans Vanderberg. 'The docs reckon he'll never come out of it. He has terrible brain damage.'

'Damn!' said Norval. 'The Americans should have taken

241

him. They're better at this sort of security than we are. They're always hiding Russian defectors.'

'Timori isn't a defector. The last thing he would want would be to go into hiding. The more publicity he got, the more he thought he could go back to Palucca.'

The Prime Minister and the Premier were in an office in the Exhibition Centre. With them were the PM's chief political adviser, a young man named Godbold, and The Dutchman's man, Ladbroke. Other aides and several Cabinet ministers, both Federal and State, were in the corridor outside. The ball in the huge hall was still going on, the music thumping the thin walls of the office like an orchestrated barrage of howitzers.

'Where's Madame Timori?'

'I believe she's gone back to Mr Hickbed's,' said Godbold. He was a plump, balding young man, his middle-aged sleek complacency already there in his paunch and his pink jowls. Some day, one guessed, when he *was* middle-aged, he would be Prime Minister with his own political adviser. But he would be far shrewder than his present master and would listen only to the advice he wished to hear. 'I think now is the time, Prime Minister, to stay well away.'

'Oh, I was going to,' said Norval hastily. 'I can't go near them – not now. Are you going to visit them, Hans?'

'Me?' He would as soon have visited the Opposition Leader in hospital. The Opposition Leader was somewhere out in the hall, hale and hearty and happy, for this night anyway, that he was not in power. 'I wouldn't touch them with forty poles, not a foot of them.'

Norval blinked, but got the point of this garbled venom. 'What are we going to do if he finishes up as a vegetable?'

'Boil him,' said The Dutchman.

There was a knock at the door and an aide looked in. 'Prime Minister, the American ambassador would like a word with you.'

'Show him in,' said Norval, glad of any interruption.

'Oh, and General Paturi is still here – he came back,' the aide added in a lower voice.

Norval looked at Vanderberg. 'He's your guest.'

'Tell him to wait,' said The Dutchman to the PM's aide and

242

sat down in the chair behind the desk. This was the Centre manager's office and the Premier, smartly and suddenly, had established who was in charge here. 'Ask Mr Cornelius to come in.'

The American ambassador came in, a very tall Texan who looked more like a Boston banker. Except for his face: that was Grant Wood gothic, thin and bony and weather-creased, with silver hair along the sides of his bald head. He had good-humoured eyes and a slow Texas drawl that, Norval had discovered to his fumbling embarrassment, could recite Roman poets and passages from European philosophers the PM had never heard of.

Cornelius looked at the Premier, then at Norval. 'Can I speak freely?'

Norval looked at Vanderberg, who just grinned and nodded. Norval said, 'Of course, Carl. Go ahead.'

'I've already spoken to the Secretary of State. He's talking to the President and he'll phone me back.'

'We want you to take Timori off our hands,' said Vanderberg, seeing that Norval was prepared to say nothing.

'Is that what you want?' Cornelius looked at Norval, giving him a chance to say something.

The PM looked at his adviser; eyes were swivelling like the numbers in a fruit-machine. 'That would be best, wouldn't it?'

'Oh, indubitably,' said Godbold, who could write the most pompous speeches.

The ambassador nodded, but looked dubious. 'You know how they feel in Washington. This is an election year. The President isn't running again, but none of the Republican candidates would want Mr Timori around their necks.'

'What about the Democrats?' said Vanderberg.

Cornelius smiled. 'Do you ever worry about how your opponents feel?'

'Only when they're hanging by their thumbs,' said The Dutchman and grinned at Norval. He and the ambassador understood each other, though their meetings rarely lasted more than fifteen minutes and then only on rare occasions. They had nothing in common except respect for each other's political ability.

'I don't think the President will welcome another request that we give the Timoris asylum.'

'Well, that's exactly what we're requesting,' said Norval, trying for some determination.

'Unless he dies,' said Vanderberg. 'Which is on the cards.'

'That still leaves Madame Timori,' said Godbold.

The others, all older men, looked at him pityingly. 'Women are never a problem,' said The Dutchman. 'They can always be got rid of.'

'She has a loud voice,' said Godbold, persisting.

'Women should be seen and not heard, so my father said.'

'I thought it was Sophocles,' said the ambassador, 'but I could be mistaken. You're a fount of wisdom, Hans. But please don't quote your opinion on women to my wife.'

'We don't want either of the Timoris,' said Norval. 'Carl, try and convince Washington we're not a country for exiles.'

'I thought that's what you're celebrating tomorrow? Weren't all your convicts exiles?'

'You don't have to mention that to Washington,' said Vanderberg. 'Your President doesn't know much about history –'

'Excuse me, Mr Premier,' said the ambassador with tall dignity, 'he *is* my President.'

Vanderberg was unembarrassed by his gaffe. 'Well, let's say he doesn't know much about *our* history. But you've got to take the Timoris off our hands. Get the CIA to look after them. America is full of ex-Presidents – another one won't be noticed.'

'The point is,' said Norval, 'you were the ones who bolstered him up for so long. You kept him in power far longer than he deserved to be.'

'I thought he was a friend of yours?' said Cornelius mildly.

'Only a personal friend,' said Norval, and for once missed a joke.

'What the Prime Minister means,' said Godbold with all a young man's superiority of intellect and education. He had three degrees and the PM had none, 'is that Australia and Palucca were never close *politically*.'

'You've been close financially. A lot of Australian investment has gone in there. Doesn't that give you a political interest?

244

Your Mr Hickbed has more money invested in Palucca than any American corporation.'

'Just let me say this –' said Norval, using the politician's favourite phrase. He bobbed his head for emphasis, as politicians always did. Ladbroke, sitting outside all this, felt he was looking at another television interview by any one of a hundred clones. He looked at his own master, who would never be anything but himself.

'Just let me say this – Hickbed isn't answerable to the Australian public as I am,' said Norval, dumping another friend. He felt terrible about it, because he was basically a loyal man; but politics was not about loyalty. That was only for the trade unionists in cloth caps and they were long gone. 'We're putting Timori on a plane as soon as the doctors say he's well enough to travel.'

'Where will you send him?' asked the ambassador.

Norval looked at Godbold, who said, 'Chad has said they will take him. They've heard he's worth three billion dollars.'

'Not in Chad he wouldn't be.' Cornelius shook his head. 'You are trying to embarrass Washington.'

'Yes,' said Vanderberg when he saw that Norval was once again going to say nothing. 'It's called being allies.'

Cornelius sighed and shrugged. Sometimes he thought these Australians should have been at the Alamo; they'd have talked Santa Anna into going back to Mexico and would have then sold the fort to Travis and Crockett. 'Okay, I'll do my best. But the President is not going to like it.'

'He's still better off than Timori,' said Vanderberg.

'Have you caught the man who did it? Seville?'

Vanderberg looked at Ladbroke, who said, 'Not yet. They've got a watch on the airport and all main railway stations and bus stations. He can't get far.'

No, except lose himself in this whole vast continent. 'Will he try again when he finds out Timori isn't dead?'

'Ah,' said Vanderberg, 'that'll be Washington's worry, won't it?'

The ambassador gave him a cold smile, said his good nights and left. He was replaced immediately by General Paturi, who had sped back from his Consulate. His face was as shiny as his medals; it was difficult to tell whether he was afraid or angry. 'Let him die!'

'Eh?' said those in the room.

'Let him die! It will solve all our problems, yours as well as ours. Order your doctors to let him die. The woman, too!'

'He's drunk,' said Vanderberg in a hoarse whisper to Ladbroke.

'He's a Muslim. He doesn't drink.'

'You can't be serious, General?' said Norval.

All the fire seemed suddenly to run out of Paturi. He would not have been a general for a protracted war: a quick victory, surrender from one side or the other, everything over. 'No, I suppose not. But it would solve everything, wouldn't it? What happens now? I heard the report from the hospital. They will be putting him on some sort of life support system.'

'Not yet,' said Ladbroke. 'He's still on the operating table. He may yet die.'

'Our doctors are as good as any in the world,' said Godbold, who knew how many doctors contributed to the Party's funds. 'They may yet save him.'

'Why?' said Paturi.

'I'm going back to the ball,' said Vanderberg, rising; the voters had been left alone long enough. 'There's nothing we can do tonight.'

'I think I'll go home,' said Norval. 'Would you go and collect my wife, Roger?'

Godbold left the room and Vanderberg nodded for Ladbroke to escort General Paturi outside. That left the two politicians alone.

Vanderberg said, 'You've got to keep up the pressure, Phil. If he doesn't die and we're stuck with him, I'm not going to have him here in New South Wales. I'm telling you, so believe me. Get the Yanks to take him, just put him on a plane and tell the pilot to fly across the Pacific until he hits America. Then when he's run out of fuel, he can ask permission to land. The hijackets do it all the time.'

Hijackets? 'I can't tell an RAAF pilot to do that! I can't tell Qantas, either –' Then Norval turned plaintive: 'Maybe we can move the Timoris somewhere else. Tasmania?'

246

'Good idea,' said the Premier of New South Wales. Tasmania, the island State, was always complaining about being left off the national map; this would put it back on the map. 'You can put him down there in one of those bloody wildernesses they're always trying to save. Anywhere but here in NSW. I've got enough bloody trouble with my police trying to find out if the Mafia has moved in here.'

'Has it?'

The Dutchman grinned. 'I wouldn't cut you in on the graft, even if they had. Get rid of the Timoris, Phil. That's all you've got to do. Get rid of them, any bloody way you can.'

Five minutes later Norval and Anita were riding home to Kirribilli House in their government Rolls-Royce. Norval's predecessor had been content with a white Ford LTD, often riding in the front with the driver; the natives always rode in the front seat of taxis, so why should the PM be any more undemocratic? It was Anita who had insisted on the Rolls-Royce and Norval, who had had one of his own for ten years, had made no argument. There had been snide comments in the press, especially Lefty rags, as Anita called them, like the *National Times* and *The Age*, but the general public, surprisingly, had tolerated the extravagance. Usually they preferred their political masters to travel in donkey-carts, but, as one voter said, that was too obvious in Norval's case.

Anita pressed a button and the glass partition between them and the chauffeur slid up. 'So what are you going to do?'

'I don't want to think about it.'

'You never want to think about anything. If you don't have your teleprompter, you shut your mind.'

'I mean I don't want to think about it *tonight*. Lay off, Anita!'

She looked at him sympathetically, a sediment of love stirring. 'Phil, I'm on your side – I always have been. But you've got to make up your mind. You've got to start acting like a bastard – like old Hans Vanderberg. Kick out the Timoris.'

'I can't – not now. That would be callous.'

'Not *now* – when he's well enough to be moved. Stand up to Washington – tell them they've got to take him. They've had Marcos and those other ones in the past, Batista and Somoza – another one won't make any difference –' She knew more about world politics than he did; she had more time to read the newspapers. She felt for his hand, pressed it. 'It'll win you votes, I promise.'

'What about Russell? He's in this with them.'

'Stuff Russell. Send him with them.'

5

When Malone got back from the hospital Zanuch had been waiting for him in the Hickbed house. 'Where have you been? You got here five minutes ago.'

'I've been checking with Sergeants Nagler and Kenthurst, sir. They've been giving me a run-down on what's been happening here.'

'Didn't they tell you I was here?'

Say no and that would put Nagler in the muck; say yes and he would be in it himself. 'I think we're all concerned, sir, that Seville got away from us again. He was in that house across the street. I gather the old people who live there are pretty upset.'

'I know that!' Zanuch was in a bad mood; his evening had been ruined. 'You should have had that house staked out. It was an obvious place for him.'

'Mr and Mrs Goodyear refused us permission to have anyone inside the house. They don't like either Mr Hickbed or the Timoris – they're pretty snobby. They've changed their minds now – after the event.'

Zanuch changed tack: 'How's President Timori?'

'It doesn't look good.'

'Madame Timori? I saw her come in and go straight upstairs.' He was miffed that he hadn't met her. He was always interested in any good-looking woman, but Delvina Timori was much more than that. He had never met her in her days with the dance company. He had not been Commissioner material then, so had had no social aspirations and had not gone to the ballet or the opera. He was also miffed that Malone, a mere inspector, had come back in the Rolls-Royce with the woman. 'How's she taking it?'

'Calmly.'

Zanuch gave him a sharp look. 'That's close to libel, Inspector.'

'Only if it gets in the papers, sir. But that's what I'm going to write in my report.'

They were interrupted as Hickbed and Sun Lee came into the kitchen where they stood. Malone had come in the back door from the garden and Zanuch had been waiting for him, sipping a cup of tea that the maid had made for him. The maid, who had been in a dressing-gown, had now disappeared, presumably to get dressed.

Hickbed pulled up short and Sun bumped into him. 'Oh! Superintendent – Zanuch, isn't it? We met a couple of years ago.'

'Assistant Commissioner.' And he'd been a *Chief* Superintendent two years ago; civilians never seemed to appreciate police rank. He refrained from reminding Hickbed that their meeting had been during enquiries into fraud in a Hickbed company, enquiries that had come to nothing.

'Of course.' But Hickbed made no apology. Rank had never meant anything to him; what you had and what you'd made were what counted. 'This is Sun Lee, President Timori's secretary.'

Zanuch and Sun acknowledged each other, then Zanuch said, 'Do the other Paluccans know what has happened to their President?'

'I have just telephoned them at their hostel,' said Sun. 'Some of them are going to the hospital to wait. A vigil, I think you call it.'

Hickbed was making a pot of tea for himself and Sun. He looked at Malone and the latter nodded; Hickbed added another spoonful of tea. Malone was looking around the big gleaming kitchen: Lisa would be sure to ask him about it, too. It seemed to have every device and gimmick that opened and shut; to him it looked more like a laboratory for the start of Star Wars. But when the tea was made it tasted like the good old-fashioned brew his mother used to make.

'The best from China,' said Hickbed. 'It was ordered specially. President Timori drinks nothing else.'

'Better than Bushells?' said Malone. But Hickbed didn't smile; he never looked at television commercials. Serves me

249

right, thought Malone: I'm starting to sound like Maureen.

Zanuch was talking to Sun: '. . . You must be finding our way of life so different.'

Oh Christ, thought Malone. A cup of tea and a little chat: what the hell does he think has been happening tonight? 'Excuse me, Mr Zanuch,' he said, putting down his cup, 'I'd like a word with Mr Sun. I have to get my report finished –'

'Sure, sure.' Zanuch turned his attention to Hickbed, the richest silvertail he'd ever met. 'I'll double the number of men here, Mr Hickbed. We don't want *you* endangered . . .'

Malone led Sun out of the kitchen and on to the back terrace. The lights in the garden had all been turned off. The harbour immediately below was a mill-pond of tiny lights, like phosphorescent water-lilies: hundreds of small craft had gathered for tomorrow's celebration. The night was still warm and the smell of the flowers and shrubs was heavy on the air. Malone put his hand on the balustrade of the terrace, but the stone had lost the heat of the day and was cold to the touch. Sun Lee was equally cold.

'What do you want with me, Inspector?'

Malone was too tired to be anything but blunt: 'When you were at Kirribilli House you made two phone calls to Beirut. You spoke to a Mr Zaid.'

'I don't recall making any phone calls to Beirut. I know no one there.' The light from the kitchen window illuminated only one side of Sun's face: it was half a mask.

'I'll jog your memory, Mr Sun. The number was 232-3344. You told Mr Zaid, who is an agent of some sort, that his client had killed the wrong man.'

'Have you spoken to this Mr – Zaid?'

'Yes.' Malone hoped his own face was a mask; he had moved a little to his left so that the kitchen light was behind him.

'I don't believe you, Inspector.' Sun was cool.

'Please yourself. But you'll believe the tapes we have when I run them for you.' He knew he would have to back down if Sun insisted on hearing the tapes, would in the end have to deny they existed. 'You told Mr Zaid that we had identified his client, though you didn't name him. You were trying to get in touch with Seville, for some reason, but Zaid didn't know

250

where he was. Why were you trying to contact Seville? Were you trying to call off the assassination?'

Sun was silent, Orientally impassive. Malone waited with Australian patience, which usually isn't durable. Then Sun said, 'I didn't organize this. I have only been the go-between.'

'Who is paying Seville?' All at once he was no longer tired; he was fired by excitement.

But Sun shook his head. 'I can't tell you that.'

'You mean you won't?'

'I suppose that is what I mean.' It was Sun who now sounded tired; or fatalistic. Malone had questioned suspects in China-town and they had always baffled him, even the ones born in Australia.

'Then you're the one I'm going to have to arrest.'

'So be it. Isn't that what you say?'

'Not me,' said Malone. 'I'm a bugger for never accepting anything. You sure you want to take the blame for this?'

'You'll have to prove it, Inspector. I have great respect for British justice.'

'This is Australia. You have no idea the tricks we can get up to here.' He was tired again, all the excitement had gone out like a fire of tissue-paper. 'Who are you protecting, Sun? Madame Timori?'

Sun Lee had turned away from the light; but there was a slight hunching of the shoulders. 'No.'

Yes! thought Malone; and felt the excitement stir again. 'Righto, let's go. We'll tell Mr Hickbed and the Assistant Commissioner.'

'No handcuffs?'

'I'm in evening dress. They're not the proper accessories.'

Sun smiled, the first time he had shown any emotion. He seemed relaxed, confident everything would turn out all right. 'You have a Chinese sense of humour, Inspector.'

'Don't bank on it, Mr Sun.'

They went back into the kitchen, but Hickbed and Zanuch were no longer there. Malone pushed Sun ahead of him and they went further into the house and found the other two in the big living-room. They were sitting in the silk-covered chairs, Zanuch lolling back as if this were his natural habitat. Which

251

was what he aspired to, but would never achieve, not since honesty had become one of the police force's better policies.

'I'm arresting Mr Sun,' said Malone, 'for conspiracy to murder.'

'Jesus!' said Zanuch and 'Christ Almighty!' said Hickbed, like a team of profane comics.

Hickbed was first to recover. 'On what grounds?'

'You'll know that when the prosecutor puts the evidence.'

Hickbed looked ready to erupt. 'We'll see about that! You can do something about this, Mr Zanuch –'

Zanuch had stood up. 'You're sure of everything, Inspector?'

'Yes, sir.' Malone returned the Assistant Commissioner's hard stare. He knew Zanuch would back him, at least for the moment. For all his ambitions, professional and social, Zanuch had the reputation of never putting his men down in front of the public. In that he was a true policeman.

Zanuch nodded, then said, 'Are you in this alone, Mr Sun?'

'I am not admitting that I am in it at all,' said Sun. He's the coolest bugger in this room, thought Malone. 'May I tell Madame Timori you are arresting me?'

'You don't need to disturb her,' said Hickbed, looking very disturbed. 'She's had enough to upset her for one night –'

'You can tell her,' Malone said to Sun, ignoring Hickbed. 'She'd want to know, I think.'

Zanuch went to say something, then thought better of it and nodded to Malone. 'A good idea, Inspector. It's the courteous thing to do.'

'That's what I thought, sir,' said Malone, who hadn't thought any such thing.

He let Sun lead the way upstairs. The stairs were marble, matching the floor in the entrance hall. On the landing a large portrait of Hickbed glowered at them; the artist, for a large fee, had been sycophantic but had still not managed to disguise his sitter's natural aggression. Sun led the way towards a door at the far end of the landing.

When Delvina sat up in bed and Sun told her he was being arrested, Malone noticed at once that she showed little surprise; there was just a slight tightening of her neck muscles. Then when she saw him standing in the doorway she turned up, like

252

a gas flame, some sudden exasperated shock: 'But you know it's that man Seville!'

'He's the one pulling the trigger. But I'm charging Sun Lee with conspiracy, with being the one who's paying Seville.'

Delvina looked at Sun and shook her head. 'I don't believe it, Sun. You love the President as much as I do. Don't worry. I'll get you the best lawyers –'

'I'm not worried, Madame,' said Sun, and didn't look to be so. 'I'm sure you'll do everything you can for me. The President would want you to.'

NINE

1

Delvina sat in bed for a few minutes after Sun and Malone had left her bedroom. Back in the palace in Bunda neither man would have been allowed within a stone's throw of her bedroom door; Abdul had had an old-fashioned Muslim attitude towards his wife's privacy. She had not been disturbed that Sun had knocked on her door and then asked if he might come in. The night's events had been such that she knew he would not have suggested such an intrusion unless something urgent had happened. At first, coming awake, she had expected it to be the news that Abdul was dead. She had lain a moment, more relieved than sad; after all, she had told herself, with that reasoning that the guiltless often need to make themselves feel better, Abdul would only have been an invalid for the rest of his life. And then Sun had given her the really bad news.

She got up, pulling her robe about her, and went downstairs. Her slippers' heels clacked hollowly on the marble; there was no dancer's glide to her walk now. She went into the living-room and saw Hickbed with a tall handsome man in a dinner suit, evidently one of his business friends.

'I'd like to see you, Russell.'

'Are you all right?' said Hickbed. 'Madame Timori, this is Assistant Police Commissioner Zanuch.'

Delvina gave him only a curt nod. 'Will you excuse us? In your study, Russell.'

She turned and walked out of the room. Zanuch felt he had been snubbed like a trainee constable. 'Excuse me, Madame Timori, I'd like a word with you –'

She stopped, looked over her shoulder. 'Not now. Russell?'

She walked across the entrance hall, her heels rapping as if she were calling Hickbed to attention. He looked at Zanuch,

254

shrugged, then followed her across the hall and into the study, closing the door behind them. Zanuch looked around for someone to vent his spleen on, but there was no one. He went out into the garden looking for a target.

In the study Delvina said, 'What happened with Sun? How did he get himself arrested?'

'I don't know. He and that guy Malone were outside for a few minutes. Then they came in and Malone just announced he was arresting him. Christ knows what was said out there on the terrace. I thought you might have guessed.'

'Why me?'

'Because I think you know more than you've told me.'

'You don't need to know everything,' she said and told him nothing. 'We have to get in touch with Philip Norval.'

Hickbed shook his head. 'He won't want to know.'

'He's *got* to know! He's got to have Sun released . . . God, don't you realize . . .' She was angry at his stupidity. 'If Sun talks, he'll tell everything! About our investments, about you and what you were going to pay Philip –'

'Keep your voice down!' His own sank to a hoarse whisper; he looked around as if he expected microphones to be hidden behind the unread books. 'You don't know Phil as well as I do . . . He can be as stubborn as hell about doing nothing. He hates to interfere –'

'He'd bloody better interfere in this!' Her accent had lapsed into the Australian she had so carefully tried to eliminate; she could have been back in the dance company arguing with a choreographer who couldn't see reason. 'I'm calling him! What's the number of Kirribilli House?'

'You're making a big mistake – he'll never listen –' But he could sense that she, too, wouldn't listen. He gave her the number. 'It's gone one-thirty. They probably won't wake him – he thinks he should work only from nine till five –'

The security guard who answered the phone said, 'I'm sorry. The Prime Minister can't be woken –'

'This is Madame Timori –' Delvina's accent was under control again; her tone was polar-cold. 'Will you tell the Prime Minister it is urgent that I speak to him. At once!'

There was a moment's hesitation; then: 'Just a moment, Madame. I'll put you on to his adviser, Mr Godbold.'

She waited impatiently while Godbold, whoever he was, was found. Then the pompous voice came on the line and she remembered him: 'Good evening, Madame Timori. Or should I say good morning?' You don't need to remind me what time it is, you pompous little upstart, she thought. 'The PM is asleep . . . Perhaps I can help?'

'No, Mr Godbold, you can't. I have to speak to the Prime Minister.'

'Is it the President? Has he passed away?'

'No, he hasn't! Get me the Prime Minister!' Her voice rose and her accent lapsed again. 'Now!'

It was almost five minutes before Norval came on the phone. She wondered with whom he had stopped for advice – Godbold, Anita? Perhaps he had stopped to consult the latest opinion poll, to see if he could afford to be seen talking to her.

'Delvina? What's the matter? Is it Abdul?'

'No, it isn't.' She told him about Sun's arrest. 'You have to have it stopped, Philip, before it gets into the papers. We can't afford to have him in the hands of the police –'

'We? I've got nothing to do with this –'

'Oh yes, you have. If he starts to talk, everything will come out. Russell has told me about his promise to you – what's in it for you –'

'There's nothing in it for me!' The golden voice sounded on the edge of hysteria. 'That's just Russell's talk – he's always trying to make out he has more influence with me than he has –'

'Philip,' she said quietly but coldly, 'have this stopped. *Now!*'

She hung up and turned to Hickbed, who said, 'I told you – you'll get nothing out of him –'

'I think I know Philip better than you do.' What she meant was that she knew men better than he did. But women have been boasting of that since Eve discussed Adam with the serpent. 'Now I'm going back to bed.'

'What about Zanuch? He wants to talk to you.'

'Let him talk to you. You claim you know nothing – you'll be safer than I would.' She gave him a thin smile, opened the door and went out of the study. Then she came back. 'I may

256

need a book to read myself to sleep. What have you here?'

She looked along the rows of books, taking her time; Hickbed could offer her no suggestions nor did he want to. Finally she took down *The Wilder Shores of Love*, tales of other adventurous women, said good night and left him. Left him wondering why he had ever been attracted to her.

2

Malone said, 'Mr Sun, why don't you call up a lawyer? Mr Quirke, maybe? He'd advise you to talk to us. It would make it easier for you and us.'

'I have no need of a lawyer, Inspector. I have nothing to hide.'

'It seems to us,' said Clements, 'you have a great deal to hide. That's why you're saying nothing. We have those tapes, you know.'

'I don't know anything about the phone calls you speak of. May I ask an academic question? Are tapes allowed as admissible evidence in your law courts?'

'You're too much of a smart-arse,' said Clements and threw his notebook, which contained nothing but Sun's name, down on the table.

They were in the interrogation room at Homicide, a bare room that made no one feel at home, not even the interrogators. They had brought Sun in here without being followed by any reporters. Most of the media men and women were at St Vincent's waiting for news of Timori; the two who had been left to hold the fort at Point Piper had either been asleep in one of their cars or gone somewhere for a cup of coffee. Bringing Sun here to Homicide had been easier than Malone had expected. It was one small break in a chain of frustrations and disasters.

'Do you work for the President or for Madame Timori?'

'For both of them, Inspector. But I am the President's private secretary.'

'What do you do for Madame Timori besides arrange her investments?'

'Just small odd tasks.'

'Like making phone calls to Beirut for her?'

Clements was too experienced to sit up at that, but out of the corner of his eye Malone saw him bite his lip. There was no reaction at all from Sun Lee.

'I don't know what you mean, Inspector.'

'Isn't Madame Timori the one who's paying for the President to be murdered?' Again there was no reaction from Sun and Malone said, 'You don't seem surprised at the suggestion, Mr Sun? Sergeant Clements is.'

'A little,' said Clements, almost as inscrutable as the Chinese.

'Oh, I am surprised,' said Sun, but still showed no change of expression. Then abruptly he smiled. 'I am *shocked*. Madame Timori would be, too. I thought you were an old friend of hers.'

'Never a friend, Mr Sun. Are all their overseas investments, the billions the newspapers say they have – are they in their joint names? Or in her name only? In any case, if the President dies, they would all be hers, wouldn't they?'

'Possibly. I have never seen the President's last will and testament.'

'His private secretary and you've never seen it?'

'Private secretaries are not privy to all secrets, Inspector.'

Malone looked at Clements, his private secretary, and grinned. 'Is that so, Sergeant?'

'I didn't know about Madame Timori being a suspect,' said Clements. 'But it's a good idea. Maybe we should bring her in?'

'That would cause an international incident.' For the first time Sun Lee showed some concern.

'We're just police,' said Clements. 'We never worry about international incidents. We leave that to the diplomats.'

Then the phone rang. Clements picked it up, said, 'Sergeant Clements, Homicide,' then frowned. 'Yes, sir. Just a moment.' He handed the phone to Malone. 'The Commissioner.'

Malone looked at his watch: 2.10. He, too, frowned. 'Inspector Malone.'

Leeds' voice was cold. 'I understand you have President Timori's secretary in for questioning.'

'Just a moment, sir.' Malone waved towards the door. Clements stood up, took Sun's arm and escorted him out of the interrogation room. Then Malone said, 'That's right, sir. I brought him in with the intention of charging him with conspiracy to murder. He's the go-between between Miguel Seville and whoever is paying for the job.'

'You have evidence?'

Malone hesitated. 'Not something I could use in court.'

Leeds didn't have to have things spelled out for him. 'Tapes? Forget them, Inspector. Let Mr Sun go.'

'Sir –?'

'Don't argue, Inspector. Let him go. Then meet me at the Premier's office, his Parliament House office, in fifteen minutes. Come in the rear entrance.'

The phone went dead and Malone sat staring at it. The Commissioner had not spelled things out for him, but the message had been clear enough. Politics had taken over the law again.

3

Philip Norval had done something he had sworn he would never do: he had called on Hans Vanderberg in the latter's office. Admittedly he had done it at 2.15 in the morning and only after he had agonized whether he should phone The Dutchman and ask the favour. He had always kept the Premier at more than arm's length and now he was trying to embrace him.

He had rung Vanderberg at his home in Glebe. He had not been surprised when Gertrude answered; she was famous for her protection of her husband. 'Mr Norval – at this hour? He's dog tired – I don't think I could raise him.'

'Please, Mrs Vanderberg –' He could call strangers all over the country by their first names; but not her. Gert and Gertrude were names that stuck on his tongue; somehow, in his ears, they never sounded like real names. Candice, Tuesday, even Delvina; but not Gert or Gertrude. 'Mrs Vanderberg, it's very important –'

She went away grumbling and a minute later The Dutchman,

grumbling, came to the phone. 'What is it, Phil? Has your mate kicked the bucket?'

'Not yet. Hans, I have to see you – *now*. Can I come to your house?'

'What's it about?'

'Sun Lee, Timori's private secretary, has just been arrested for conspiracy to murder. Some smart-arse cop named Malone has taken him in.'

'What do you want me to do?'

'Stop it. Pull strings, use your influence. Can I come and see you?'

'Not here. The missus won't allow any politicians in the house.' He pondered a moment. 'See me at my office in Parliament House. Come in the back way. I take it you don't want to be seen in my company?' The chuckle down the line was full of malice.

'I'll be there. Twenty minutes.'

Norval went alone, not wanting any of Godbold's advice on this matter. The duty chauffeur was used to being called out at odd hours, but he had never had to deliver the PM to the back door of State Parliament House. He pulled the car in below the office block that backed the old colonial building and wondered if he was expected to stay out here parked on the edge of the Domain, the big park where anyone might come out from under the shadow of the trees and hold a knife to your throat. The chauffeur came from Canberra and was prepared to believe all the stories he read about Sydney being the crime capital of Australia.

'Better not stay here,' said Norval as he got out. But he was not thinking of the chauffeur's safety, only that the Rolls-Royce might be recognized. Though why any reporter should be prowling around the back of Parliament House in the middle of the night, he didn't stop to consider. He was becoming paranoid about secrecy, though he was just about to go in and confide in a man who used secrets like bullets. 'Come back in half an hour.'

A security guard met him at the rear entrance and conducted him upstairs. The Premier's office was a small suite where he attended to his parliamentary business; the rooms in the State office block were for departmental business. This, Norval knew, was where what The Dutchman called skulbuggery occurred. He was in the right place for it, but he wished he were somewhere else.

The lights were on, but the curtains were drawn. The Dutchman, in trousers, pyjama jacket and a brown suit jacket, was waiting for him. With him was Police Commissioner Leeds, still in evening dress, as immaculate as if the night were just beginning.

'Oh.' Norval pulled up as the door closed behind him. 'I thought this was just between you and me, Hans. No offence, Commissioner.'

'I don't run my police force like that,' said Vanderberg, sounding pious but smiling like a devil who had just been given the keys to the Vatican. 'John Leeds has got to be in on this. It's his bailiwickle you're asking me to butt into.'

Norval shrugged resignedly. 'Okay, I asked for it. You know what's happened, Mr Leeds?'

The Commissioner nodded. 'I've been in touch with Inspector Malone, who made the arrest. He's on his way here.'

'Jesus! Do we have to have him in on it, too?'

'He has the evidence, so he says. We need to know what that is before I decide what to do.' There was a knock at the door and Leeds went to it and opened it. 'Ah, Inspector Malone. You didn't take long.'

'I was curious, sir –' Then Malone saw who else was in the room. He had expected to see the Premier, but not the Prime Minister. He nodded respectfully to both political leaders, neither of whom he had ever voted for. He had the feeling his respect was not going to last very long. The room smelled of politics, as if something – morals, decency, honesty – had died in it. My nose is too sensitive, he thought.

Norval, out of character for him, plunged in off the deep end. 'What's this about arresting Sun Lee for – what do you call it? – conspiracy to murder? You have a hide, Inspector. Christ, don't you know what this can do to our foreign relations?' He wasn't sure himself, but most Australians, Neil Kissing had told him, knew next to nothing about foreign relations.

'I was only looking at it from the viewpoint of the law, sir.'

'Jesus, if we did that, where would we be?'

261

The two policemen looked at each other. The two politicians looked at each other. Only the latter were in agreement on the sentiment just expressed.

Malone, feeling he was floating in mid-air now, said, 'This man Seville has killed three people, two of them Australians. He's all but killed President Timori tonight. He's not here of his own accord –'

'How do you know that?'

'He's not a Lone Ranger, sir, not in terms of carrying out a killing campaign of his own. Someone's employing him.'

'Nobody's claimed credit. They usually do within an hour of whatever has happened.'

'Those are terrorist gangs. More than half the claims come from gangs that had nothing to do with the bombing or assassination or whatever it happens to be – all they want is publicity for themselves and the media are stupid enough to give it to them. Nobody's issued any claim or any warning on this attempt.'

'So you think Sun Lee is the one who's employing Seville?'

'No, sir. I think he's just the go-between.'

Vanderberg had sat silent through all this, his bare-ankled feet in scuffed leather slippers propped up on his desk. Behind him a silver-framed photo of Gertrude watched him with a wifely smile.

'What's your evidence, Inspector?' he said.

Malone hesitated, looked at Leeds, then back at the Premier. 'I'd rather not say, for the moment.'

'Why not?'

Malone was acutely aware of his situation. He could not confess in front of the Prime Minister that he had listened to tapes of phone taps on the PM's own Sydney residence. It could be that the PM knew the phone lines were tapped when visitors were in residence; it was also just as likely that he didn't know. ASIO, like intelligence organizations all over the world, didn't trust the intelligence of its political leaders. The CIA and the KGB were forever proving that.

Vanderberg glanced at Leeds. 'Can you make him tell us?'

'I could order him to, yes,' said the Commissioner. 'But I trust his judgement.'

262

Thank you, said Malone silently. Leeds had stood by him in the past and he had not spoiled the record now. Some day Malone hoped he could repay the Commissioner's loyalty, but he could never imagine Leeds being in a situation where he would need a junior officer to defend him.

The Dutchman, surprisingly, accepted Leeds' answer. Perhaps he was tired, too old at seventy to want to fight in the shank of the night. He threw the fishing line back to Norval. 'You satisfied, Phil?'

Norval knew that he was out-numbered and in the wrong territory. He was Sydney born and bred, but when he had gone to Canberra he had lost his citizenship as far as these three were concerned. He had never been brave, so he was not going to be foolish. 'I guess I have to be. But do you have a suspect, Inspector? I mean, who's paying Seville?'

Malone hesitated again; then decided to be brave if foolish. 'I think it is Madame Timori.'

'*What?*' The golden voice turned tinny. Even Vanderberg sat up, taking his feet off the desk so fast he kicked off one of his slippers and had to grope under the desk for it. Leeds, who knew his man, just pursed his lips.

He said, 'That's quite a charge, Inspector.'

'I know that, sir. I have no hard evidence, but I'm sure I'm right.'

'Then you can't prove it?' Norval sounded relieved. 'Why bring it up then?'

'You asked me, sir. I thought you might take it as a warning.'

'What do you mean by that?' The PM's voice was sharp. The Dutchman, slipper on again, looked up, eyes unblinking. Even the Commissioner looked perturbed, as if his man had gone too far.

Malone was surprised at the reaction; he had not meant to imply any under-meaning. 'Politically, sir. It won't look good, will it, if one of the government's guests turns out to be a murderer?'

'It's ridiculous,' said Norval and tried to look convincing; but he had begun to think that Delvina was capable of anything. 'It's someone from Palucca, I'm sure.'

'She's from Palucca,' said the Premier, all at once wide awake. 'Or her money is.'

Norval shook his head, but there was no emphasis to it.

'Have you faced her with the charge?' said Leeds.

'No, sir. I'd like more hard evidence before I do that. I thought I was on the way to getting it from Sun Lee.'

'I want it stopped,' said Norval, suddenly decisive. 'Everything. Call off the whole investigation. I'll try Washington again, we'll get rid of them.'

'What if Timori dies?' said Vanderberg. 'The Yanks won't want her, not if we let 'em know she paid to do him in. Fegan only likes little old ladies with blue hair.'

'I don't know. We may have to let her stay, if he dies. Neil Kissing tells me she's kept her Australian passport. She has dual nationality.'

'Is that allowable?' said Leeds.

'Would you question the wife of a President about her passport?'

'Inspector Malone wants to question her about being a murderess,' said Vanderberg.

'There's such a thing as protocol,' said Norval, sounding as pompous as his absent political adviser.

'Ah, we never worry about that at State level,' said the Premier and grinned. 'Well, I think you and I had better do some talking, Phil. Good night, John, thanks for coming in. 'Night, Inspector. You'll keep your trap shut, won't you? No leaks about this.'

'Are you talking to me or Inspector Malone?' Leeds was indignant at his abrupt dismissal, but it only showed in his cold demeanour.

Vanderberg saw his mistake. 'Sorry, John. No, I was talking to the Inspector.' He didn't apologize to Malone; magnanimity hurt him if he was too liberal with it. 'Keep it to yourself, right? If I read about it in the *National Times*, I'll know where it came from.'

As Malone went out the door with Leeds he heard the Premier say, 'Okay, Phil, let's you and me get down to a little skulbuggery.'

In the outer office Leeds said, 'I'm sorry I had to put you through that, Scobie.'

'You get used to it, sir,' said Malone, knowing the Commissioner would remember two other cases when they had been caught up in politics.

'One shouldn't have to. You're sure about Madame Timori?'

'As sure as I can be without proof. Another twenty-four hours with Sun Lee and I think I could have got the proof. He's worried about his own skin.'

'Does he know about the tapes?'

'No.'

'Were they illegal tapes?'

'I don't know. Probably.'

'Then I don't want to know about them, either. Can I give you a lift home?'

'Thanks, but I've got my car. I'm going back to Homicide – Russ Clements is still there. I'll have a kip on the floor. If I went home now, my wife wouldn't let me into bed.'

Leeds smiled. 'My wife would understand how she feels. Good night, Scobie. Let's hope you collar Seville. You'll need some satisfaction out of this.'

Malone went back to Homicide and woke up Clements, who was asleep with his head resting on his arms on his desk. He told him what had been said in the Premier's office and Clements, another veteran of political interference, just smiled. 'So we keep our traps shut?'

'The Dutchman's very words.'

'You going home now?'

'No, I'll take a kip here. I'll go home at six, when Lisa will be awake.'

They both settled down, heads down on their desks. Malone kicked off what Claire called his party shoes and took off his dinner jacket. Five minutes later, sound asleep at his desk, he could have been mistaken for an all-night reveller who had been brought in drunk and had passed out before he could be hauled off to the nearest cells up at Darlinghurst.

His phone rang at 6.15, but it was Clements, already awake, who picked it up. He listened, massaging his stiff neck while he did so, then he put down the phone after saying, 'Okay, thanks for the info.'

Malone, awake now, looked up. 'What was that?'

'Seville's been sighted. He's kidnapped Dallas Pinjarri.'

265

TEN

1

Seville was fumbling with the ignition wires, trying to start the motor, when Pinjarri loomed up beside the open window. He was dressed in a checked shirt and jeans, but his face was painted so that he looked wild and fearsome.

'Where you going, Mick? I wanna talk to you –'

Seville connected the wires, got the car started. Then he looked at the dark, striped face close to his own and knew he was not going to get rid of Pinjarri without trouble. He looked down the long line of parked cars, their occupants getting out of them with the stiffness of people who had slept in spaces too small for them, and saw the burly policeman from last night standing there with a loud-hailer projecting from his face like a yellow snout.

'What's he saying?'

'There's been some sorta balls-up. He's telling everyone they gotta move their cars. Fuck him. What about you and me, Mick? You still owe me four thousand dollars.'

The policeman had begun to walk along the line of cars; his words were clearer now. In a minute or two there would be confusion as the angry motorists, who had thought they would be allowed to stay here for this Day of Days, began to drive their cars away to look for another parking space. Seville felt the canvas bag on the seat beside him. He pushed it on to the floor in front of the passenger's seat and slid across the seat.

'Get in, Dallas, if you want to talk.'

Pinjarri, unsuspicious, opened the driver's door and slid in behind the wheel. Seville reached down, took Malone's Smith and Wesson from the bag and said, 'You drive, Dallas. Hurry.'

Pinjarri looked shocked; the white markings on his dark face

266

seemed to stretch. But he didn't argue. He put the car in gear and carefully took it out from the kerb.

'Do a U-turn,' said Seville. 'Away from the policeman.'

Pinjarri did so, not very skilfully; a man in a parked car yelled for him to be careful. Then they were heading back under the bridge. Out of the corner of his eye Seville caught a glimpse of the Aborigines, all with painted faces, running down the slope through the crowd. 'Speed up!' he said. 'Faster!'

They went under the bridge, leaving the Aborigines, led by the young boy, standing in the middle of the road shouting. 'Put your seat-belt on,' said Seville, and Pinjarri did so, fumbling with it as he drove one-handed past the wharves and up into the city.

'Where are we going?'

Seville hadn't put on his own seat-belt; he didn't want to be constricted if Pinjarri decided to fight. 'Out of the city. Head west.' He had no idea where west was or what was there.

'Parramatta?'

'What?'

'Do you want me to drive to Parramatta?'

'Yes.' Wherever or whatever Parramatta was. The Aboriginal names confused him, as if they had some secret meaning that he, a foreigner and a white one, could never fathom.

Pinjarri drove in silence for a while, then said, 'You didn't finish him off.'

'Timori? No.' He now accepted the fact that he had failed again. He would make no further attempts, he would fly out of here some time today, go straight to Damascus and hole up there till he had recovered. He felt as wounded as Timori. 'I'll send you the money I owe you, Dallas.'

'Like fucking hell you will.'

Seville lifted the gun; he was losing patience with Pinjarri, with everything in this godforsaken country. 'Moderate your language, Dallas. You're with a gentleman.'

'You – a fucking murderer?' Pinjarri laughed; then saw that Seville was serious. 'Okay, okay. How long am I gunna have to wait for the money? We could of done with it today. We could of staged a decent fuck – a decent demo.'

'You'd be wasting your money. That war paint, or whatever

267

it is, won't frighten them.' He had seen enough of the country, or at least its attitudes, to know who were the inevitable winners. 'I should tell you about the Indians in my own country.' He said something in Guaraní.

'What's that mean?'

'It's something I once heard an Indian say. A revolution does not guarantee freedom.' The Indian had probably heard it from a white man; they weren't natural political philosophers.

'We don't want a revolution – we're not stupid. We want 'em to just hand back what's ours.'

'The land? All of it?' Seville laughed. 'They'd give you freedom before they'd give you land. Freedom doesn't cost them anything.'

'We've got that.' Then Pinjarri saw the argument and nodded bitterly. He drove in silence for some miles, then he said, 'We're coming into Parramatta.'

It was another city, once a suburb of the capital city; now they merged, like lakes joined by a permanent flood of red-roofed houses and iron-roofed factories. Seville saw an arrowed sign: *Katoomba*; and said, 'Keep going. We'll go to Katoomba. I'll let you go there. You can be free.' He smiled, but Pinjarri didn't smile back. 'Where's the nearest airport?'

'We're going the wrong way if you're looking for an airport. The nearest one this way would be, I dunno, Bathurst, I guess.'

'How far is that?'

'I dunno. A hundred and twenty, a hundred and fifty ks. Maybe more.'

'Ks?'

'Kilometres.'

Seville was dismayed. He had expected Sydney, a city of more than three million people, to be surrounded by small airports. He had been deceived by the superficial resemblance of life here to American life: the used car lots with their twinkling bunting, like a whore's come-on; the fast-food outlets spreading like an international attack of indigestion; the brashness of the people who were not always as friendly as they first appeared. In California or Texas and on the East Coast it had seemed there was an airport of some sort, public or private,

every thirty or forty miles. Now he was going to have to drive
150 ks to Bathurst, wherever that was.

'Where is it?'

'Over the mountains, the Blue Mountains. The road may be
closed if the bushfires are still burning.'

'We'll take another road.'

'There's only the one road.'

God, he thought, and they boast of their standard of living!
It was like Syria. Or Argentina, where the airlines never ran to
time and the roads petered out into nowhere, like tracks into
a vast swamp. He had forgotten too much of where he had
come from.

'Why do you want me? Let me out, Mick. Forget about the
money, just let me out.'

They had pulled up at a traffic light. A car, with four youths
in it, pulled up beside them, and the driver, skin and bones
held together by a T-shirt, looked across at Pinjarri, saw the
painted face and laughed.

'G'day, darky! On your way to a corroboree? Who's your
mate – Crocodile Dundee?'

All four youths hooted with laughter and Seville said quietly
to Pinjarri, 'Shall I shoot them?'

'Christ, no!'

'You see, Dallas? You'll never beat them.'

The light turned green and Pinjarri drove on, ignoring the
challenge from the other driver to race him. 'Let me go, Mick.'

Seville shook his head. 'Ah no, Dallas. You'd tell the police
where they could pick me up, at Bathurst. There must be a
reward out for me, trying to kill a President. You'd make more
than four thousand dollars.'

'They haven't said anything about a reward. Me go to the
pigs? Jesus, Mick, that's fucking insulting –'

'Drive on, Dallas.'

They skirted Parramatta and soon were on a long straight
freeway that ran between rolling fields where isolated housing
developments stood out like herds of giant box-like cattle. The
grass fields in between were all black, smoke rising in some
places like steam from a dark thermal swamp. They passed a
big amusement park on their left, the Big Dipper rising above

269

it like the skeleton of some ancient Loch Ness monster brought here for display. The fires seemed to have skirted the park, saving it for another day.

Up ahead smoke was billowing thickly into the sky, turning it yellow. They came down a long incline at speed, slowed to a crawl as they came to a T-junction and Pinjarri turned right. Seville looked out and up at the escarpment of mountains ahead of them. And saw the police helicopter overshoot them.

2

Clements had said, 'A young Abo kid told the constable on duty down at the bridge what happened. He got on to Police Centre right away and they've got an alert out. The car is a brown Mazda, number-plate HBT-651. They've got the chopper airborne and the SWOS guys are standing by.'

Five minutes later the phone rang again. Clements took the call, said, 'Thanks,' and hung up. 'The Mazda's been spotted. At Leichhardt, on Parramatta Road, heading west. The chopper will pick it up.'

On their way out they picked up Andy Graham coming on early morning duty. Somehow he produced a marked car with a driver. 'We can move faster in this, Inspector. The siren and the blue light –'

'Right,' said Malone and grinned at Clements. Despite his tiredness he felt better this morning than when he had gone to sleep. Hope is a good pick-me-up.

Now they were coming out of Parramatta on to the Great Western Highway, the siren screaming and the blue light flashing. Two Highway Patrol cars joined them and Malone knew that the SWOS wagons could not be far behind. The young driver was handling the car beautifully, but Malone, a bad passenger at the best of times and the slowest of speeds, sat nervously hunched in the back seat. It didn't help to see Andy Graham, up front, grinning like an 18-year-old let loose in his first sports car.

The radio was on, the reports being relayed through Police Centre. 'The suspect is now beginning the climb up the mountains from Emu Plains. He is still under aerial surveillance.'

270

'We'll get the bastard this time!' said Graham, no longer grinning.

They went down the long stretch of freeway at 150 kilometres an hour, siren wailing, light flashing. At this time of morning there was virtually no traffic going their way; in the opposite lane there were already cars heading for Sydney and the Big Day. Up ahead Malone could see the Blue Mountains, no longer blue, and the thick clouds of smoke, like yellow-grey thunderheads, hanging above them.

'The highway is blocked a mile out of Springwood,' the radio reported. 'The bushfires have crossed the road. Police are turning back all traffic. The suspect is in for a shock,' said the police radio officer cheerfully.

'I bloody hope so,' said Malone.

'Right,' said Graham up front and grinned again.

Clements looked at Malone. 'Did you call Lisa?'

'Bugger!' Malone threw up his hands. He looked at his watch. 'Never mind, I'll call her as soon as this is over.'

In the Mazda Seville was urging Pinjarri to increase his speed, but the Aborigine was taking no notice. It was as if he had gone back to his tribal heritage; he sat behind his bars of paint, fatalistic as an old man. The bone had been pointed and he had accepted it.

'We're never gunna get away from that chopper, Mick. I just wanna stay on the road and make sure we don't crack our fucking necks. I ain't the world's best driver. You don't get much practice when you don't own a car.'

'I thought you'd be stealing one every chance you got.' It would be about the level of Pinjarri's rebellion: he was still contemptuous of the Aborigine and his hopeless cause.

Pinjarri didn't answer that, just concentrated on taking the car up the wide curving road. They came up behind a big semi-trailer labouring up the steep grade and Pinjarri slowed.

'Go past him!'

'I can't! There's a double-line and a bend up ahead – there's too much traffic coming this way!'

'Pass him!' The gun came up.

Pinjarri, sweat glistening on his face so that the stripes were now beginning to smudge, changed down, took the car out

271

from behind the semi-trailer and trod hard on the accelerator. Without believing in any god, he said a prayer: the old primitive instinct at work again. They roared by the huge truck and squeezed in in front of it just as three cars, nose to tail, came round the curve. There was a scream of tyres, a blaring of horns but no accident.

Pinjarri let out a gasp of relief. 'That's the last time, Mick! You can shoot me, if you like. That'll be better than running head-on into something.'

Seville hadn't yet thought of death. He still believed in his skill and his good fortune; his invincibility, if you like. The skill had been less than perfect the past few days, but that had been at killing, not at escaping. He had been caught only once, back in his Tupamaros days; there had been three days of police torture, but then he had escaped, even with the handicap of his broken knee-cap. Since then he had evaded better and more sophisticated police forces than the amateurs who were chasing him.

The road twisted through cuttings and steep banks. The land on either side was rocky and last week might have been dense bush; now it was a black forest of stumps and bare trunks, highlighted in places with red where logs still glowed. Smoke wraiths danced in slow motion amongst the dark trunks and the acrid smell of smoke began to invade the car. Then they ran into a dense yellow pall blocking the road; Pinjarri slowed the car and they crept through it. When they came out of it they saw the police cars and the fire engines drawn up across the roadway a quarter of a mile ahead. Beyond the road-block the forest on either side of the road was a red-and-yellow inferno, flames leaping sixty and seventy feet towards the dense, billowing clouds of smoke above it.

Pinjarri slammed the car to a halt and at once they heard the clatter of the helicopter above them.

Two miles behind them the police convoy had slowed to a crawl behind the labouring semi-trailer. The sirens were blowing and the blue lights flashing, but the traffic coming downhill couldn't hear or see because of the curves and consequently neither slowed down nor pulled over on to the road's shoulders.

The young driver cursed. 'Sorry, Inspector. It's not worth the risk.'

'Just take it easy,' said Malone. 'He won't get past that road-block.'

Then the road widened, the semi-trailer pulled over into the slow lane and the police convoy, now caught up by the two SWOS wagons, accelerated past. At the same moment there was suddenly no traffic coming from the other direction.

Clements looked out at the devastated countryside, at several houses that were now just charred ruins, standing like rough charcoal sketches of what they had once been.

'He won't get far in country like this.'

'We're lucky,' said the young driver. 'I was up here a couple of weeks ago, bush-walking. We got lost and they had to send in a rescue party for us. I never been so bloody embarrassed in my life. If the bush was like it was a couple of weeks ago, he could lose himself in there for weeks and we'd never pick him up.'

'I'm glad we're getting a break at last,' said Malone and looked out at the smouldering homes of people who had had no breaks at all.

Then they came round a bend and ran into the thick barrier of smoke. The young driver braked sharply, glanced in his rear-vision mirror, said, 'Christ, I hope they don't run into my bum!' and drove cautiously through the thirty or forty yards of dense smoke. Everyone had hastily wound up their windows, but the smoke, or at least its smell, still leaked in and they all took out handkerchiefs and put them over their faces. Then they came out into the clear and there was the brown Mazda, the passenger door wide open, blocking the roadway in front of them.

Malone was out of the police car on the run, his gun already drawn. Clements and Graham went out their doors, drawing their guns as they did so. Police were running down from the road-block up ahead.

Dallas Pinjarri sat in the driver's seat of the Mazda, his hands on the wheel, his seat-belt still on and his face streaked into a horrible mask as if he had run a hand wildly over the paint on it. He looked at Malone as the latter came up beside him, but his eyes were lost in the crazy abstract of his face.

'Thank Christ, mate. I never thought I'd be glad to see youse pigs.'

273

'Any time, Dallas,' said Malone. 'Where is he?'

Pinjarri nodded off to his left. 'He went down there. He's got the Sako and two hand-pieces.' Then, reluctantly, sounding as if it hurt him to warn the pigs, he said, 'You better be careful – he's a cold-blooded bastard.'

'I know,' said Malone, aware of Pinjarri's awkward gratitude and trying not to sound awkward in return. 'We'll be careful.'

The helicopter had disappeared, but now it came back, riding along the front of the clouds of smoke. Clements was using the hand-radio from the police car. 'Where is he?'

There was a lot of static and noise, but the observer's reply could be heard: 'He's heading south down into a gully. It runs down into the valley proper.'

'Is there any fire down there?'

'Not so far. Keep an eye on us. We'll hover over him.'

'Watch out he doesn't start shooting at you. He's got a high-powered rifle.'

The helicopter swung away, dropping down below the level of the roadway. There was no traffic at all on this section of the highway now; one of the Highway Patrol cars had swung round and gone back half a mile to halt all traffic coming up from Sydney. Beyond the huge fire and the towering boiling smoke the traffic was banked up for at least a mile. Their Big Day, it seemed, had finished before it had even begun. History was just a repeat performance: every summer these fires broke out, homes were lost, people's lives ruined.

The SWOS men, flak jackets on, properly booted, automatic weapons at the ready, were already leaving the roadway and plunging down the rocky slope towards the deep gully where the trees and bushes were still green and uncharred. Malone, in his dinner jacket and party shoes, his gun in his hand, went after them.

Clements yelled, 'Scobie! Where the hell are you going?'

'I'm not going to miss the end of this!'

'Shit!' said Clements and followed him.

Graham looked at the young driver. 'There's no fools like old fools. Right?'

'I know where I'm going to stay,' said the driver, and did.

Down in the gully Seville, the canvas bag hanging by its strap

274

from his shoulder, was beginning to panic again. Suddenly all his confidence had gone; he had chosen the wrong territory in which to match his skill against that of the New South Wales police. He was not a novice in rough terrain. As a youth he had tramped through the Enchanted Valley in Patagonia, through its forests of conifers and false beeches and past its strangely shaped rocks; he had climbed in the Andes that separated Argentina from Chile and had done the same in the Alps of Switzerland when he had lived there some years ago. He had trained in the guerrilla camps of the Bekaa valley, clambering over the rocky, treeless hills above Baalbek; and once, escaping from a betrayed Red Brigade bomb plot in Naples, he had walked over the southern Appenines from Salerno to Bari. But this Australian bush was something else again.

The rocks seemed to have done little to hinder the growth of the forest. The trees appeared to grow out of the rocks; every step between them had to be negotiated carefully. There could be no striding out, no sliding down a leaf-covered slope. And above him the tall canopies shut out all landmarks, so very soon he had no idea where he was heading except downwards.

He could hear the helicopter somewhere overhead and when it swung away he could hear the shouts of men up the steep slope behind him. Though it was still early, down here the heat was humid and heavy, as if the fires on the ridges had kept it from escaping during the night. His knee was hurting, hampering him each time he put weight on it. He was sweating profusely and it shocked him that it was not all from the heat: he was afraid, too. This dense forest was trapping him, closing in on him. He slid off a rock into a patch of dead brown leaves; a thick stick turned into a large brown snake and slid away from beneath him. He gasped, choking on the breath.

Then he came to a rocky stream, narrow and beginning to dry up. He bent down, scooped cool water into his face from a clear pool, then drank some. He straightened up, took the Sako out of the canvas bag and quickly assembled it. He loaded it and shoved the extra ammunition into his trouser pockets. He dumped his jacket and the canvas bag, debated whether to take the second Smith and Wesson with him, decided against it and left it.

The helicopter came back, seen now above the narrow patch of open sky above the creek, and he ducked back under the trees. Then he started to clamber up the opposite slope towards the top of the second ridge. He had no idea how many ridges he would have to climb before he was safe; for all he knew they might stretch to the western borders of the State. He knew nothing of the vast plains that, like the pampas of Argentina, began less than a hundred miles from here. He had not expected to have to battle the continent: he had come expecting to travel no further than the limits of the city on the harbour.

Malone, reasonably fit but no bush walker and certainly not shod properly, was having just as much difficulty as Seville in negotiating the down slope of the gully. The SWOS men, younger and more agile, had gone ahead of him. Clements, younger but out of condition and not in the least agile, was somewhere up above him, stumbling over rock, crashing into trees and swearing all the time. Malone, sweating profusely, tore off his jacket and dropped it over a bush; Lisa, a careful guardian of clothes, would ask him tonight where it was and he had better remember. His party shoes, he knew, would be useless after this, but that couldn't be helped. If needs be, he would go after Seville in his bare feet. He hadn't attempted to analyse his passion to capture Seville. He just knew it had to be done and he had to be there when it was done.

He could hear the clatter of the helicopter as he came down to a thin creek; it was up above the facing slope, so that meant Seville was heading for the top of the opposite ridge. He wondered why, as he crossed the creek, Seville hadn't gone down it: the going would have been easier. Then he heard the automatics firing.

He clambered up between the trees, slipping on the smooth rocks, panting like an old man making love. Christ, he thought, I'm going to die of a bloody heart attack! He paused, gulping for breath, and looked back down through the trees. Clements had just reached the creek. He was lying flat on the ground, like a black crocodile, his face buried in one of the pools of the creek. Then he rolled over and dipped his head backwards into the water. He looked as if he was prepared to lie there all day.

The automatic firing broke out again. Malone turned and

clambered on, praying desperately he would be there before Seville died. Sweat was blinding him, his breath came out of his lungs like fire. He came up behind a SWOS man, fell against a tree and managed to gasp, 'Where is he?'

The SWOS man, for all his youth and fitness, was also sweating and gasping; Malone felt a little better, psychologically if not physically. The SWOS man pointed and Malone looked up through the striped trunks of the eucalypts. 'I can't see him.'

'He's in that nest of rocks, sir. He's just got one of our men.'

'Killed or wounded?'

'Killed, I think. I saw him go down – he'd been hit in the face.' He looked at Malone. 'Did you want this guy alive?'

'Preferably.'

The man looked disappointed; he nodded reluctantly. 'Okay, we'll do our best.'

Up in the jumble of rough-edged rocks Seville knew he had at last come to the end of the road. Though he had spent a third of his life in alien lands, often at risk, it had never occurred to him that he might die in a land as alien as this. Yet he knew it was about to happen. There was no death penalty here in Australia; with the killings he had committed they would send him to prison for ever. Death was a much better prospect than that.

The heat and exhaustion were affecting him; and he could smell smoke, like acrid dust in his nostrils. He looked up, but the trees above him weren't burning. There were short gusts of breeze and the leaves turned in the early morning sunlight, silver-green like water flung into the air. He reached out and touched the trunk of a tree that grew out of the rocks behind him; its thin grey bark peeled away like strips of sun-burned skin. He could hear no birds, see no animals: they had all fled, fearful of the fire on the opposite ridge. He looked across there, saw the flames and smoke there and imagined he could feel the heat.

But what he felt most was loneliness. He didn't recognize it at first; it was so long since he had felt lonely. Now all at once he wished there was someone beside him he knew: Juan, his best friend at university, who had persuaded him to join the Tupamaros; Gabriella, the girl he had worked with in the Red Brigade in Milan and with whom he had almost fallen in love; anyone at all from the old days. Even his mother: he looked down the slope and thought he saw her come out from behind a tree. He raised the Sako, but he couldn't shoot her: she wasn't to blame for what she had been or what he had become. He began to weep.

Then he heard the faint crackle above him. He looked up, his mind and his eyes suddenly clearing. The tree-tops were bursting into flame. First, there were wisps of smoke amongst the silver-green leaves; then the leaves turned to bright red as if blossoms had suddenly burst. All at once, as if someone had run a giant match along the tops of the trees, the whole top of the ridge burst into flames. Fire took hold of the forest and thick smoke, as if the top of the ridge were a volcano crater, belched into the morning sky.

The crackling roar was suddenly deafening. The air down here on the slope all at once dried out, became a searing pain in the lungs. Seville, terrified, stood up and the one shot from the SWOS man down by Malone hit him in the chest. He shuddered and dropped the Sako and the hand-gun. Then he looked up again, saw the burning limb fall off the tree and drop towards him and he screamed. He began to run, stumble, fall down the slope, sliding off rocks, crashing into trees, but feeling nothing as he tried to flee the worst death of all. The countryside itself was going to kill him.

Malone saw the crown fire break out and was about to turn and race down the slope when he saw Seville plunging towards him. He waited; he didn't know why. He didn't attempt to raise his gun; he just opened his arms and Seville ran straight into them. Malone thudded back against a tree, but managed to remain on his feet. Seville's face was close against his own. He stared into it, into the eyes that were already beginning to empty; there was a flash of recognition, but that was all. Nothing of defiance or surrender: Seville died wondering, as most of us will.

Malone picked him up and carried him, twice falling and losing his grip on the dead man, down to the creek where the SWOS men and Clements were yelling at him to hurry.

He fell the last few yards and two of the SWOS men grabbed Seville.

'The bastard's dead!' one of them yelled.

'Bring him!' Malone croaked and let Clements help him down the creek towards the deep pool under the overhanging rock where the other SWOS men were already in the water.

The fire came racing down the slope; the very air beneath it seemed to burn. Tree trunks burst into flame as if they had been soaked in kerosene; burning branches fell from on high like flaming spears. There was the terrible roaring crackle and the men in the creek felt the skin on their faces and necks begin to tighten as if about to split. Malone, his lungs on fire, his eyes feeling as if they might boil in their sockets, fell into the pool beside Clements.

'Duck!' yelled the sergeant in charge of the SWOS and everyone fell under the bank and dived as deeply as they could, two men dragging Seville's body down with them. The fire leapt the creek, killing the air above it; the surface of the water sizzled for a moment, then was still again. The air, hot but breathable, rushed back to fill the vacuum.

Malone, still with a little air in his lungs, half-swam, half-crawled along the bottom of the pool, heading downstream. It was about twenty yards long and ended in a tiny waterfall that dropped about four feet over some smooth rocks. He came up gasping, his lungs on the point of bursting, and slid head first over the slippery rocks and down into another pool. He stood there, aware of the blackened earth on either side of him and the small fires burning in the underbrush, feeling the burning heat and smelling the smoke and scorched air, but knowing that, for the moment, they had survived.

Clements flopped into the water beside him. 'Jesus, Scobie, I thought we were gone then!'

The SWOS sergeant was leading the way downstream. 'Another hundred yards and we'll be okay! The fire's going the other way!'

The two men carrying Seville's body stopped and looked at Malone. 'You still want him, Inspector?'

Malone looked at the soaked and bedraggled figure, at the grey strained face with the staring empty eyes and the open mouth: there was no threat of terror there any more. I'd have liked to say goodbye to you, Seville, he thought with

279

out-of-character malice; but the malice died suddenly, like an aberrant thought. *No, all I would have done was ask who was paying you? Was it Madame Timori?* But perhaps Seville had never known. Hit-men often never knew for whom they committed their crimes. History was full of innocent murderers.

'Yes,' he said, 'bring him along.' He looked at Clements. 'Right?'

'Right.'

3

'It was wonderful, Daddy,' said Claire. 'Absolutely wonderful!'

'Yes,' he said. 'I saw it on TV.'

'Ah, it wouldn't have been as good on TV,' said Maureen traitorously. 'You should've been there.'

'Yes,' said Lisa. 'You should have been. Instead of where you were. What happened to your jacket?'

'I lost it.' He felt her hand press his.

'Where were you, Daddy?' said Tom.

'At work. Just at work.'

'Everybody was there,' said Claire. 'The Prime Minister, the Premier, the Queen, cricketers, golfers, footballers, yachtsmen, jockeys – Captain Mack pointed them out to me when we sailed past the – what do they call it?'

'The 'ficial 'closure,' said Tom.

'Yes. Everybody's heroes, Captain Mack called them.'

'No police heroes,' said Lisa.

'I saw it all on TV,' said Malone. 'Especially the Prime Minister and the Premier. Everybody's heroes.'

He had not made it after all to the excursion on the tug-boat on the harbour. It had been almost two hours before he, Clements, the SWOS men and the dead Seville had all been lifted out of the valley into which they had retreated from the fire. An emergency rescue helicopter had flown in and, two by two, they had been hoisted up to the top of the valley's escarpment. He had been the last to go up, swinging up through the hot smoke-tinged air with Seville's body in the sling beside him. He had looked down on the grey-green forest below him and then along to the huge black scar where the fire had roared through. The fire was still burning along the tops of several ridges, but a slight wind had sprung up and turned it back on itself. With some luck it may have burned itself out by this evening and the firefighters, professionals and volunteers, could rest up and think about whether they had anything to celebrate.

There had been some bitterness amongst the SWOS men that their dead mate, shot by Seville, had been left to burn in the fire while Seville's body had been carried out. Why? they asked angrily; and Malone had not been able to answer them. It had nothing to do with justice. On the way back to Sydney, with Seville's corpse following in an ambulance, he pondered the question. Then he recognized a reason, though it may have been only subconscious. He wanted to present Delvina, if only in a photograph, with a view of her employee's body. It would be some sort of revenge, if not justice.

'Let's go to the morgue with the body,' he said.

Graham, in the front seat beside the young driver, turned round. 'Why?'

'I want his photo in tonight's papers. And on TV.'

Graham looked blank, then nodded. 'Right.'

Malone looked at Clements beside him and grinned resignedly. But Clements, too, looked blank.

There was one press photographer and one TV cameraman waiting for them at the City Morgue. They took their shots and then hurried off. Dead terrorists weren't as interesting as live partygoers falling off yachts into the harbour or Aboriginal demonstrators being heckled by fellow Aussies, including the lately arrived ethnics. 'They probably won't run it,' said the press photographer.

'They'd better,' said Malone, then added recklessly, 'There could be a bigger story to follow.'

'Do you think there will be?' said Clements as the photographer hurried away.

'No.'

They went back to Homicide where Zanuch, out of evening dress now and in uniform, all silver buttons and silver braid, looking as if he was brushed up for more climbing, professional and social, was waiting for them. 'Good work, Malone, good work. That wraps it up.'

'We go no further?' Malone all at once found he no longer cared.

'No. The PM has got the Americans to agree to a deal. He's going to announce it this evening.'

'What deal?'

'Timori is never going to recover full consciousness. He's out of the operating theatre and in intensive care. But it will be at least a month before he wakes up. He's going to be a virtual vegetable for the rest of his life, be on a life support system. The Mexicans have agreed to take him and his wife – evidently the Americans put some pressure on. They're going to put them on some island in the Gulf of Mexico.'

'Timori can't speak? Or recognize anyone?'

'He'll never speak, they say. He'll have amnesia, but not about everything or everyone. For instance, he'll probably always recognize his wife.'

'He'll enjoy that,' said Clements.

'Yes,' said Zanuch and looked at the rumpled, smoke-begrimed sergeant as if he wasn't sure whether Clements was making a joke or not. 'Well, I've got to be off. I'm taking the salute. There's a march past on the way down to the harbour. Take the day off.'

'Thank you, sir,' said Malone and Clements and only just stopped themselves from saluting.

Malone had gone home, was glad to find that Lisa, angry though she might have been at his once again failing them, had taken the children off to their outing on Eric Mack's tug-boat. He showered, standing under the water for twenty minutes, got into his pyjamas and climbed into bed. He propped himself up with pillows and switched on the television set facing the bed. Conservative in his living, if not his police work, he had objected to their buying a second set, but Lisa had convinced him it was the only way to avoid arguments with the children.

'You're spoiling them,' he had said.

'I know. It's because I have to spend so much time alone with them.'

There had been no answer to that and so they had a second

TV set in their bedroom. As he looked at the spectacle on the harbour, with the hundreds, maybe thousands of small craft gathered on what had been sparkling blue water but was now a frothing, constantly changing pattern of white wakes, he wished he were actually there. The kids must be out of their minds with delight and excitement and it hurt like a stab wound that he wasn't there to share it with them. National pride swelled in him: he was proud to belong to what was being celebrated.

Then he saw the big Maritime Services launch pulling into the Kirribilli wharf. Norval and his wife stepped aboard; even in long shot the PM's smile seemed to take up the whole screen. As the launch swung round and went out into the harbour towards the opposite shore, to the point known as Mrs Macquarie's Chair where the enclosure for official guests had been set up, Malone saw the Premier standing on deck. He and Norval were smiling at each other, like old soldier mates reunited after a long separation. Malone waited for them to throw their arms round each other. Bloody hell, he thought, what sort of skulbuggery went on this morning in The Dutchman's office after the Commissioner and I left? Whatever it was, the voters would never know.

Malone, falling asleep, switched off the set before the tall ships began their stately procession down the harbour and out through the Heads. He was just too tired to say farewell to the country's second century.

Now Lisa was saying, 'I wish you'd been there.'

'So do I,' he said, heart full.

She leaned across and kissed him in front of the children; but they said nothing this time, just stared at the two of them. Then she looked at them and smiled. 'He's okay.'

'Right,' said Maureen, and Malone smiled and winced.

4

Two months later President and Madame Timori flew out of Sydney on a specially chartered aircraft, bound for Mexico. With them went Sun Lee. Russell Hickbed went to the airport to see them off.

So did Malone. He went out to the Boeing 747 and climbed the steps to the front section, where Abdul Timori, under the care of a doctor and two nurses, lay in a bed with a life support system attached. Malone paused by the thin, inert figure and the dull black eyes stared back at him. For a moment he thought there was a spark of recognition in them, but he would never know.

'Does he recognize his wife?'

'We don't know,' said the doctor. 'We can't be sure. Maybe in time . . .' He shrugged.

Malone went into the next section where Delvina, Sun and Hickbed sat quietly, like mourners waiting for the hearse to move off.

Delvina looked up and a frown crossed her smooth face. 'Not you again, Inspector! What do you want now?'

'Nothing,' said Malone. 'I've just come to say goodbye.'

'Why?' said Hickbed.

'I thought Madame Timori might like to know the case is closed.'

'It was closed when that guy Seville was killed.'

'Not officially.' He looked at Delvina. 'If ever the President wakes up, tell him we know who was paying the man who tried to kill him. Goodbye, Delvina. Enjoy Mexico.'

She tensed in her seat and for a moment he thought she was going to jump at him; he would have welcomed the chance to manhandle her. Then she relaxed and sat back, had the control to be able to smile.

'Anywhere will be better than here.'

Without your billions? he wanted to ask; but didn't. All their Australian holdings had been frozen and it looked as if the fortune was going to be returned to Palucca; the Swiss were talking of offering access to what the Timoris held in the Zurich banks. There would still be a million or two left in other havens around the world, but life at the top level was finished for Delvina. Soon she would be no more than a footnote on the gossip pages. Unless, of course, Timori died or, somehow, was disconnected from his life support system. In which case she might find another dictator looking for someone to manage his life.

Malone turned his back on her and left the aircraft. That evening on the news he saw the 747 take off and disappear, a gradually diminishing dot ahead of its fading plume, into the bright blue sky.

'Who goes there?' challenged Tom, not interested in TV, playing his own game. 'Fred or foe?'

'Foes,' said Malone. 'For ever.'